Memories of Ivy

Memories of Ivy

a novel

JAMES E. HARF

Ivy House
Publishing Group
www.ivyhousebooks.com

PUBLISHED BY IVY HOUSE PUBLISHING GROUP
5122 Bur Oak Circle, Raleigh, NC 27612
United States of America
919-782-0281
www.ivyhousebooks.com

ISBN: 1-57197-437-7
Library of Congress Control Number: 2004096750

Printed in the United States of America

To my daughter, Marie.
May your journey lead you to your Jonathan.

Prologue

Jonathan never ceased to express wonder at the simple beauty of the scene below him. It was as if he was viewing a Monet painting of the French coastline at Etretat. The waves of the sea, so powerful yet paradoxically peaceful, splashing against the shore. The seagulls seemingly riding on a carpet held aloft by a gentle breeze, oblivious to everything except morsels of food casually dropped by bathers or marine delicacies coughed up by the throbbing surf. The few boats offshore dancing to the cadence of the ocean's seductive melody.

Children of all sizes and shapes playing in a world measured simply in terms of school time and holiday. Individuals stealing an idle moment without an apparent care or purpose. Couples lying on the beach or strolling along the shoreline, obviously happy only to share the rhythm of the waves together. All appeared to be content, enjoying the apparent freedom of finding themselves far-removed from the worries of everyday life, as if the pounding blue waves could wash away all cares.

The familiar combination of the ocean's sounds and smells especially captured Jonathan's senses. The salt air piercing his eyes. The faint smells of the sea twitching his nostrils. The laughter of children disrupting the natural flow of the ocean's message, particularly the constant thunder of the waves hitting the shore.

All of these scenes awakened in Jonathan that summer of 1992 an ever-changing collage of vivid memories—some happy and deliciously wonderful, and others melancholy and so painful. Recollections of times that began far away from where the ocean met land. Far away on a university campus whose ivy-covered beauty rivaled that of the scenery in front of him. Far away from that moment in time, yet memories that were as freshly painted on his brain as if they had been recorded only yesterday.

As much into one another as those couples below him appeared to be, in his heart Jonathan believed—really believed—that none possessed the intensity and totality of love he had always felt for Sarah, even after all these years. None, he was convinced, could possibly have achieved the perfect mix of physical desire and passion, and of psychological intimacy and serenity, that experiencing unconditional love with one's best friend and soul mate had brought him for all these many years—if only perhaps in his dreams.

Jonathan loved the view from the top of the hill. In the short time since he had discovered that place, he had spent countless hours absorbing its splendor. He often thought that if he had to spend the rest of time in one place, that would be the chosen spot. The vast, open space touched previously only by God and nature had evolved into the perfect setting for a retreat away from all his cares. It had become the perfect escape.

As Jonathan wandered across the huge, grassy expanse, his hand reached into his pocket and removed a piece of paper. It was the first page of a rather lengthy letter from Sarah. She had composed it when he asked her to marry him, which now seemed like a long time ago. It was her way of responding to his proposal—or more precisely, of explaining her decision. Jonathan glanced at its first three paragraphs.

My dearest Jonathan,

Last evening you asked me to marry you. Such a simple question, yet one that stirred my heart and soul like no other. As your words filled the night air, the most incredible set of emotions I'd felt in my forty-three years overtook me. I haven't been able to stop thinking about their effect on me since I first heard them.

Now, then, how might I best describe it? Well, let me try—although it might not be easy, and maybe even a little silly. It seemed at first like a late spring's gentle breeze blowing softly against my skin. Then like a ray of bright sunshine warming each side of my heart. Finally, like a sweetness inhaled that traveled a lengthy path to the far corners of my soul.

You dear, sweet man! Let me explain my answer and the complicated and even nonsensical reasoning behind it. Let me also tell you about my remarkable journey—from the first day we met as professor and student to that extraordinary moment years later, when I realized with the most incredible sense of amazement that you loved me more intensely than the midday August sun. . . .

A smile initially graced Jonathan's face as he gazed at Sarah's response, followed soon by a peculiar calmness as, with his eyes closed, he contemplated her message.

But soon an incredibly strange feeling began to overtake him, as it had virtually every time he had begun to peruse her answer. In reality, he wasn't certain that what he had just "read" was actually written on the sheet in front of him. Had she really said yes? Or was his desire for her so strong that he had once again willed those beautiful words onto his brain, refusing to accept what he really found on the paper? Had the words he longed to find replaced hers? The ones Sarah crafted to let him down gently.

Was his mind playing tricks on him, as it had so many times previously? He had desired her for so long that he simply couldn't take yet another major disappointment. Particularly one that would totally define the rest of his life in a way that he wanted so much to avoid— what remained of his life alone, without Sarah. Over the years, his mind had often protected him as he sifted through the implications of his many encounters with her. Was it doing so now at this pivotal juncture?

As he stared at the letter and then toward the hillside a short distance away, his thoughts turned to that day twenty-five years earlier when he first laid eyes on her.

PART ONE

~ 1 ~

The First Glance

Nineteen sixty-seven. Durham, North Carolina. The time and place were vividly etched on Jonathan's brain as if it was only yesterday. When the year began, Jonathan had high expectations, but nowhere on his list was the prospect of falling in love. After all, his professional career had already begun to consume him. He welcomed the challenges it brought. The idea that personal feelings, particularly those that might bring vulnerability and even heartbreak, would intrude on his focused sense of purpose was ludicrous. But 1967 would bring Sarah into his life. It would never be the same again, nor would he have wanted it to be. The year would be so pivotal that he would always view everything thereafter in pre-1967 and post-1967 terms. Frank Sinatra had it right: "It was a very good year."

Professor Jonathan B. Hawthorne, Ph.D., was in his second year as a member of the faculty at Duke University, a highly respected southern private institution catering to well-to-do students from all over the United States. He was twenty-seven years old, six feet tall, handsome in a somewhat subtle sort of way, with golden hair and blue eyes that glistened like sapphires. His finely tuned physique, unlike those of most campus professors, reflected the long hours of exercise and outdoor activities that characterized much of his free time away from campus. His social life had found him unattached, without a serious relationship—or any relationship for that matter—since his graduate student days.

Jonathan held the rank of assistant professor of political science.

That entitled him to nothing but the opportunity to work hard and publish his research. If he was successful, he might some day acquire tenure, that sacred word signifying lifetime job security at a university. On the other hand, if he did not satisfy the senior members of his department that his research and teaching record merited a permanent position, they would cast him aside and replace him with another equally promising young scholar. "Publish or perish" was the popular phrase describing this expectation in universities across the country. Publish or perish was alive and well at Duke. He understood this and accepted it without hesitation.

Jonathan had established himself in one short year as a popular teacher. His research agenda had also begun to bear fruit. He already had two articles published in respected academic journals, two others were in the works, and a partially completed book manuscript lay on the corner of his desk. He was looking forward to the end of the academic year, nine months hence, when he could devote three months of uninterrupted attention to his research. But first he had four classes to teach, two during each semester.

Jonathan enjoyed teaching. He took great satisfaction in watching young minds at work in search of answers to the world's weighty political mysteries, his particular specialty. In fact, it was the love of teaching, not research, that had led him to pursue a faculty position. Although he had underestimated the importance of research at a major university when he first entered graduate school, particularly when compared to teaching, he was not sorry he had opted for such a career. Because of Sarah, he would later be more thankful than he could ever imagine at his choice, no matter what the outcome of his "affair of the heart."

Duke University was simply icing on the cake. As a graduate student at Penn State, he had hoped only to acquire a position at a respected institution of higher learning. He knew full well that unlike the idyllic setting of PSU, nestled at the foot of Mt. Nittany among the rolling hills of central Pennsylvania, many universities stood in places considered marginally desirable at best. Most had other shortcomings as well.

So when the letter with a job offer from Duke arrived in the winter of 1966, Jonathan immediately realized his good fortune. The university was simply perfect. Its setting appeared to be carved from the pen of the author of *Love Story*. The buildings exceeded the expectations of the university's founder, James B. Duke, who had set out to create the Princeton of the south. The climate of the eastern fringe of the North Carolina Piedmont region suited his lifestyle—one that kept him outdoors when he wasn't pursuing his dream of tenure. And the ocean, his special escape from the rigors of everyday life, was but a few hours away.

It was the Duke student body, though, that most captivated the young professor. The doors of the university were open to such a small percentage of those who applied that he knew they were the cream of America's high school graduates. They absorbed every word that flowed from his lecture notes and constantly engaged him in debate, challenging his every assertion. Students sought his advice on personal affairs as well as professional matters. They made him feel as if he, a young second-year professor, made a difference in their lives. He took the latter role seriously—too seriously, some of his colleagues would say.

While Jonathan thought himself immune to feelings of gender differences, particularly when it came to assessing student performance, his first-year experience had led him to coin an unusual phrase in describing Duke students. When his friends from graduate school days asked him about the coeds on campus, he simply said with a slight smile that the "Duke boys are boys, but the Duke girls are women." Jonathan did not mean that in a sexist or disparaging manner. Rather, it conveyed his belief campus females were much more mature, focused, and in touch with what quite possibly lay ahead of them than the males were. By 1967, the women's movement had just begun to make significant inroads at the more prestigious universities. It was this newfound freedom to explore uncharted waters that made Duke women so interesting, both in matters relating to their undergraduate careers and in situations of a more personal nature. This last characteristic would change his life forever.

The autumn semester of 1967 opened innocuously enough. Jonathan arrived for the first day of class tanned and relaxed, but excited to be back on campus. Two weeks at the beach had rejuvenated his mind and body. He had vacationed in Avon, a sleepy little town near the southern end of North Carolina's Outer Banks—a thin stretch of land separating the mainland and two adjacent bays, Pamlico Sound and Albemarle Sound, from the Atlantic Ocean. He cherished his two weeks there. Avon was a desolated place. He could stroll on the beach in the early morning hours or late at night without crossing paths with another living soul. He could sit for hours during the heat of the day reading his favorite authors without interruption.

Jonathan's two courses, an introductory class in international politics for undergraduates and a graduate seminar on the major theories of war and peace, were both in his field of international affairs. He was pleased that the department chair, Lawrence Farrell, allowed him to offer courses in his specialty. He was convinced his teaching was cutting-edge quality when he focused on topics of interest to him. His undergraduate class was to meet twice a week on Monday and Wednesday mornings for ninety minutes. Thirty students, the cutoff number, were enrolled, and he expected most of them to show up for the first class. His graduate seminar, scheduled for three hours every Thursday afternoon, would have ten students at most. While Duke had a highly respected graduate program in political science, its attention to undergraduate education was nationally recognized.

As Jonathan prepared his first week's lectures, he felt the normal excitement of a new semester beginning. He wondered what his students would be like and what the next fifteen weeks would bring. But nothing prepared him for what would happen between the first day of class and the end of the academic year in May.

The second Monday in September broke beautifully, with the North Carolina sun burning brightly despite the passing of the worst of the summer heat. Jonathan was still not used to summer being so delightfully long. Even the nights would not witness temperatures that required one to wear a sweater for several weeks. His undergraduate class was assigned one of the classrooms in Perkins Library, the same building that housed the political science department in one of its wings. It was thus only a short walk from his office.

The library was in the middle of West Campus, the newer part of the university that had been constructed when its trustees decided to expand in the late 1920s. The older part, known as East Campus, now housed mainly auxiliary services such as Duke Press and most freshmen.

Perkins lay on a pedestrian walkway just east of the point that served as the main intersection for the academic buildings housing the liberal arts departments and most housing for upperclass students. Around the corner to the northwest of the intersection was Duke Chapel, the large edifice used for weekly worship service and for weddings by current students or alumni who met on campus, fell in love, and subsequently married. The entire area was reserved for pedestrians alone, automobiles having been relegated to a drop-off circle about fifty yards southwest of the intersection.

Jonathan arrived at the assigned classroom and made his way to the lectern, where he placed his first day's lecture notes and class roster. The beginning of class was five minutes away. It was time to start perusing the new group of students as they made their way one by one to their seats for the first time. He could instantly sense their initial reactions— much anticipation and even some anxiety about both the instructor and the course. *Typical,* he thought. He enjoyed the excitement of the first contact between professor and class. He liked to identify (privately of course) male or female students who appeared interesting at first glance—for whatever reason. This first day's ritual had quickly become a game with him in his short teaching career.

His eyes, already focused on the doorway, caught sight of her as she appeared at the entrance. Almost immediately, she looked toward him, and their stares locked in on each other. He thought her scrutiny somewhat prolonged, certainly not of the typical length he expected from a student. He wondered what the reason for it was, as he had never seen her before. The obvious plausible answer escaped him—a student's normal curiosity about her new professor coupled with, he would later discover, his rapidly growing reputation as a superb instructor on campus, particularly among Duke coeds.

His heart skipped a beat or two as he inhaled her intoxicating beauty. *Strange,* he thought, as she was not the first attractive woman to walk into his classroom during his short time at Duke. Afterward, he would reflect on the phenomenon, concluding that the eternal mystery of what made one's heart flutter at such moments was just that—an inexplicable enigma. Still later, far into the future, he would figure it all out. It was more than simple beauty that began to captivate him that first morning. Much, much more.

Jonathan soon caught himself, however, and his eyes returned to the lectern and his notes. It was time for class to start. He took a deep breath, introduced himself to the thirty students who had taken their seats, and began to call out each name on the class roster. As was his custom, his initial order of business the first day was to take roll. The young professor believed it essential to learn who each member of the class was as quickly as possible, so when he called on them, he could do so by name. He had come to understand early how much students appreciated this gesture. It also helped him place faces with names when he read his students' papers or graded their exams. Taking daily roll was the fastest way to accomplish it.

About a third of the way through the roster, Jonathan came upon her name. Sarah Joan Matthews. The twenty-year-old junior acknowledged his roll call with a subtle smile and a look that an astute observer would characterize as falling somewhat closer to a pointedly extended stare rather than a fleeting glance.

In the days following that first class, memories of their first eye contact often occupied his mind. He amused himself with the notion that Sarah had never quite smiled at another man like she had toward him then. Although he knew better, it warmed his soul to think she might view him in a special way, as he had her on that first day.

As Jonathan thought about her smile twenty-five years later, he knew he was right about its uniqueness, although he would discover that quality only much later. The beam that graced her face every time he encountered her was like no other he had ever experienced. It was a smile that his fantasy seemed to suggest, "My sweetheart, there is no greater feeling of happiness and fulfillment than to be in love with one's best friend and have that love returned." After all those years, its memory was embedded in his mind as if it had occurred only yesterday.

For the first time in his young life that early September morning in 1967, Jonathan had experienced an unusual phenomenon that both scared and moved him. His first encounter with Sarah had an inexplicable effect on him, causing all manner of silly reactions, he would muse—a fluttering of the heart, a lump in his throat, a slight flushness in the face, a momentary loss of his train of thought, and constant reflection thereafter.

From that moment on, no matter how much he initially denied it, his every contact with her differed from any he had with another human being. He could not rationalize this phenomenon away. At first it unnerved him, but he eventually learned to accept it. Although it was perhaps a bit melodramatic, the word "destiny" kept intruding on his mind. It was destiny, he later told her, that brought them together that fateful semester. And it was destiny that led to other encounters from time to time, rekindling the fire that had made their initial time together—her last two years at Duke—the most fulfilling and happiest period of his life.

In moments of reflection in the years since then, Jonathan would take great delight in trying to remember every detail of their first meeting that beautiful September morning. His memory never failed him. Her eyes came to mind first. They were dark green, almost as black as coal yet as warm as a welcome ray of sunshine through a frost-covered window on a cold winter's day. They seemed to display both a shyness and a security that belied her young age of twenty. He later discovered that he was only half right about these two traits.

Jonathan was not used to female students flirting with him. After all, there was nothing extraordinary about his appearance, at least in his own eyes. Moreover, he had always designed his behavior, both in and out of the classroom, to prevent such occurrences. Nothing about Sarah's behavior suggested flirtation even remotely. Quite the contrary. It was as if, he tried to convince himself sometime later, she was saying, "Your looks are pleasing, Professor Hawthorne, but I have much more stringent tests for you to pass before you can become a part—any part—of my world." Of course, at the time he thought nothing of the kind. He simply concluded that she had a puzzling innocence about her, which eventually only heightened his desire for her.

Jonathan was on target about the stringent part, however. Sarah turned out later to be quite simply the most remarkable person he had ever met. Her standards were high. He constantly reflected on this quality whenever he fantasized about lying in bed with her. As feelings of utter exhaustion and total sexual fulfillment overwhelmed him in his dreams, he could not help but think how fortunate he was that she had allowed him into her life, and that he had, indeed, passed her test.

Jonathan also remembered Sarah's hair that September morning. It was deep black with a shine that made it glisten, probably even in the moonlight. It provided a frame for her small face, covering just enough of it to convey a sense of mystery. The way her hair fell about her strikingly beautiful features rendered them even more so. He never tired, years later, of fantasizing about kissing every inch of her face slowly and gently as he inhaled her intoxicating scent. He did not know, of course, at that first meeting how special her lips might be. He later dreamt about what they could do to make him feel like the most desired man in the universe.

Graphic images of Sarah's stature that first day of class next came to mind. "Petite" probably best captured his perception. But Jonathan would not have thought to use that term in 1967. Instead, he simply observed the remarkable combination of slimness and curvature discretely revealed by the matching skirt and blouse accompanied by loafers and knee socks—the style of the day.

Long after that first encounter, Jonathan still grew excited at seeing her in loafers and knee socks. They always seemed to give a special bounce to her walk, as if to say, "I love life!" They fit so perfectly with her calf muscles, which conveyed a serious athleticism to them. How he loved, over the years, to contemplate kissing and caressing her beautiful calves as he worked his way toward warmer pleasures.

All of those first memories of Sarah registered in Jonathan's subconscious that opening day of his second year at Duke. His brain stored them and then, over the years, eagerly recalled them in total clarity whenever he wanted to relive that initial moment when he first laid eyes on her.

While Jonathan remembered how their first meeting had touched him in some unfathomable manner, he had no way of knowing then, of course, how Sarah felt about that fateful September morning in 1967. Years later he would discover her initial reaction when he read her letter answering his marriage proposal, assuming again that the words he "saw" on the pages in front of him were the ones that she had penned in her letter to him.

> . . . *I remember when I first saw you. It was not the initial day of class the beginning of my junior year, as you have probably always suspected. Rather, it was the year before when you had just arrived at Duke.*

Word spread quickly among the women on campus about this handsome new political science professor with an intellect, charm, and wit, as well as a beautiful body and face. I was as curious as the rest of my friends were to find out what you looked like. So a group of us waited one day after one of your classes to see what all the fuss was about. Quite frankly, I was only moderately impressed with what I saw at first glance.

It wasn't until I walked into your class, sat, and listened to you lecture for the first time that I began to sense what my friends who had already taken your course meant when they said you were different from other professors. You had a presence about you that made students come alive, both intellectually and emotionally.

I left class that first day really excited about the course. I couldn't wait for your next lecture. I already loved world politics, but I had a feeling that your influence would help me love it even more. So I was determined to reap as many benefits as possible from being your student. Little did I realize how many would come my way over the years, including one for which I was not prepared—your heart. . . .

Time stopped only for a moment during that initial class, however. Jonathan moved past Sarah Joan Matthews' name on the roster and on to the next one on the list. He tried to think no more of her that first day.

~ 2 ~

The First Meeting

The semester flowed smoothly. Jonathan faced the normal number of student problems crossing the desk of a university professor during the school term. Students became ill; mono was common on college campuses. Some encountered personal crises often associated with the beginning or ending of personal relationships. Others did not deal well with breakups of their parents' marriages. And finally, a handful wanted to switch their majors from the hard sciences or humanities to political science because they were better-suited to politics or had developed new career aspirations.

But Jonathan also saw students learning. The world of international politics fascinated him. He took great pleasure in awakening in his undergraduates a love of this world. Nothing exhilarated him more than seeing their eyes come alive as he expounded theory after theory.

One topic especially absorbed his students. Nineteen sixty-seven was the height of the Cold War, the name given to the nonmilitary struggle for global dominance between two bitter enemies, the United States and the Soviet Union. It was also a time when students were growing more aware of the escalating danger facing them from newly developed intercontinental ballistic missiles (ICBMs). Now missiles—far-reaching missiles carrying nuclear weapons capable of widespread destruction much greater than what the United States unleashed at Hiroshima and Nagasaki—launched from thousands of miles away could easily violate the borders of both superpowers in a matter of minutes. The threat of nuclear war called into question the survival of the planet itself.

Even more difficult for students to comprehend was that both superpower governments had given tacit approval to allowing their own citizens to be vulnerable to such a nuclear attack, whether from another country's surprising "bolt out of the blue" first strike shattering the peaceful calm without warning, or from an enemy's counterattack in retaliation against its own initial nuclear strike. Civilian defense against a nuclear assault, popular during the 1950s, was fast becoming a dim memory, a victim of a change in official government policy. Their reasoning for governments holding their own people as nuclear hostages was simple. Leaders on both sides hoped that failure to protect their own population against an adversary's weapons of mass destruction would suggest they had no intention of striking another country with nuclear weapons in the first place and inviting certain heavy casualties in a retaliatory second strike.

Allowing, even endorsing, one's own vulnerability was part of a bold strategy called "deterrence." Policymakers coined the term "mutual assured destruction" (MAD) to describe the conditions allowing deterrence to work. MAD was the rather appropriate acronym penned by some insightful journalist. MAD meant that no matter which side initiated a nuclear attack, the target country would be able to withstand the initial assault, retaliate against the aggressor, and inflict unacceptable damage on the aggressor's population and industrial capacity. The reason was simple. The aggressor nation had left the very things it valued most unprotected.

The key word was "unacceptable." MAD assumed that any country contemplating a nuclear attack would think twice about it, and then likely abandon the idea because of the fear of resultant damage to its own people and property at a level deemed too unacceptable a price. On the other hand, if a country ignored the dire retaliatory consequences and launched a first strike on its enemy, millions of innocent civilians on both sides would perish in the ensuing nuclear exchange. The latter decision was deemed irrational behavior by scholars and policymakers alike, but history, the critics of MAD would charge, was replete with fanatical leaders. The threat of such dire consequences would deter rational rulers, on the other hand. War—at least nuclear war—would be averted. Deterrence had worked.

The uncertainty of it all was an unsettling feeling for those who had given it any serious thought. Students came to Jonathan's class already interested in the topic because of their fears that they might someday witness the destruction of the planet in a global nuclear war. They wanted to do something, anything, to change the grim forecast. But first they had to learn about this frightening phenomenon. That was Jonathan's role—to teach the facts and theory behind this modern-day monster. He always found class discussion about the superpowers' nuclear strategy the most exciting and challenging of the semester.

Autumn 1967 was no different. It was during such give-and-take between professor and class that he observed Sarah Joan Matthews in action for the first time. He liked what he saw. He clearly remembered her first query.

"But, Professor Hawthorne, what right has our government to use us—just ordinary citizens—as nuclear hostages in this mind game of deterrence with the Soviet Union?" she asked.

Sarah's question was a difficult one that cut to the core of the moral issues surrounding nuclear deterrence. Jonathan had no ready answer, at least one that he knew would be completely satisfactory to her and the rest of the class.

Before he could respond, she continued, "The whole concept of deterrence appears to be predicated on the assumption that leaders of both superpowers are rational human beings. That's a pretty huge assumption. Look at the Cuban Missile Crisis. Many would argue Khrushchev was not rational when he challenged the U.S. by putting missiles in Cuba. Some critics even believe President Kennedy took us far closer to war than was necessary because he wanted to get back at Khrushchev for the terrible way the Soviet leader treated him at Vienna the previous June. JFK's ego got in the way. That's not my view, though. At least not the part about JFK's ego."

Jonathan smiled to himself. Here was a woman who could take one international situation and apply it to another. Sarah was obviously well-read and bright. And she captivated him more and more each day. There was a spunk about her that fascinated him.

"You're absolutely right, Sarah," he said. He made certain he uttered her name. He wanted her to know he was aware of who she was, or at least that he knew her name. "It's a clear moral dilemma," he continued. "The best minds have calculated that neither superpower would jeopardize the lives of its own citizens by launching a first strike because of the near certainty that it would, in effect, sentence a large number of its own citizens to death in an enemy retaliatory or second strike. So far, these minds have been right on target. Neither the United States nor the Soviet Union has seen fit to use nuclear weapons against the other."

"So far," Sarah countered. "But we're putting an awful lot of trust in a group of leaders who, we have always said, cannot be trusted. I just think there's a better way. Why not develop a defensive system to protect ourselves from a nuclear attack, no matter how the Soviets attempt to deliver the weapons?"

Jonathan continued to marvel at Sarah's logic and her willingness to engage him in debate.

"I believe self-interest or self-preservation is the key here, Sarah," he responded. Again he deliberately uttered her name. He continued, "The first law of a ruling group is to remain in power. We bank on the assumption that any Soviet leader desires to stay in power at all costs. And he doesn't want his country destroyed. Besides, both the Soviet Union and the United States have been trying to build a defensive system to protect their citizens, but the technology doesn't yet exist for such a guarantee. So MAD is the best alternative today."

"I hope it works, Dr. Hawthorne," Sarah said. "I hope twenty-five years from now we are all here congratulating ourselves on how smart we were."

Sarah was clearly not backing down on her point about the uncertainties of the situation. Jonathan allowed a devilish thought to enter his mind. He imagined her being with him twenty-five years down the road contemplating the merits of MAD. But he thought it was silly to ponder such fantasies. His professionalism then got the best of him. Sarah clearly had a solid grasp of the issue. The rest of the semester was going to be fun if this was the kind of intellectual exchange he could expect, particularly from her.

That evening he replayed the day's events in his mind as he lay in bed. Dancing throughout Jonathan's brain was the image of a woman whose beauty had begun to move him in ways quite different from any he had ever experienced, and yet whose mind excited him in the conventional way that bright students inspired professors. Not surprisingly, sleep was slow in coming that night.

◆ ◆ ◆

The semester continued. Several weeks passed by quickly. Jonathan found that his excitement and anticipation grew on Sunday and Tuesday evenings, for he knew he would once again gaze upon Sarah the following day in class. He was quick to tell himself that what he was experiencing was natural. It would probably occur often throughout his teaching career.

He also knew he was doing nothing wrong. Sexual harassment was not a common term in 1967, but even if it was and he was so accused, he would deny any culpability. After all, Sarah had no idea Jonathan— Dr. Hawthorne to her—thought of her any differently than he did any other student. He had given her no cause to think otherwise. Probably a good idea that she didn't, too. She was the kind of person, he would find out later, who would have had great difficulty knowing her professor was fantasizing about her. No telling what her reaction might have been had she known.

He also suspected he might even be disappointed if he came to know Sarah—really know her—in any way other than as her instructor. Wasn't that how it worked? The person imagined in one's dreams was always perfect. Reality was always flawed. Better to know Sarah in the real world simply as his student and leave it to his dreams to create the perfect relationship for lovers.

He didn't yet have much sense of her persona other than what little he had observed in his course. While she had asked and answered questions with enthusiasm during that time and had eagerly participated in discussion, Jonathan and Sarah had had no contact, even of a casual nature, outside of class. Duke was a medium-sized university, so he expected to see her around campus. But students and professors had daily routines, adjusted only once a year as one semester's responsibilities and schedules replaced another's. They crossed paths with the same people every day for almost half a year, yet went unseen by individuals who took different routes. The next semester, everyone's routines changed due to new class schedules, and different sets of faces greeted one another daily for the following four or five months.

Sarah's and Jonathan's schedules did not intersect that first semester. Not once had he seen her outside the classroom, even from afar, although he had looked for her. From time to time he stopped by the commons in the student union, a favorite hangout of most students, hoping to catch a glimpse of her. He knew that was silly, but he didn't care. But to no avail. No matter. He sensed it was only a matter of time until they bumped into each other. After all, destiny was on his side, he remembered.

And, besides, Jonathan enjoyed the increasingly vivid fantasies that had begun to flood his mind. He was in no hurry to replace the perfect world of his dreams with the flaws of reality. His fantasies did not detract from his daily set of professional responsibilities. They did not make him vulnerable. He would not be hurt. They simply amused him, particularly at first. This playful game was a new experience for him.

But then a thought began to emerge, ever so slowly, until he could ignore it no longer. Perhaps there were consequences. At first, he balked at the idea. Only if he allowed something to happen, he rationalized. Jonathan had no idea how Sarah would eventually change his life. Had he realized that and had he known the possible joy and fulfillment she might bring him, he would have jumped in head-first, taken his chances, and damned the consequences to his personal and professional lives. Although he soon recognized his physical and emotional need for Sarah, he was slow to act. Instead, he made decision after decision that delayed or even prevented the happiness and contentment he could likely find with her.

Duke University expected its professors to hold a number of office hours each week. It was important that students believed they had adequate access to their instructors. Tuition was high at most private universities, and Duke was no exception. The powers in the central administration did not want disgruntled parents complaining that their children had been shortchanged by absentee professors. No matter that students rarely took advantage of this opportunity to meet one on one with an instructor—unless, of course, it was to question a test grade. Professors knew that until the semester's first exam, they could use the time set aside for office hours for personal matters, to catch up on their reading, to write a few pages for a journal article or book, or to simply keep up with their correspondence.

Jonathan spent most of his work time outside of class in his office or in the library stacks doing research. He loved his office. It was small by most standards—he would use the word "cozy"—and it contained a desk, telephone, typewriter stand with typewriter, desk light, visitor's chair, and comfortable desk chair. No ashtray, however. Jonathan was a nonsmoker. While not smoking was not that unusual in 1967, it was certainly ironic since James B. Duke, the benefactor of the university, had made his money in tobacco. Bookshelves filled with volumes that revealed Jonathan's specialty of international politics covered three walls from top to bottom. The fourth wall displayed mostly photographs, each one cataloguing one of his many trips abroad over the years—to London, Paris, Quebec, Brussels, Rome, Madrid, Frankfurt, Athens, Rio, Hong Kong, Tokyo, and Bangkok. Each picture showed Jonathan in a typical tourist spot posing for the camera. His reason for displaying what he jokingly called The Jonathan Hawthorne Travel Portrait Gallery was to show students the glamour and excitement of careers in international affairs, whether as policymakers or research scholars. It worked. Students often gazed at the pictures and then felt compelled to describe one of their own trips abroad or talk about their future international career plans.

❧ ❧ ❧

It was the fifth week of the semester, immediately before the first midterm examination, when it finally happened. His first out-of-class contact with Sarah. Jonathan was in his office perusing an article in one of his favorite professional journals while waiting for his office hours to end. The knock at the door could not have given it away, but somehow he knew. It was Sarah, and they would be alone, face to face for the first time. It could be no one else. It was destiny, he remembered, and he had no choice in the matter. His heart began to beat rapidly, more so than ever before. He hoped its racing wasn't obvious. He didn't want to reveal the excitement overtaking his body. The door opened. He was right.

"Hi, I'm . . ." Sarah began.

But before she could utter her name, Jonathan replied, "I know who you are, Sarah Joan Matthews."

She appeared to be taken aback by his quick response.

"Please come in," he said. His heart beat faster still. *This is not going to be easy,* he thought as he found himself overwhelmed by the exhilaration of a moment that he had fantasized about since that first day of class.

In the weeks to come, Jonathan's memory of Sarah's first visit to his office was as clear as if it had transpired only yesterday. And years later it was still fresh on his mind, much like the moment when he initially laid eyes on her. Her physical details caught his attention first. Loafers and knee socks, always the same combination. October in North Carolina still meant shorts, and Sarah did not disappoint. Her wheat-print blouse matched her khaki shorts.

Sarah's shining black hair framed her beautiful face. And for the first time, Jonathan really noticed her breasts. They were medium-sized and appeared firm. His initial image of her breasts proved accurate years later—at least in his mind—when he first held them gently in his hands, caressing them until the nipples stood erect, as they now seemed to against her blouse. His mind later took great pleasure in exploring every inch of their pinkness with both his fingers and tongue, telling her each time they made love how much he adored them. He meant every word of it.

Jonathan stared at Sarah, careful to do so in a way appropriate for someone in a position of authority. He took the conventional moral restrictions on professor-student behavior seriously. While some members of the faculty and student body at Duke had begun to take advantage of the new sexual mores then just starting to take hold on college campuses, particularly outside the South, Jonathan was conservative and even a bit old-fashioned. He was somewhat good-looking, which made him ripe for every possible compromising situation and even scandal. He had learned early during his teaching assistantship days at Penn State that he had better be "more pure than Caesar's wife." Sarah later chided him again and again that he had, unfortunately, overachieved for far too many years, well beyond the time when they found themselves cast in the roles of professor and student.

"I have a few questions about the midterm, Professor Hawthorne," Sarah said.

Jonathan imagined her voice different from what he had heard in class. It sounded softer, more friendly and yet reserved. He tried without success to figure it out. She asked question after question. He simply sat there mesmerized, now not by her physical attributes, but by her riveting intellect.

Jonathan remembered there were two kinds of student queries. There were inappropriate or stupid ones that lazy students who had not put forth much effort asked, thereby using the instructor as a crutch. Duke had few students of this type, though. Its standards were too high. Much more common were relevant and sophisticated inquiries borne out of minds vigorously at work. Sarah's questions definitely fell into the second category. He was not surprised. Although she was impressive in class, she amazed him even more with how much she had grasped from his lectures. Despite her status as a junior, she demonstrated the ability of an advanced graduate student to work through the complexities of international affairs.

Seconds grew into minutes, and minutes turned into an hour. Sarah moved the conversation from specific questions to the joys and frustrations of analyzing world events. Jonathan could not remember when he had had such an exhilarating intellectual exchange with a student. The session appeared to be coming to an end, though. He had answered her queries. There were no more questions. He had no more "wisdom" to impart. Sarah was getting ready to leave.

Jonathan started to panic. He didn't want their session to end, but he couldn't be obvious about it. His brain kicked into high gear, probing for some subtle way to prolong the meeting. At first, nothing came to mind. He racked his brain for a way to keep her in his office a bit longer. Finally, an idea took hold. Why not move the discussion toward her current academic activities or more personal queries about her background? What about her course load that semester? Her major? Extracurricular activities? Hometown? What high school did she attend? Why did she select Duke? Did she have other options? What about her family? Had she traveled abroad? Where? What were her goals? The list that raced across his mind was endless.

Not on Jonathan's inventory, however, were two important questions borne out of his fantasy. Was she seeing anyone? If so, was it a serious relationship? In a way, he hoped the answer to both questions was yes. It just might keep his life much simpler. Even the best of relationships were not uncomplicated. Add the professor-student factor, and simplicity was out of the question. As their friendship grew, however, he came to welcome the astonishing complexity an intimate relationship with Sarah could bring.

"Tell me, Sarah." Jonathan had begun his probe. "Where are you from? How did you happen to end up at Duke? Did your parents go here?"

Her answers—both what she said and the way she said them—only heightened his attraction to her.

"I'm from Pennsylvania Dutch country," Sarah replied. "It's not really Dutch, you know. That's just a mispronunciation of 'Deutsche.' The region's first white settlers were from Germany. Many of them were Amish, that strange religious sect that avoids any modern conveniences like electricity or cars. Lancaster's the city. Named for Lancaster, England. I guess by early British settlers to whom the king formally deeded the land. It's in eastern Pennsylvania, about fifty or sixty miles west of Philadelphia. I've lived there all my life—all twenty years of it," Sarah laughed. "Do you know the area?"

"A little bit," Jonathan said. "I was an undergraduate at Pitt. Named for William Pitt, the great British general. It's obviously in Pittsburgh, in the western part of the state. Old man Pitt probably named the city after himself, although it might have been only a fort in his day. Called Fort Pitt."

They were both amused at Jonathan's rather pathetic attempt at humor. A blush crossed each of their faces, a fact that seemed to unnerve Jonathan somewhat.

"Why do you say 'obviously'"? Sarah interjected. "Wake Forest University isn't in Wake Forest, North Carolina."

"No, but it used to be until recently, when the Winston-Salem tobacco people donated mega-dollars to the university to move it to their town." Jonathan was giving Sarah a local history lesson.

"My father's an executive with Hamilton Watch Company in Lancaster," Sarah said. "Mom's a professor at Millersville State College, about three miles southwest of the city. It's a former teacher's college— part of the Pennsylvania system of fourteen such places. We live halfway between their work. Mom doesn't teach political science, though."

"Not all of us are so lucky," Jonathan interjected. "What's her field?"

"She's in library science. It's one of their specialties. That's why I spend all of my time at the Duke library studying. Just kidding," Sarah said.

Their dialogue was reaching a solid comfort level, Jonathan thought. He was enjoying Sarah.

"I graduated from the main high school in town, McCaskey High School," she continued. She was serious once more. "I applied to three universities, Duke, Smith, and Miami of Ohio. This place was my first choice, for all the right reasons, of course. I wasn't following some old boyfriend down here. Nor was I searching for a warmer spot where I could get a tan. I didn't buy that old story that southern guys are more gentleman-like. None of that silly stuff. Instead, I investigated the three schools, and do you know what I discovered? Duke's student body's brighter, the faculty is more famous, and the campus is more beautiful. That's it. Quite simple. No other reason. My folks were pleased."

"Impressive. Very impressive, Sarah Joan Matthews," Jonathan said. He pretended at first to be serious, but after a few seconds he couldn't contain himself. The wry smile on his face gave him away.

Sarah continued her story. She was an only child. Her parents, both highly educated with three advanced degrees between them, including her mother's doctorate in library science, had obviously opened many worlds for their only child.

"I just love the pictures on the wall, Dr. Hawthorne," she commented. Her voice grew more excited. Sarah was now really into the more personal exchange. "You must have been everywhere," she continued.

"Not quite," Jonathan replied. "But I do love to travel. Maybe that's why I chose international politics. It gives me an excuse to go off somewhere in search of 'the truth,' as we professors like to say. If I had chosen to study the American political scene, then I would spend all my free time in Washington. Now don't get me wrong. I love D.C. But I get there enough anyway to satisfy my appetite. It's the rest of the world I really want to see."

"Me too. I'm the same way," Sarah said. "I guess it's because my parents and I often traveled when I was growing up. We went to lots of exciting places, all around the U.S. and even overseas too—to Europe and even the Middle East. I guess many of our trips were what one might call 'different' or 'unusual.'"

Indeed they were unconventional, particularly for the 1950s and early 1960s. This became clear as Sarah continued talking. She related three of her childhood travels in the course of her first visit to Jonathan's office. Together her stories would provide a good clue to the worldliness and dauntless nature of the woman in front of him.

"I don't see any picture of Cairo on your wall, Professor Hawthorne," Sarah commented. "Have you visited there?"

"I came close. Athens," Jonathan said. "But I didn't quite make it to Egypt. I guess I wasn't adventurous enough. Tell me. You've been there, I'll bet. Otherwise, you wouldn't have asked the question."

"You just saw right through me, Professor Hawthorne," Sarah admitted. "It was a leading question. I have been to Egypt." She then proceeded to describe her trip to the land of pyramids—the obvious highlight of her many youthful travels. "It was near the end of third grade. My parents asked me where I wanted to visit that summer. So on a lark, I told them in my best serious voice, never dreaming for a moment they would indulge me, 'I think we study the pyramids next year in school, so let's visit Egypt.' And do you know what? Off to Cairo went the Matthews family in 1955. I know now it was a time when Egypt's political climate did not put that country high on the list of vacation destinations for Western tourists. But I didn't know it then. All I knew or cared about was that I was going to see and climb the pyramids, and maybe even ride a camel. I was really excited!"

"You're right about one thing, Sarah," Jonathan observed. "I'm not certain I would have gone to Egypt in '55. But I guess the Matthews family was just braver than the Hawthorne clan."

"I guess so," Sarah said.

Laughter flowed from both of them. Jonathan was enjoying this exchange. It was obvious Sarah was also.

Her face grew more expressive and her voice more animated as she continued her story of the family's wondrous journey to Egypt. The trip to the pyramids at Giza, with the last mile covered by camel. A boat cruise on the Nile River. The incessant bargaining at Khan el-Khalili, the most famous bazaar in the world. Purchasing cartouches, the Egyptian necklaces with their names carved in gold hieroglyphics on them. Dinner overlooking the Nile. All of it seemed to come to life as Sarah described the favorite trip of her youth. Her voice grew more animated as she relayed the details of each part of her Cairo adventure.

Her tales of the land of the pyramids began to fill Jonathan's mind with marvelous images of Sarah as a young girl. He tried to imagine her as she passed through the various stages of childhood and young adulthood. A warmth came over him, as all thoughts of her now seemed to cause, as he visualized how the sweetness of her preteen years had now been transformed into a ravishing beauty of twenty.

Jonathan's mind soon filled with visions of a future exotic excursion to the northeast tip of Africa with Sarah at his side. He imagined Cairo with its Arab influence permeating every sector of life. A romantic dinner complete with water pipe on their hotel balcony, perhaps the Nile Hilton, overlooking the famous river. A visit to the Museum of Antiquities with its overflowing collection of artifacts from the three ancient Egyptian dynasties. A long descent deep inside the pyramids among the ghosts of centuries past. Daily strolls on the crowded, narrow streets with the singular sounds of Egyptian music always in the air until dawn. Watching the faithful pray at centuries-old mosques. A cruise south to Luxor and Abu Simbel to see the wonders of earlier times.

Sarah's voice interrupted Jonathan's daydreaming. "I see from that picture over there you've been to London."

She was pointing to a frame on the left side of the wall. The office portrait gallery gave it away. Jonathan had been to England many times. The picture showed him in front of his favorite pub, The Hat in Hand, with a huge grin on his face fueled by some tasty English lager that suggested the photograph had been taken after a rather long visit inside, a mug ever by his side.

"I've been there too," Sarah enthused. "When I was five." She began to recall another trip of her youth. It included a splendid tale of father and daughter sharing her dad's favorite obsession, the game of golf. So Sarah first provided some background to her London trip. As a young girl, she had spent countless hours with her dad at the country club. Not content simply to play in the swimming pool, she frequented the putting green or the driving range just to watch the golfers. Her father noticed her fascination with the game and nurtured it.

Jonathan was intrigued because the mid-1950s were still too early for most fathers to take any athletic interest of their daughters seriously. *Sarah's father was clearly ahead of his time,* Jonathan thought as she detailed the story.

Mr. Matthews allowed her to follow along as he played, particularly on Saturday and Sunday evenings when the course was virtually deserted. It was their special time, a period when her mother did not intrude. She preferred instead to give father and daughter time alone together.

Sarah then turned to the London portion of her story. It was the winter of her kindergarten year. Her father had an important meeting in the British capital with executives of Harrods, the largest and grandest department store in the world. His company was trying to convince the store to carry Hamilton watches. The entire family made the trip across the ocean. It was two weeks before Christmas, so Sarah only had to miss a week of school. Her mother had already finished her semester. Her father's dealings with Harrods brought only limited success, but everything else about the trip was wonderful.

Sarah remembered the details of the journey as if it had only taken place yesterday, despite the fact that she was only five at the time. Her mother had helped her with details over the years.

"It was in London where I was introduced to the West End musical with all its elegance," Sarah continued. "It was mostly a blur at the time, but Mom later described it to me so I would always remember it. The ornate but intimate theaters, the honor system used during 'interval'— the English term for a theater intermission—for purchasing drinks, a dress code calling for one's finest evening wear, and the quintessential black English taxis lined up outside afterward to take everyone back to their hotels. In my family's case, it was the Hotel Savoy."

Jonathan was familiar with West End musicals but chose not to interrupt her. He liked listening to her tales of youth. In fact, if truth be told, he liked everything he observed about Sarah.

Sarah went on with her story. "A revival of *Oklahoma* was the hit attraction that season, so I convinced my parents to take me to see it—not once but twice. In fact, I saw a musical every night that week in London, except the one day the theaters were closed. After we returned to the hotel each evening, I fell asleep with visions of performers singing and dancing in front of me. I was very, very happy."

"I guess you're majoring in theater as a consequence of London's West End," Jonathan said.

The idea amused her. "If you heard me sing or saw me act, Professor Hawthorne, you would realize that about the only thing I would be good for is a stage hand or set designer. Not much else," Sarah answered.

Jonathan thought her reply funny.

"Tell me more about your trip to England," Jonathan said. "I guess I'm an Anglophile at heart, because I never tire of listening to people's travels there."

"Well, I really find the English so interesting," Sarah replied. "'They speak a language of which I'm not familiar,' an American once said. I think that's true. I just love to listen to them talk. I would deliberately make up what I thought were really grown-up questions for department store clerks so I could hear their delightful accents when they answered. Then I would try to copy them. I don't think I was very good at mimicking them though."

Sarah continued her tale in the same animated voice. The second week found the Matthews family boarding the *Flying Scot* at King's Crossing Station for a train trip north to Edinburgh in the southeast corner of Scotland. The family had a first-class compartment all to itself. Sarah was simply in heaven. "I just loved the British trains, especially the private compartments in first class. As soon as we were settled, I managed to spread all my belongings until I had covered every horizontal space. This didn't make my dad very happy, I can tell you that."

As she recounted the details of the *Flying Scot* speeding north past

York, past Newcastle-upon-tyne, Sarah's level of excitement rose. She began to wonder whether Scotland would be different from England. "I kept looking for Hadrian's Wall—you know, the stone barrier separating England and Scotland. We had learned about it in school. But by the time we came upon it, I was fast asleep. The rhythmic clicking of the wheels had done its job."

"That's a neat way of putting it, Sarah," Jonathan said.

"Actually, that's what my mom suggested when I woke up and cried when I found out I had missed Hadrian's Wall. All these years I have never forgotten what she said." Sarah continued the story of her trip to the land of bagpipes and kilts. "The real reason for going to Scotland, as Dad and I constantly reminded Mother at the time, was to visit St. Andrews. It's the birthplace of golf."

"I know. I play a lot of golf, when the time permits," Jonathan said. "It's a little difficult now because of all the work, but I hope to play more in a year or two."

"I don't play as much here at Duke as I would like to either," Sarah said. "Last spring was a washout, but I'm hoping to get some rounds in before this spring semester ends. But let me tell you about St. Andrews. It's a good tale."

Sarah's attitude amused Jonathan. He was in no hurry for her stories to end, and he implied such. So she continued her account of the time she spent in Scotland fifteen years earlier. After an overnight stay in Edinburgh at the Royal Caledonian Hotel at the end of Princes Street, father and daughter rented a car for the seventy-five minute trip northeast to St. Andrews. It was with anticipation—his borne out of a passionate love of the game and hers growing out of the opportunity to do something new that excited her father—that the two of them made their way to the hallowed ground of the Old Course at St. Andrews. Not to play a round, but simply to witness the place where man first struck a golf ball.

It was early Sunday afternoon, an unusually warm December day with temperatures in the mid-fifties. The sun rapidly made its way westward and soon set over the horizon. The church spires of the town came into view first. It reminded her father of a scene typically found in picture books of merry old Scotland. The buildings snug against one another and smoke emanating from the stacks warming the occupants against the winter cold, even on a day when the thermometer reached temperatures higher than usual. A clear blue sky in the background. The Firth of Forth, the name given to the bay of water in the North Sea that abuts the town off in the distance. The Old Course, crafted only by God and nature.

Sarah's father drove rather impatiently—"recklessly" might be a better word—toward the clubhouse of the Royal and Ancient Golf Club, the imperious structure that stood just beyond both the first tee and eighteenth green of the Old Course. Their first landmark suddenly came into view. The seventeenth green, part of the most famous hole on the course and probably in the world, was but a few feet from the road. Thus the name "the road hole," her father reminded her. Its reputation as one of the world's toughest holes was well-documented. Many a British Open had been won or lost at the road hole.

Sarah's face lit up as she related the next part, a tale only one who loved the game of golf would fully understand. Jonathan's affection for the game qualified him for membership in the club. "We both quickly got out of the car, then walked to the flag stick right in the middle of the seventeenth green. We knelt and slowly kissed the green right next to the cup. My dad remarked, with a tear in his eye, that we had completed the journey to 'the Mecca of golf.' I didn't know what that meant, so Dad told me about the real Mecca. Said we had acted no differently than those who traveled to worship there." Sarah and her dad inhaled deep breaths, then smiled to one another. Father had kept the promise he made a year earlier to her. They had touched the sacred ground of St. Andrews.

A tear came to Jonathan's eye. He brushed it away with the back of his hand. "That's really a beautiful story," he said.

"Oh, but there's more," Sarah remarked excitedly. She then told of their stroll across the Swilcan Bridge, the thirteenth-century walkway crossing the Swilcan Burn, a little creek that traversed the eighteenth fairway. Made of stone and only about twenty-five feet long, it was bowed toward the sky in the middle. Golfers had first left footprints on the bridge some seven hundred years earlier as they made their final journey of the day's round in the company of friends or competitors.

Years later, Jonathan came across an unusual photograph of the bridge with the clubhouse in the background, taken by the famous Scottish photographer Brian Morgan. The gift touched Sarah greatly.

Still later, Arnold Palmer, the professional golfer's golfer, stopped and paused one last time on the Swilcan Bridge as he played the eighteenth hole in his final British Open—the British term it simply the Open—after over thirty years of exciting the golf crowds of the British Isles with his majestic charisma both on and off the course. It was the most famous golf photograph of the year.

Sarah's story kept Jonathan spellbound. Father and daughter slowly walked hand in hand up the fairway toward the eighteenth green, seemingly satisfied that they had completed their pilgrimage. They ate fish and chips by a window at the Hotel Scores—no hotel was more aptly named—across the road from the clubhouse before returning to Edinburgh. Sarah's dad washed the Scottish fare down with a combination of some local single-malt scotch and draft ale, while she drank some local soda that was unfortunately only a few degrees cooler than room temperature. The hotel was perfectly situated. Their vantage point allowed them to alternate looks between the Old Course on the left and the beach by the Firth of Forth on the right.

Jonathan was moved as a small tear appeared in a corner of Sarah's eye when she had finished her story. He was touched by her emotion. Later he came to understand more clearly both her passion for the game of golf and her love for her dad. "Father's daughter" is an overused phrase, but in Sarah's case he came to the conclusion that it captured the essence of her relationship with her father.

Jonathan's mind once again fantasized about a trip he and Sarah might take one day to golf's holiest of shrines. He thought of the shoreline beyond the Old Course, a view he remembered from an earlier visit to the University of St. Andrews. The beach, later made famous in the Academy Award winning movie *Chariots of Fire,* stretched for miles. It reminded him in many ways of Rye Beach in New Hampshire. He longed to walk with her among the Scottish dunes as lovers, his arm draped over her shoulder, at the birthplace of the game they both loved.

Jonathan emerged once again from deep contemplation as Sarah began to relate a third travel adventure of her early years. "Do we have time for another trip, Dr. Hawthorne?" she asked. She clearly wanted to continue.

"Of course. I have no plans," Jonathan answered. "Please tell me more about that adventurous girl from Lancaster, Pennsylvania." He laughed loudly at his remark.

"It was to Paris, divinely beautiful Paris, city of lovers," Sarah began. "The summer when I was thirteen. It was a family vacation to the city that has inspired more romance than any other."

Sarah was clearly becoming dramatic, but Jonathan didn't care. He was enjoying himself too much to worry about the increasing theatrics.

"We walked every inch of the city, at least it seemed so to me," she continued. She then laughingly related how she had phoned her two best friends from the first level of the Eiffel Tower. Her father, trembling, would climb no higher.

Sarah told of her family's special interest in the works of Claude Monet, the most famous of the nineteenth-century Impressionist painters. Off to Giverny they went, some fifty miles west of Paris, where Monet had spent the last decades of his life. His home and studio did not disappoint the Matthews family, but the water lilies and Japanese bridge over the nearby pond made the trip even more special. Both were subjects of numerous Monet paintings, and each appeared in real life exactly as it did on his canvases. Sarah had her picture taken while standing on the bridge. From that day forward, she would have a Monet reproduction of the acclaimed gardens on the bedroom wall above her bed.

Following Giverny, the family traveled by train to Rouen, a small city in the west of France. Again they were in search of Monet, this time the famous cathedral that the French Impressionist painted some thirty times over a two-year period and was badly damaged during World War II. After a day-long visit, they returned on a late train to Paris.

Jonathan began to fantasize yet again, this time about how he and Sarah would experience this city made especially for lovers. Images came easily. A quiet walk along the banks of the Seine, laughing and kissing, stopping often to hold each other. A boat ride on the river at dusk, with its spotlights on the adjacent buildings. The Cathedral of Notre Dame would be the highlight of the ride, of course. Climbing the many steps hand in hand with her to Sacré-Cœur, the magnificent church high atop Montmartre. Sharing a baguette, the elongated piece of bread filled with cheese and/or ham, and a bottle of wine while taking in the beauty of the city spread out before them like a giant landscape painted by a French master. A glass of wine at his favorite outdoor café on a warm spring evening. Café de Flore offered a splendid vantage point for watching the locals stroll along the Boulevard San Germain.

But back to reality. Sarah had finished the last of her three stories. Jonathan paused for a moment before speaking. Already he was beginning to see what a special person she was. He marveled at her way of revealing just enough of herself to make him want to know more. "Well, Sarah Matthews. Those were three wonderful tales. Do you have any more for another time?" he asked.

"Sure, Professor Hawthorne," Sarah replied. "But perhaps you will reveal your stories behind all those pictures on your wall."

"Come back sometime and I'll tell you all about them," he said. Jonathan could hardly contain his excitement.

"Well, I'll be off then. Thanks for spending so much time with me," Sarah replied.

"Actually, it didn't seem like much time. Besides, I enjoyed it. I hope I answered all your questions," Jonathan said.

As Sarah left his office, Jonathan knew he wanted to spend more time with her. Much, much more time. And he was impatient to start.

And Sarah's reaction?

. . . I remember my first visit to your office. I was so scared I would do or say something stupid. I wanted so much to make a good impression. You see, I had already come to develop such great respect for you. The thought that you would think less of me for whatever reason was unbearable. I know I babbled on about my travels as a child. But I guess I wanted you to know I was no neophyte about the world. Quite the contrary.

You did understand, I hope, that I had legitimate questions that brought me to your office. I simply didn't make up some excuse to see you. Well, maybe a little. However, once I was there, I was glad I had come. I was pleased when you began to ask me lots of questions about myself. . . .

Jonathan sensed, or rather hoped, that there would be many more meetings with Sarah in the weeks and months ahead. He was right. The seeds of friendship had just barely been planted. He would have to travel many more roads, though, before he could ever begin to entertain hope that their bond would someday move beyond friendship into the total giving—sexually, intellectually, emotionally—that defines a perfect relationship.

~ 3 ~

The First Time Away from Sarah

Jonathan returned to his apartment after the initial meeting with Sarah emotionally exhausted but more excited than he could remember. So many thoughts, feelings, and images raced through his brain. Visions of every aspect of Sarah—her face, her body, her voice, her questions, her stories—took over. They kept dancing in his mind as he strained to place each one in its proper sequence. He tried to remember every detail, but it was difficult, at least that evening. Years later, all of it still burned brightly on his brain. She had made an impact, of that he was certain. Little did he know at that moment what her ultimate effect on him would be. Jonathan tried hard to remind himself, however, that he should not make too much of Sarah's first visit to his office. He knew he was infatuated with her—hopelessly infatuated—but he tried to convince himself it was only a momentary feeling. It would soon vanish as later events overtook this initial feeling.

The pace of the semester quickened. Soon it was late November, Thanksgiving break. Jonathan returned to his parents' home in Colorado Springs for the traditional feast in a somewhat melancholy mood. Sarah had not been back to his office since her initial mid-October visit. He had given the second midterm examination the Monday before Thanksgiving and had hoped and expected that she would make a return visit prior to the test. Although many students had begun to take advantage of his office hours, she had not been among them. He wondered why she hadn't returned. Had she had some inkling that he had been fantasizing about her? Or had she simply sensed that he had shown an unusual amount of attention at their first out-of-class encounter and thus felt somewhat uncomfortable about it all? He finally concluded it had nothing to do with him. She simply had no questions. No other explanation was acceptable.

Jonathan pondered how Sarah was spending her Thanksgiving break. He assumed she was back home in Pennsylvania and tried to visualize her with family. The holiday was a special one across the country, but people in the Middle Atlantic and New England states seemed to take particular care to celebrate it properly. They certainly appeared to take the occasion more seriously. Perhaps it was related to the origins of the holiday that those two adjacent regions enjoyed it with much fanfare. They were the first areas of the country to celebrate the success of the early settlers. He hoped she was with relatives rather than somewhere else. This last feeling seemed silly, he knew, but he took comfort in a picture of Sarah that emphasized family.

All those private thoughts drew Jonathan's attention inward as he went through the motions of the holiday season. His parents did not suspect anything amiss, as he successfully hid his state of mind from everyone. He wanted to shout to all those gathered around the Thanksgiving table—twelve relatives were present—that he had the most bizarre case of infatuation ever to grace the heart of an adult male, certainly one with his advanced educational level. He thought better of it, however, as the family finished the pre-meal blessing. He had no idea how he might broach the subject. Besides, he did not want them to think him a fool. Better they envision him in deep contemplation about his responsibilities at Duke.

Fortunately, the dinner conversation didn't address any weighty subjects. His parents and other relatives asked lots of questions. But they were the usual ones, borne of simple curiosity about his recent life as a university professor. No one asked him about his social life. It had been a couple of years since his parents had raised the subject of marriage with him. Their last attempt had resulted in Jonathan's carefully crafted response about how his graduate school obligations prohibited any meaningful relationship. He assumed they now understood that the early years of an untenured professorship created the same time constraints.

There was another reason why the dinner table talk focused on either his new job or simply frivolous subjects. Jonathan's brother, Benjamin, was in Vietnam fighting a war few understood. Ben, as everyone called him, was a graduate of the United States Military Academy, class of 1965. He had dreamed of a military career since he was a small boy.

Because he chose the Point, his parents had always asked where they had gone wrong. They always posed the question with clearly exaggerated, raised eyebrows to give the distinct impression that they might not be completely serious. Actually, it was very much tongue-in-cheek. Jonathan's father had been a career U.S. Air Force officer who fought the enemy in the skies over both the Pacific and Europe during World War II. Despite being slightly older than most pilots, he was quite successful in both theaters, with eight "kills" before the war ended. That achievement had earned him the title of "ace," given only to those with at least five such successes.

After General Joseph Hawthorne retired from the service in 1959, his family settled in Colorado Springs. The nearby Air Force Academy was just a newborn child when Ben was completing high school. Most of the future complex was still on the drawing boards in 1960, although twenty-five years later its physical facilities would rival the other two major service academies.

The Hawthornes had probably assumed—although they had never raised the issue directly—that if either son embarked on a military career, he would follow family tradition and become a pilot. But a father's influence was no match for the West Point recruiter who convinced Ben of the glamour of the army's academy, situated high above the banks of New York State's Hudson River. It was an easy sale. Already inclined toward the Point, Ben was also a football fan. Autumn Saturdays in the late 1950s brought the American football public the likes of Bob Anderson, Pete Dawkins, and Bill Carpenter. Each was an All-American as a member of Colonel Earl "Red" Blaik's Black Knights football squad. The recruiter painted a colorful picture of Ben as part of the cadet corps cheering wildly at Michie Stadium, and he was seduced.

In reality, his parents were proud of his decision, as proud as they would have been if he had decided to follow in his father's footsteps and join the Air Force. While both parents understood that Jonathan was not cut out for the strict military life—he was always more preoccupied with the political aspects of international relations—they sensed Ben's avid interest in military affairs early on. They had long before prepared themselves, and Ben, for the eventuality that he would one day pursue a military career. They were not surprised or disappointed when his appointment to West Point arrived in the mail in the spring of his senior year of high school. USMA it would be for son number two.

As the Hawthorne family gathered around the Thanksgiving table that crisp November morning in 1967, however, fears of all parents who waited for their sons and daughters to return from combat zones around the world replaced the joys of seeing Ben perform so well during his four years at the Point. Nowhere was America's military more engaged than in Southeast Asia. Vietnam was especially troublesome for several reasons. It was a war the United States was not prepared to wage, either politically or militarily. The conflict had begun to divide the country as no war before it had done. It was a war whose casualty list grew daily.

As the conflict dragged on, loved ones back home answered knocks on their doors from military officers representing the U.S. government at an increasingly alarming rate. The officer's presence meant only bad news. The soldier had died in the service of his or her country or was missing in action. By 1967 more and more Americans with relatives in Vietnam were coming to understand Pentagon procedures for notifying families. A telegram signified injury to a loved one; a personal visit meant death or MIA status.

Lt. Ben Hawthorne was a platoon leader who implemented the U.S. military's strategy of "search and destroy" in the Mekong Delta on a daily basis. His job was to find the enemy and kill it. His letters home minimized the danger, but both Jonathan and his father knew enough about the war to be concerned. Only his mother was unaware of the assignment's extreme danger. General Hawthorne saw no reason to alarm his wife.

After General Hawthorne offered a special prayer of Thanksgiving for Ben's good health, the family mentioned him no more. The other relatives sensed his parents wanted it that way. Soon the turkey gave way to pumpkin pie, coffee, and after-dinner drinks. After a couple of glasses of the smoothest brandy Jonathan had ever tasted, his mind once again returned to thoughts of Sarah. For the rest of the day he participated little in the conversation surrounding him. Instead, he tried to isolate himself as much as possible in the corner of the living room so that he could indulge himself in his private fantasies. At last the events of the day came to a close, and his contented relatives retired to their homes or motel rooms to sleep off their Thanksgiving Day meals. Jonathan also fell into a deep sleep, but his mind wandered beyond the day's feast.

He awoke the next day refreshed and ready to take on all Colorado had to offer. He had looked forward to a return trip home since after his last visit the previous May. He wanted to drive deep into the mountains west of Colorado Springs and hike until he could go no further, physically exhausted but psychologically recharged. Although he had planned the day's trip six months earlier, Jonathan especially looked forward to it now because of his desire to be alone. He wanted the opportunity to contemplate the personal intrusions of the semester away from friends, away from relatives, and away from the day-to-day rigors of his role as a young professor.

Jonathan drove the family four-wheel-drive jeep up Ute Pass to the first set of mountain ranges, then on to Wilkerson Pass, where he paused to reflect upon the hardships of the early white settlers. Finally, Independence Pass, the last obstacle to the old mining town of Aspen, by 1967 a ballooning ski resort, stood majestically in front of him. Snow was everywhere, but the pass had not yet been closed for the season as he had feared.

Aspen of the 1960s still possessed some of the charm of the Old West. Jonathan liked to use it as a base for climbing one of the nearby mountain peaks. His favorite was the Maroon Bells, the most-photographed mountain range in the Colorado Rockies. Pike's Peak might have been more famous, but "the Bells" were more pleasing to the camera's eye.

On that day, however, he simply wanted to make his way through the snows of the lower elevations, absorbing the cold, dry air not found in his new home state of North Carolina. He drove past the center of town out Route 82 toward Glenwood Springs. This stretch of road was

flat for some thirty miles, but good hiking could be found on the western side of the road among the rolling hills at the base of the mountains. The Roaring Fork River formed the boundary on the eastern
flank. Soon Jonathan was in half a foot of snow, but it proved no match
for the pace of his strong stride. The higher elevations would be different, he knew, but it was not a day for such a challenge.

After about an hour he found a spot that invited him to pause and
sit. It was at a point a few miles from the highway that a decade later
would form the base of Fanny Hill at the new Snowmass Ski Resort.
Jonathan spread his waterproof cover and blanket on the ground,
opened his backpack, and produced a bottle of white wine, a California
chardonnay, and a packet of camembert cheese. He had selected the latter because it reminded him of the region of Normandy in western
France where he had first tasted it at the urging of the local cheese-
makers, who convinced him no other cheese could match camembert's
sweetness. Subconsciously, he might have also been influenced by
Sarah's tale of her trip to western France as a young teenager.

His thoughts turned to her, or more precisely to a future trip they
might take together. He had fantasized about it since their mid-
October encounter in his office. They were on a late train back to Paris
after a day of sightseeing at the battle sites of Normandy. They had
walked the vast expanse of the beach made forever famous on the sixth
day of June, 1944. They had followed the footsteps of those brave soldiers up the steep slopes toward the German gunnery positions at the
top of the bank, constantly visualizing the danger that confronted those
young men at every turn. They had then spent an hour reflecting on
their experiences before starting their return trip back to Paris.

The somber mood that had characterized their pilgrimage to the
World War II battlefield became but a memory. The chardonnay and
camembert they bought at a small store across the street from the rail-
road station in the little town of Bayeux—the departure point for those
coming by train to the most famous of the war's battlefields—were very
much in evidence. As Sarah and Jonathan drank the wine and fed
morsels of cheese to each other, they talked and laughed about how
happy they were. Their laughter was interspersed with long passionate
kisses. It was a wonderfully good feeling that warmed every inch of his
body and soul, that made him feel like a man deeply in love whose

affection was being returned as enthusiastically as it was given. Oh, to be in love on a night train bound for Paris!

Jonathan allowed this fanciful game to continue for the duration of lunch, about thirty more minutes. But he soon became reflective, asking himself repeatedly what purpose all of this daydreaming served. He had no ready answer, of course, but the constant questioning helped bring him back to some semblance of reality. He vowed that when he returned to Duke, he would not become a slave to his fantasies. Although this kind of vulnerability was different from that imposed by a serious relationship with a woman, it was, nonetheless, potentially destructive. Jonathan was not going to let that happen. Too much was at stake. His career meant everything to him, and nothing, nobody, was going to interfere with it. At least that's what he convinced himself of as he breathed in the panoramic beauty surrounding him.

He completed the trip back to his car in little over an hour. The chardonnay he consumed at lunch accounted for the ten-minute difference. Snow and wine don't mix very well, and one's legs are the first to realize that. He arrived back in Colorado Springs five hours later with a firm resolve that his life was on track and that nothing was going to change that.

Two days later, Jonathan returned to Durham prepared to finish the semester without any intrusive thoughts about Sarah. But his resolve melted the instant she walked into class the Monday after Thanksgiving.

~ 4 ~

The First Outside Contact

Sarah looked lovelier than ever as she took her seat in the third row. Jonathan watched out of the corner of his eye as she placed her books on the floor and took out her notebook and pen. She appeared to be all business, waiting for him to begin his lecture so she could take notes. Jonathan hoped her demeanor was due to a strong work ethic and not to some concern about first impressions—his or hers—during the initial office visit. He hoped he hadn't offended or scared her in any way. That would be unfortunate, perhaps even devastating, if it was the case. He already had forgotten about his new resolve to discontinue his fantasies about her.

The day's topic focused on the emergence of international organizations as newly influential players in world politics. Jonathan emphasized the role envisaged for the most important of these new bodies, the United Nations. He discussed the high hopes of the men and women who gathered in San Francisco during the final days of World War II searching for a way to prevent future wars. These aspiring architects of peace had concluded that nations of the world needed a special place where their representatives could meet on a continuing basis and resolve problems without resorting to violence. A formal arena that might even have sufficient power of its own to prevent military conflict. Their answer was a new global actor, the U.N., to be located in New York City on land donated by the Rockefeller family. The young professor described how the U.N. had struggled since its inception to carve out a meaningful role for itself. Reasonable individuals debated whether or not it had been successful. The major problem, of course, was that while national rulers were willing to assign this new international organization responsibility for world peace, they were not ready to give it the means to achieve such a noble goal. That would require countries to relinquish some of their own national power to the larger political body. This idea flew in the face of one of world politics' most sacred ideas, national sovereignty.

This meant that ultimate power resided in a nation's governmental leadership, with no higher authority above it. National leaders were thus accountable to no one. They selected their foreign policy goals according to whether they had sufficient force to achieve them. If their neighbors had the power to prevent certain actions, then they would refrain from provoking them. But they were not deterred by some higher power, for none existed. The international system was thus controlled by a group of independent nations that, on paper at least, accepted the idea that all countries were equal to one another, particularly in a legal sense. But they were not averse to bullying any country that appeared to be weaker. It was a global system inclined toward anarchy.

In earlier times, the Roman Catholic Church as well as several national leaders—Julius Caesar and Alexander the Great among them—had attempted to rule the world through empire-building. But since the 1500s, the world had accepted the notion of nation-state dominance. The model had been reaffirmed on several occasions since then in response to challenges from individuals, like Napoleon or Hitler, who sought to have their own single nations dominate the planet, or from religious leaders who wanted their own paramount positions of influence.

Now as a consequence of the devastation of two world wars, however, some scholars and world leaders questioned the future viability of the nation-state system itself, blaming the structure for causing most conflict witnessed during the previous century or so. Creating the U.N. and giving it the responsibility, if not the means, for world peace was their response to the emerging doubt about the ability of nations themselves to avoid global strife.

As Jonathan searched for just the right words to keep his students enthralled, he could not help but steal glance after glance at Sarah.

Although she was seated in the third row, he had an unbroken, clear view of her from top to bottom. He had ambled across the room as he lectured in an apparently aimless fashion, but in reality he calculated the direction of each step in such a way so as to keep her constantly in sight.

Jonathan wondered if students knew that professors' meanderings around classrooms were often not random wanderings at all but probably had clear purposes to them. The objective was usually to acquire a better view of an interesting student, or less often, to sneak a glance out the window at some fascinating sight below. At exam time, watching for inappropriate behavior from suspected cheaters was a common reason for such sauntering.

Jonathan had not in his short teaching career been one to engage in looking for "interesting sights" in or out of the lecture room as he spoke to the class. He had always felt the need to concentrate on his next thought. But things were different now. One seated not fifteen feet away had smitten him. There was now a purpose to such behavior. Moreover, he had already discovered he was developing great skill in disguising his salacious thoughts. That was fortunate, because he found himself unable to control it.

A wool skirt had replaced the shorts Sarah wore in October. She crossed her legs in such a way so as to convey a sense of modesty rather than provocation. Her demure manner could not hide her sensuality, however. Quite the contrary. It made her more desirable than if she was sitting before him completely naked or wearing some lewd, erotic out-fit. Jonathan found that even the simplest of her moves excited him. He had concluded early in his teaching career that female students were really quite sexy when, lost in concentration, they were completely unaware of both their movements and their subsequent effects on male observers. With Sarah, the impact was even more pronounced.

Jonathan's heart raced just a little faster, for example, whenever he observed her eyes darting back and forth between her notebook and the lectern in what seemed, subconsciously, like a slightly mischievous motion as she absorbed what he was saying. Or when he saw her inno-cently trying to become more comfortable in her seat, oblivious to what she was doing or to the fact that she was being watched. He hoped his efforts to keep her in sight went unnoticed.

As class ended, Jonathan, careful to avoid detection, watched as Sarah disappeared beyond the exit. As was his custom, he addressed a couple of questions from a handful of students who approached him after the lecture. He always enjoyed the opportunity at the end of class to pontificate further on the topic of the day. That was what teaching was all about. He hoped those who stayed after his lectures did so because he had piqued their interest that day. He knew that after the next class period, when he handed back the second midterm examination, a few students would likely ask for clarification about their grades. That was not a pleasant situation for him, but post-lecture questions were a different matter. If only professors didn't have to grade exams.

After the last student left, Jonathan gathered his notes together and began to make his way to the door. Before he reached it, however, he sensed Sarah's presence nearby, although he couldn't see her. Immediately he remembered he had felt the same way when she knocked at his office door that first time, before he actually knew who was there. His intuition was on target. As he scurried into the hallway, there she was, with that same look on her face that had captured his soul when he first laid eyes on her.

"Hi, Professor Hawthorne," she said.

Jonathan's heart began to pound, much as it had at their last face to face encounter. He couldn't help it.

"I have a question about the lecture," she said, and proceeded to elaborate.

She is so perceptive, he thought. Jonathan answered her, although he later would not be able to remember what he had said. No matter. It wasn't important, for Sarah was again standing in front of him. He had to seize the moment.

But before he could, she spoke once again, this time with another question. "I finished some of the future reading assignments when I was home at Thanksgiving. One thing puzzled me about the Wright reading though."

Quincy Wright had been one of the giants in the academic field of international politics since World War II. Students usually found him a bit difficult, as they did most thinkers on the frontiers of their research disciplines. Jonathan was certain, however, that Sarah's problem grew not out of her inability to understand Wright, but from the implications of what he had to say. He was right. Her question was a good one. He answered her query with enthusiasm.

"So that's how you spent your vacation," he asked almost rhetorically. "Reading international politics?"

Although Jonathan had not really called upon her to answer, Sarah made some humorous reply that suggested her life did, indeed, center around her responsibilities as a student. Rather than describe how she had spent her remaining time at home over Thanksgiving, however, she took a different path. "I bet you spent your Thanksgiving working. Don't all professors? Or do you have a life outside the office? Students, you know, aren't quite certain what faculty do when they're away from campus. Actually, I'm just joking. I'm sure you do—that is have a life outside Duke. Did you go play somewhere or visit relatives?"

Jonathan was taken aback by her probe into a personal aspect of his life—although, if truth be told, asking about one's holiday did not exactly constitute prying into one's private self. This small detail was lost on him in the excitement of the moment, however. Sarah wanted to know about his Thanksgiving vacation. Was she just being polite, or did she have a genuine curiosity? And if she was curious, what kind of interest did she have? Did she view him simply as just another professor—albeit a young one—who stimulated students in class? Or had she sensed some of the obsession that had engulfed him?

It didn't really matter. Sarah now stood in front of him. Jonathan was not going to lose such a golden opportunity to spend some more time with her. He quickly took the initiative and spoke. The words poured from his mouth as if he had rehearsed them for weeks. He told of his trip home to Colorado Springs, of the family gathering on Thanksgiving Day, and of his desire for some solitude both then and the following day when he went up into the mountains.

He did not, of course, relate the reason for his yearning, even need, to be alone—so that he might reflect on a personal matter, the obsession with her that was overtaking him. The thought never crossed his mind to tell her, although if it had he would have dismissed it. He believed Sarah would have thought him bizarre and the entire idea absurd.

Jonathan elaborated on his trip into the mountains, secretly hoping that such an adventure would fascinate her. If Sarah was interested, she gave little clue. This intrigued him. So he continued, painting a colorful picture of the snow-capped mountain peaks in the distance, the crisp, dry air nipping at his face, and the snow-covered ground on which he reclined with his bottle of California wine and French cheese.

Sarah grinned when he related how the combination of extreme altitude, low temperatures, and a covering of snow—mixed with the consumption of a full bottle of wine—gave him a rather less-than-balanced sense of reality. The grin was subtle—not one designed, Jonathan knew, to impress him. It merely conveyed the simple message he had amused her with his story. It was reward enough for his efforts, though.

"Do tell me about the rest of your holiday," Jonathan inquired next. He wanted her to stay. "Did you go home to Lancaster?" He sensed that Sarah was surprised and even somewhat pleased that he had remembered details about her background. Whether his perception was accurate or not was beside the point. He was eager to grasp at anything that conveyed something beyond the traditional professor-student relationship.

At the same time, their somewhat personal exchange was beginning to create cross-pressures for Jonathan. He had strong convictions about the inappropriateness of certain situations in which faculty and students sometimes found themselves. He understood that a friendship between student and professor could be proper behavior for both parties. It depended on the circumstances. If it developed after the end of the semester in which the student was enrolled in the professor's class, it probably didn't cross the line. At Penn State he had observed several examples of faculty-student relationships that appeared to blossom, at least publicly, after a class had ended. He often wondered what, if anything, had transpired in more private settings during the semester.

But Sarah was still in his class. Given this point, he saw some ambiguity about his proper role at that time. So he stopped short of asking her to join him in the student union for coffee. He didn't want to give off even the slightest appearance of impropriety. Maybe after the semester finished, when she was no longer his student. But not now. So their conversation continued in the hallway.

"I went back home for the holidays," Sarah said. "It was wonderful. All my grandparents were there, as well as my aunt and uncle and their kids." She grew livelier as she related the events of the weekend. Her extended family was in a jovial mood the entire time, which made for a rather relaxing time. She welcomed that, as she needed the escape from the rigors of Duke for a few days. Many of her high school friends had also returned home for the holiday. She spent Friday night with them at the Colt Inn, enjoying a few beers and the best beef tips sandwiches in Lancaster County.

The Colt Inn was one of many local bars where one could get by with a fake ID card. Sarah's generation had long since learned how to fool the Pennsylvania authorities with their illegal driver's licenses, which made it much easier to pass for the legal drinking age of twenty-one. She had but a short six months before she reached that age, she rationalized, so what harm could come from consuming a few beers while she was slightly under age?

The Saturday after Thanksgiving was a day for serious adventure, though. The revelation surprised Jonathan. "It was all your influence, Professor Hawthorne," Sarah said. She then related how she and a couple of friends had traveled to Gettysburg, some fifty miles away, to view the Civil War battlefield.

Jonathan did not see the connection, so she elaborated. "Remember your lecture on the difference between nationhood and statehood? Nationhood meant a sense of consciousness among people who shared a number of similar characteristics, such as language and religion, and consequently wished to be governed only by their own kind. Statehood, on the other hand, signified a legal government with a clearly defined territory. By the middle of the nineteenth century, the U.S. South was one nation and the U.S. North a different nation—divided by opposing views on the issue of slavery—although both parts of the country were legally under the control of one big 'state' or government, the United States. So I wanted to experience how the incompatibility between the two concepts of nationhood and statehood led to a violent civil war."

Jonathan was speechless, and it was no act. He remembered when he had explained those two important concepts in class, using obvious examples such as the Soviet Union with its hundreds of nationalities or the two nations within Canada, the French-speaking and English-speaking sectors. Sarah had taken the concepts of statehood and nation-hood one step further, and by using her powers of application, had identified an unusual but highly relevant example from her own coun-try's history. Jonathan just smiled to himself when she finished her tale. *What an extraordinary mind at work,* he thought. More importantly, she had been thinking of him over the holidays, he reflected, even if only in their conventional roles of professor and student rather than in some more intriguing way, as his fantasies had promised.

Jonathan then shared his own travel story of the previous summer when he toured the eastern third of Canada. His purpose was to emphasize the point about nationhood and statehood once more. He also wanted to show what an interesting guy he was. Canada was cele-brating the one-hundredth anniversary of its sovereignty that year. The countrywide festivities had prompted him to spend almost three weeks in June traveling there—from the predominantly English-oriented part of western Ontario through the mixed sectors of eastern Ontario and the Francophile province of Quebec, and concluding in Anglophile New Brunswick. Montreal hosted Expo '67, and Jonathan passed one week there absorbing the atmosphere of the World's Fair. He loved the excitement and distinctiveness of the various country exhibits.

Jonathan amused himself with the sudden idea—privately, of course—that he ought to take Sarah on a tour of Canada. There they could experience firsthand the tension between two proud cultures tied to one ruling government. It occurred to him that she might have been reading his mind.

"What a great way to do a comparative analysis of statehood and nationhood," Sarah remarked. "A genuine academic road trip disguised as a vacation, or was it vice versa? I bet you even wrote it off on your tax return, didn't you? I would have."

It took most of Jonathan's willpower to refrain from blurting out that perhaps the two of them ought to retrace his steps from the previ-ous summer during spring break that year. He had enough sense to realize the stupidity and futility of such a move. It shocked him, how-ever, to think he could readily conjure up such a potentially romantic trip with someone who was his student and who probably had no inkling of his complete infatuation with her.

Not knowing what else to say, Jonathan mumbled something about having to meet a colleague in ten minutes and that he had better be going. As he told Sarah, he watched for any sign of disappointment. His powers of observation were not developed enough to discern any meaningful reaction, positive or negative.

"Good-bye. Stop by again when you're free," he said.

Sarah grabbed her books and with a final glance turned and walked away. She had made no commitment to return. He watched her for a few moments until she was out of sight.

But Sarah had made such a promise to herself.

. . . You may have wondered, my dear Jonathan, why I was in the hallway the first day back from Thanksgiving vacation that first semester. The fact of the matter was that I had missed you when I was home. It wasn't a loneliness created by being away from one's love. Rather, I had come to appreciate your mind, both in and out of the classroom. I kept thinking about my first visit to your office. I missed listening to you talk, both in front of the whole class and just to me. It took me three days of being home before I realized it. And it surprised me—really surprised me. I didn't quite know what to make of it.

So I decided I wanted to learn more about you. Not just about your professional career, but about your personal life as well. I hadn't yet been fortunate to come to know any other professor well. But it seemed so natural talking to you.

I returned from Thanksgiving convinced I would benefit from seeing you more often, perhaps even on a regular basis. My actions the Monday after Thanksgiving were the first step in my new plan. . . .

~ 5 ~

The First Off-Campus Encounter

Jonathan returned the second midterm exam to Sarah's class the next period. Her score was excellent, easily the best in the class in his judgment. He wondered if he was being totally objective. But a colleague whom Jonathan asked to read it, without stating the real reason for doing so, confirmed the exam's merit. This meant that, coupled with her outstanding performance on the first midterm, Sarah was going into the final examination at the top of the class.

The external assessment pleased him, as he wanted her to do well. His motive was a bit different from the usual one, though. He told himself, in a somewhat amused manner, that if he was going to fall madly in love with someone in his class, better she be an A student than a C one. His colleagues would think better of him for it. He wasn't sure about his parents, though, particularly his mother. The key for her probably wouldn't be the A. It would be "student." The thought crossed his mind that he would relish the opportunity some day to convince his mom that falling in love with a student was okay—more than okay actually—if it brought him total happiness. He knew she would approve, perhaps not right away but eventually.

The last weeks of the semester went by quickly. Soon Jonathan had delivered the term's final lecture, and students began preparing for the end-of-semester tests. This was a stressful time for all, and Jonathan hoped it would go smoothly. Duke had a special week-long schedule for final examinations. As bad luck would have it, Sarah's class was scheduled for the last time slot of the week, eight to ten o'clock the Thursday evening before Christmas. That meant that while most Dukies were already home preparing for the holidays, his students were among a handful who had to endure a few more stressful days on campus.

Jonathan decided to do something special for them since they would be feeling sorry for themselves because of their later departure time from campus during the Christmas season. He would give a small party in an adjacent room after the exam was over. It would be his way of saying "happy holidays!" The menu would include what had already become well-known on campus, at least among faculty who had sampled it a year earlier, as "Hawthorne's famous eggnog." Sister Al, as she was called, was a Polish nun and former classmate of Jonathan's in graduate school. She had given him the recipe for this popular winter holiday season drink. He first tasted it when his Russian language class celebrated one Christmas during his Penn State days. The eggnog was well-fortified with three different kinds of alcohol—whiskey, brandy, and rum—in abundant quantities, as well as more sugar than an average teenager consumed in any given week. Also on the menu were assorted Christmas cookies.

Since none of his students would leave campus until the morning after the exam because of the late hour, Jonathan was not really concerned about any post-party problems. Besides, he would monitor students' consumption carefully. He knew his gesture of a party might be out of character, if not for him, at least for the typical faculty member. But he didn't care. Perhaps the Duke administration would not look kindly on his behavior. If confronted, he would argue, somewhat tongue-in-cheek, that it was just the kind of gesture that would please parents who shelled out thousands of dollars for their children's education and thus expected faculty to go "the extra mile."

The eggnog was a huge hit at the Duke faculty Christmas party the preceding year, and Jonathan wanted to share it with his students. He did not consciously consider what role Sarah's presence in the class played in his decision. If he was honest with himself, though, he would probably admit he was trying to make an impression on her.

Jonathan was clearly vying for most popular Duke teacher, most of his colleagues would jokingly say if they knew about the post-exam celebration. A few might raise some eyebrows, particularly because some of the students were underage, but they were mostly the "old guard" who had spent a quarter of a century or more on campus and whose careers were rapidly coming to an end. While he didn't want to alienate any of them—after all, a few still served on the university-wide tenure committee—he wasn't about to let a few stodgy old professors who had probably forgotten why they had joined the profession in the first place shackle him.

Old Roland Peterson was a perfect example of a faculty member whose time had come and gone. He arrived on campus in the mid-1930s straight out of graduate school. Yale, of course. His specialty was Japanese history and politics, and he spoke perfect Japanese. He left briefly during the war to serve in military intelligence but returned to campus the very day General Douglas MacArthur accepted the Japanese surrender. He had always remained secretive through the years about his specific duties but clearly left the impression that he had defeated America's Pacific menace single-handedly with some important and unusual sleuth work.

In those early years, Peterson was well-liked by students and colleagues alike. He even won the coveted Martha Duke Teacher of the Year award. His acceptance speech was brilliant. Quotes from both ancient and modern philosophers sprinkled his remarks, which praised the glorious profession that had become his life's calling.

As the decades rolled by, however, Peterson had come to dislike students. First the average students. Later, even the better students. Finally, even the younger faculty began to sense his coldness toward them. The word "bitterness" didn't quite capture his attitude, at least at first. "Detachment" or "aloofness" were better descriptions. Increasingly, though, signs of clear and undisguised disdain toward everyone and everything marked his behavior. His tongue became more caustic toward both students and colleagues alike. He had become a cancer in both the department and the broader campus community.

University mores were such, however, that his type of behavior was tolerated. Some would say it was even encouraged as long as it wasn't too disruptive. Kept the faculty more mysterious, more in control. Students soon stopped enrolling in Peterson's classes. Exactly the response the disenchanted professor desired, because the fewer students he had to deal with, the better. Then younger colleagues found excuses to avoid him, and his committee assignments became fewer. "All the better," he would say. That left more time for research or simply total absorption in whatever interested him. And less reason to interact with anyone.

Except for the university-wide tenure committee. That institution remained the senior faculty member's greatest authority—determining the final fate of a younger colleague. An applicant's department must first approve tenure, but that was only the first step. A necessary one, to be sure, but clearly not a sufficient enough step. The real "keepers of the gate" were the campus-wide tenure committee members who could ignore the peer evaluation of colleagues in the candidate's own department or external assessments from scholars in the same research areas at other universities. Senior faculty became intellectual custodians of the university. If a junior colleague didn't fit the desired mold as defined by the "old guard," no matter how outstanding the research and teaching records, he or she was denied tenure. The candidate was sent packing.

Some faculty would deem the system arbitrary, but most agreed only that there were some intangible criteria at work in the final stage. These defenders of the system would argue that because tenure brought lifetime job security, a candidate must be deemed not only worthy of such an honor, but must also be judged a potential contributor to the broader intellectual community that comprised the essence of the university. Who better to protect the institution than those with a lifetime of service?

Senior faculty thus took their role on the university-wide tenure committee more seriously than any other task. Peterson relished his time on the panel and actively campaigned for the assignment. Despite his increasingly negative reputation, no one had ever dared vote against him because the selection process took place in public. The old professor had a long memory, a very long one, and no one wanted to feel the lengthy reach of his vindictive wrath sometime down the road.

Jonathan understood all of this as he sat watching his class hard at work on their exams. The evening went as planned. Most students took at least an hour and a half to complete the test. Why did they have to write everything they knew about the topic, he wondered? Why couldn't they just answer the questions directly, without extraneous information? He had explained to the class on numerous occasions that they should always think in terms of high-powered rifle responses— ones that focused only on writing the specific information that the question called for. They were to avoid a shotgun approach—jotting down everything they knew about the topic. But he realized his suggestion had fallen on deaf ears. That didn't surprise him. Duke students wanted nothing left to chance in their answers. He had to prod many of them to hand in their exam booklets at the end of two hours.

The department secretary had agreed to return to campus that evening and to set up the food, Cokes, and eggnog. Jonathan knew that some students would finish the exam earlier than others. These early finishers would make their way into the adjacent classroom before the rest of the students. So he needed help.

At last the allotted time was up. Jonathan hurried into the party room and filled the cookie plates. He then added more eggnog into the huge punch bowl, careful to explain that the alcohol level was far greater than one could taste. The entire class could now relax. Soon the students were into the mood of the party. Not a loud, boisterous celebration, but one in which they just seemed to unwind and engage in relaxed conversation. The first semester of 1967–1968 had finally come to an end and a major load had been lifted from their shoulders.

Most students stayed for just a short time because they had to pack for the trip home the next day. About ten of them remained for almost an hour, with most drifting out the door shortly thereafter. A couple of students delayed their departures a little longer. Sarah was among this last group. Soon all were saying their thank-yous and good-byes and moving toward the exit. All except Sarah, that is. She paused for a moment, then asked if Jonathan needed any help cleaning up after the party since the department secretary had long since left. Her offer clearly caught him off guard, but he gained control of himself quickly.

"That would be great! I need to conserve most of my energy for that big task tomorrow. You know, grading all those exams. You want me in tip-top shape, don't you? I mustn't miss any of the subtle pearls of wisdom now, must I? So thanks for offering," he said.

Both laughed as they set about straightening up the room and transporting the remaining food and drink to Jonathan's car, parked behind the library about five hundred feet from the entrance to the building. As they loaded the leftovers into the trunk, he feverishly wondered what to do next. Again he was torn between wishing somehow to signal his desire to know her better and his belief any romantic relationship with her was forbidden territory—at least until she was no longer his student. He "bit the bullet," as the saying goes, and indicated he was hungry. It was a little white lie, as he had had his fill of eggnog and cookies. But such lies are permissible in these circumstances, he rationalized.

"Would you like to join me for a quick burger and fries?" he asked. Jonathan had just taken the next step in their relationship. He knew the few glasses of eggnog had given him the courage to suggest they grab some food, but he didn't care. Part of the reason for drinking eggnog, of course, was to enable him to ignore his inhibitions. Sarah's face lit up when he asked her. It was all the answer he needed.

Unlike most major universities, Duke didn't have any student-oriented businesses within walking distance of the campus, so they jumped into his car and headed off to find a place to eat. No fast-food restaurants were open at this late hour—it was then almost midnight—but they found Tom's Diner, an all-night establishment about a mile from campus. Jonathan would have preferred an upscale restaurant or bar, but he knew he was already pushing his good fortune.

A couple of cheeseburgers and Cokes later, they were deep in conversation. Sarah was eager to discuss the final examination because she was concerned about one of her answers.

Jonathan quickly dismissed her anxiety, though, with his analysis of her overall performance to date. "Don't worry. You probably did just fine. Don't sell yourself short. Besides, you may well be the best student I've yet had at Duke. Of course, I haven't been here long enough to have taught a whole lot of students."

Jonathan's serious remark caught Sarah off-guard, and her face appeared to blush. She had never thought of herself that way, she told him.

But he stated the point again, this time emphasizing she was simply outstanding, both in absolute terms and in comparison with her classmates. He hoped it was his mind, not his heart, talking. "Let me repeat. You're as good as or better than any student I've had since I've been at Duke." Jonathan uttered his words slowly and emphatically, trying to drive the point home.

Sarah thought about it for a few moments, her face turning deeper shades of crimson red with each passing second. "Thanks for the compliment, Dr. Hawthorne. I'm not used to such comments. No one has ever suggested that to me before. Look, I know I'm smart, but so is everyone else here. I've been on the dean's list every semester, but I assume most everyone else has been too."

Jonathan took another sip from his Coke as he surveyed what effect his last comment had had on her. He decided it had had the desired impact. It was time to shift gears. He tried to think of a way to signify the end of the semester and the beginning, hopefully, of a new stage in their relationship. So he changed directions. "What are your plans for next semester? Are you taking any political science courses?"

"In a way, I am," Sarah said. "I'm enrolled in Duke's internship program over in Raleigh. I'll be working in Senator Erwin's North Carolina office, spending about twenty hours a week learning about politics in the real world."

Sam Erwin had represented the state in the U.S. Senate for fourteen years. Jonathan thought him a good man.

"The Senator is interested in bringing more international business to America, with the not-so-hidden agenda of helping North Carolina companies. I'll be involved with some research projects relating to it. That's about as close as I'll get to international politics next semester," Sarah said.

Sarah was also taking two morning classes—general courses to fulfill the university's basic education requirements. She would spend the bulk of her time during the day, however, at the federal government complex thirty miles away in the state capital.

Her plans intrigued Jonathan for both professional and personal reasons. He, of course, loved international politics but really knew little about the mercantile aspects of world affairs. Perhaps Sarah could teach him something. But her internship also gave him the potential opportunity of seeing her more often, as they now had something in common. *Carpe diem!* He seized the moment.

"I worked as an intern in Pennsylvania Senator Hugh Scott's office one summer during my undergraduate days at Pitt. Perhaps I can help by telling you some of my 'war stories.' If you need someone to share your experiences with, to bounce off some ideas of, or simply just to let off some steam to, stop by the office sometime. Maybe I can help a little," Jonathan offered.

"I'd like that," Sarah replied. "I'm really looking forward to the internship, but to tell you the truth, I'm scared about it too."

"What are you afraid of?" Jonathan asked. "In a month you'll know more about the subject than anyone in the office, maybe even more than the good Senator himself."

Sarah was amused at that possibility. "I don't know about that, but I can tell you I will work hard."

"It'll also give you an opportunity to meet lots of new people," Jonathan observed. "Perhaps it'll open some doors for a future job once you graduate too."

"Perhaps, but graduation seems so far away. I'm not yet thinking about what I want to do when that day finally arrives," Sarah said. "In the meantime, I'm just trying to get as many different experiences as I can while I'm at Duke. I'll cross the employment bridge in due course."

Jonathan paused for a moment. He now wanted to change the subject completely away from the academic side of their relationship onto more personal grounds. But he wished to be subtle about it. After all, it was still much too early to reveal what had been going through his mind for the entire semester—fifteen long weeks. He found the answer in the season of the year.

"Do you have any special plans for Christmas?" he asked. Jonathan now sought to establish a more equal give-and-take between them. He wanted to throw aside their respective roles of professor and student. He yearned for Sarah to view him as a person, as a man—maybe even as one capable of delectable thoughts about women, and particularly about her. His pulse rate began to climb and his heart started to beat more rapidly. It was the heartbeat of one whose level of excitement was rising. It always did when they moved into more personal conversation.

"The usual," Sarah answered. "I'll arrive home too late to get a part-time job over the holidays, like most of my friends. In fact, I'll have to hustle just to complete my Christmas shopping. I haven't even had time to start yet. We tend to spend a quiet time at Christmas, especially before Christmas Day. Mom is always ready for a break from teaching by mid-December, so she doesn't do much. And Dad is busy with increasing responsibilities at work. I like to put my mind to rest and do those things that don't tax my brain so much."

Jonathan listened intently as Sarah spoke. It was really good to hear her talk about herself. He wanted to learn as much as he could about her, as if that would lead to what he hoped would be the next phase in their relationship.

"I'm the same way," Jonathan said. "I don't open a book between the time I get home until about the twenty-eighth."

"It's the only time of the year I bake," Sarah said, laughing. "Cookies, cranberry bread, nut mixes, casseroles, roasts, fancy desserts, you name it. I lose myself in the kitchen. Mom says I really have a hidden desire to become a chef at a famous French restaurant. But I always tell her that she, being a professor, should know that cooking is really an escape from college.

"Just the three of us—Mom, Dad, and me—spend Christmas Eve together. No other relatives. We are victims of tradition, I guess. We have a favorite restaurant where the family has a scrumptious meal at noon, including a bottle of wine. Rather decadent, don't you think?" she asked rhetorically. "That usually puts us to sleep for a few hours. Then we attend church service at seven o'clock followed by a huge snack at home—shrimp, crab, cheese, meat tips, spreads. We end the evening by opening our gifts from one another while we listen to the *Messiah* in the background. Any gifts from others are left until Christmas morning."

As Sarah rambled on, Jonathan fantasized what it would be like to be included in her family celebration. All sorts of thoughts entered his mind. He would be in charge of making the eggnog and would wear an apron appropriate to the occasion around his waist. The first step was to separate the whites and the yokes of a dozen eggs. It was a very important procedure in the eggnog recipe, and it always caused him the most difficulty, particularly if he had had a few drinks in the process.

Sarah's job would be the cookies. Jonathan's role in that venture would be chief taster of the finished product, sort of a quality control engineer. He thought that title funny. He had always assumed that task at home for his mom and wanted to repeat it for Sarah. Of course, a half-gallon of milk was a prerequisite for the test. The cookies had to be dipped in a glass of milk ever so slowly soon after being removed from the oven. The final key to a successful test was rescuing the cook-ies from the milk just before they began to crumble. That way he could put them into his mouth at the very moment they fell apart. Of course, he held a spoon in his free hand just in case. That was always how Jonathan had performed the ritual with his mom's chocolate chip cookies, his favorite. He cherished his time as chief tester of her sweet delicacies.

He had second thoughts, however, about performing the same task at Sarah's house. Better to wait until much later when their relationship was on far firmer ground. Their tenth wedding anniversary seemed soon enough. He wasn't about to take any chances.

He imagined Sarah opening her gifts by the Christmas tree to the sounds of traditional holiday music filling the background with the spirit of the season. He pondered what he might give her that first Christmas. Something thoughtful and somewhat personal, if discrete. A gift that captured some special memory or something she valued. Perhaps a book about the essence of St. Andrews or one of the other trips she had taken with her family as a child.

Jonathan had learned early that the key to good gift-giving was the thought that went into the selection. His parents had often remarked that they were struck by how uniquely appropriate his selections always seemed to be. He usually sensed that they opened his gifts with just a little extra anticipation.

Of course, sometimes he missed the mark completely. Witness the baseball he gave his mom for Mother's Day when he was eight years old. Jonathan had just joined his first baseball team and was convinced that his mother coveted a baseball more than anything else in the world. After all, that's what he wanted. The choice had been between flowers and the ball. It had been an easy decision for an eight year old. His mother accepted the gift with all the graciousness a loving parent could muster, but the baseball was his within a week.

Sarah's voice interrupted Jonathan's daydreaming. "On Christmas Day, the relatives get together at someone's house. It rotates each year, at least among those who live nearby. We all exchange gifts and then spend the day playing and eating, including a traditional holiday dinner. The designated chief cook of that particular Christmas dinner prepares a traditional feast from some country in the world. Nobody can reuse the menu for four or five years, nor can a cook repeat his or her menu the next time around. I know it seems like a huge chore, but it really isn't. Everyone pitches in and helps the main chef."

"Sounds really exciting," Jonathan remarked as he thought of all the wonderful meals he had eaten abroad. "What's been the most fascinating Christmas meal?"

"Tough question," Sarah said. "The cooks do fairly well when they stick to western European countries. I especially like the English dinner. I guess I'm just a bona fide Anglophile. My trip to England during the Christmas season when I was little must have influenced me. I remember a holiday dinner at the fourth floor restaurant in Harrods. What a feast! Chestnut and apple soup, roast goose with fruit and chestnut stuffing, Yorkshire pudding, spiced cranberries, brussels sprouts, plum pudding with hard sauce, fruitcake, and mince pies. I ate so much that day, except the brussels sprouts, of course. But each country seems to have some special dish—an appetizer, entrée, dessert, or whatever—that I remember really well. I'd like to combine the best of all the menus some year. Kind of an international Christmas smorgasbord."

Sarah continued with her vacation plans. "I'll probably spend the rest of the holidays, now that I'm away at college, with all my friends whom I haven't seen for awhile. We'll visit all the old stomping grounds and find some new ones. I guess as soon as we're all old enough to drink legally, we'll have a whole new list of places to visit."

"That's how it works," Jonathan suggested. "I remember the first holiday season home from Pitt after I turned twenty-one. My friends and I went from bar to bar flaunting our ID cards. A whole new world opened up to us, although it became 'old hat' rather quickly."

"How are you spending the Christmas season, Professor Hawthorne?" Sarah asked.

He wished Sarah would call him Jonathan, but of course that would be inappropriate, at least for now. He longed to move beyond the traditional roles in which they now found themselves. As he later learned, it would take quite a while for that to happen, and it would be he, not she, who would be slow to make the transition.

"I'm off to Colorado again," he said. "Our house literally becomes a motel for all the relatives, but fortunately it's our second home in the mountains, not the one in Colorado Springs, and it's not until after Christmas. The time before the big day is spent pretty much like yours—a quiet family dinner at home on Christmas Eve with our own exchange of presents. The difference between your schedule and mine is that I'll probably spend the afternoon before Christmas skiing on a small nearby slope by the Broadmoor Hotel or else ice skating in the hotel's famous rink. Many Olympians practice there most of the year, but the Christmas season is down time for them."

Jonathan and the rest of the family were also content to spend time skiing on Christmas Day. It was practice for the long list of outdoor activities they would enjoy in the mountains the week after Christmas. The nearest ski slope of any size was two hours away from his parents' home. Most easterners who had begun in the last decade to make their way to Colorado at Christmastime traveled to resorts in the higher elevations, so the Broadmoor slope was not crowded on either the twenty-fourth or the twenty-fifth.

"Christmas dinner is late, after dark, so that all of us can hit the slopes all day if we wish," he continued. "We have a ham that's already cooked so no one need miss out on skiing because they're in front of a hot stove all day. Most locals don't ski much on Christmas Day, so my family has the slopes pretty much to itself."

Jonathan then described the rest of the holidays. "The day after Christmas, we go up to our house in the mountains northwest of Denver, just east of the Continental Divide. There we spend the rest of the holidays hiking, skiing, ice skating, or snowmobiling—just the usual stuff when you have the most breathtaking snow-covered mountain setting in the world right outside your window. And you're entertaining lots of relatives who seem to make it to the mountain home. By week's end we're always exhausted physically, but we're also re-energized. It's so exhilarating to push oneself until every muscle says, 'No more.' Then we retire to the outdoor Jacuzzi to let the hot waters soothe each one of them while the cold air bites away at our faces, maybe a snowflake or two circles our noses, and glasses of wine rest in our hands, of course."

"You paint an inviting picture, Professor Hawthorne," Sarah remarked. "I wish I could escape over the holidays to some mountain retreat like yours."

It took every ounce of discipline for Jonathan to acknowledge her comment with only a slight smile rather than an invitation to join him. He had better watch himself, he thought. He looked at his watch. "My goodness," he said. "It's almost two o'clock. I'd better get you back to the dorm so you can get at least a few hours of sleep before you take off tomorrow."

While Sarah made no attempt to disagree, it seemed to him she would not have minded continuing their conversation. But cooler heads prevailed, and back to campus they drove. As they approached her dorm, Jonathan reiterated his earlier invitation to stop by his office during the next semester. Sarah assured him she would.

"Have a really good time when you're home, Sarah. I hope your holidays are wonderful and that next year will be your best year ever," he said.

"And you too, Professor Hawthorne. Merry Christmas. If you make some more eggnog—I guess I should say, 'when you make it'—toast our class. And think about me when you're at the top of the mountain looking down on the rest of civilization, just before you ride off down the slope. That way, I'll get to ski this Christmas, if only vicariously," Sarah said.

As she made her way into the dorm, Jonathan thought to himself, *Don't worry, Sarah. I'll think about you. In fact, I'll have you totally in my thoughts every minute of my entire vacation. Fantasies of us together. Making passionate but tender love at dusk by the fireplace at our winter home with a panoramic scene of the snow-capped Rockies in full view, then lying in bed*

together, basking in the warm glow of love fulfilled. Wine glasses in hand, of
course.

Jonathan knew he was becoming a bit theatrical, but he didn't care.
He continued to dream such thoughts. Other equally welcome ideas
flowed into his brain as he made his way back to his place. He felt a
warm glow deep inside, and nothing that night would be able to
remove it. He had experienced Sarah in a new way, and he liked—really liked—what had transpired. He would go to Colorado as always and
enjoy himself immeasurably. But he would return to Duke after the first
of the year eager to follow wherever his obsessive fantasy took him.
Nineteen sixty-seven had been a very good year!

And, although Jonathan was unaware of it, Sarah also looked upon
1967 as a good year.

> . . . *It was no accident, my dear, that I was the last person to leave*
> *the party you threw for the class after our final exam. By the way, that*
> *was really a wonderful gesture. I was determined to outstay everyone that*
> *night. I viewed it as an excellent opportunity to get to know you better*
> *and to experience those little ways in which you had begun to reveal*
> *yourself.*
>
> *You must understand that none of my feelings were romantic or sex-*
> *ual. At least, I don't think so. They would appear later. I would not yet*
> *call us friends either. Well, maybe new friends. But we were also still in*
> *the mentor-student phase of our relationship. I felt special, however,*
> *because I believed, really believed, you didn't have another relationship*
> *like ours. I don't know why I felt that way. I just did.*
>
> *You must appreciate that you had begun to have some kind of dra-*
> *matic effect on me. I found myself thinking about what had happened at*
> *our encounters. I had begun to share them, ever so briefly, with my room-*
> *mates. They, of course, were envious and suspicious at the same time. They*
> *wondered what your motives (or mine, for that matter) were. But I was*
> *determined, apparently as resolutely as you were, to continue our contact*
> *after the semester.*
>
> *That's why I was so happy to learn about your internship when you*
> *were an undergraduate. That gave me the "in" I needed to maintain the*
> *connection. That's also why I asked you, as I made my way into the dorm*

that evening, to think about me over the Christmas holidays. When I was home then, I hoped I was on your mind. I now know, of course, that you were probably obsessive about it, which makes me feel good.

Frank Sinatra was right. "It was a very good year." I knew I wanted 1968 to pick up where 1967 had finished. . . .

~ 6 ~

First Revelations

Jonathan's Christmas holidays were no different than they were any other year, just as he had described them to Sarah earlier. He spent much time in the snowy outdoors, particularly after the twenty-fifth, at the family's second place up in the mountains. He plunged into all sorts of physical activity while in Colorado. There was one discernible difference from years past, though. He wanted the season to pass quickly so he might return to campus. He longed to see Sarah once again, but hopefully under a new set of ground rules.

Seeing her in the new semester, however, would pose a basic dilemma for Jonathan, one that he could not easily resolve. Sarah was no longer enrolled in one of his classes. Therefore, he was under no strict obligation to follow a hands-off policy. But he was still a member of the faculty, and Sarah was still a part of the student body. The Duke administration, particularly its most conservative members, would probably argue that an unequal power base existed between them, and therefore he had to maintain his personal distance.

The concept of *in loco parentis* was becoming increasingly outdated, however, so perhaps the more enlightened among the central powers might look at the situation differently. If he really worked at it, Jonathan might even be able to rationalize a liaison with Sarah. But he had a long way to go before reaching that position, he would likely admit if he was being truly honest with himself. In the final analysis, then, justifying a romance with Sarah was well into the future.

After all, while Jonathan often had moments of romantic fantasy about her, in reality, he also knew a bona fide friendship was only in its early stages. Perhaps his best course of action was simply to nurture it. At the very least, much happiness and fulfillment could come from just such a relationship with Sarah. And, moreover, who knew what might happen then? Although he had had no such experience, friendship could eventually evolve into love. They would not be the first couple to travel that most treasured of roads. *Being in love with one's best friend must be the ultimate feeling,* he thought.

What Jonathan did not know was that at that very moment Sarah was involved with another man, a student who had entered Duke the same year as she had. They had dated off and on for almost a year. She later told Jonathan she enjoyed her friend's company, although she recognized it was probably a relationship of convenience. They had not, for example, seen each other the previous summer, as each had been in different parts of the country.

Such low intensity relationships that outlive the initial passion were not unusual for most college students. It was sometimes easier to let such affairs continue than to dissolve them. After all, there was usually no pressure during one's undergraduate career, particularly when each partner entertained aspirations of post-graduate work, to move to the next stage of a lifelong commitment. Being in a relationship, however, provided a sense of belonging, particularly on a large campus with its typical impersonal nature. Many students tended to gravitate to liaisons and then remain in them far longer than they might have if they were out in "the real world." Not terminating them allowed students to avoid having to expend the necessary energy to deal with a situation that usually turned unpleasant or even ugly quickly. Better to focus on the daily task of getting good grades.

Years later Sarah described it this way:

> . . . *I know I didn't tell you about Michael at first, but there were several reasons why. I was excited about the series of events that seemed to bring us continuously together, all of them leading to the most fascinating conversations, at least fascinating to me. It soon was apparent our meetings were becoming an important, even essential, part of my life. It was a situation I had never encountered before, and, quite frankly, its meaning puzzled me.*

Besides, you hadn't asked me if I was seeing anyone. I came to understand after awhile that you had apparently set certain parameters about what we would discuss at our get-togethers. There were definite ground rules that seemed to make certain subjects off limits. Personal relationships—yours or mine—were one of those areas, despite there being nothing romantic between us. In fact, I hadn't really thought about that possibility. I was so enthralled with you in so many other ways that I hadn't contemplated you as my lover, at least consciously. Although, quite frankly, if I had been honest with myself, I would have figured it out that I was also attracted to you in some physical sense, for reasons that had nothing to do with the intellectual stimulation that I took away from our encounters.

As I look back on it now, I realize I was in no hurry to tell you about Michael. At least at first. Goodness knows what the real reason was. Maybe I wanted you to think me uncomplicated. Or possibly it was an ego thing. Maybe Michael wasn't that important in my life. Perhaps I really did want you to desire me. Who knows? I only knew I found it easier, for the first time ever, to compartmentalize my life. I know that probably surprises you. Women don't usually compartmentalize things; men do. But I guess that was one time I succumbed to the temptation.

As I look back on it now, it is increasingly clear that you were having an effect on me. A really pronounced effect. Feelings began to emerge that were quite different from those of a student toward her professor . . .

When Jonathan returned to campus after the holidays, he was ready for another semester. He had two courses to teach, one a graduate seminar in the classical literature from his field of international politics and the second a new undergraduate course on the emerging new global agenda. The second course particularly excited him. The field of international relations was about to embark on a fresh emphasis—how to deal with a set of problems that had until then occupied the attention only of specialists but would shortly spill over into the mainstream of world politics.

The U.N. had begun to address many of these emerging issues, particularly in the specialized agencies within the global institution. Uppermost among these problems, of course, was how to save the planet from nuclear annihilation. But there were others. The behavior of the

Nazis during World War II drove home the need for greater attention to human rights violations around the globe. Many private groups also pressured the United Nations to become more involved with environmental issues. They would finally be successful four years later when the organization convened a global conference at Stockholm on the environment and set an ecological plan of action into motion. A few individuals within the U.N. had also already recognized the potential for future global disaster because of rising birth rates throughout the poorer sectors of the planet. Population growth in the developing world not only stunted economic development in those countries, but it was beginning to threaten the global resource base. The U.N. would soon take major steps to help reverse this fertility trend.

Jonathan's tasks were to trace the history of this new set of issues and to examine the international community's current efforts to address them. It was a difficult course to prepare, as no useful textbook—or any textbook for that matter—existed on the subject. Rather, students would read from a wide range of sources, primarily articles in professional journals and more popular magazines, as well as official government documents.

Jonathan thought it good that he would have to spend a huge amount of time preparing his lectures. It would leave less time and energy to engage in his fantasies about Sarah. He had already decided he would wait for her to visit his office. He would not phone her. He considered such a move a major step, one he was not yet prepared to take. He suspected, though, that his resolve was probably more a function of his expecting her to show up at his door anyhow, rather than due to his strong conviction about the impropriety of such behavior. Their last encounter had convinced him she would not walk out of his life altogether.

The semester was not yet a week old when Sarah appeared at Jonathan's office. "Hi, Professor Hawthorne," she uttered with her usual inviting grin. "Are you free?"

"Hi, Sarah. Of course. Come in. It's really good to see you," he answered. "I was wondering if you were ever going to make it down this hallway again now that you're finished with my class. How's your semester going? Has your internship started yet?"

"Oh yes! I just returned from Raleigh," Sarah answered. "I've been there every afternoon this week. It's so interesting, but I feel so lost. There's so much to read just to get to where everyone else is. But I'm glad I'm interning. How's your semester going? Off and running, I'll bet."

They chatted for about twenty minutes about their respective new semester responsibilities, then moved on to describing their holidays. There were no surprises. Jonathan was eager to hear all about her every move while she was home. It gave him a special insight into her character and personality. He waited for the mention of a special friend—the term "significant other" was not yet in popular usage—but Sarah made no reference to anyone. He still refrained from direct questions about a boyfriend. After about an hour, Sarah had to leave. Dinner, she said. But she promised to return the next week to bring him up to date on her comings and goings in Raleigh.

After she left, Jonathan pondered their meeting for quite awhile. He was pleased that she had dropped by. While he had thought she probably would based on their last conversation before Christmas, his heart wasn't quite as certain. So he felt a huge sense of relief. Beyond that, he sensed a slightly different Sarah—a more open or more mature Sarah, perhaps. She seemed to treat him less like a professor and more like a friend, even a confidant. Maybe he was wrong about his perception, but he didn't think so.

She also appeared to be more relaxed, more outgoing. Jonathan had begun to notice the change at Tom's Diner the night of the final examination, but he had attributed it to the freedom brought on by the end of the semester, not to mention the eggnog. For the time being, he would allow events simply to unfold. He would not push matters, nor would he shy away from Sarah either. He was just content to spend time—it didn't matter what kind of time—with her on campus.

Conversation between them came easily. It was clear that Sarah was as comfortable discussing how she spent her vacation time as she was examining abstract theories of world politics. Jonathan was also much more at ease in her presence, except, of course, for the heightened excitement the feelings gnawing in his stomach brought on.

It was certainly true that their conversations had not yet addressed matters of a deep personal nature. While they had talked about how they had spent their time away from Duke and other rather trivial things, neither had really opened up to the other much. Indirectly, though, each was coming to know the other. But they still hadn't detailed anything really important or revealing about their personalities or characters, not to mention their souls. Jonathan had no way of knowing, of course, that the situation was about to change. Despite the lack of such familiarity, he could still see a close friendship eventually developing between them.

He had never had that kind of a relationship with a woman before. All his friends for as long as he could remember had been guys. Not that he had many friends, though. He knew that, while he was well-liked, he allowed very few people inside the imaginary wall behind which he kept his most personal thoughts and feelings. He preferred it that way. He was a private person who, paradoxically, was outgoing and well-liked in a social sense by most everyone who came into contact with him. Party-givers invariably included him on their invitation lists. His colleagues always asked him to join them for lunch at the union. In short, people sought him out for social situations. Jonathan figured people gravitated to his dry sense of humor or his self-deprecating style, but that didn't mean that he was obligated to reveal much else, and certainly anything important about himself.

He had never been one to reveal much about himself to others, male or female. Most men didn't, but Jonathan was even more secretive than the average guy. Some would call it shyness, but Jonathan knew that wasn't the case. It was a question of style, perhaps, or even a more basic decision of not allowing himself to become vulnerable. He certainly had never allowed that to happen in his romantic relationships, but he also believed that being vulnerable could create problems in matters of pure friendship as well. He had been burned once by a presumed friend who turned on him somewhat viciously over, as it turned out, a rather silly matter. The outcome had quite an impact on him. Although he didn't go so far as to pledge off future friendships, it would likely be a long time before he gave of himself as best friends expect of each other.

The result was that many called Jonathan their friend, although when pressed, all but a few would admit they knew little about what made him tick. Only one man, a boy from his childhood days by the name of John Evans, could call him a true friend.

Somehow, he had the feeling Sarah was going to be different. It was inexplicable, he told himself. Here was a woman—a very young woman at that and a student of his, for goodness' sake—who had begun to touch his soul in larger and more meaningful ways than anyone before her. Who had made him begin to talk about himself, albeit not yet as intimately as he might. Who was likely to unlock the door to the wall that had shielded him all those years. Add to his increased comfort level his continuously growing infatuation with her, and it was no wonder Jonathan was both excited and confused.

• • •

The semester rolled into high gear. True to her word, Sarah returned the next week, and the week after, and again the fourth week. She shared the progress of her internship with him, while he talked about his two new classes. He asked question after question about her work in Raleigh. She answered with a contagious enthusiasm. He began to develop somewhat of a proprietary interest in what she was doing for Senator Erwin and offered advice about her research. He volunteered to read initial drafts of her reports. Sarah was delighted with his offer and accepted it on the spot. She would have something for him in about two weeks.

What Jonathan found so intriguing, however, was that Sarah expressed the same level of interest in how his semester was going. She wanted to know about his students. Were they as good as the ones in her class? Did any come around to his office hours on a regular basis? And then came the question that caught him off guard. "Dr. Hawthorne, are any of the women attractive? You know. Drop-dead gorgeous, or maybe seductively beautiful in some mysterious way?" she asked.

Sarah's inquiry floored Jonathan. He began to blush, and his hands seemed to move nervously. "Why do you ask? I haven't thought about any of my female students that way," he said. "Either way, for that matter. If I did, it would be tough lecturing. Remember, a professor must have total concentration when he's in front of a class. He doesn't have the luxury of allowing his mind to wander, particularly down that road. We can't have what the Catholic Church calls 'impure thoughts.'"

Jonathan tried to make light of the question. He didn't know what else to say. His mind began to ponder the implication behind it. Was it an innocent query, or was there some motive behind it? If so, what kind?

Before he could speak again, Sarah interjected. "I just wondered. I'm surprised you haven't noticed any women in your class yet. That is, if you're really telling me the truth. After all, you're not exactly old, Professor Hawthorne," she said, laughing. "I assume you're not married and probably don't even have a girlfriend, or whatever you real adults call them."

"Why do you say that?" Jonathan asked. "I've not said anything about my personal life, at least as it relates to a special relationship with a woman. Besides, it's really boring anyhow. My personal life, I mean. And what do you mean 'real adults'? What's a fake adult anyhow?"

Sarah smiled again, ignoring the question about real versus fake adults and preferring instead to address the first part regarding his personal life. "It's really quite simple. You have a picture of what I assume are your parents and your brother on your desk, but no photo of anyone who looks even remotely like the current love of your life. So I just made an easy assumption. No girlfriend, no fiancée, no wife."

It was Jonathan's turn to smile. "You're very perceptive, Sarah Joan Matthews, but I already told you how observant you are, at least as it relates to political science. I guess it carries over into other areas as well. No, I don't have a girlfriend. We 'real adults' actually use many names for our partners in romantic relationships—'female friend,' 'girlfriend,' 'current love,' one's 'steady,' and a new one that I just heard—'significant other.' You pick which one you think is appropriate for someone my age," he challenged her while grinning again. *This is fun,* he thought to himself.

"You're not really that old, are you?" Sarah asked. "I've calculated that if you graduated from Pitt on time, and if you went through graduate school in four years—that's how long it's supposed to take, right?—and you've been at Duke for a year and a half, you're probably around twenty-seven or twenty-eight." Sarah gave off the air of someone who had completed an important piece of research and wanted to impress her instructor.

"Twenty-seven," Jonathan admitted. "I guess I'm over the hill, or, as they say, finished. Too old to enjoy life anymore. Find me the nearest nursing home."

"Hardly. I don't mean to pry. But if you don't have one now—I mean a girlfriend—have you recently been involved with a woman—in a serious way, I mean? Have you had a real girlfriend sometime in your adult life? Surely you must have," Sarah said

Jonathan gazed at her with one of those long, slow looks, accompanied by a slightly red face. The question should have offended him, and if it had come from anyone else, it probably would have. But, emanating from Sarah, it did not. Quite the contrary. It was the first real sign that their conversations might move into new terrain that would allow him to get to know her better. His response moved from her specific question of his having a special person in his life to a more general focus on the meaning of true love. Jonathan seemed to become more animated, even dramatic, as he answered.

"It depends how one defines the word 'serious,'" he said. "I saw someone for awhile when I was at Penn State, but, if the truth be told, my heart really wasn't in it. I've never experienced what true love is, so I don't know what to look for. But I have this belief that when it arrives, I'll know what it is. It'll feel, I'm sure, like a ton of bricks hitting me over the head."

Sarah, suddenly serious, jumped in. "But what exactly will hit you, Professor Hawthorne? What really is true love? I really don't know either."

"Tough question," Jonathan answered. "The emotions will be so different, I'm certain, from anything else I've ever experienced that I'll have no doubt I've found it. Let's see. How shall I describe it? Well, the feeling will make my heart pound as it has never pounded. It will make me want her intellectually, physically, emotionally, and in every other way possible. Every fiber of my body will cry out for her. Quite simply, she will touch my soul in a way so profound that I will know in an instant this woman is the one true love of my life. I will suddenly feel both total contentment and a rush of anticipation about the future.

"She will soon become so much a part of me in every way. Together we will create a third being—us. Each morning will begin with desires for her. Each evening will end with dreams of her. Everything that happens between the first moment I open my eyes at daybreak and the last time I close them at night will be done and viewed in the context of her. My complete focus will be on giving—giving of myself, my love, my total being. That's what I believe true love means . . . No, I haven't experienced that wonderful feeling yet."

Sarah said nothing at first. She appeared stunned at Jonathan's answer. "Wow! I know why you haven't had a serious relationship up till now," she finally commented. "You've set such high expectations that it's going to be difficult to meet women, at least one who will pass your test. But the girl, the woman, who does manage to reach your soul will be a very, very lucky person, I imagine."

Jonathan pondered Sarah's last remark for a moment. He briefly allowed himself the luxury of contemplating that if the woman was Sarah, he would be the fortunate one. "Actually, we'll both be lucky," he said. "I suspect few couples ever achieve what I would describe as true love. Instead they've 'satisficed' in their searches for mates."

"'Satisfice'—I've never heard that word before. What's it mean?" Sarah inquired.

"It's a combination of two words, actually, 'satisfy' and 'sacrifice,'" Jonathan replied. "You accept the lowest acceptable condition or common denominator. That is, you become satisfied with what you have so you don't do what's necessary or sacrifice enough to achieve the best or optimal result. That's what 'satisficing' is. With respect to finding your true love, you must search and search until that magic moment happens. You mustn't let fool's gold deceive you. It's easy to think you've discovered true love, when in reality you might have only found temporary lust. But if you maintain a proper perspective about your initial feelings, you'll be able to tell soon enough. Just don't stop your search prematurely. Your true love is out there somewhere. So don't 'satisfice' when it comes to love . . . There, I don't know if I've explained it well enough, Sarah."

"Oh, I understand it now," she said. "I think you're right, Professor Hawthorne. I look around at many of my friends' parents, and it's clear they're just going through the motions of love."

"That's a good way to put it, actually," Jonathan said. "I have this view, probably a naive one, that everyone has a true love, a soul mate, out there somewhere. The catch is to find that individual, to never be satisfied until you're successful. The secret, of course, is to be patient. Most people will never find that one special person because they become impatient and therefore 'satisfice.' They either lower their expectations, or they don't set them high enough in the first place. They marry the first one who comes along who is satisfactory. That's good enough for them.

"The unfortunate part of all of this, of course, is that since most of us haven't yet experienced true love, we won't know of our lost opportunity at total happiness, bliss, and contentment. Even when we discover, sometimes years after our wedding day, that something is missing, we still don't know what it is. Inertia takes over, and we decide to do nothing about it. It's simply easier to accept our present situation—to 'satisfice'—than to search for the perfect relationship. If we knew precisely what we were missing, however, I believe it would be a different story." Jonathan was amazed at his philosophizing about love and life, but it seemed so natural talking about the subject with Sarah. He decided to take the big plunge. "What about yourself? Are you involved with anyone, here or back home?"

Sarah paused and then proceeded to tell him about Michael. She was quick to point out, however, that her friend didn't come close to meeting Jonathan's minimum definition of one's true love. In fact, she seemed to downplay Michael's importance in her life. Nonetheless, her mention of a relationship, however trivial in the grand scheme of things, both surprised and disappointed him. He always knew it was a possibility, of course, but until he heard it from her own mouth, he had entertained the notion that Sarah was free of such entanglements.

   . . . You must remember the first time we talked, really talked, about our personal lives—that is, about whether either of us had a significant other. It was early in the spring semester after I had just taken your class. I considered myself rather bold that day. I know you were taken aback by my frank assertion you had no such person in your life. I was rather proud of myself for saying it.

   You must have wondered why I was so forward. Good question. I had already decided I wanted to know you better, as I told you earlier. Not just better in the subject areas that we had talked about, but also in uncharted waters. I was convinced you were not going to move very fast, for whatever reason, beyond the rather inconsequential conversations that had characterized our socializing so far. I knew I had to take the next step and move us beyond unimportant topics to themes much closer to your heart and to mine.

I also knew my raising the issue of your romantic involvement with another would lead to your asking me the same question. I was prepared for that likelihood. As you must remember, I downplayed the significance and long-term viability of my relationship with Michael. I had to take the chance that my revelation would not drive you away from any interest in me. Remember, I had not yet really harbored any sexual desire for you, at least consciously. Although in retrospect, I now know that I was attracted to you for some reason other than your intellect.

I was your student, not in the formal sense, but certainly anyone at Duke would have defined me as such. I would be your student until the day I graduated. It was becoming increasingly clear, as a consequence, that you had set certain parameters for our conversations. I viewed you as someone who could affect my life greatly, but I must confess I had not given much thought to the nature of that impact. And I wanted to take full advantage of that potential. I had to get us moving toward new terrain.

It felt surprisingly comfortable talking to you about more personal matters. I left you that day thinking that we had made progress, although I wasn't certain about where the progress would take us. I did realize a change in how we viewed each other was about to occur. Little did I know how circumstances we dearly wished had passed you by would force us into such dramatic change . . .

Jonathan looked at his watch. It had been more than an hour since Sarah had arrived at his office door. The meeting should probably be drawing to a close. He had to digest what she had told him that day. It was silly to be upset that she had a special friend her own age. Why should having such a relationship affect their behavior toward each other? He had no right to expect anything else. After all, he and Sarah were only in the early stages of friendship. Perhaps later, when and if matters advanced to the next phase, he could be sad or even take some offense. But certainly not now. He would try to accept her liaison with another stoically, without remorse. But he knew it would not be easy. His major hope lay in the fact that he was now convinced they would move through a major passage shortly.

Jonathan had no way of knowing, of course, that it would take a tragedy of the most monumental proportions to set in motion such a journey. It would be the saddest day of his young life.

~ 7 ~

Jonathan's First Need of Sarah

A piercing telephone ring shattered Jonathan's deep sleep. Disoriented, he reached for the receiver. At the same time, he struggled to open his eyes so that he might see what time it was. It seemed awfully late. The numbers "11:30" stared back at him from the clock-radio on the dresser. All of his friends knew he went to bed early, unless he was in the middle of a huge writing effort. Obviously, it wasn't one of them, unless there was a problem that couldn't wait until morning. Probably a wrong number, he concluded as he mumbled hello.

"Jonathan?" said the voice at the other end. "This is Chuck Taylor, next door to your parents."

Immediately Jonathan's adrenaline began to flow like lava from an erupting volcano. He sensed a major problem, one involving his parents. Why hadn't they made the call? He quickly gauged the time at the other end. Colorado was on Mountain time, two hours behind Durham. That meant it was only nine-thirty in Colorado Springs. Perhaps it wasn't as bad as he originally thought.

Before he could ask the obvious question, Taylor began to speak, his voice quivering as the words rolled off his tongue. "I'm afraid we may have a problem, Jonathan. Your mom and dad are away, and no one knows how to get a hold of them. They are due back tomorrow late morning—at least that's what they told me when they pulled out of the driveway last week and hit the road."

"Chuck, I know," Jonathan replied. "I talked to them before they left. They were going to travel south, then west toward Phoenix, then retrace the route. They wanted some warmer temperatures." He was hesitant to ask the next question, fearful of what the reply might bring. "What's the matter? Why do you have to get in touch with them? Can't it wait until they get home tomorrow?"

The neighbor's reply shot through him as devastatingly as if a large bullet had struck him. "Your parents had a visitor just a little while ago," Taylor said. "It was a man in military uniform. When he couldn't reach your parents, he knocked on my door. He's really anxious to get a hold of them."

Ben. Jonathan's mind turned immediately to his brother in Vietnam. Something had happened to Ben. What was it? "Is there a problem? Did he tell you anything?" he wanted to know.

Jonathan's heart was pounding faster than the German cuckoo clock in his study. He feared the worst, but he didn't know what that might be, at least at first.

"No, he didn't," Taylor said. "But he did say he would be back after grabbing a late snack to see if I had been able to get a phone number where he could reach your mom and dad. What should I tell him?"

Jonathan thought for a moment. He had to find out why the military officer was there. And he didn't want to wait until his parents returned home the next day. "I don't know how to reach Mom and Dad either. Have the guy call me as soon as he gets back," he said. "When do you think that will be?"

"He just left, so I suspect it'll be at least an hour before he returns," came Taylor's reply.

"Thanks, Chuck, for getting a hold of me," Jonathan said. "Tell the officer I'll be here waiting for his call. Also watch for my parents in case they've decided to come home early. If anything else happens, call me collect as soon as possible. Okay?"

As Jonathan placed the receiver down, his mind was already working overtime. Obviously the officer's visit involved Ben. But in what way? When did the government send someone to the parents' or spouse's home? When a loved one is wounded? Or does the reason have to be more serious—like when the soldier is missing or killed? Jonathan wasn't certain, although deep in his heart he suspected that a knock on the door meant the news was very grave. Missing or killed in action were the only two situations that probably qualified for a personal visit to the door. If a relative was only wounded, he thought the Pentagon opted for a telegram, perhaps followed later by an official visit.

He suddenly realized the questions were probably pointless. He thought he already knew the answer. How could he find out for certain? He thought for a moment until a light suddenly came on in his brain. He would call Denver Smith, a former classmate of his in graduate school. Colonel Denver Smith, United States Army, was spending four years on the Penn State campus heading the Army ROTC program while studying for his doctorate in Soviet studies. Jonathan quickly calculated that Denver was in his fourth year, so he should still be in State College.

One of the duties of the heads of the ROTC programs on campuses across the country was the sad responsibility of notifying local families about tragedies involving their loved ones serving in the military. The Pentagon contacted the head of the program whose service— army, navy, or air force—matched that of the victim's. Then the Pentagon gave the ROTC head the relevant information and instructions on how to carry out the assignment. It was not a task that ROTC heads relished. Their regular duties on campus did not entail such a difficult task. It was not why they had joined the military. But delivering bad news about soldiers was an important assignment, nonetheless. Officers carried out the responsibility with dignity, but it never became any easier for them, no matter how many doorbells they rang.

Due to the war in Vietnam, Colonel Smith had faced the unpleasant task of delivering tragic news to relatives fifteen times since his arrival at Penn State three years earlier. There were no other major military installations within a hundred miles of the campus, so the Pentagon had often called upon ROTC heads on campus to be the bearers of bad news. Smith had traveled east to west from Lewistown to Altoona and north to south from DuBois to Bedford to relay the message that a loved one had been killed or was missing in action. Delivering the sad news had been particularly difficult for Smith, a proud black man, because a majority of the victims in Vietnam seemed to be black. It was an issue—wealthy, white, high-level government policymakers sending poor young blacks to their death on the battlefield—

he hoped would be addressed by the nation's leaders before any future wars.

Jonathan found Smith's phone number and gave him a call, hoping against hope he would be home and would have the answer he wanted to hear. At last he heard someone pick up the receiver.

"Hello," came the sleepy response on the other end, reminding Jonathan that it was almost midnight in the Eastern time zone. It was Arlene, Denver's wife, whom Jonathan knew fairly well.

"Arlene, this is Jonathan Hawthorne, from Duke. I used to be in the same Ph.D. program as Denver," he began. He waited for some sign of recognition, which came almost immediately.

Arlene had remembered him. "Hi, Jonathan. What's going on?"

"There's a critical problem here, and I need some information from Denver. I know it's late and I apologize, but it couldn't wait until morning," Jonathan said.

Perceiving an emergency, Arlene quickly awakened Colonel Smith, whose voice was soon on the line. He sounded wide awake, although he had been sound asleep only a few minutes earlier.

"Hello, Jonathan. What's up?" he asked. Denver was never one to mince words.

"Denver, it's good to talk with you. But I wish it was under different circumstances," Jonathan answered. He then told Denver the whole story, ending with the question to which he did not want to hear the answer. "So I need to know. In what situations does the Pentagon send someone to the house? Does it happen only when a soldier is killed or missing in action, or also when he's wounded?" Jonathan asked hesitantly.

Colonel Smith seemed to pause before answering. "I think the regulations are quite specific on this. It's only the two former tragic circumstances when we are sent to deliver the news in person. The soldier has been killed or is missing in action. At least it's been that way in every case in my experience since arriving here. I'm afraid the news is quite likely bad. Jonathan, I'm really sorry."

Jonathan's heart sank, and tears began to roll down his face. "Could you do me a big favor, Denver? Is it possible to check with Washington at this late hour and confirm what you just told me? Tell them the situation—that my parents are not due home until tomorrow and I need to know—so in the event of the worst-case scenario, I can begin to make plans to get home ASAP. I would catch a flight first thing in the morning. If they won't confirm Ben's condition, at least find out their general policy and if they ever deviate from it. I would really appreciate it."

Denver agreed to do so, and they both said good-bye. Jonathan waited for the longest thirty minutes of his life before the telephone ring suddenly jumped out at him again. It was Colonel Smith on the other end.

"My contact at the Pentagon confirmed what I told you," Denver said. "A representative goes to the house only when the soldier is dead or missing in action. He couldn't or wouldn't—I don't know which—give me any specific information about your brother, however. He did remind me to tell you there could be other reasons why the soldier was at the door."

But when Jonathan pressed him for examples, Denver couldn't think of any. He had all the information he needed. Ben had died or was missing in Vietnam. His intuition had been correct. There was no other explanation for the military officer's visit. He thanked Denver and hung up. He now waited for another call—a call he would have gone to any length to avoid.

Ten minutes later, the phone rang again. This time it was Taylor on the other end of the line with Major Anthony Lombardi. The major was back after a quick bite to eat. He repeated the sparse information he had given Taylor earlier. Jonathan pressed him, saying his parents would not return until the next day. It was important he be told something so he could be with them as soon as possible if the news was as bad as he feared.

Major Lombardi hesitated, explaining that his official instructions were to give his information only to the parents of Lt. Hawthorne and to no one else.

The major's mention of his brother's name only confirmed what Jonathan had already sadly suspected. He repeated his argument, and this time the Pentagon representative appeared to be more sympathetic. "Look, Dr. Hawthorne. I have my orders, and I could get in trouble for violating them. But I'll tell you what I'll do. You ask me some questions, and I'll answer them truthfully. If the answer is no, I will so indicate by answering the question directly. If the answer is yes, I will say nothing. In that way I may be able to help you. But please phrase your questions so I can truthfully say to my superiors that I literally told you nothing. And give me a couple of practice questions first so we're both certain we're on the same wavelength. Do you understand?"

Jonathan acknowledged he understood and wrote down the major's instructions on a piece of paper. An oral response would indicate a negative answer, while the major would leave a positive response unspoken.

"Are you a civilian, Major Lombardi?" Jonathan asked.

"No," came the major's reply.

"Are you now a member of the military?" Jonathan continued.

Major Lombardi said nothing.

The trial run was over. Both men understood the rules. Jonathan hesitated for a moment. He thought of how he might phrase his questions so there would be no ambiguity about Major Lombardi's responses.

"Is Ben missing in action?" Jonathan asked hesitantly.

"No," the major replied. His voice was loud, and it was distinct.

Jonathan's heart sank even further. The words to the next question flowed haltingly from his lips. He struggled to maintain his composure, but it was a battle he knew he would lose. How he dreaded to continue. Its answer, he was certain, would drive him into the deepest abyss of anguish he had ever experienced. "Has Ben been killed in Vietnam?" he finally asked the major.

Jonathan waited for what seemed like an eternity, but only silence—total silence—greeted him. He repeated the question. Same response. Nothing. Not a sound coming from the other end of the line.

"Thank you very much, Major Lombardi," he concluded. "I appreciate your understanding my situation and accommodating me."

"I'm terribly sorry, sir," the major replied.

Jonathan fell rapidly into the depths of grief—for Ben, for himself, and for his poor parents who he knew would be devastated by the news. But he needed to press forward with some questions regarding the next day's procedures as well as those for the next couple of weeks.

Major Lombardi was most cooperative while remaining faithful to his instructions. He would arrive at the home of Jonathan's parents early in the morning and stay there until they returned. He would give them "the information he was carrying," and then remain to help them as long as they needed him. He asked for the name of their minister so the latter could be there immediately after he delivered the tragic message.

He expected the family could "begin the final process in about a week and complete it in about ten days." It was his way of revealing, without really saying so, that the body would arrive in Colorado Springs in about a week, and that the funeral and burial could be held three days later.

"Major Lombardi, I'll be flying home tomorrow," Jonathan said. "When you talk to my parents, I would appreciate your telling them that I know about Ben and am on my way home. Tell them I don't know my exact schedule yet, but I should arrive sometime late morning or early afternoon. I'll get a ride from the airport. I'll try to reach them with my plans if I can."

"Sir, I'll give them the information," the military representative promised.

"Thanks, Major Lombardi," Jonathan said.

There was nothing else to say, so Jonathan bid the major good-bye and put down the phone. As the receiver dropped into place, he felt himself cascading into the hollow depths of grief and despair. His world had just fallen apart, and no one or nothing could put it back as it had been just a short time ago. Ben. Dear Ben. His younger brother dead. Killed in a war that had no rhyme or reason to it. Jonathan sobbed uncontrollably for a few minutes, then tried to compose himself. The hurt was unbearable. Little did he know the pain would get worse— much worse—before the grieving process ran its course.

But what about his parents? His thoughts now turned to them. Nothing could be worse than burying one's child, even if that child was an adult. He knew of similar situations and remembered how crushed, how totally crushed, the parents of the victims had been. He remembered, too, the short- and long-term aftereffects on the grieving parents. Denial. Sadness. Anguish. Torment. Pain. Suffering. Emptiness. Anger. All these emotions bore deeply into their hearts like bullets from a machine-gun that never seemed to stop. Despondency and depression soon followed, in some cases never to leave.

Jonathan began to cry once again as he thought of his parents experiencing those terrible emotions. And he knew neither he nor anyone else would be able to soften the blow. They would be devastated, simply devastated. His heart ached as he thought about them. They were probably enjoying themselves as they made their way back to Colorado Springs, happy and refreshed from a week's vacation. In about twelve hours their world would turn upside down, never to be righted. It was sad beyond measure.

Jonathan called the ticket office at the airport and made arrangements to fly home the next morning. The flight was scheduled for ten o'clock. It would get him into Colorado Springs by early afternoon. He knew he would get little sleep between then and the plane's departure, but that was of little consequence. He had never felt so alone in his entire life. Nothing coming close to this tragedy had ever happened to him before, and he was simply lost. He needed to be with someone to talk about what had just transpired and to share his grief.

Jonathan thought about his faculty colleagues but quickly dismissed the idea. He was on good terms with all of them and had visited the homes of several in his year and a half on campus. He had discovered, however, that, unlike at Penn State, the members of his department at Duke went their own ways at the end of the day. They rarely socialized with one another. When they did, it bordered on obligatory, command-type performances expected of faculty, particularly junior faculty. The conversation at such formal gatherings was best described, in the words of Shakespeare, as "much ado about nothing."

There was also the age difference. Jonathan was the youngest in the department by almost five years. His interests, particularly those involving the outdoors, were not widely shared by his fellow faculty. Moreover, he was the only unmarried member, if you discounted several divorcees who were at least twenty years older than he. So he was not close to any of his peers—at least close enough with whom to share the most tragic day in his life. And there really wasn't anyone from his pre-Duke days who could console him. His reluctance to reveal himself to all but a few over the years would now come back to haunt him.

Although Jonathan didn't want to admit it to himself, at least not right away, there was only one person with whom he wanted, perhaps even needed, to share this time. His thoughts turned to Sarah. At that moment he realized he wanted to be with her to share the agony that permeated every strand of his body and soul and to have her comfort him as he tried to make sense out of the nonsensical.

He hesitated to call her at first, however. He wondered if their relationship had reached a stage where it was all right to ask her to help him through the tragedy of his brother's death. After all, a truly personal relationship had existed primarily in his mind and in his fantasies. Granted, they had increasingly talked about non-academic matters. But they had not really communicated in ways beyond those of a typical professor-student relationship. Well, perhaps a little. But their conversations had remained within the bounds of appropriateness. He decided to risk a phone call to her.

It was now a half hour past midnight. It had only been an hour since Taylor first awakened him, but those sixty minutes seemed like an eternity. Fortunately it was Friday night, so Sarah probably didn't have to get up early the next day. He hoped she would be back in the dorm for the evening. He dialed her number and waited impatiently for a response on the other end. She answered almost immediately. Her soft voice was a most welcome sound. He instantly knew he had made the right decision when he thought to call her. He needed to talk to her—needed, in fact, to be with her.

"Hi. This is Jonathan Hawthorne. Sorry to bother you at such a late hour, but something has happened. I wonder if you could meet me. I really need to talk to someone, and I immediately thought of you. I hope you don't think me too forward," he said.

"Forward? Of course not. I'm glad you thought of me," Sarah replied. "I can be ready in fifteen minutes. Why don't you meet me at the same place where you dropped me off after the final exam. Do you remember where it was?"

Jonathan knew the spot. He was glad Sarah had the good sense not to probe over the phone about what was troubling him. He had been prepared to ask her to wait until they were face to face, but it proved to be unnecessary. It also pleased him that she was so quick to agree to meet him, despite the lateness of the hour and the short notice. She had not shown the slightest hint of hesitation. She was going to be a true friend. Maybe she already was.

Jonathan left his condo, and, traveling as fast as he could, arrived at her dorm in about fifteen minutes. Sarah appeared in the walkway two minutes later and slid into the front seat of his car. She instinctively reached over and touched his forearm, squeezing it ever so slightly before releasing her grip. He reciprocated briefly on the back of her extended hand. It was a welcome touch, and under any other circumstances would have raised his desire for her tenfold. But not tonight. His needs for her were now of another kind.

She turned to him and tried a faint smile, but none materialized. Instead, her expression had worry written all over it. "I know something is bothering you, but I hope our getting together tonight will somehow make things right. Thanks for thinking of me. That makes me feel special," she remarked softly.

"No, I'm the one who should thank you," Jonathan said. "It was really good of you to drop everything when I called. I shall never forget it."

"Drop everything? All I had to drop was my nightgown and throw on some clothes," Sarah replied. "I could immediately tell from your voice that something was really troubling you. I don't know you very well yet, but I do know you well enough to realize when something is terribly wrong. I hope my intuition is way off base."

Jonathan did not respond. After a few seconds, he suggested they visit an all-night restaurant, not Tom's but another one about a mile away. He selected Gail's Cafe because it would be less crowded and thus afforded more privacy in a more dimly lit atmosphere. He was right about the place. Only a few people were there, over in the far corner away from where they were now headed.

They said nothing until they were seated. "Sarah . . ." Jonathan started to talk, but it was clear he was having difficulty. He had to pause for a moment. After a few seconds he continued. "I'll just give it to you straight. My brother Ben has been killed in Vietnam. I just got word right before I called you."

Sarah's mouth opened wide in a state of disbelief. Jonathan suddenly started to sob, as his attempts to prevent it were unsuccessful. She instinctively reached for a napkin on the table and handed it to him.

Just as spontaneously, he took it and patted his cheek, thanking her as he did. "Sorry about that. I can't seem to help it," he apologized.

Sarah appeared to be at a loss for words, so she simply grabbed his forearm once again and squeezed it as a sign of sympathy.

The rest of the story unfolded from Jonathan's lips in an agonizingly slow fashion. From time to time he stopped as his voice cracked. He appeared to choke up from the intensity of the emotions that had captured his heart. When he had finished, Sarah was already crying, having failed to hold back her tears for fear of upsetting Jonathan even more. She seemed to feel so sorry for him, and a huge sense of helplessness appeared to engulf her.

They talked for almost two hours. Jonathan told Sarah story after story about his brother, from their early childhood years to his time at West Point. Clearly he loved Ben a great deal, even though they seemed different in so many ways. His mood swung from denial to deep sorrow to outright rage at the unfairness of it all. Sarah watched closely as he tried to come to grips with the reality of the tragedy. She knew he would be unsuccessful, that night and for many nights thereafter, but she listened patiently while extending words of support as often as she could.

Sarah offered to drive Jonathan to the airport the next day. Her gesture surprised and pleased him, and he readily accepted. He didn't know how long he would be home, and he welcomed the opportunity to avoid the daily parking fee at the airport. More importantly, he wanted and needed her presence the next morning. It was time, though, to try to catch whatever few winks of sleep were possible.

"Thanks for being here for me tonight," he said. "I didn't want to be alone. I needed to talk with someone, a friend. I may have been presumptuous, but you were the one person who immediately came to mind. I don't know what I would have done had you not been at the dorm when I called."

Sarah did not respond at first, yet Jonathan's words seemed to touch her. "I haven't done anything except listen," she replied.

"Perhaps, but you have no idea how much it has helped tonight. I feel so helpless and empty. My own brother killed in Vietnam. It hurts so much," Jonathan said.

He took Sarah back to the dorm, parked the car, and walked her to the front entrance. As he began to say good night, each of them reached for the other simultaneously, falling into the other's arms. Tears flowed freely from both, as if unleashed by a dam finally giving way to the flooded waters of a raging river. Neither said anything. It was not a time for speaking, only for holding and comforting each other. It seemed as if the embrace lasted an eternity, but in reality it was less than a minute. It was an embrace borne out of shared grief, not passion. But it was a welcome feeling to Jonathan, nonetheless. What he needed more than anything else at that moment was the support of another human being—someone who could reach out and touch him, a friend. Sarah was now such a person, quite likely the only one who could do so.

She turned and opened the door to her dorm, looking back with an expression of support. Jonathan waved good-bye and then ambled slowly toward the car. The cool air against his face stirred his consciousness. He would return to the late winter snows of Colorado the next day. But, unlike the two previous trips that school year, he was not looking forward to what awaited him there. There would be no skiing among the magnificent evergreens dotting the sides of the slopes. No climbing among the trails whose beauty belied the excitement brought on by the challenge of the ascent. No incredible high delivered by the combination of the extreme altitude and glorious splendor of the Colorado Rockies.

Instead, his return would lead only to deeper sorrow and emptiness as he came face to face with the stark reality of his brother's death. It would bring him the terrible anguish of his parents as they tried to cope with the loss of a son. It was a trip he would have gone to almost any length to avoid if it was in his power. But he had no choice. He slammed his car into gear and roared away, trying to see through the tears blurring his vision.

The next day arrived soon enough. Unlike on the other occasions when he had left Sarah, Jonathan's thoughts were not now of her. He did not replay every moment of their time together, as was his custom. Not that her effect on him had lessened. Quite the contrary, as he would come to realize later when he took stock of the events surrounding his brother's death. But his mind was still trying to come to grips with the harsh blow that had struck him like a runaway freight train just a few hours earlier.

Not so with Sarah. She was consumed with thoughts about Jonathan.

    . . . My sweet Jonathan, as I contemplate how our relationship evolved, how it moved from stage to stage, I remember so well the awful time when Ben died. His death had such an impact on me and on how I began to view you, to see our relationship.

    It had been awhile, more than a month, since I was your student, at least in the usual sense of the word. In the short time since then, we had already moved into a more comfortable relationship. The subjects of our talks had expanded, and the parameters had stretched. You were having such an effect on my professional growth. But there was a bonus. We were developing a friendship. I could sense it happening, and I welcomed it.

    It also scared me, of course. You were seven years older than I was, a huge difference for someone of only twenty. You were a professor. And you were such an intellectual, so worldly! I was so in awe of you. But I knew that had to change, or at least be channeled in productive ways, because I wanted to be able to offer you something.

    After all, friendships are based on giving, by both parties. You were giving me so much, and I wanted to reciprocate. Your brother's death, as terrible as it was, gave me the opportunity to give something to you. And I believe—no, I know—that I gave. I wanted so much to fulfill the role you had apparently thrust upon me. I was glad to be there to comfort you in the early hours after you learned of the tragedy.

    After you dropped me off at the dorm that night, I tried to sleep but couldn't. I was surprised at how your sadness had become my sadness. I felt so sorry for you and frustrated at my inability to do anything about it. It was my first experience with death, at least the death of someone near my own age, and I didn't know what to expect. I know that I kidded you about being so much older than I, but you know I didn't mean it. And Ben was even closer to my age.

    Your stories of Ben had made him seem so real to me, although I had never met him. You were in such anguish that I was also overcome with emotion. I don't believe I slept for more than an hour that night. Had you been in a normal state when you picked me up the next morning to go to the airport, you would have noticed. My entire thoughts as I lay in bed were of you, of what you must be going through. I wanted so much to reach out to you, to comfort you. I was frustrated that I could do so little.

As morning approached, I came to understand that you were more important in my life than I had realized. I had come to care about you. And, again, I wanted to know so much more about you. I wanted our friendship to grow, and grow, and grow. You, Jonathan Hawthorne, were someone so exceptional, and I wanted to benefit from that specialness. . . .

~ 8 ~

Jonathan's Sad Trip Home

Jonathan arrived back at Sarah's dorm at seven-thirty in the morning, still emotionally drained from the events of the previous evening. She was outside waiting for him. She would drive him to the airport, then keep his car until his return. He stepped out of his Monza and opened the passenger door. As she was about to get in, they hugged each other, much like the embrace from the previous night.

"Thanks for everything last night," Jonathan said. "It really helped to be able to talk to someone about Ben's death—someone with whom I've been sharing a large part of myself recently."

"I wish there was more I could have done. How do you feel this morning?" Sarah asked.

"Quite frankly, like I've been run over by a truck. I've had to push myself to function. Then the next moment I'm in total denial, followed by rage. Then back to denial again," Jonathan replied.

Jonathan drove off toward the airport, about half an hour away. As the car made its way toward Raleigh, he had a strong need to continue talking about the tragedy. He sensed Sarah's attention and her ability to respond to him with just the appropriate reply, drawing his feelings out. She simply seemed to know the right thing to say. It comforted him, at least as much as he could be consoled. Just having Sarah beside him gave him strength to face what lay ahead.

They arrived at the airport in time not only for Jonathan to purchase his ticket but also to catch a bite to eat. So they grabbed a quick snack at the airport cafeteria. He wasn't hungry yet, but he wanted some solid food anyhow—something besides the several cups of coffee he knew he would have before the plane touched down in Colorado Springs. It was soon time to board.

As they made their way to the gate area, Sarah took Jonathan by the arm and offered her help if he needed it. She even implied that she would fly to Colorado Springs after things settled down a bit if that's what he wanted. "Feel free to call me anytime when you're home. You know how to reach me. Please don't hesitate," she insisted. "Sometimes it helps to talk to a friendly voice, particularly one that's not physically there. It might be therapeutic for you."

Jonathan thanked her, adding that he probably would. The touch of her hand on his arm felt good. Really good.

"I've come to lean on you the last two days, Sarah Joan Matthews. I hope I'm no bother," Jonathan said.

Sarah appeared surprised, and pleased, that Jonathan once again remembered her middle name. "Of course you're no bother. Quite the contrary. I'm happy I can help. I wish I could do more."

Again they hugged each other. Sarah wished him luck and offered the hope all would go as well as could be expected under the circumstances. Then Jonathan turned and walked down the steps and out into the cool, North Carolina late-winter morning to meet the plane. It sat about a hundred yards from the terminal, so he slowly made his way across the tarmac. He sluggishly climbed the steps and disappeared through the door.

. . . I ached for you, my dear, as I watched you walk across the tarmac and climb the stairs to the plane that would take you home to be with your brother.

I guess bonds develop much more quickly in times of turmoil. Clearly the tragedy that had come your way led to our friendship evolving much faster than it probably would have under normal circumstances.

But the important point is that some force had brought us together, and consequently I was there when you needed someone. And you turned to me, not someone else. You needed me, and I was able to come through. I wanted always to be there for you. . . .

The flight home was uneventful, although it seemed to take much longer than usual. Jonathan tried to reach his parents when he changed planes in Atlanta, but there was no answer. He looked at his watch. It was still too early for their return home. *They still don't know,* he thought to himself.

The next leg of the trip led Jonathan to Denver. It had taken four hours. As the plane circled the airport at the base of the Rockies, he found himself staring out the window at the eastern part of the mountain range. How majestic they appeared! Yet he also thought how sad they must be that one who had loved them so much, Ben, would never again see their beauty, feel their warmth, or meet their challenges. His mind turned to the many occasions he and his brother had passed the test of those mountain peaks as they enjoyed life to the fullest. How he was going to miss all their splendid times together.

Jonathan had but ten minutes to catch the third and last leg of his flight home, so he ran across the airport to the commuter gate for the trip to Colorado Springs. He barely made it, but soon he was seated for the thirty-five minute ride. It was almost two o'clock in the afternoon. Surely his parents must now know about Ben. Tears came to Jonathan's eyes once again. This time he allowed them to flow freely. He had to be strong for his parents, so it was best to get all the tears out of his system before he arrived home. It was not fashionable for men to be seen crying. It was thought—at least to the supposedly stronger gender—to be a sign of weakness. But he didn't care what others on the plane thought.

The plane touched down on time. Jonathan looked around for a familiar face but saw no one. He was not surprised. No one knew of his arrival time. After renting a car, he headed for his parents' home. In many ways he hoped they had not yet arrived. As difficult as it would be, he wanted to be the one to tell them about Ben rather than to have some stranger—no matter how well-intended or how well-trained—give them the news.

But as Jonathan pulled into his parents' driveway, he saw their car as well as what he assumed to be a military vehicle. His heart sank as he tried to hold back the tears. Rushing into the house, he found them both pacing, his mother in the kitchen and his father in the living room. Major Lombardi was with his dad. He knew instantly the major had relayed the news. Jonathan was too late. Both parents turned to their son as soon as they saw him. All three quickly embraced as their anguished cries broke the silence. Finally, they stopped hugging and moved slightly apart.

Jonathan's mother was first to speak. "Oh, Jonathan. I can't believe it. Ben dead. It can't be true."

Disbelief was always the first reaction in times of tragedy for the victim's loved ones. His mother was no different. Its power could be overwhelming. If left unchecked, it could hinder the natural course of the grieving process. The seeds of denial had clearly captured his mother. He knew the feeling. He had experienced it several times the previous evening. And he had a long way to go before he would even come close to conquering that emotion for good.

After what seemed like a long exchange with his parents, Jonathan went over and introduced himself to Major Lombardi. Over the course of the next hour, the major filled Jonathan in on the details of Ben's death, at least those that he had.

Much of what happened over the next ten days would remain forever a blur. Major Lombardi was pretty much on target about the schedule. Ben's body arrived home in a week, and the funeral took place three days later. Jonathan remained in Colorado Springs for a couple of extra days to help with a number of matters related to Ben's death and to serve as a crutch for his parents. Although his grief was unbearable, he tried to hide it, as he had to be strong for them.

Only a few memories of his time home would remain in his mind. The first was the identification of the body. Jonathan had asked his parents if he might be the one officially to identify Ben's remains. His chief concern, of course, was that Ben would be so disfigured that it would be impossible to identify him visually. His parents would be devastated if that was the case. Moreover, he wanted to make certain Ben "looked" like himself. It would be difficult enough when his parents cast their eyes on the body for the first time. No need to make it even more trying for them. Fortunately, Ben "looked" like himself. And there appeared to be no external wounds. At least none on the exposed parts of the body.

Major Lombardi was helpful in that regard. Ben had been leading his platoon on a standard "search and destroy" mission when a single bullet from a sniper ripped through his heart. He was dead within seconds. For that Jonathan was thankful. He hoped the major was telling the truth and conveyed the message to his parents that Ben had not suffered. His father wanted more specific details. The military representative took him aside and satisfied his concern about the lack of any suffering before the last breath left him. His parents could see Ben. A public viewing could be held.

Jonathan remembered bits and pieces of the wake. It was only one night, the day before the funeral. Hundreds of mourners, many unknown to members of the family, made their way to the small chapel where the body lay in state. It was obvious that Ben's death had touched many, many people. He was so proud of his brother, and he knew his parents were also.

But the pain. It was so intense. He could not imagine what his parents were going through at that moment. Their son—the younger of their two children and their baby—gone so young at twenty-four. What a waste! And he, Jonathan, had been cheated out of being a big brother for the rest of his life. He would never experience nieces and nephews—at least those of his own flesh—or enjoy the camaraderie of a brother. He would never again endure sibling rivalry. He felt guilty for thinking such thoughts, but he was, after all, only human, he told himself.

The evening passed slowly but finally ended. He breathed a sigh of relief as the family headed home from the chapel. He heard his mother's soft sobs above the hum of the car's engine as they made their way westward toward the foothills above Colorado Springs, just south of the newly sprawling grounds of the Air Force Academy.

The next morning dawned with a full sun in a cloudless sky, perfect weather for the usual activities on a late winter day in the Rockies. But it was not a normal day. It was the day when Jonathan would say his final good-bye to his only brother. When he would experience an emptiness that would tear at his stomach until the pain was almost unbearable. When he would watch his mother and father brave the most difficult task forced upon a parent—burying one's child before his or her time.

Much of what happened that day remained vague to Jonathan. While the succeeding months helped the grieving process, the haze of the first days of his brother's death and burial never lifted. It was just as well. The music ringing in his ear as he entered the chapel, his elegant eulogy (as others reminded him later), the military honor guard, the flag-draped coffin, the shots ringing out in unison from rifles pointed toward the heavens, the playing of "Taps." Blurred images of these elements danced fleetingly across Jonathan's brain, but their foggy nature left him with an out-of-focus picture of what had transpired.

Jonathan finally recalled a short time later that it seemed to be a really beautiful ceremony, although the details were still blurry. If it did not hurt so much, he might even have enjoyed it. The military had perfected a style that aimed to shift one's attention from the horrible aspects of the cause of death to the solemn nature of the burial. If the strategy was intended to convince family and friends that the loss of a loved one was worth it, then it was rarely successful for more than a transitory moment.

That evening Jonathan told himself he had waited as long as he could. He longed to hear a familiar voice. One voice in particular—Sarah's voice. He needed to reflect about events since his arrival home. He wanted so much to share with her all the disparate thoughts going through his mind. He dialed her number, hoping she was in her room. He could not bear to wait until the next day. It was becoming increasingly clear to him that a recognition that he wanted her, needed her, as a friend as well as a lover, was superseding or at least complementing his romantic infatuation with her. He had drawn much strength from her in the hours following the fateful phone call about his brother and knew he would need her even more when he returned to Durham.

The changing nature of Jonathan's feelings for Sarah did not mean he desired her less in a physical sense. Quite the contrary. Dramatic thoughts of the two of them locked in passionate embrace were never far from his mind. His fantasies had come into even sharper focus as he spent more and more time with her. But his current needs fell in a different direction, and she had been able to meet them. Had he had high expectations about what their growing friendship would mean to him in his hour of need, she would have exceeded all of them. Sarah had had such a pronounced effect on him, and he could not, nor did he want to, deny her strong influence.

"Hello." The familiar sound of her voice on the other end of the line instantly lifted Jonathan's spirits. "Hi, it's Jonathan Hawthorne," he said.

"I recognize your voice. How are you? I've been thinking about you virtually every minute since you left. I'm really glad you called," Sarah said.

Under other circumstances, he would have viewed Sarah's remark as a come-on. But he knew that was not the case this time. She was simply concerned about how he was coping.

"How are you doing? I've been so worried," she continued.

Her tone seems so genuine, Jonathan told himself. She clearly considered him a friend.

"Fine, under the circumstances," he replied. It was a little white lie. He knew he probably hadn't fooled her. "Actually, it's been tough. The most difficult part was waiting for Ben's body to arrive and worrying the entire time about how he would look, as if it really mattered. Nonetheless, it was very important to my parents, and I guess also to me, that we be able to recognize Ben—that he looked, shall we say, okay."

"I hope that part worked out all right," Sarah said.

"It was fine. The body arrived in about a week. Ben looked like himself. Fortunately, the wound was away from his face and head. In fact, you could not tell he had been hurt at all. He looked as if he was just sleeping and would wake up any moment. It was really difficult trying to convince myself that Ben would never wake up," Jonathan said.

"Denial is the usual initial reaction in times like this," Sarah suggested. Her voice was already beginning to soothe his pain.

"I know. I keep telling myself that Ben's gone, he's not coming back, and we have to move on. But it is so hard. I'm learning the grieving process has no shortcuts. The best you can hope for is that you don't get stuck in a particular stage. Better that you are able to move through each passage in due course without any prolonged or unusual delays. But darn it. I don't really care about moving through this stage or that stage of the grieving process. All that matters is that Ben is gone and I'm having trouble coping with it. My pain is simply too great."

"You must try to get beyond the simple mourning of your loss and start reflecting on how you are a better, happier, and more complete person from having had Ben as your brother," Sarah advised.

Jonathan pondered what she had said for a moment. "You're right,

Sarah. That's a really good way to put it. I've got to focus on the cele-bration of Ben's life, not on the tragedy of his death."

"That's good. I like that phrase, 'the celebration of life.' Think about it rather than lamenting a premature death." Sarah was right on target.

"I will. You're absolutely right. By the way, I anticipate I'll be home on Saturday night. That will give me another three days to help my par-ents with all the loose ends," Jonathan said.

"And simply to be there for them," Sarah interjected.

"Right," he agreed. "I can't forget they may really need me. Tomorrow they will wake up and remember what they had to do the day before—bury a son. Moreover, quite frankly, I need them too."

"Of course you need one another. You're the only remaining child. They will no doubt cling to you. And they are your only remaining family. It will be difficult leaving them on Saturday," Sarah observed.

"I know," Jonathan answered. "You're right, as I've come to realize most if not all of the time." Sarah's perception and sense of timing never ceased to amaze him. For the first time since he heard about Ben, a slight smile came to his face.

"Do you know what time your plane gets in to Raleigh Saturday evening, Dr. Hawthorne?" Sarah asked.

Jonathan was uncertain, but it seemed as if she was now having a somewhat more difficult time calling him by his professorial title. He hoped his impression was correct. If so, he wanted her inhibition to result from her viewing him in a different light than she had when she took his class the previous semester.

"I think it's around eight. Let me check it. . . . Yeah, two minutes after eight. I'll tell you what. Why don't we plan on dinner after I arrive? I'll probably be hungry. Besides, I want to repay you for all you've done," Jonathan said.

"I'd like that. I'll meet you at the gate then. Have courage the rest of your visit. And have a good flight on Saturday," Sarah said.

"Thanks. I'll try. See you then," Jonathan replied.

Jonathan replaced the receiver. It was really good to talk to her. Sarah just seemed to anticipate what he was about to say and instantly had the right answer for him. He liked that. He had never experienced anyone, man or woman, who could forecast what was on the tip of his tongue. It scared him a little that she appeared to have the power to do so. But a great feeling of comfort immediately replaced his trepidation. He wanted so much at that moment to hold her. Not the grasp of one passionate lover to another. Rather, the squeeze of one dear friend consoling another.

Jonathan lay in bed that evening, not able to fall immediately asleep but not really minding it. He wanted to reflect on the events of the last week and a half. His life would never be the same again. His brother gone. He would not share with Ben those many passages he would experience throughout the rest of his life. His years at Duke or wherever he might go. His marriage. It was always understood he and Ben would each be best man for the other. His children greeting Uncle Ben. A slight smile came to his lips as he remembered how he used to kid his brother about his nieces and nephews calling their uncle by the name of a rice product. Nor would he be able to take delight in those good things that would have come Ben's way. A wife. Children. "Uncle Jonathan," they would have called him. Grandchildren. Success. All those wonderful things that would have happened to a man of Ben's talents and character, now never to occur.

Jonathan thought about his parents spending the rest of their time on earth in deep remorse over the death of a son. No matter what joy he, Jonathan, would bring them, he knew they would always feel the emptiness of their loss. In the backs of their minds, even as they took great pride and joy in his accomplishments, would lurk thoughts of what might have been with Ben.

It was not going to be easy, Jonathan told himself. He also wanted to contemplate the evolving friendship with Sarah, but his tired body would not allow it. Perhaps the following day. His eyes grew steadily heavy, and he drifted off to sleep.

He didn't know it, of course, but Sarah's mind was working overtime reflecting on the tragedy that had befallen him. She was also pondering what was happening in her life. Years later, as Jonathan read her letter, he came to appreciate how she was then dealing with his entering her life.

. . . As I lay awake at nights during that awful week when you were home for Ben's funeral, I tried to visualize you and your parents dealing with the tragic loss. I tried to picture how you must have looked when

you first saw his body. I tried to imagine you as you said your final good-bye at the cemetery.

I ached for you, so deeply that it soon puzzled me, then frightened me. What was the meaning of all of this, I asked myself. I pondered it for several nights before I came to the realization you were by far the most fascinating man I had ever met. Clearly, our relationship was the most intriguing and most exciting one of my young life.

The thought of romance had probably entered my mind, although barely in its far recesses. Had I been more perceptive, I would have understood that my feelings had a touch of physical yearning for you.

But what did come to me loud and clear was the recognition you were someone whose friendship I ought to allow to grow. In fact, I knew I ought to cultivate it, perhaps even vigorously. And when I had—really had—your friendship, I ought to treasure it more than anything else that would later befall me. I ought to treasure you, my friend, more than anyone else who would come into my life. . . .

~ 9 ~

Confronting Initial Friendship

Jonathan's plane touched down in Raleigh on time. He was happy for such small favors. True to her word, Sarah was waiting for him. As he disembarked and started across the tarmac, she walked briskly toward him and extended her arms. The moment of her embrace was the most welcome one since he had left North Carolina two weeks earlier. How he had missed her, he thought, as he held onto her for what seemed like eternity.

"Thanks for coming." The words flowed haltingly from Jonathan's lips at first. He wasn't quite ready to reenter his world of the past two years, that of a university professor. It was much too sudden. Duke had been far removed from his mind the past couple of weeks, except for thoughts of Sarah, of course. But the next sentence came easier, hastened by her bright smile. "It's so good to see the warm face of a friend."

Sarah said nothing at first. Instead, she squeezed a little harder, then released her grip. They turned from each other and walked arm in arm toward the terminal. After a moment, she broke the silence. "I hope it went okay this morning at the airport when you left."

"About as well as one could expect, I guess. I tried to be as upbeat as possible," Jonathan said. "It took every bit of acting talent I could muster to achieve some semblance of normalcy. But I have to shake my parents out of the malaise into which they have fallen since Ben's death. They need to accept their loss and allow the grieving process to continue. I really worry about them. And I have to deal with my own grief as well." Jonathan sighed. He looked like he had aged ten years.

Sarah looked intently into his eyes and remarked, "It's going to be a difficult several months. I hope you can take time away from work to give it the attention it needs."

"I really have no choice," Jonathan replied. "But there is some good news, albeit a small amount in a huge bucket of sadness. My graduate course is the same one I taught last spring, so I am, by and large, already prepared. The undergraduate course, on the other hand, is a new one for me, but I'm on top of it. So perhaps I can handle it okay the remainder of the semester. I can put my book project on hold until summer. It's been at a near-standstill anyhow for awhile. It's really hard to find a block of time long enough in which to write a whole book chapter when one has to prepare several lectures a week. So I had pretty much decided I would put it aside until May when I could concentrate full-time on it without the interruptions of class."

"What can I do to help?" Sarah asked.

Sarah's question pleased Jonathan. He immediately thought of many things she could do to enhance his life. In fact, his mind wandered far and wide for a few moments thinking about her playing a dual role of friend and lover. But his words did not betray his private thoughts. "Just keep doing what you're doing. It really is a big help."

"I'll be there. You can count on me," Sarah assured him. Her words were a much needed antidote to the emptiness that had enveloped him the last two weeks. He grasped the implications of her remarks like one stranded on a deserted island would at the sight of a ship sailing toward him from offshore.

Jonathan's luggage arrived in about ten minutes. As they made their way to the car, he broached their eating plans. "Are we still on for dinner?"

Sarah smiled. "We certainly are. I'm going to keep you to your word." There was a pause. Then, with a sly grin on her face, she revealed her scheme. "I want you to know I have been very presumptuous, Dr. Hawthorne. I did a lot of checking and found the perfect restaurant for tonight. It's about thirty minutes from Durham, ten miles south of Chapel Hill. It's a French restaurant, La Chandelle, converted from a beautiful old Victorian home. I checked it out myself this afternoon. Its menu's authentic. So's the atmosphere. I also took care of the wine. One of my friends in the dorm who's twenty-one picked up a bottle this afternoon. I didn't give her any specific clue as to why I wanted it, only that it was for a special occasion."

Jonathan suddenly remembered North Carolina's antiquated liquor laws. One could not buy alcohol for onsite consumption. It was only available at state stores for drinking in the privacy of one's home or to bring to a restaurant in a brown paper bag for consumption during dinner. There was a way around the law, however. Establishments sold pseudo-memberships in private clubs. They then could serve liquor in little miniature bottles. But Sarah's answer to the problem was much more imaginative, and much more personal, Jonathan thought. They would enjoy a good bottle of wine that night.

"I hope you don't mind all of this," Sarah said half-heartedly, as if she already knew the answer.

"Mind? I think it's terrific," Jonathan assured her. "To tell you the truth, I hadn't thought about a place to eat. And I haven't had much experience since I've been at Duke searching for good eateries, other than the 'greasy spoons' I tend to frequent. La Chandelle will be a welcome change. I'm putty in your hands tonight, Sarah Joan Matthews. Lead me to your restaurant."

Sarah was right on target. La Chandelle was a lovely place in an exquisite setting. The original owners of the estate had set the home back about a hundred yards from the road. Giant oak trees formed a canopy on both sides of the entry road for the entire distance, which reminded diners of Oak Alley outside New Orleans. It was perfect for a meal among good friends and even more suited to dinner for lovers.

"*Bonsoir, madame. Bonsoir, monsieur.*" The doorman seemed to appear out of nowhere as they approached the entrance to the restaurant. "*Comment allez-vous?*"

"*Très bien, merci,*" Jonathan replied. He thought to himself that at this moment he was very well, indeed. He then asked the same question about the doorman's general condition as he took Sarah by the arm and directed her into the anteroom.

The doorman answered in the expected fashion. "*Très bien, merci.*"

"This is wonderful, Sarah. A really terrific choice," Jonathan said.

"I'm glad you're pleased," Sarah replied. "I was worried you wouldn't think this place appropriate for tonight."

"Silly woman! Of course, it's appropriate. It's great!" Jonathan exclaimed. "I love it. I needed something like this to take my mind off all that's happened the past two weeks, to unwind. How did you find it?"

"Just call me Nancy Drew. The usual sleuth work. I called the concierge at the Hotel South in Raleigh. Asked him for the name of the restaurant in the area with the combination of best setting and wonderful food. *Et, nous voici!* And here we are!"

Once again Jonathan was astounded at the behavior of the woman in front of him. Sarah was really something, he thought to himself. How lucky he was that she had entered his life. Although he knew he was exaggerating her talent, he didn't care. He was enjoying the moment too much.

The maitre d' approached and asked, "*Bonsoir, madame. Bonsoir, monsieur. Avez-vous une réservation?*" Jonathan looked at Sarah. He had not thought to ask her. If he had pondered it for a moment, however, he would have known her answer.

"*Oui, une réservation pour deux, Monsieur Hawthorne et une amie,*" she answered. Her assertiveness and smooth use of the French language brought a warm glow to Jonathan. Sarah was simply amazing, once again. She impressed him in so many ways, helped along of course by his strong desire for anything and everything she did to impress him. Jonathan continued speaking in the continental tongue. "I didn't know you spoke French," he remarked.

Sarah took the cue and also responded in the same language. "I didn't know you did either. But I should have known. You have a doctorate in international politics, which, I assume, required you to know a language or two. French is the language of international diplomacy, so I made the logical conclusion."

Jonathan returned to English. "Your assumption is correct. Russian and French were my two languages in grad school. Russian was by far the hardest because I didn't begin studying it until then. French, on the other hand, has been part of my life since grade school. My mother started me with the language when I was six, then turned me over to tutors until I reached high school. By the time I had graduated, I was fairly fluent.

"But it was during the summer between high school and college that I really made the big jump speaking the language. Two of my friends, John Evans and Alden Thomason, and I had saved our money for three years so we could go to Europe on our own. We begged and badgered our parents for two years until they agreed that, if we had enough money, we could go the summer we graduated from high school. I really think they didn't believe we could raise the funds, but we fooled them. They must have been so brave to let us attempt it.

"So off to Europe we went. We had an ambitious goal—one country a summer until we graduated from college. First country, France. Initial stop, Paris. We were so young and naive. But our parents had helped with hotel and train reservations along our intended route, so that relieved a lot of the anxiety.

"We traveled every inch of France, trying to sound like the locals, particularly to every teenage girl we could find. Without much success, I might add. We saw a new French city every three days. But we certainly got our feet wet. And once we left Paris, the good-natured locals responded so positively to our attempts to speak French. We did not feel the disdain we felt from the Parisians. People in the capital seemed to dislike tourists, particularly Americans, but also anyone else who couldn't speak the language perfectly.

"It makes me mad after all we did for them during World War II. I've already decided I'm going to be in Paris at the end of August 1994 when the city celebrates the fiftieth anniversary of its liberation from the Nazis. Let's see them try to hide America's contribution. *L'avenue des Champs-Elysées* had better be full of "thank-you-America" signs hanging from every building lining the boulevard. And the parade had better include U.S. military units, not like the one on Bastille Day, which glorifies every piece of hardware—plane, tank, jeep, weapon— that French forces ever deployed. There are none from any other country. I must admit, though, the July 14 celebration is one impressive sight after another. And the fireworks that evening are simply breathtaking, like the displays of our Fourth of July. But that's beside the point.

"I'll bet the citizens of Normandy and every other city on the route from there to Paris are grateful for what American GIs did in 1944. The British and the Canadians too. The Allies paid an awful price to kick Hitler's troops out of France.

"I guess that's why, as much as I love Paris, the object of my affection is really the city's physical beauty—both natural and man-made—not Parisians. When I want to get close to the French people, I much prefer the ones who live outside of Paris. But no matter. Now I can always greet waiters at French restaurants in the U.S. and Quebec, and order from a menu written entirely in French."

Jonathan feared he had been too hard on Parisians, so he tried to lighten the conversation a little with his last remark.

Sarah joined him in laughter. "You'll get your big chance tonight," she said.

"You too, Sarah Joan Matthews," he replied.

"But don't you now find it exciting, Professor Hawthorne, when you go to Paris or Brussels, that you can converse in the native language?" Sarah asked. "I find that to be an incredible high."

"You're exactly right. I do too," Jonathan agreed.

The waiter interrupted their discussion about the merits of language skills. He asked if they wanted their bottle of wine opened so that it might breathe. Jonathan nodded yes, and he accommodated them. He then placed a menu in front of each of them.

This intrusion caused Jonathan to reflect upon what had just happened. Sarah was a clever woman. She had channeled his thoughts away from the tragic events of the past two weeks to topics far-removed from Colorado and his brother. He was certain it was deliberate. He was grateful for her strategy and decided to allow her to continue such pleasant diversions. But first he wanted to get something off his mind. "Sarah, I have one request of you, and I hope it doesn't offend."

Her face suddenly took on an aura of puzzlement. An astute observer might have detected just a little acting, though. "What is it? Have I done something wrong? I'd be just crestfallen if that was the case." She spoke the last sentence in such a way so as to convey her intuition that what Jonathan had to get "off his mind" wasn't really such a big deal.

"No, no, no," he said, laughing. "Nothing like that. Don't worry." It was silly, he knew, but he suddenly felt extremely nervous. That emotion always seemed to appear when he moved into more serious conversation with Sarah. "Look, you and I have developed a friendship during the past two or three months. It's becoming far different from a simple professor-student relationship. I can't have someone who is my friend calling me 'Professor' or 'Doctor' now, can I?"

Sarah said nothing. Jonathan couldn't tell from her expression whether or not she had ever thought about how she greeted him before.

"So let's make a deal," he continued. "When we're alone, on campus or off, please call me 'Jonathan,' okay? I'd like that a lot more."

She paused for a moment and then replied, "Okay, but it will take some getting used to. After all, conventions are pretty formal around here."

"I know," Jonathan said. "But I suspect there aren't many professor-student friendships like ours either."

"I agree, Jonathan. Well, that wasn't as difficult as I thought. Let me try that again, Jonathan. There, I can do it," she said and laughed.

Jonathan sensed immediately they had just traversed another in what would be a long series of transitions in their relationship. He was surprised at how much her calling him by his first name pleased him, how it made him almost euphoric. But then he came to realize it was only natural that their relationship should take this course. And it seemed so right, so very right. Years later he would look back at the endless trail of progressions and reflect that they all seemed so seamless, so right.

Dinner went smoothly, Jonathan thought. Sarah allowed him to set the tone and the pace of conversation. He smiled to himself as he observed her initial hesitancy to address him by his first name, then her eventual transition into a more comfortable atmosphere in which she seemed to find excuses to utter "Jonathan."

Later he kidded her about it, which always seemed to turn her face a rich shade of crimson. Sarah laughingly denied it, but of course Jonathan knew he was right about her reaction. And, just as importantly, he was confident she knew he was correct.

The evening was the perfect antidote to the recent events still so fresh in his mind. For a long while, his conversation alternated between a strong need to talk through what had happened back home and his struggle to come to grips with the reality of his brother's death. For the first time since leaving Colorado, he came to realize he still suffered from moments of denial. It frustrated him because he knew, as painful as the thought was, he would never see Ben again. And he had to get to the point where he accepted the reality of that fact intellectually, if not emotionally.

It helped immensely that Sarah was sitting across from him at that moment. He felt so comfortable, so at ease, in discussing such incredibly personal feelings with her—emotions that cut to the very core of his heart. He tried to think of another with whom he might be able to share such intimate feelings so easily. Try as he might, though, he came up empty. Sarah was, in fact, the only person to whom he could or wanted to bare his soul. "Sarah," Jonathan said and then paused. He wanted to convey the uniqueness of their relationship, yet he hesitated, fearful of her reaction. It might be too soon. Indecision overtook him at first, but his emotions were too powerful that particular evening. He hoped he was not making a wrong turn.

"I want you to know I typically don't open up to others like I'm doing tonight." Again he paused, searching for just the right set of words. They came to him, but ever so slowly. "But I have a real need to talk about these things that are affecting me so much. There was really no one at home to share my sorrow with except my parents, but I wanted to remain strong for them. So I kept a stiff upper lip, as they say."

Sarah stared at him intensely, speaking with her eyes as much as with her voice. "Look, Jonathan," she said. "You've been carrying a heavy burden on your shoulders from the time you got off the plane in Colorado Springs until you boarded it again to return back here. And it has probably stayed with you even after you landed in Raleigh. Maybe even up until we sat down here at La Chandelle and you began to talk about it.

"You need to go though your own grieving as well as help your parents though theirs. And to do that, it's obvious you need to talk though the entire episode, from beginning to end. You loved your brother, and it must really hurt. So bare your soul. I want to help, and I sense tonight that I can be of help, if only in a small way, by listening to you. So don't hesitate, please. And drink some of my share of the wine. That will help too."

Jonathan returned her stare, not moving away from the eye contact she had initiated seconds earlier. At that moment he didn't want to focus on the tragedy of Ben's death. Instead he had a strong desire, even need, to convey to Sarah how he had come to view her as even more than a confidant—as a dear, dear friend on whom he could count. On whom he had relied since that fateful phone call from home. "Sarah. I don't really know how to say it, so I'll just go ahead and blurt it out. Okay? For some strange reason, or perhaps not so strange, I have leaned on you for solace. I have come to really need you in the fullest sense of the word. Inexplicably, you seem to occupy an incredibly important spot in my life, in my heart. I don't think it's just the unfortunate circumstances that have accelerated these feelings. They may have contributed to them, but only in a small way. I only know no one has ever touched me like you have these few short months."

Sarah was now the one to assert herself. "Jonathan," she began. How the words now seemed to flow so effortlessly and so eagerly off her lips, he thought.

"I sense what you sense," Sarah continued. "We have been talking to one another in a variety of settings since early last semester. I have returned each time because I found our meetings to be the most rewarding and fulfilling of my life, here at Duke or anywhere for that matter. Simple as that. I enjoy you. I cherish our talks. That's why I came back to visit you after last semester was over. You have so much to give, you are so interesting and knowledgeable, and let's not forget that you're so funny. As least I think you're humorous. In a subtle sort of way, which I really enjoy. I have a good feeling each time I leave you. I can't explain it any more than that.

"I've really been the one benefiting from our 'get-togethers.' It's been a special bonus, I guess, and it wasn't even mentioned in the university catalog sent to all prospective Dukies. James B. Duke would be proud.

"I'm glad I can give something back to you, although I wish the circumstances behind my giving could be different. I have come to view you in a special way, Jonathan Hawthorne, and I'm happy you have used the word 'friend.' I like that. I like the thought of being your friend. And the more I think about it, I relish the idea I am fast becoming your special friend."

They were entering new terrain, Jonathan thought. And while it was not a movement toward sexual fulfillment, it might even be better. After all, friends, real friends, were harder to come by, more rare than lovers. Lovers come and go, sometimes sooner, oftentimes later. But most often they go—far, far away. True friends are different. They are always there. One can count on them. They rarely, if ever, fail you. If truth be told, friends, not lovers, are a more valuable commodity. Jonathan didn't pause to contemplate the most desirable condition of all—having both friend and lover wrapped up in the same person. Much later, he would consider himself the most fortunate man in the world as the possibility of his becoming both friend and lover to Sarah appeared more likely. He welcomed Sarah's comments. The slight grin now permanently affixed on his face gave it away. He grew more and more excited as he contemplated the implications of their relationship.

Both eased comfortably into their new roles as the evening played itself out. Sarah was right about La Chandelle. Clearly a restaurant for lovers. For a brief moment Jonathan allowed himself the luxury of thinking about a return trip someday with Sarah at his side, playing yet a new role, that of lover or even wife. The setting—the giant oaks towering over the entry road, a small intimate room, the dim lighting, music for lovers, classical French cuisine, a waiter standing at attention a discrete distance away poised to fulfill every request—all contributed to the most vivid amorous fantasies. His imagination ran wildly. It would have taken a most unusual person, one not given to any kind of romanticism whatsoever, to withstand the effects of La Chandelle.

Jonathan began to feel guilty. He was supposed to be grieving for his brother, and yet here he was thinking lustful thoughts of himself and Sarah locked in a passionate embrace somewhere, each eagerly exploring the other's body, probing widely and deeply. How could he possibly allow himself the pleasure of such fantasies when his brother lay recently buried sixteen hundred miles away? He didn't deserve such joy.

But he understood that life must go on and that meant moving beyond Ben's death. Only then could the healing begin and the awful pain that had stuck with him since that fateful phone call two weeks earlier start to dissipate. And what better way to heal than by taking advantage of this wonderful moment to let his mind roam in pursuit of forbidden pleasures? Intellectually, he began to come to terms with the feelings of guilt, rationalizing that while they might very well be legitimate, he had every right to get on with his life. After all, Ben would want it that way.

Time at La Chandelle was coming to a close. The dinner wine had had its proper effect. Jonathan was mellowing, accepting wherever the moment took him. As they made their way to the parking lot, he took Sarah's arm. As he did, she snuggled close to him—the movement of a friend consoling another.

It felt good, awfully good, he thought, as they made their way toward the car. Soon they were standing next to it. Instinctively they turned toward each other. Jonathan spoke in a soft, almost pleading voice, yet one accompanied with a wry smile. "I need a hug. A big bear hug."

"Oh, Jonathan! I'm so sorry about Ben. I don't know what else to say," Sarah said in an anguished voice.

"There's nothing else to say. Just hug me for a minute. I need that more than anything else right now," Jonathan replied.

That instant cemented their friendship and its accompanying commitment to one another in times of need. From that moment on, Jonathan knew he could count on Sarah to be there when he needed her, no matter where their respective paths might take them over the coming years. And he pledged to himself to be there for her when circumstances called upon him.

"That's what friends are for," the lyrics to a Dionne Warwick song later reminded listeners. Each time he heard it, Jonathan thought back to that night outside La Chandelle where he and Sarah made a mutual commitment to one another and sealed it with an extended, emotional embrace. Little did he know a call from Sarah for help would come sooner rather than later.

And Sarah?

. . . There were many transitions in our relationship over the years, but none surpassed our first visit to La Chandelle—until some time later, of course. I made reservations there because I knew you needed something

dramatic to take your mind off Ben's death. There was little I could do. I knew that. But I thought a special evening at an exceptional restaurant might help.

I wasn't looking for romance, and it didn't enter my mind that evening. But I welcomed the direction the evening took. I must admit you caught me off guard with your request that I call you by your first name. That was new territory for me, but I was thrilled. It symbolized, I guess, that you were now thinking of me in a different light. I know I hesitated at first, but you should have noticed that I soon felt comfortable with it. In fact, I sought out excuses to call you "Jonathan." Now, of course, I prefer more interesting terms, some of then even scandalous.

More importantly, I sensed as the evening wore on that our relationship was changing, and quickly at that. I'm sure the sad circumstances had something to do with it. But it was bound to happen anyhow, I know. By the time we made it to the parking lot, I probably was ready for anything—well, almost anything. It seemed so natural that you would want me to hug you, and it seemed so right when we did it. I fully understood that it was borne out of a newly committed friendship.

Looking back on it, I have often wondered if there was any sexual tension that night during our, by now, memorable embrace. But I don't really think so. Well, perhaps a little. I felt a warmth, a really wonderful warmth, but friendship brings with it such feelings. I did sense a closeness to you, a special closeness. I guess it was because you had allowed me into your life at a most critical time. The intimacy of sharing your tragedy was not lost on me. It had such an effect then, and it still does today when I think about those times.

It would be years before I came to realize just how much of an effect it had on me, however. Because you allowed me to get so close to you at a time when most men would have shunned contact with another, and certainly with someone who until recently had only been an acquaintance, it made the foundation for our friendship more substantial and firm. And it has been that foundation that has sustained me through all of my travails. I knew then, without a doubt, that you would always be there for me, no matter what the circumstances and no matter where our respective journeys took us.

I made the commitment that evening to always be there for you as well. I hoped you would call on me, rather than another, whenever you needed someone. I had enough confidence in myself, and in our evolving friendship, that I believed I and not someone else was the one to help you.

Initially I feared I had read more into the embrace and the circumstances surrounding it than I should have, but events proved me wrong over the years. Thank you, my sweet, sweet Jonathan, for recognizing I could be such a comfort, then and during all those other times over the years when you called on me.

As we drove back to Durham that evening, I felt euphoric about what had transpired. I had a new friend, and I had really helped him that evening. Somehow I knew he would be a friend for life. I knew you would never disappoint me. And I wanted so desperately to believe I would never fail you. It suddenly made me fear that I would let you down in some future crisis, and I prayed that would not be the case.

When you dropped me off at the dorm, I wanted to shout, "Thank you, thank you, thank you," for making me feel so special, for giving me—a somewhat insecure, not very self-confident girl—a sense of purpose and a sense of being wanted. Yes, although I tried to fool people, I was all of those things and more. What a boost for my ego, I tell you that, Dr. Jonathan Hawthorne!

I really now think that, unbeknownst to me, I had just started a long, wonderful journey. But it would be quite a while before I would admit that was the case. For the time being, I was simply so excited about our friendship because I knew it would bring me only good things. I would benefit in so many ways as yet undreamed of as a consequence of our relationship. So let me say once again, as I have often said to you, thank you, thank you, my sweet man, for entering my life . . .

Jonathan, of course, had no idea what Sarah was thinking as he released his hug and opened the car door. Unlike with Sarah, their embrace had reawakened in him an unequivocally sexual desire for her. He allowed himself a slight moment to indulge in such feelings before coming back to reality. It was a good evening, he reflected. He had not given much thought to what might take place when Sarah met him at the airport, so he had no expectation of what might unfold. Clearly he welcomed—more than welcomed, actually—the events of the night. They gave him a warm and secure feeling, about then and about the future.

Jonathan did not want the drive back to Durham to end. He found himself traveling at about ten miles under the speed limit in order to prolong the evening. He was in no hurry to return to the emptiness of his condo, though he later relished some time alone to ponder the consequences of the past two weeks. And, although he would not admit it, he also welcomed the solitude in order to sort through the implications of the changing circumstances with Sarah.

As they neared the campus, Jonathan felt the need to reiterate what he had said earlier. "Thank you, dear friend, for all you've done, for being there for me. I shall never forget it."

Sarah responded in a way that left no doubt, he inferred, that she understood the implications of the evening's exchange.

As they approached the entrance to the dorm, Jonathan could see several couples making their way back from wherever they might have spent the past several hours. He could picture Sarah as part of such a group, but he didn't want to. He liked it better when she was part of his world. But he knew that was too much to ask. Besides, he was determined to do nothing that would infringe on their newfound friendship. It was much too important to him.

Years later he would realize that expressing one's love to one's best friend need not be a recipe for disaster, for ending the relationship. Instead, it could be a formula for total happiness if the friend returned the love in kind. But he learned that lesson much later. Whether or not he learned it too late is another story.

~ 10 ~

Sarah's First Need of Jonathan

Jonathan arrived at the office bright and early Monday morning ready to delve into his classes. He wanted a return to normalcy as soon as possible as a way of moving the grieving process along. Word about Ben had spread quickly around Duke, and he returned to a mailbox full of sympathy cards and letters. He was surprised at the outpouring of condolences from faculty colleagues and students alike. It made him feel good that the campus had responded as it did, despite an overwhelming sentiment among both students and faculty against the Vietnam War itself.

Not surprisingly, he found it difficult returning to second semester's normal routine, though. A colleague had covered for him in his two classes while he was gone, for which he was grateful, so his absence presented no problem. But his heart and mind simply weren't in his lectures. Thoughts of Ben's death kept intruding. And, of course, any research was out of the question, at least until summer when he would be free of his teaching duties and his grieving process would be further along.

The semester continued, nonetheless, and Jonathan dealt with it as best he could. Preparing lectures turned out to be rather therapeutic. March had just arrived, and the campus was showing signs of spring. Jonathan loved the early exit from winter, preferring to take his gulps of cold weather in one-week chunks in Colorado rather than to spread them out over several long, dreary months. The sun's new warmth helped his frame of mind.

Also aiding it was Sarah. While Jonathan did not see or talk to her every day, their number of contacts came close to that. Usually it was a late-night phone call, mostly but not always initiated by Sarah. In fact, he had come to anticipate the friendly sound of her soft, warm voice filling his ear before he drifted off to sleep. On those nights when they failed to connect, he felt like something was missing from the day's itinerary. Sarah also stopped by his office often, about once a week. He cherished them as much as, if not more than, the nightly calls. There in his office he could look into her eyes and catch their sparkle. How he loved to gaze at her.

The conversations were a bonus. Sarah shared everything about her day, most of which centered around the internship in Raleigh. It was an exciting time for her, and she included Jonathan in all of it. He suspected, though, that she had an ulterior motive for doing so. The more he focused on Sarah's Raleigh, the less Ben's Colorado occupied his mind.

Sarah's principal assignment in the Senator's North Carolina office was to research the domestic benefits of U.S. business investment abroad. If she could help provide evidence that more American jobs were created if the United States could entice foreign countries to buy American, then Congress might consider allocating funds to promote international trade. Simple as that. Jonathan never tired of listening to Sarah as she grew more animated with each description of her work.

They managed to steal away on a few occasions for an off-campus meal, although the ambience and the food of these eateries never approached that of La Chandelle. Despite the pleasure Jonathan took from simply being with her, he knew Sarah's major contribution during this period was as listener to his ventilating about the misfortune that had befallen him. She had just the right knack for knowing when to speak and when to remain silent. When she did say something, it was always just the right phrase. As the days turned into weeks, Jonathan came to appreciate just how valuable Sarah had become in helping him through the grieving process.

It was becoming more and more evident that she understood him— his moods, his insecurities, his current state of mind—better than anyone ever had. It was almost scary just how well Sarah could anticipate what he was going through at any given moment, or what he was about to say. At first it made him uncomfortable. Soon, though, it had just the opposite effect. He came to appreciate, like even, that someone was there—a dear friend who understood him so well, even though she was a student and he a professor.

He had not stopped coveting her, but the rewards of their friendship were so fulfilling that he wanted nothing to stand in its way. That included a sexual relationship if it meant lessening what they already had. He couldn't explain his reasoning. In fact, he experienced moments when he thought it rather stupid. But he couldn't ignore the voice inside of him warning that if he and Sarah crossed the line, its effect on their friendship would be negative, even destructive. He had seen it happen to others over the years, and he didn't want to chance it. He was, purely and simply, afraid.

Of course he had also not forgotten about Michael. Sarah never talked about him, although he thought she was still seeing him on a somewhat regular basis. Jonathan believed he could plot their schedule based on when she called him at night. He guessed that when her calls approached midnight—once or twice a week—rather than the normal eleven o'clock, she had just returned from a date. But he asked no questions. He did not want to know about that part of Sarah's world. And she apparently was able to compartmentalize her life enough so she felt no need to relate any of the details to him.

Thus, Jonathan was not prepared for that Sunday evening when she appeared at his office door, her eyes reddened from what had obviously been a major bout of crying. Her knock sounded like it always did—two soft touches of the wooden part of the door followed by one louder tap on the glass. They had developed this unique signal as a way to distinguish her from anyone else at the door. While he might ignore a regular knock from another student because he was knee deep in some important analysis, he wanted to make certain that he never missed a visit from Sarah.

Jonathan immediately knew something was amiss. "What's wrong, Sarah?" he asked. He pondered all the possible terrible things that could have happened to her. Did one of her parents die? Or a best friend? Was someone she loved in a terrible accident? Whatever it was, it had to be serious.

"I've been dumped. Michael told me he no longer wanted to see me. And he offered no reason. He just said it was over between us. That was it," Sarah said.

The tears started down her cheeks once more, and Jonathan rose quickly to offer her a handkerchief. Instead, he found himself holding her as he tried to console her. But he knew no words could remove the hurt. Sarah was upset, and there was little he could do. It was raining outside and he only had a small umbrella, but he suggested they go for a walk so that she could then vent to him.

Sarah agreed, and soon they made their way across the darkened campus, rendered more so by the light rain drops falling about them. Jonathan put his arm around her, as much to shrink the space they jointly occupied so that the umbrella would shield them from the rain as to provide a strong shoulder on which to lean. Off they went, heading across the quad toward the south side of the campus, past Cameron Indoor Stadium, the home of the Blue Devils basketball team. Soon the Duke golf course, situated among the tall North Carolina pines so familiar in the Piedmont region, loomed in the short distance. The course would offer an uninterrupted stroll for as long as Sarah needed to deal with Michael's surprising action.

At first they walked in silence. Jonathan had decided he would wait until she was ready to talk before he said anything. Sometimes it was best, he understood all too well from his recent experience, to let silence have its way. A full ten minutes passed before Sarah spoke.

"I really appreciate your dropping what you were doing at the office and helping me. You didn't have to do that, you know," she said.

"But I want to," came Jonathan's quick reply. "Besides, I have relied on you so much this past month that I'll have great difficulty ever repaying you."

"Who's counting? Friends don't keep score to see whose turn it is to help the other. The situation dictates who's the helper and who's the helpee. It just feels good to know you're here and will help me through this mess I find myself in somehow."

During the next couple of hours, Sarah exhibited several different kinds of feelings. It was clear that her first reaction was a combination of anger and hurt. "How could he do this to me?" she said in a cracking voice. "Out of the blue, too. No warning. Just a simple, 'That's it. It's over.' How dare he?" On and on she ranted, until she had exhausted all the venom she held toward Michael inside of her.

Jonathan could see Sarah also slowly assume an air of vulnerability. The word "helplessness" did not quite capture her mood swing. But clearly she was moving from rage to self-pity.

"Why me?" she continued. "Why does it always have to happen to me? This isn't the first time, Jonathan, that some guy has dropped me. But it doesn't get any easier, I can tell you that."

Jonathan listened and absorbed. His first reaction was one of surprise. Sarah had always appeared so confident, both in and out of the classroom. But matters of the heart are unlike any other experiences. Rejection is never good for the soul, not to mention the ego, no matter how indifferent one might be toward the rejecter. His heart ached for Sarah. He wanted to reach out, lift her off the ground, and tell her what fools all those guys who had walked out on her had been. He was also eager to confess that if she would let him love her as only he wanted to and could, he would worship her for the rest of their time together.

But, of course, he said nothing of the kind. Years later Jonathan lamented that he had missed a golden opportunity. He knew, though, that it would have been unfair of him to take advantage of her heightened vulnerability at that moment. He also later admitted that the real reason for his inaction was a lack of courage.

Sarah later chided him for not baring his soul that fateful evening. But she also reiterated in her most serious voice that the time would not have been right. She immediately added that Jonathan's revealing his love for her might have made the succeeding years very different—much more rewarding with far less heartache.

As Jonathan and Sarah continued their stroll throughout the golf course, she began to recover from her self-pity. She appeared to gain strength as they reached the far corner of the golf course. There, away from everyone, away from reminders of Michael, Sarah began to philosophize about her situation. A whole new attitude emerged.

"You know, Jonathan," she said, "it's not like I was madly in love with him. I wasn't. Yeah, I enjoyed being with him, although I might be hard-pressed to give you a solid reason as to why. I guess I just enjoyed his company. But it is a coincidence that I have been assessing the situation recently, as it turns out. And I think I had already figured it out. Being in a relationship does provide a sense of belonging, particularly on a large campus with its usual impersonal nature. I know Duke isn't as big as other campuses and everyone makes an effort to get to know one another—not like it probably is at a giant school like Ohio State, for example—but it's large enough to create some feelings of isolation."

Jonathan agreed and laid out his full-blown inertia theory of campus relationships—that is, how they continue beyond their normal "shelf lives" because staying in them is easier than enduring the fallout of a break-up.

Sarah was intrigued by his theory and pressed him about its origin. "How do you know so much about this?" she asked rather light-heartedly.

"I've been there, more than once, back in my Pitt days," he said. "Although I confess I was less inclined than the women I was involved with to stay together. But I do think I let them down somewhat more gently than Michael did you. Maybe he decided that continuing on was harder than making a clean break. Nonetheless, as your friend, of course, I must now show righteous indignation, come to your defense, confront Michael, and demand an explanation on your behalf. If he refuses, a dual it will be, with weapons of his choice. I will not be denied an opportunity to protect your honor!"

Sarah laughed out loud at Jonathan's fake outburst of anger. "That's it. Protect my honor."

"I'll do more than simply protect your honor, my dear Sarah," Jonathan uttered in his most formal voice. "I'll be more chivalrous than *Camelot's* Sir Lancelot in coming to your aid. No stone will be left unturned in my effort to right this wrong. Michael will pay dearly for his actions. I'll even flunk him if he dares show up in my course some day. No mercy. Not for him. Ever!"

Jonathan's antics increasingly amused Sarah. But it was her turn to theorize once more about campus relationships, particularly about their endings. "Even though you're probably right about the rationale behind campus romances, that doesn't make being dropped any less traumatic. Being rejected is never easy, even if in our most rational moments we understand that it's better in the long run, and maybe even in the short run, to have the other person out of our lives.

"Pride also plays a role. We like to think we possess qualities that make us desirable to others. We're eager to assume that this yearning will never weaken and eventually disappear, but instead will always grow stronger. The rude awakening of being told it's over drives a dagger into one's heart, even if its painful effects are felt only momentarily or even if one really doesn't even care."

"You're saying your relationship with Michael had been like those we just described—essentially one of convenience or one held in place by simple inertia?" Jonathan queried.

"I guess that's right. I am saying just that," Sarah agreed. "Of course, it would be a lot easier if I didn't have a healthy dose of insecurity along with my confidence. Sounds confusing, doesn't it? Well, I think both emotions—confidence and insecurity—wage war with each other to see who can get the upper hand and influence me more. Sometimes I'm full of confidence, while at other times I'm so uncertain of myself. This business with Michael certainly can't help but exacerbate that latter condition of mine. Oh well. I'll just have to deal with it," Sarah sighed.

"Let me help you, okay? I think you are one terrific person. There, how's that?" Jonathan asked triumphantly.

Sarah smiled, trying to hide her embarrassment. "Sounds good. But come on, Jonathan. I know my imperfections and limitations. The list is miles long. Maybe even endless."

A seriousness suddenly came over Jonathan as he responded. "Sarah, once before I told you that you, and I quote, 'may well be the best student I've yet had at Duke.' I meant it then, and if I was to repeat the same phrase now, I would drop the word 'may.' You are the best student I've had, period. Let me expand on the accolade. You are, moreover, simply the most remarkable person I've ever known. I treasure our friendship. I can't begin to tell you how much I have benefited from knowing you the way I do. I stop and think sometimes about how fortunate I am our paths have crossed. Don't ever sell yourself short. What more can I say?"

"That's quite enough, thank you," Sarah answered. "I won't be able to stop blushing for a week. Even though I don't believe a word you say. Remember my insecurities? They are winning right now—so it is really nice of you to say such things. Maybe some day I'll begin to think of myself a little like you described. But not if I have many more episodes like tonight."

Sarah tried to make light of the situation, and Jonathan quickly joined her. They continued walking. He sensed a stronger gait to her stride. She was coming to grips with the events of the day. She was working through rejection and rationalizing that the loss was really not much of a loss. Sarah suddenly looked at her watch and said, "Jonathan, we have been walking for almost three hours. Can you believe that? You must be exhausted."

"What do you mean, 'You must be exhausted?' What about you?" Jonathan asked.

They both chuckled at his remark. Around they turned and headed back toward her dorm. Although they hadn't noticed, it had been raining constantly since they left his office. Also unacknowledged by both of them was Jonathan's arm around Sarah's shoulder the entire time.

She later reminisced about that rainy night:

> *. . . I remember well that evening when I appeared at your office door in a rather sorry state, courtesy of Michael. You were so good to me, so understanding. I have this image of a strong arm around my shoulders, holding me up against the evil forces that threatened to crush me.*
>
> *In retrospect, Michael meant little to me, as we quickly came to understand. But his action had reinforced my insecurities. You were so wonderful in trying to counteract what he had done to me. I still remember your words.*
>
> *When I returned to the dorm that evening, I reflected for the longest time on what you said. For the first time in my life, someone had looked me straight in the eyes and said, "You're okay. You're more than okay. You're terrific." Even though I told you I didn't believe a word of it, that's not exactly true. To the extent that I have dealt successfully with my insecurities over the years, it is because of your treasured comments that night. Whenever I develop pains of self-doubt, I try to think of your soothing words. I admit, though, it took me almost two decades before I completely accepted what you said as the truth, at least as you saw it. . . .*

~ 11 ~
First Experience with Public Tragedy

The coming weeks proved Jonathan and Sarah right about campus romances. She told him a month later that Michael was ancient history, no problem. They celebrated by sharing a bottle of wine and a few laughs over the long walk in the rain.

The semester was winding down. It was early April when tragedy struck again. This time though, it was not a personal adversity but a national one. Sarah's call broke the news to Jonathan. Martin Luther King, Jr., had been gunned down in Memphis that evening. He died immediately.

Sarah was visibly upset. "What is wrong with this country?" her anguished voice asked, not expecting an answer. She was in high school when President Kennedy was assassinated. "Now there's another political murder. Why is this happening?"

She and Jonathan had talked earlier about the first modern assassination on "the day," as it was called, November 22, 1963. King's murder reminded her of their earlier conversation. That exchange had led them to recount how each had become interested in political science. The common circumstances that influenced their long-term career commitments struck both of them.

Jonathan had related how JFK's campaign for the presidency had led him to political science. He was a math major when the summer of 1960 rolled around. But he became caught up in all of the hoopla surrounding the Democratic convention in Los Angeles, and later the most exciting presidential campaign in decades. Kennedy's charisma captivated him as much as it did millions of other young Americans and inspired many of that generation to study or enter politics. When Jonathan returned to Pitt for his junior year, he had made up his mind. Gone was a career in mathematics. Replaced with a lifelong journey in political science. He never once regretted his decision.

His first political activity was passing out JFK campaign leaflets on the street corners of Pittsburgh. Predominately Democratic Pittsburghers welcomed him with open arms. He joined fellow Allegheny County Democrats long into the wee hours of election night and the next morning, first on the edges of their seats waiting for the final returns, then rising from catching a few winks on the floor to toast JFK's national victory. Kennedy's win reinforced his decision to change careers.

Sarah had a similar story. She had even seen Kennedy in the flesh during the 1960 campaign. She was in the eighth grade at the time and skipped school one September afternoon to catch a glimpse of the Democratic Party candidate as he made a campaign swing through Pennsylvania. She remembered that, as handsome as he looked in pictures, photos didn't come close to capturing his good looks in person. More importantly, even to an eighth-grader, when JFK spoke, he did so with such vitality and such conviction. Sarah was swept away with enthusiasm, for him and for the causes he advanced. She returned home that night with a new interest, politics, most certainly from a Democratic Party perspective. Seven years later she officially declared political science her major at Duke.

She too had worked for JFK's election. Despite her apparent shyness, she had gone door-to-door in Lancaster passing out campaign literature, hoping to keep the Nixon vote in predominately Republican Lancaster County as low as possible. Her parents even allowed her to go to the county Democratic Party headquarters on election night.

There, Sarah, along with about a hundred other hopefuls, waited for the final results. She called her parents several times in the initial hours after the polls closed, pleading to be allowed to stay longer because returns were coming in slowly and the race was close. Finally, her father joined her around midnight. Together they waited until early morning, when he convinced her to go home and catch some sleep. Joy followed a few hours later when she awoke to find the outcome fell in Kennedy's favor.

Jonathan was in graduate school and Sarah in eleventh grade three years later when Lee Harvey Oswald struck. America's consequent loss of political innocence greatly affected them both, and it took an enormous amount of time for them to recover from events in Dallas. Both had eventually recaptured enthusiasm for America's political way of life, but the assassination of Martin Luther King, Jr., had just shaken them badly again.

They agreed to meet in the television room at the student union, where they knew many students and even some faculty still on campus would gather to learn more about King's assassination. Each arrived about twenty minutes later and spent about an hour together watching the news. When it became clear no more information would be available, they crossed the hall to the commons, where they grabbed a bite to eat.

There they engaged in the type of conversation that thrilled both of them—lively, animated, and placing the day's terrible event in some sort of historical context and theoretical perspective. They each fed off the other's intellect and helped the other deal with the sadness that had overtaken both of them. Sarah went home that evening well-prepared to discuss the entire context of the King assassination with her dorm friends. Jonathan left better able to impart words of wisdom to his class the next morning.

In the days that followed, Jonathan and Sarah talked often about what had happened in Memphis and its consequences for the country as well as the civil rights movement. She learned for the first time that Jonathan was present on the Mall in Washington on that late August day in 1963 when Dr. King had mesmerized the crowd with his "I Have a Dream" speech at the Lincoln Memorial. She appeared surprised about his revelation since he had not told her of his special interest—more of an avocation really—in civil rights and civil liberties.

Although his specialty was international politics, Jonathan always harbored a curiosity about one of the fundamental principles of America's form of government—the protection of individual and minority group rights from the tyranny of both the majority and the government. It was a strange combination, he knew, but he reminded

Sarah that President Kennedy had emphasized the same two areas—foreign affairs and civil rights—during his presidency. "So I was in good company," he told her.

Television also played a role in Jonathan's dual interests. It had burnt on his brain images of violence against American citizens perpetrated by government officials who had sworn to uphold the law. They targeted individuals who were only exercising their rights to assemble peacefully and petition their government to champion constitutional guarantees of individual rights and liberties.

Television had also brought vivid pictures of the horrors of modern warfare from the jungles and villages in Vietnam into living rooms across the nation. The latter intrusion changed the attitudes of a large segment of American society from indifference to vocal opposition to the U.S. government's role in Southeast Asia.

Television's portrayal of the violence perpetrated on both civil rights protestors and on the people and countryside of Vietnam had profoundly affected Jonathan. By far the most important consequence was his decision to become a professor of international politics. Whenever he could, he also read about the civil rights movement and other historical efforts by American citizens to obtain civil liberties. As a student, he had even enrolled in two courses—one that dealt with constitutional constraints on governmental abuse of power and another that focused specifically on civil liberties and the role that the courts and Congress played in them.

Jonathan also took the opportunity to observe firsthand civil rights activities around the country whenever his schedule and wallet permitted. That was how he happened to find himself on the Mall on August 28, 1963. He tried to capture for Sarah the excitement of that momentous day in Washington, which firmly established Martin Luther King, Jr., as the undisputed leader of the civil rights movement.

Spring 1968 thus found both Sarah and Jonathan continuously caught up in national political events. It was good for both of them, as it helped to put Ben's death and Michael's departure further and further behind them. The Vietnam conflict and King's assassination were having a major impact on their ability to deal with their two personal tragedies. Also sharing center stage was Lyndon Johnson's decision not to seek re-election to the White House. Its effect on the upcoming presidential election and the Democratic Party convention in Chicago preceding it would be enormous.

Johnson's action had thrown the race for the party's nominee for president wide open. He had already faced opposition in his run for another term from within his own party, most notably from Senator Gene McCarthy from Minnesota. Now President Kennedy's brother, Bobby, a senator from New York, sought the nomination as well. Vice President Hubert Humphrey stood in for Johnson, although he would take pains to distance himself—at least late in the campaign—from some of the President's policies, particularly those relating to Vietnam.

Jonathan and Sarah watched from afar as the spring political primaries kicked into high gear. Second semester was also winding down, so they found themselves attending more and more to academic concerns for a few weeks in late April. He was happy the semester was drawing to a close. Its passing would leave two memories, one wonderful and one devastating. He would always associate spring 1968 with the death of his brother. He still experienced moments when it was difficult not to despair. But he also recognized, as most did in those situations, that time had a way of helping the grieving process run its course so life could go on.

His other memory would also be with him for the rest of his life. Spring 1968 had solidified his friendship with Sarah. She was now the most important person in his life, as he was in hers, she would tell him. Again, there was nothing overtly lascivious about their relationship, although sexual tension was clearly present. The ground rules were clear to both of them.

Sarah understood that as well as Jonathan.

. . . *Spring 1968 was a pivotal time in our relationship. When the semester began, I had only recently made the decision to visit you from time to time in your office, as I had found you intriguing. Nothing more than that. So there I was, one week into the semester, scared to death as I knocked on your office door.*

By the time the semester ended, however, I was secure in the most meaningful friendship of my life. What made it so special was that you had asked nothing of me, and certainly not for my body. You only want-

ed to give, and what you had to offer was the most precious present of all, the desire to be my friend. I soon came to realize there was no more cherished gift than that of friendship.

We had endured two personal crises by late spring, well, certainly one. My breakup with Michael wasn't such a misfortune. More of an annoyance really, and perhaps even a relief. But you had suffered a profound loss with Ben's death. We had experienced a national tragedy as well, the King assassination. Through all of this, you shared yourself with me and opened up to me, drawing me closer and closer to you. I saw such a remarkable man coming to grips with all these events. And I also saw how you valued my reaction and my views on what was happening. You quickly began to treat me as an intellectual equal, which, in turn, allowed me to view you differently.

You also showed me a side of you few had seen. Vulnerability was part of that side. Love for a brother was another. Anger at social injustice was a third. And such sensitivity for a friend. You worked at our friendship. You made me feel as if I was the most significant part of your life. I became so secure in our friendship that it gave me strength in other areas as well.

That is why I made the decision to get involved in politics again, for the first time since autumn 1960 when I was in the eighth grade. Thank you, my dear, for the gift of courage you gave me. . . .

Sarah decided to once again become part of a political campaign as the semester drew to a close. She related her new idea to Jonathan the day after she had completed her coursework and the internship in Raleigh. "Jonathan, I have what I think is a really great opportunity, but I want your opinion. It's very important to me what you think about it. This is really exciting!"

"What's that, Sarah?" he asked. Jonathan had come to expect the unusual of her, so he thought nothing would surprise him. But he was wrong.

"Bobby Kennedy's office has put out a call for volunteers to go to Indiana to help the senator with his primary campaign there. The election's the first week in May, so I would work for about two weeks. They need to get the vote out among people, particularly college students against the war, who want to show their opposition to Vietnam by voting for Kennedy," Sarah said.

"But what about McCarthy? After all, he's an anti-war candidate as well," Jonathan observed.

"Yes, but he doesn't have a chance to win, and Bobby Kennedy does. Oh, this is really exciting!" Sarah exclaimed.

"You're right about McCarthy," Jonathan agreed. "Kennedy is the only one who can derail Humphrey. But he has to win big somewhere during the primaries. If not in Indiana, certainly in California in June." Jonathan knew the politics of primaries well.

"See. It is important. And it would be like old times. Like it was in eighth grade," Sarah said.

"Well, not exactly," Jonathan interjected. "Times are different. For one thing, Bobby Kennedy is not the choice of the party elders like his brother was after he had captured the convention nomination. For another, we're talking about convention delegate votes. That's different from electoral votes, which are based on the November popular vote. Delegates to the convention are selected on a couple of criteria, only one of which is the primary popular vote total."

"Oh, that's right," Sarah said as she suddenly remembered earlier lectures about presidential primaries. "And after one ballot, state delegates are no longer committed to the candidate who won their primary. So it's more of an uphill struggle then."

"Precisely," Jonathan was quick to add. "And remember, Bobby Kennedy entered the campaign late—much too late, in my judgment. But if he can score some impressive primary victories, particularly in California with its large number of November electoral votes, then he has a good chance not only of winning the party nomination but also of capturing the White House in November."

Sarah had something else to point out. "It seems to me that the most important goal in the minds of the Democratic Party leaders is a victory in November. That is more critical than who the candidate is. If one of them has the best shot at defeating Nixon, then that person will get the support of party leaders, particularly after the first ballot."

"Good point. And Bobby Kennedy is more popular than Humphrey," Jonathan observed.

"So do you think, Jonathan, that my idea of going to Indiana is a good one?" Sarah asked. "After all, the timing's perfect. The semester's over, and I was just going home to Lancaster for a month anyhow before I returned for summer school. This is much better. The practical experience will help me in the long run, no matter what I end up doing with my political science degree." Sarah was clearly getting more and more excited by the minute.

"I do, Sarah," Jonathan answered. "What have you got to lose? And if Bobby Kennedy becomes president, who knows? There might be a job a year from now for a young, bright, attractive female political science graduate of one of the best universities in the country. It won't be a top job, but if you're interested in the Washington political scene, it would be a great step."

So Sarah made her decision. She was off to the Midwest to help get the student vote out at Indiana University. The state's flagship campus, IU was situated about fifty miles south of Indianapolis among the rolling hills of southern Indiana. She had two weeks to help turn the tide against the establishment. Jonathan was happy for her. He knew it would be good experience—one that would help her later.

As for Jonathan, he planned to abandon North Carolina for Colorado during the month of May. Then he would return to Duke for a summer of research and writing. Under normal circumstances, he would have looked forward to a month home with little to do but head off into the mountains every other day or so. But this year was different. His primary function was to check on his parents to see how they were coping with Ben's death. In his phone conversations with them since he had returned from the funeral, he sensed they were doing about as well as could be expected. But he wanted to see that firsthand. Once he was satisfied that they were okay, he would head for the mountains.

Jonathan and Sarah decided to spend their last night in Durham at dinner together before taking off on their respective journeys. Independently of each other, they both thought La Chandelle the perfect place to end spring semester. It had served a very useful purpose almost two months earlier, but they wanted to experience the restaurant in a somewhat different light. Not that their first dinner there had not been special. Indeed, they had come to realize that evening that the bond between them was extraordinary. It just seemed fitting now that they would close this particular chapter in their relationship by returning to the spot that had forever changed their lives.

La Chandelle once again lived up to its expectations. All the right emotions surfaced that evening. Jonathan and Sarah talked at length about how their lives were so different from the way they had been the previous September when the school year began. He recalled three major changes in his life. The most important one, and the most traumatic, was the death of his brother. Although he was dealing with his loss as well as could be expected, it took a long time before thinking about his childhood days with Ben brought a smile to his face rather than a tear to his eye.

A second change was more subtle. He had now settled comfortably into the role of professor at a leading research university. His colleagues respected him both for his teaching and his research. His student ratings were now the highest in the department, and scholars around the country had already begun to cite one of his published articles. His reputation as a researcher would go a long way toward helping him achieve tenure in a few years. Letters of evaluation from external scholars were important components of Duke's evaluation process. He had also grown to love the campus and the people who worked and studied there. It stimulated him to perform at his best. And beautiful North Carolina made it even more perfect.

Sarah really knew nothing about the politics of being a professor, so his story of faculty life at a major university fascinated her. Most students did not understand the role of research as the lifeblood of an institution of higher learning. Nor did they see the connection between a scholar's search for truth in the laboratory, library, or field and good teaching in the classroom.

Students' lack of awareness about the importance of the research-teaching nexus was not surprising, since most parents who footed the huge tuition bills and most legislators who voted the requisite funds for public institutions of higher learning did not understand this relationship either. Many believed time spent on research was time taken away from student contact hours in and out of the classroom and thus hurt the educational process. As a consequence, universities had a constant public relations job on their hands to address this misperception.

Even many young professors underestimated the predominance of research in their professional lives when they began their careers. Those who could not make the research grade or who did not like it soon left, of their own choosing or by their colleagues' decision. Jonathan had no fears, though, about not succeeding at Duke. His job security level had risen dramatically during this, his second year.

But if he was honest with himself, the principal reason for his good feeling about Duke rested with the third change that academic year. Sarah. His friendship with her was the highlight of the year. Tops without a doubt. She had provided him with the most fulfilling and rewarding experience of that or any other year. Jonathan reflected on their evolving relationship. He was forced—no, he was eager—to admit that no friend, male or female, had ever quite touched his soul like Sarah had. He felt at ease conveying these thoughts to her as they made their way through their last dinner together that academic year. "It certainly has been a year like no other," he said.

Sarah also projected a sense of comfort as she talked about how the year had affected her. She told of arriving the previous September as a junior, pleased that Duke had been good to her the first two years and even a little confident it would continue to be so for her remaining time on campus. "But I was not prepared for what happened between us," she related to Jonathan. "Had someone told me last summer that I would be best friends with the new, young political science professor— or any professor for that matter—I might not have returned to campus, so scared would I have been. But here I am, acting as if we have known each other for years. It is simply unbelievable."

Jonathan laughed at her admission. He suggested he had the same feeling about what had happened.

"It's been a great year for other reasons as well," Sarah related. "My semester working on the project for Senator Erwin went really well. It convinced me that I want a career in some kind of government work. I'm hoping to spend my last semester at Duke next year in the university's Washington program in public policy."

"That's a great idea, Sarah," Jonathan said. He knew how seductive the nation's capital could be. He was convinced Sarah would some day find a life there. The thought of her far away in Washington saddened him a little as he suddenly remembered she was not a permanent fixture at Duke. At some point in the future—it would be sooner rather than later—she would say good-bye to Duke and probably to him as well. Once again, he tried to put such melancholy thoughts out of his mind. He would be happy for his best friend but full of self-pity.

A warm glow came over him as he digested their last campus conversation before going their separate ways for the summer. He returned home to his condo that evening with feelings unparalleled to any he had felt in his entire life. Oh, how good it was to have a special, special friend!

~ 12 ~

First Time Really Apart

Jonathan's trip back home to Colorado the next day was uneventful. As he made his way across the country, he thought back to the last time he had taken the journey not quite three months earlier. That flight had been the saddest of his life. This time it was different as the plane passed over the familiar flat farmland of the Midwest. Although the trip had a serious purpose as well, time had begun to dull the hurt in his heart that felt so new and so overwhelming just a short time before. But it would never leave, and, quite frankly, he didn't want it to. It would always be a reminder of his loss.

Ben was more than a brother. He and Jonathan were close friends, although not in the way that non-relatives befriend one another. Separated in age by three years, they nonetheless had grown up to be close to each other. While Ben admired and looked up to his brother, he didn't always try to emulate him. He was very much his own person. But the differences between them complemented each other rather than drove a wedge between them. They formed quite a pair, and adults rarely saw one Hawthorne boy outside of school without the other. Their bond wasn't just a case of Ben tagging along after his older brother. Jonathan liked including his younger sibling in his life as much as possible. As Ben entered his late teens, Jonathan became more willing and even eager to seek his perspective on things, while the younger of the Hawthorne boys grew to accept advice more easily from his elder sibling.

Their different career paths within the same substantive area, world affairs, also served to heighten their desire to spend time together. Those moments allowed each of them to unwind a little—Jonathan from the often-found intellectual snobbery of the university and Ben from the sometimes mindless rigidity of the military. Their laughter rang out late into the night as each told one story after another about life back at school or work, their attitudes fortified by the consumption of Colorado's favorite beer, Coors. Both always returned to their positions reenergized and with a better sense of balance about conditions in their own particular worlds.

While the trip home brought back memories of Ben, his heart had made room for other feelings as well. The flight across America's heartland proved to be a time of reflection and assessment for Jonathan. Life was, after all, good to him. He understood personal tragedy was part of life. And he accepted it, although he didn't have to like it. But he had to look at the total picture. His health was good, although he made a promise to himself to be much more vigilant about working out. Second semester had not found him in the gym often, but there was good reason for this. He just didn't want his lack of regular exercise to continue.

His career was going smoothly, which brought him special satisfaction. He had no doubt he would spend the rest of his life on a university campus instructing young people about the joys of international politics. His camaraderie with Sarah had brought him much fulfillment as well. Add to that friendship the sexual infatuation for her that burned inside of him, and he had a complete set of emotions wrapped up in that one person. Life was, indeed, good.

Another thought occurred to him, one that had not entered his mind for the entire year. It was one, he knew, his parents, especially his mother, would raise during the course of his stay at home. He had not had one date the entire academic year, if one didn't count his time with Sarah as dates—and he did not. He may have been kidding himself on this last point, but that was how he saw it.

Not one single date! No women had invited him anywhere, even as part of a larger group. Nor had he asked anyone out—to a ball game, to dinner, to a movie, to a concert, to anywhere. It suddenly struck him he had been celibate the entire year. He laughed as he pondered why Sarah's presence always so excited him sexually. He had not slept with a woman in more than a year. In fact, it had been almost two years, since graduate school at Penn State. His last sexual encounter was but a distant memory. He jokingly wondered whether he had forgotten how "to do it." Remembering the analogy of riding a bicycle, he came to the quick conclusion that you never forget certain skills.

The incredible part of his subconscious celibacy, he realized, was that he had not missed sex nearly as much as he would have had Sarah not been the center of his attention the past year. In fact, it now seemed strange to think about being with another woman in any setting, romantic or otherwise. He pondered its implication as the Rockies came into focus out of the left window of the plane.

His parents greeted him at the airport. He was pleased to see them and hoped their presence there meant they were getting out and about town. He didn't want them to stay cooped up in the house too much. He knew older people often stopped living life as they had known it after the death of a loved one, and he didn't want that to happen to his parents.

"Hi, Jonathan," His mom said. She was the first to greet him.

"Welcome home, son. It's good to see you," his dad chipped in.

Jonathan couldn't be certain, but he thought his father had emphasized the word "son." "It's good to be home. How are you both doing?" he asked.

"Fine," was the collective response. Jonathan hoped it was true. It was almost noon, Colorado time, so his parents suggested lunch at the Broadmoor. Jonathan was not ready for such opulence, but he didn't want to offend them, so he agreed. Off they drove to one of the country's most famous resorts, nestled at the foot of Cheyenne Mountain. Lunch went as expected. The conversation centered at first on what each of them had been doing the past couple of months. The key phrase was "keeping busy." All three had been doing just that. Left unsaid was that keeping busy was the way each dealt with the family's huge loss.

But talk finally got around to Ben just as their entrées were served. For about fifteen minutes, each told revealing stories about him and experiences that had some particular impact on each of them. They each tried to find humorous anecdotes about Ben, as if somehow laughter would ease the pain, now greater as a consequence of the three of them being together again.

His mother recalled Ben's sheer mortification when his female teacher caught him zipping up his fly as he came running out of the lavatory in second grade. As she was in the midst of sternly correcting him, he caught the zipper—not on his pants, unfortunately, but on the exposed flesh. The school nurse, also a female, had to use a Band-Aid to stop the bleeding. Ben never told his parents about the incident. He went to his grave not realizing that it had been topic number one at the next teacher-parent conference. He would have been mortified, had he known—even as an adult—about his teacher's revelation to his parents.

His dad then recounted the time his younger son, the ink on his new driver's license not yet dry, took some girl by the name of Kim up the winding dirt road to the old mining town of Cripple Creek just as dusk approached. His intentions were obviously typical of those of any sixteen-year-old boy who had been given the old family convertible for the first time. He was searching for a secluded spot on the way back to Colorado Springs after darkness fell.

He had figured it all out from some old 1940s movie. Step number one: find a quiet place on a clear, full moonlit night high on a mountain with a spectacular portrait of the city below. Inch the car—top down, of course—slowly toward the edge of the cliff to maximize the view of the scene below.

The front range of the Rockies was perfect for such an occasion. It was high above the city, was deserted after dark, and harbored plenty of secluded turnoff points that were not visible from the road. Ben found such a site without any problem and undertook step two of the two dozen steps every teenaged boy with raging hormones thinks about but never masters.

He was well on his way through step five—unfasten the second button from the top of Kim's blouse so his hand could reach inside more comfortably—when he forgot to read that step's fine print. "Be careful not to disengage the car's emergency brake as you reposition your hand and body." Too late. As Ben maneuvered himself to maximize his hand's groping range, his knee clipped the brake, dislodging it immediately. Before he could recover, the convertible lurched forward, just enough so that the front wheels moved over the edge. Momentum, which Ben had figured was on his side only a moment earlier, was now with the car. Ten seconds later and twenty feet lower, the 1963 Ford Falcon came to rest 1,400 feet short of the bottom. Thick brush had slowed its speed, so the only damage Ben suffered was to his pride.

Kim escaped injury too, but her blouse was in shreds, ripped in several places after Ben's hand got caught inside it during the descent. The shirt had kept him from being thrown from the car. Never had a blouse given up its life for so noble a cause!

The car was almost in the same shape as Ben was, with only a few dents here and there. It had lodged between a couple of trees—not mature ones, but mere youngsters with highly underdeveloped trunks. That was both good news and bad news. As long as Ben and Kim didn't move, they would probably drop no further. That was the good news. As long as they remained immobile, they would be there until morning at the earliest. That was the bad news. The road was sparsely traveled at night, and only the mountain creatures of the dark would hear their shouts. The nearest house was more than five miles away.

Needless to say, Ben's and Kim's parents had a most eventful night, without any success whatsoever in finding the two teenagers. None of their kids' friends knew of their plans. A passing motorist finally heard their screams around noon the next day. Two hours later, a tow truck with a long chain successfully rescued the Ford Falcon and its two occupants from pending disaster. Ben never lived that episode down.

Jonathan smiled as his parents related the two incidents. They both took comfort in remembering such stories. It helped slow down the fading memories of their younger son. When they had finished, he chipped in with two tales of his own, neither of which his parents knew. They listened intently, eager to learn new things about Ben. It helped fuel the illusion that he was still alive and his adventures had occurred only a short time earlier.

After a while, the conversation took a more serious turn. One after another grieved out loud for the loss. It proved to be cathartic. Within twenty minutes, they were able to move on to other subjects.

Jonathan's mother was, of course, most interested in his personal life. It occurred to him that the loss of Ben had probably placed an urgency on her desire to have grandchildren and to carry on the family line.

He was now her only hope. "Are you seeing anyone?" came the first question.

As Jonathan answered it, he wondered whether or not he ought to tell his parents about Sarah. The desire or need to tell anyone about her had not yet confronted him. In fact, he rather enjoyed that their relationship was their little secret. Perhaps that gave a mysterious quality to it or allowed for a greater degree of fantasizing. He wasn't certain. But he had felt no need to tell the world, or simply even one other person, about this wonderful intrusion into his life. While some of his colleagues had seen the two of them together around campus from time to time, their discretion had resulted in no raised eyebrows.

Sarah had confided to him that none of her friends or her parents knew anything about the depth of their friendship either, although several were aware they talked from time to time and even got together on occasion. Her roommate had initially probed but now did not raise the subject—only her eyebrows—whenever Sarah told her she was meeting "her professor friend."

Her parents simply knew, based on her letters and a couple of phone conversations, that Sarah had been in Jonathan's class and thought him terrific, and had also visited his office from time to time since then. She gave them no other details. She had barely singled out Jonathan among her list of professors, other than to mention his brother's death in Vietnam and her "small" role in helping him cope with the tragedy. Sarah left the details somewhat sketchy. Her father, with the ears of a protective lioness guarding her young, suspected that Sarah hadn't told the whole story about Jonathan, but he didn't press the issue.

"Actually, Mom, I'm not dating anyone," Jonathan said. "I haven't come across any woman at Duke yet who interests me, not even a little bit. But I'm still looking."

His dad coughed at his answer—it was a deliberate and animated cough—but his mother only furrowed her brow. Jonathan tried to make light of the situation by describing the kinds of women found at Duke and in the surrounding community.

"Mom, you've got to realize that there aren't many female faculty members at Duke. And most of them are already married or have made it clear to everyone within earshot they have no interest in tying the knot. That leaves basically only secretaries and librarians, and all the secretaries in my department are also married. And I really don't interact with any women in other departments. I obviously visit the library, but my eye hasn't yet caught anyone working there who looks interesting. And the bottom line is that my hectic schedule just won't allow me to spend time looking for a mate let alone have a casual date, although I must admit, Mom, that I haven't taken any initiative."

For the first time, the desire to confide in someone about Sarah crossed his mind, but he chose to ignore it, at least for awhile. He was not ready to do so. But he decided to have some fun, particularly with his mother.

"But you should see the Duke female students, Mom. Most of them are, quite simply, stunning. I don't think I've seen a homely one yet."

"Oh, Jonathan," his mother uttered. "You shouldn't think thoughts like that. You could get into trouble."

But his father simply laughed and said, "Really, Kathleen. Jonathan's only kidding. You are, aren't you, son?"

"I don't know about that, Dad," Jonathan said. "You can't stroll across the quad at any given moment without observing at least twenty or thirty coeds who are simply knockouts." He continued the humorous theme at his mother's expense. "When I walk into class to lecture, Mom, I have to be really careful. The beautiful ones are everywhere, but mostly they sit up front. It's hard to concentrate on what I want to say with some beauty sitting provocatively right in front of me. What's a poor fellow to do?"

"Stop it, Jonathan. That's awful," his mom said. "What if those poor girls knew you were thinking about them like that?"

"I'm sure they do," Jonathan teased her. "Remember, it's hard to get into Duke. Only the brightest ones are admitted, and then only if they have something else going for them. Coeds must realize that the young, virile professor in front of them notices how seductive they can look."

Jonathan was satisfied with his answer, but his mother was rather annoyed. "Oh hush. I don't want to hear it," she said.

"But, Mom, I'm only twenty-seven years old. What if one of them caught my eye? What's wrong with my asking her out after she graduates?" Jonathan asked her. He posed the question somewhat playfully. It wasn't entirely rhetorical, but his parents had no clue of that.

"Well, I guess there's nothing wrong with that. But how would your colleagues take it if they knew you were dating someone who had just graduated? Would they be upset?" she asked. His mother was not going to let go of the conversation just yet.

"Heck, they probably wouldn't care if I dated someone while she was a student as long as I was discrete about it and she wasn't in my class," Jonathan answered. "I probably wouldn't take an undergraduate to the big faculty party at the end of the year. Actually, there isn't any big faculty party, at the end of the year or at any other time for that matter. We don't socialize that much with one another. I really haven't had much time to think about dating."

Jonathan knew it was a little white lie, but he just wasn't quite ready to confide in them yet. He suddenly put on a more serious face. "Under normal circumstances the first few years of a professor's life are really tough," he continued. "I've had to develop new courses to teach. I've also had to make certain I have a solid research agenda underway, with some products already emerging. I've been successful on both counts, but it has come at a huge price to my personal life. And remember, this has been an extraordinary year because of what happened to Ben. It's probably a good thing a woman wasn't in the picture. She would have been lost in the shuffle."

"You're right about that, son," his dad interjected. "Best you haven't had a girlfriend this past year. Too complicated."

"Okay. I hear what you're saying," his mother said. "But you mustn't wait too long, Jonathan. You aren't getting any younger."

"I know, Mom," Jonathan replied. "But times are different now. People don't get married as young as they did in your generation. So I'm not worried. It'll come in due course."

The check for lunch arrived, so they paid and made their way to the exit. Soon they were comfortably situated in his parents' home. It was a welcome sight.

Jonathan had planned to do nothing for the first few days and he overachieved. He read a little, worked out a lot, and slept even more. He wanted to return to Duke physically and mentally rested. His initial schedule ensured that would be the case. He knew that in a few days' time he would get restless and turn west toward the mountains.

He also thought about Sarah. Actually, he indulged himself in romantic images of her. It was as if being away from her heightened his desire for her. He knew it was unrealistic to think of them as lovers, at least any time soon, no matter what he had told his parents at the Broadmoor lunch. But he would take Sarah under any circumstances. And right now, friendship was what they had. So that's what it would be. Dream he would of a romantic liaison with her, but friendship was a reality that he enthusiastically embraced.

And what about Sarah? She had told Jonathan she would travel home to drop off her clothes and other belongings, and then head to Indiana the same day. She promised she would contact him as soon as she was settled. Her call came the evening of Jonathan's second day home. General Hawthorne took the call and, with a somewhat wicked look on his face, gave Jonathan the receiver. Sarah's voice was a welcome sound.

"Hi, Jonathan. How are things at home?" she asked.

It is just like Sarah, he thought. Here she was in the midst of what was probably an exciting adventure, and she asked about him first.

"Fine," he said. "My parents are doing okay, it appears. I have just been hanging around the house since I arrived, but I'm getting antsy for the mountains. What's happening with you? How's it going?"

"Just great!" Sarah exclaimed. "I arrived late yesterday. A rather exhausting day, I'll tell you. We started early this morning with a briefing, then went out into the field, as they say. I'm in charge of an information booth outside, of all places, the political science building, Woodburn Hall. My job is to provide information about how students can register to vote or to give them absentee ballots if they are registered back home. Assuming they're from Indiana, of course. It sounds dull, but it's really exciting.

"And do you know what? Bobby Kennedy will be on campus next week. He's going to speak in the auditorium on Wednesday afternoon. Isn't that great? All the workers will have a private session with him for a short time. Private if you count a hundred people as an intimate gathering. I want to see how he looks compared to his brother. You remember I saw JFK during the 1960 campaign."

Sarah was staying at the Poplars, a privately owned hotel that had served ever so briefly as a private dorm for students. It was now being transformed into a conference center, but rooms were available for the Kennedy volunteers.

Jonathan was delighted to hear her voice again. Sarah seemed to be doing well. He wished he was there working side by side with her. Although he was a university professor, he was not beyond campaigning for a political candidate in whom he believed. They talked for about an hour before she had to go. It felt good to hear her voice, even though they had seen each other only a few days earlier. They agreed to talk after he got back from the mountains in about a week. He told her to call person-to-person collect then so she would not have to pay. Secretly he hoped it would encourage her to phone more often.

When Jonathan was finished, the look on his face told the whole story. But his parents never saw it, as they had retired to the other room when he took the call. When they returned, he answered their obvious query by saying it was a friend who was working for Bobby Kennedy in the Indiana primary. They didn't probe further, so he offered no additional details.

A few days later, Jonathan was ready for the mountains, so off he went. One could still ski in the highest elevations, so he enjoyed one of his favorite sports. Spring break had found him remaining on campus, so the sojourn into the mountains represented his first real getaway since last summer—if one didn't count the day trip to the Aspen area over Thanksgiving. He was gone for five days, camping out in an isolated area of cabins owned by a friend of his dad's.

Jonathan and Sarah talked right after he returned to his parents' home. Her excitement when he picked up the receiver told him everything. All was going well. Senator Kennedy had been to campus that day. Different from his brother, the former president, he was nonetheless equally impressive. The Senator spent about thirty minutes with the volunteers. She was even able to shake his hand.

"I'll never wash my hand again," she laughingly related. More importantly, she told of his inspiring speech to the volunteers. The Senator had talked of a new day, one that would put the country back on the path that his brother had originally carved out a few short years earlier. Sarah had been thinking of what Bobby Kennedy had to say continuously since he had finished speaking. She was convinced it was very important that he be the next president, and she was going to do what she could to help him—even if that meant taking a semester off from school if he won the Democratic Party's nomination. But first things first. He had to win the Indiana and California primaries, then go on to the Chicago convention and derail the party machine's first choice for the nomination, Hubert Humphrey.

"I can't tell you how exciting today was," she continued. "It convinced me that politics and government are in my veins. I can't wait until I can go at it full-time. And there's something else. I found the perfect bar. It's called Nick's. It has the best stromboli sandwiches and an ancient, simply ancient, barmaid by the name of Ruth. I have been there the last four nights, and she has yet to crack a smile. But she is an institution. I'll bet we can come back in twenty years and she'll still be there."

Jonathan and Sarah talked for about an hour and a half. It was the start of a daily routine until after the primary. He was excited that she wanted to share her experience with him.

Sarah waited with anticipation for primary day. She was so happy when the final results declared Senator Kennedy the winner. The volunteers celebrated long into the night with visions of a successful march through Chicago running through their minds. She interrupted her celebration to call him.

"Oh, Jonathan, we did it! We did it!" she shouted. "I can't believe it. Nobody thought we had a chance, but we fooled them, just like in 1960. California is next." Some volunteers had decided to go on to California, but Sarah opted for home. She was tired, she said, and needed some rest before she jumped into her summer schedule.

Again they talked for more than an hour. Jonathan told her he would be in Colorado for another three weeks, so she could reach him at his parents' home. Sarah would remain in Pennsylvania for just about as long. Both were scheduled to return to Duke at about the same time, so they arranged to get together the first of June. He was eager to hear her stories in person.

Jonathan's remaining time in Colorado passed quickly. How he enjoyed the mountains as, indeed, he relished the beach. The ocean would come later that summer. For now, he was content to roam the Rockies as the spring thaw kicked into high gear. As he hiked among the most beautiful vistas in the world, thoughts of Sarah never strayed far from his mind. As much as he fancied his outdoor adventures in the Rockies, he was anxious to get back to Durham.

Sarah was also in a hurry to return to campus.

. . . Jonathan, you remember when I went out to Indiana University to work in the Bobby Kennedy campaign. It was one of the highlights of my life up till then. We were so excited when he won. We were certain he would go all the way to the White House, just like his brother had.

But I must confess that I missed you when I was in Indiana. We had spent so much time together as the semester wound down that I had gotten used to you. So, even though I was really busy at IU, thoughts of you, Jonathan Hawthorne, were always with me.

You can imagine how it was when I returned to the relative quiet of Lancaster. I tried to keep busy, but in reality, I wanted to just sit back and relax. So that's what I did. The problem is that it left too much time on my hands. So I thought about you even more then. I couldn't wait until the end of May when I would return to campus. It couldn't come soon enough. . . .

~ 13 ~

Sarah's Taste of Tragedy

The first of June could not come fast enough for Jonathan either. He and Sarah celebrated their return to campus with dinner at a new place in Raleigh called George's. It provided the same kind of intimacy and privacy found at La Chandelle, although the ambiance was not quite as good. No matter. They both fell into their old patterns immediately, almost as if they had not been apart for more than a month. Their ability to pick up where they had left off at their most recent rendezvous would become a defining characteristic of their relationship, no matter how long it had been between visits or what was happening in their lives.

It was good to see Sarah again, and Jonathan had the courage to tell her so. He instantly realized how much he had missed her. Dinner stretched over several hours, as they had so much catching up to do. She regaled him with tale after tale of Indiana, especially the university. Its beauty matched that of Duke's, although the campus was much larger. Its student union reminded her of several old English inns attached to one another. Greek row on Third Street was like no other she had ever seen, particularly the Alpha Phi sorority house. She told Jonathan that, had she gone to IU, she would have tried to pledge Alpha Phi. She even befriended a fellow campaign worker, herself a member of Alpha Phi, who later made it big in the Washington world of politics as both an astute commentator of the global political scene and as a political novelist. Still later, this IU Alpha Phi sister would represent Ohio in the

U.S. House of Representatives before becoming the first woman Senator from the Buckeye State.

Unlike at Duke, immediately adjacent to the main entrance to the campus was a street lined with store after store that catered to college students. Kirkwood was always crowded, as both students and parents gravitated to it. Nick's sat in a prime location on the north side of the street just a short distance from campus. IU seemed neat.

The next morning, both were busy preparing for the start of summer school—still almost a week away. But not far from their minds, especially Sarah's, was the California presidential primary, then only a few days away. She watched the news religiously to see how Senator Kennedy was faring. The polls showed Kennedy in the lead, so she was in fine spirits.

They agreed to catch the voting returns in the student union. East Coast viewers would not know the winner until late into the night because of the time difference with California. They watched with anticipation as the first results were posted. It looked good for Bobby Kennedy, but both knew there was a long way to go before anyone could be declared the winner. Predicting election winners in 1968 was not the science it would become later, particularly the polling of voters as they were leaving the voting precinct. Exit polling would someday allow the news media to predict a winner almost immediately after the polls closed. But at last the final ballot was counted. Senator Kennedy had won. Sarah was so excited, and Jonathan shared her elation as if he, too, had been in Indiana.

"Now it's on to Chicago!" she shouted. Her joy appeared boundless.

It is going to be one exhilarating summer, Jonathan thought.

They soon left the student union in order to celebrate with something stronger than Coke. Sarah had turned twenty-one while she was home in Lancaster—not that her lack of official drinking-age status had stopped her from imbibing earlier. They parked at the entrance to the golf course and walked to the back of the first hole, giggling the entire route. Behind the green was a slight mound, which served as a grassy pedestal on which to toast the victory. Out came the chardonnay and two wine glasses—Jonathan had placed them in the car earlier without telling her in anticipation of the night's celebration.

As they slowly sipped the wine, Sarah commented on their circumstances. "I can just see the headlines now. 'Professor and student caught on the first green drinking alcohol. Thought to be drunk since both appeared to be having so much fun.' What would your colleagues and my friends think of that, Dr. Jonathan B. Hawthorne?"

"They would be extremely jealous, Sarah Joan Matthews," Jonathan responded in his best formal voice. "Of course, they would hide their envy well and instead feign righteous indignation at our behavior. And I would be summarily fired."

"Really?" Sarah asked.

"Really. Well, maybe not, but I would have to do some high-powered groveling to the right people. But don't worry about it. Nothing's going to happen. I've been here lots of times with women at night. No one ever bothers you."

"What? You've been here with lots of women?" Sarah looked shocked.

"No, no, no. Just kidding," Jonathan said. "I've never brought a woman here before, day or night. But I know the golf course well. My errant shots have taken me all over this place. If we have to, we can keep going further into the far corners of the course until we lose those who might come after us. Okay?"

Sarah laughed at his strategy, but nobody bothered them as they finished the bottle of wine. Feeling good as well as tired, the two of them headed back to the car, singing the Sonny and Cher hit "I've Got You, Babe" verse after verse as they strolled beneath the Carolina pines lining the first fairway. It had been a perfect evening, Jonathan thought, as they slid into the car. Their candidate had won, and he had celebrated with the woman he loved. He dropped Sarah off at her dorm, hesitating for a moment before deciding against a kiss, then headed home. He was tired and needed a good night's sleep.

But it never happened. As he lay asleep for about an hour at most, a loud series of knocks on the door awakened him. Jonathan jumped from his bed, wondering who could be disturbing him at that late hour. Opening the door, he found Sarah in a rather disheveled state. Her presence caught him off guard. She had never been to his condo before. It was one of the unspoken parameters she had not yet crossed. Jonathan immediately sensed something was wrong. Terribly wrong. What else would bring her to his door at that time of night? Her eyes caught his attention first. She had been crying heavily, he quickly surmised. And she was currently sobbing almost out of control.

"Sarah, what happened? What's wrong?" he asked.

"It's Bobby Kennedy. He's been shot. Oh, what's wrong with this country?"

Sarah's remarks hit Jonathan right between the eyes. "How is he? Where was he hit? Is he badly hurt? Is he alive?" Jonathan asked question after question in rapid-fire fashion.

"I think so, but I don't know how bad it is," Sarah replied.

"Come on in. Let's turn on the television. It must be all over the news," Jonathan said. He was right. Every station was covering the breaking story. Information about the Senator's condition was sketchy, but what little they did hear did not sound good. An assailant had shot him in the head soon after he delivered a short victory speech. *How ironic,* Jonathan thought. Bobby Kennedy was celebrating his finest moment since his brother's election to the presidency, and he was gunned down. Few details were known or had been made public about the shooting. The attacker was apparently of Middle Eastern descent, although nothing else was known about him at that time. Roosevelt Grier, the former professional football star, was at the Senator's side when it happened and helped disarm the assailant.

The assassination attempt was already beginning to affect Sarah and Jonathan greatly—particularly Sarah—even more so than the King murder had. She had worked for Kennedy's election, had just seen him and shaken his hand, and had just been mesmerized by his eloquence. Now her dreams had been dashed, just as they had been five years earlier on a sunny November Friday afternoon in Dallas. As much as President Kennedy's death hurt, however, she felt this senseless act more deeply. Sarah was older and thus better able to understand the far-reaching consequences for the country. She was also at an age where she was ready to let a political leader who promised a new world and had a plan to deliver it—one who spoke out against injustice at home and abroad and whose charisma knew no bounds—sweep her away.

Sarah had cried periodically since she first heard the news, but now the reality of the event unfolding in front of her proved too much. She broke down completely, unable to gain control of her emotions. Jonathan sat beside her and held her for what seemed like an hour before she was able to acquire some measure of control. Exhausted, she simply fell asleep in his arms right there on the sofa.

Under different circumstances, Jonathan would have been delirious with joy. But not this time. Sarah had fallen into a deep slumber, and he was content to hold her for as long as she slept. It felt really good. He inhaled her perfumed aroma as she dozed, dreaming his usual fantasy, this time fortified by her intoxicating scent. But soon he gave in to his own body's plea for rest. His eyes slowly closed, and he, too, entered a sound sleep.

Five hours passed before either of them awoke. Neither one had stirred the entire time—not as surprising as one might expect, as their bodies paid the price of fatigue. As pending consciousness began to push away the effects of a deep sleep, Jonathan and Sarah slowly came to realize the compromising situation in which they found themselves. But neither made a move to retreat. It was as if each took great comfort from the touch of the other. Jonathan finally grew alert enough to remember why he was locked in an embrace with Sarah.

He jumped up quickly and turned on both the television and the radio. In the days before CNN, television was not as timely as radio was in its presentation of news. Unfortunately, details were slow in coming from either medium. Jonathan shouted at both to tell them something, anything, about the Senator's condition. Finally, the television commentator's message cut through both of them like a dagger deep in the heart. The assailant's shot had gravely wounded Bobby Kennedy, and he was near death. Cut down by Sirhan Sirhan, a Jerusalem-born Jordanian, who wanted to get even for what he believed to be Kennedy's pro-Israel stance. The bullet entered his head just behind the ear.

They both stared at the picture in front of them. Neither could say anything for a few minutes. Then Sarah began to slowly emit sounds of anguish. Reality was quickly sinking in. Jonathan reached for her and tried to console her, his heart also heavy with grief. She was his best friend, so her anguish had become his anguish.

They spent the rest of the day together trying to come to grips with what had happened in Los Angeles. They left campus and drove east toward the ocean. Jonathan had decided a walk on the sandy beaches of the Outer Banks would be the perfect antidote to the tragic news. The five-hour drive went by quickly as Sarah bared her feelings throughout the trip. *The grieving process will not be easy,* Jonathan thought.

Soon they were at Nags Head, a small Outer Banks town just across from the northwest entrance to the Banks. It was not far from Kill Devil Hills, the spot where the Wright brothers of Dayton, Ohio, took to the air for the first time. Early June was still too soon for the tourist season, so the long, sandy beach was virtually empty. Jonathan and Sarah ambled along the shoreline, his arm draped over her shoulders. It brought back memories of that long, nocturnal walk across the Duke golf course two months earlier after Michael had delivered his bad news to Sarah.

They were in no hurry to leave the comfort of the waves beating at their feet, though they always remained several paces back from where the surf pounded hard against the shore. They strolled aimlessly for a couple of hours, having no particular destination in mind. Once and a while they would stop to scan the view beyond the surf or pick up a wayward seashell that had made its way to shore.

"I seem to return to the ocean in difficult times for solace," Jonathan confided to Sarah. "This is certainly one of those moments. I always find the peaceful nature of this scene in front of us therapeutic. I don't know why, but I do."

"I get the same feeling, although I haven't been to the ocean nearly as much as you have," Sarah said. "And it's my first time to the Outer Banks. It's so beautiful. It's as if your troubles get washed out to sea, gone for good."

"That's a good way to put it," Jonathan observed.

"Jonathan, what's going to happen now?" Sarah asked. "I mean, Bobby Kennedy won primaries in Indiana, Nebraska, and California, and he picked up a lot of votes in other states as well."

"First of all," Jonathan said, "you probably already know this, but party leaders still handpick many if not most of the delegates to the convention. The popular or preference vote in a primary does not bind them to the winner. It would have been a problem even if this tragedy had not happened. Now the delegates are under no pressure or moral obligation to give their votes to Kennedy in the unlikely event he's still alive by convention time.

"But it does raise an interesting question. The McCarthy people could argue that since their candidate was closest in philosophy to Bobby Kennedy, they should get his delegates, not Humphrey. They might make quite a stink about this over the next several weeks before Chicago. It's no doubt too late, though, for any other candidate to come forward after an appropriate mourning period following the burial. I'm sure Bobby's brother, Ted, wouldn't have the stomach for a national political campaign so soon after his second brother's death. So it's probably going to be Humphrey and Nixon in November. I don't see any other scenario." Jonathan seemed resigned to the eventuality of both Kennedy's death and Humphrey's victory.

"That's so depressing," Sarah sighed.

She is now showing anger—a healthy sign, Jonathan thought. Anger moves one along on the path of recovery. He knew it well. It had helped him a few months earlier when he was faced with dealing with Ben's death. Anger hadn't been present immediately, however. It only emerged after he had pondered the senselessness of America's involvement in Vietnam. No matter whether its war aims were justified, Washington never took the necessary steps to achieve them, to "win," whatever that meant. The more he thought about this failure, the madder he became.

Jonathan had been a student of Carl von Clausewitz, the famous Prussian military analyst of the early nineteenth century. He knew his famous argument well—a nation must know what it's fighting for if it's considering going to war, and then it had better allocate sufficient resources to achieve its goals. It was also important to bring its own citizens on board in support of the war initiative. Finally, even under the best of circumstances, strategy and tactics never went as planned—what Clausewitz had called "the fog of war."

To Jonathan, it was unfortunate that the Johnson administration officials had never read Clausewitz. Pentagon advisors should have spent more time educating their civilian superiors about the Prussian's theories and less on trying to make a convincing case that America was actually winning the war. From the moment he was notified of Ben's death, he would look at U.S. national security decision-making with a jaundiced eye.

Their long stroll along the beautiful coastline of the Outer Banks finally produced a few twinges of hunger, despite their distraught conditions. Jonathan suggested they stop for food. "I'm starting to get hungry. Actually, I think I'm starved. What do you say we grab something to eat? That will give us just enough time to get back to campus around one or two in the morning. That's not too late, is it?"

"No. It's a great idea," Sarah said. "I have no dorm curfew, and I'm beginning to get hungry too. I assume you have a place all picked out. I'm right, aren't I? I'm beginning to know you so well, Jonathan Hawthorne."

For the first time since she appeared at his condo door early that morning, a sense of normalcy appeared. It was a welcome relief for both of them.

"As a matter of fact, I do," Jonathan confessed. "I guess I can't feign spontaneity here. It's my favorite on the Outer Banks. Owens. It's just south of here, about a ten-minute ride. Seafood is obviously the specialty. They really know how to cook it there. I guess I've eaten at Owens at least half a dozen times since I arrived at Duke. Nothing fancy, but great nonetheless. What do you say?"

"I say it sounds perfect. I'm with you," Sarah replied.

Owens did not disappoint. As it had for several decades, the restaurant satisfied its two customers that early June evening. They had not realized how hungry they both were until they sat down to eat. Dinner conversation focused on small talk, as the agonizing that had characterized their day drained each of them mentally and emotionally.

After dinner they headed back to Durham. Long stretches of silence filled the car ride as they made their way westward. But the return trip was also not without conversation.

"Jonathan." Sarah finally opened up after they had been on the road for about an hour. "Thanks for everything today. For being there for me. I know Bobby Kennedy's tragedy has affected you too. But because I feel I've had a personal stake in his election bid, I guess it has just hit me extra hard. You've been here, once again, for me. I am rapidly developing assurances that you will always be there for me when I need someone, no matter what. I really treasure our friendship. Thanks for coming into my life." Sarah's smile was like that of one resting comfortably on a dear friend's shoulder after having been rescued from the perils of the sea.

"It's been good for both of us," Jonathan said. "I've gained as much from our friendship as I've given. Maybe more, perhaps. And besides, wasn't it you not so long ago who remarked, 'Who's keeping score?'"

"I think we're both lucky you appeared in my class last autumn and we kept in contact with each other after the course. Maybe it was fate, but each of us has really needed someone these past several months. I shudder to think how lonely and difficult it would have been if you hadn't been there for me when Ben died. Do you understand what I'm saying?"

"I do. I feel the same way. But you have been really wonderful. I really believe our friendship will be part of our lives forever. At least, I hope so," Sarah said.

"Me too," Jonathan agreed.

As the drive back to campus continued, they both settled back into rather somber moods. The radio kept them up to date. Senator Kennedy was clinging to life, but the outlook was grim. His head injury was simply too serious. Sirhan had used a twenty-two caliber gun, which normally was hardly big enough to inflict the kind of harm it did on the Senator. But the trajectory of the wound allowed it to inflict the maximum damage. It was clear from the reports—many of them unsubstantiated, but devastating nonetheless—that the Senator would have major brain damage even in the unlikely event he survived.

But it was not to be. As Jonathan and Sarah pulled onto campus and neared Sarah's building, the news flash spread across the airwaves. Senator Kennedy had just died, at 1:44 A.M. Sobs emanated from both sides of the front seat. When they arrived at her dorm, Sarah hesitated before making a move to leave the car.

Finally, Jonathan, sensing her loneliness, spoke. "Do you want to stay at my place again tonight? I have a second bedroom. That way, if you want to talk anytime during the night or first thing in the morning, I'll be right there."

"Thanks. I'd like that. The dorm is virtually empty anyhow since summer school doesn't start for a few days yet. I'd rather not stay there," Sarah replied.

So Jonathan made a 180-degree turn and headed toward his condo. As they settled into his place, Jonathan opened a beer. He would have three more before he went to sleep.

"How about a stiff drink, Sarah?" he offered.

"Sounds great. Do you have any vodka? And kahlua? If so, add some milk. Make it a strong one. I want to sleep well tonight. That'll do the trick, for sure," she said.

Jonathan made her drink as she requested. He obliged with two huge shots of each, rather than the normal single one. Sarah was pleased with the finished product. They sat in the living room, he on the sofa and she on the chair, and allowed the alcohol to do its job. Sarah would have another as Jonathan moved on to his third and fourth beers. They had earned this indulgence. Sleep came easily for both of them that night.

Sarah recalled the moment years later.

. . . I remember how understanding you were when Bobby Kennedy was shot. That episode was so hard on me, driving me deep into the pits of depression. I needed you so much during that awful time. And you were wonderful, as always. Your conversations alternated between directly addressing my emotional needs and discussing the national political implications of the assassination.

I remember waking that second morning at your condo—the night I slept in a real bed instead of using you as my pillow—and thinking what an incredible guy you were. I thought for the first time what a great catch you would make for some lucky woman.

The thought did not quite enter my mind then that I wanted to be that woman. But it was close, and yet so far away. . . .

~ 14 ~

First Summer

The next week saw the final chapter in the life of Senator Robert Kennedy. His body was flown to New York where it lay in state, followed by a funeral at St. Patrick's Cathedral. Then he traveled on via train to Washington, where he was buried near his brother at Arlington National Cemetery.

Sarah and Jonathan watched the events at his condo. They had decided it would be better if they limited their time together to his office, condo, or some other place off campus. They didn't want people to read more into their relationship than what it was, at least the official version.

As Jonathan observed Sarah's reactions, he could tell she had had the political wind knocked out of her. He hoped she would regain it before it led to her changing career plans. He needn't have worried. She was back in the political swing of things before too long.

Summer officially began at Duke soon after Senator Kennedy's burial. Jonathan's only responsibility for the next three months was his research agenda. He planned to pursue it with every ounce of energy he could muster. He had lost too much time already that year, and he had some major catching up to do.

Sarah was enrolled in one summer course, a survey of English literature, that filled a general education requirement. She wanted to take a second class, but none counted toward graduation or fit her major program. She and Jonathan debated about her taking an independent study from him, primarily because of fears of impropriety if those in authority discovered their close friendship. After some hesitation, they decided to go ahead with it.

Sarah was going to investigate the recent history of political assassinations around the globe. It was a daunting task, but she argued she was up to it. Jonathan thought the topic would be a good way for her to deal with her grief over Bobby Kennedy's murder. Although it was not one of his areas of expertise, he could at least point her in the right direction for her research materials.

Jonathan also knew that as the presidential nominating conventions approached later that summer, memories of recent events would push to the forefront once again. It would not be easy. Unless Sarah was already working through her grief, she would end up back where she was on June 6, the day Bobby Kennedy died. He didn't want that to happen.

As for Jonathan, he was eager to get back to his research. His book, well underway, investigated how successful the United Nations had been over its first two decades in mediating conflict situations around the globe. He focused on sixty-eight cases for his study and was particularly interested in what conditions had led to successful U.N. intervention.

Jonathan's goal was to complete a few pieces of research that he'd had already underway for some time, then finish a rough draft of the entire manuscript on successful U.N. intervention by the end of the summer. Or at least when it was time to go on vacation. He knew he would have to spend a week in Colorado, which would cut short his time at the beach. But he was determined to once again spend two weeks at Avon on the Outer Banks, as he had done the previous summer.

Jonathan hoped the allure of the summer national political scene would not seduce him. He knew he had to discipline himself in order to avoid putting his research aside in favor of a choice seat in front of the television set. He did not yet realize, of course, how difficult it would be for a professor of political science to ignore the Democratic national convention in Chicago. It would go down in history as a classic confrontation between the establishment—city officials, local police, and old-time party "hacks"—and the younger generation of "rebels," who had gone to the Windy City to protest the war.

Summer began on a positive note. Jonathan jump-started his

research. By the second week, he was already in the computer lab running some analyses for his U.N. study. His research method was a combination of case studies about a handful of the sixty-eight conflicts under investigation and statistical analyses of large bodies of information relating to the entire group of cases. The first strategy represented the traditional way of doing research in international politics. The latter approach, however, was relatively new. Jonathan was one of a handful of scholars around the country, most of whom were young, who had mastered the statistical techniques necessary for such analyses. He hoped to make his mark in the profession by leading the way in a whole new approach to research. Until the advent of personal computers some two decades later, it meant long hours at the university's computer lab, usually late at night when it was least crowded.

He went to the library early in the morning to examine the few remaining cases to be completed. Lunch followed. Then it was back to the library once again. Late afternoon found him at the gym. Jonathan had returned to his exercise routine, which made him feel much better, both psychologically and physically. He vowed never again to be far-removed from the rigors of daily exercise. After dinner, it was off to the computer lab for another long evening.

Sarah was also doing fine. She was a little slow getting into her independent study but was on top of it by the third week. Her one regular course was not too difficult, so her study responsibilities placed few demands on her. She was going over to Raleigh once or twice a week to finish work left over from the internship the previous semester. She also had some individual projects she wanted to complete. The hectic events throughout spring semester had slowed her somewhat, and she didn't like to see work undone.

Sarah's strong work ethic was a trait Jonathan liked. It was important. He had always tried to follow one. It made him mad when fellow colleagues and students did not do likewise. But Sarah was different. He already knew that.

They both settled into what one might call normal routines. Spring semester had wreaked havoc on any semblance of normalcy they might have expected. Jonathan hoped summer would be different. He would not be disappointed, and for that he was thankful. It meant, though, that he probably would not see Sarah as much as he had in the spring. After all, the tragic events of that time thrust both of them into a need for each other. They had readily accepted this dual dependency, this bonding. It had helped them both through a most difficult period.

Jonathan was wrong in one sense, though. Sarah was taking an independent study from him. This meant they had to meet each week, one of the rules the university had for such courses. So, at the very least, there would be one contact per week. This formal meeting had been taking place in his office. Both he and Sarah were now experimenting with playing two different roles simultaneously. One moment, friend to friend. The next time, professor to student. This dual role was uncharted water for him, and he knew it was for Sarah as well. But the bond that had developed between them over the spring, he was convinced, would keep the periodic transition from one role to another smooth. The primary reason for the ability to switch roles was the comfort zone in which they now found themselves.

In some ways, their get-togethers so far that summer were even more wonderful than those of the spring. The latter ones were, of necessity, intense, growing out of a crisis mode that intruded virtually the entire semester. Their time together during the summer, however, was much more relaxed. Both of them, and particularly Sarah, were still working their way through the Bobby Kennedy assassination. The King murder seemed like ancient history, but of course it wasn't. And Jonathan was still coming to grips with Ben's death. But time was on their side, helping them move forward.

He had his good moments and his bad ones. From time to time, some innocent thought about his brother entered his mind and lingered there for a short while. A current incident usually triggered the memory. Once in a while, though, recollections of Ben took over his brain, pushing all other thoughts aside. He tried not to dwell on his brother's death though. After all, he still had a full life ahead of him—one in which, he hoped and assumed, would bring him love, marriage, children, and fulfillment. Ben had no future. He was gone, forever. All that remained were memories.

His parents would spend what time they had left on earth grieving for a lost son. There would be no beautiful tomorrows for them, only memories of better yesterdays and trepidations of sad todays. And nothing could change that. Not even the most wonderful of things that would befall him in the future would make a dent in the void his mom and dad constantly felt. Jonathan vowed never to forget what his parents were experiencing. He had to do what he could for as long as they lived to bring as much joy as possible from his life to theirs.

Fortunately, thoughts of Ben did not consume him. He meant no disrespect to his dead brother, but he had to go on living his own life. Sarah Matthews was part of that life, a huge part. Both of them fell into a regular routine as the summer progressed. They talked on the phone almost daily, usually late at night. Both described their days and shared thoughts about anything that interested them.

They did not meet on campus except for her independent study sessions, but did manage to get together for a movie once and a while. Dinner or a late night drink was also part of the routine. Twice a week seemed to be the norm. Jonathan was concerned, not about what his peers would think, but about suffocating Sarah with too much attention. Otherwise he would have tried to be with her every day.

He need not have worried.

. . . Summer 1968 was a wonderful relief, particularly after the awful spring we both had experienced. I returned to campus at that time determined to enjoy myself to the fullest. But then Bobby Kennedy was shot just as summer began. It seemed like tragedy was starting all over again. But we got through that terrible episode, and life began to return to normal.

It was then that I saw a different Jonathan beginning to emerge. Your work ethic caught my attention first. I really admired the contribution you were trying to make toward world peace in your own way. World leaders twice in this century had put their hopes for peace in a new arrangement, a global organization whose major role was helping nations either avoid war, or, should they be unsuccessful in that endeavor, find resolutions to end conflicts. Your research that summer examined how successful the U.N. was as a third-party intervener. I loved it when you took the time to share your research—its goals, its frustrations, its dreams, and its successes—with me. You were terribly patient in explaining just how you were going about investigating the problem you had chosen for yourself. It was so fascinating listening to accounts of your progress.

A different Jonathan also manifested itself during our social interactions. You were much more easygoing, as they say, in those circumstances than you had been during the spring. You were much more at ease, as well. And funny. I loved your sense of humor! I came to expect you would have a humorous remark for every situation in which we found ourselves. It felt good to laugh after so much heartache. It was wonderful just to act normal, with no surprises dumped into our laps.

In some ways, I was content not to have the national political conventions arrive. That meant some serious events were about to happen, so I would have to put on my solemn face again.

Part of acting normal for a soon-to-be senior in college was also running around with other students at Duke. Although it might have seemed our friendship occupied every waking moment of my time, that wasn't the case. Granted we saw each other often. But I also had a life away from you. Not nearly as exciting as our relationship, but a separate existence nonetheless. Summer school was a particularly good time to be involved with classmates. There were fewer students on campus, which led to closer involvement with those who were there. Moreover, the work pace was somewhat slower, and there were more activities to take advantage of, particularly off-campus.

As you know, there were two people with whom I spent a lot of time that summer—Laura Rutter from Delaware and Marie Hart from Indiana. When I wasn't with you, the three of us often hung out together. Movies were a big part of our time together. And we were then all old enough to drink, although those stupid North Carolina laws meant there were no bars like the ones we had back home.

So I had, in effect, two lives. My normal life as a student doing those things students do, and my friendship with you. Laura and Marie became increasingly curious about our relationship as summer moved forward. In fact, they continuously warned me about you. Said you were only interested in one thing—my body.

Years later I decided to have some fun with them for all the grief they caused me that first summer we were friends. I hinted to both of them during one of our periodic get-togethers that they had been partly right. I teased them, not really letting on whether I was being serious or just toying with them when I described the evolution of our relationship. I laughed this devilish chuckle as I suggested that you did, indeed, desire my body back then (and today), but you also wanted my heart and soul, all of me. I told them that you were then making me feel alive and wonderfully satisfied in so many ways I had never experienced before. And that you knew exactly how to make me feel like the most desirable woman in the universe. With a sly grin, I painted a revealing picture of just exactly what all that meant, particularly your desire for my body. I sighed as I revealed that no man had come close to satisfying me as you had. We laughed and laughed about it. They apologized, rather tongue-in-cheek I think, about imposing their concerns on me two decades ago. But they still weren't sure I was telling them the truth. And I never divulged the real story to them, at least in a way in which they could tell I was serious.

But back then they thought you were just a sleazy professor trying to take advantage of a poor, innocent student. They always asked right after we had been together whether you had made the "big move," but I would just smile and say no. There wasn't going to be any big move, I was certain. I tried to tell them then our friendship wasn't like that at all, although deep down I was beginning to contemplate alternatives. After awhile they finally began to believe me. Then I think they grew very jealous of the fact I was on such close terms with a professor. Neither of them had such a relationship.

But I can now tell you that it was just about that time I started to think of you in ways other than as a professor. Looking back at it now, it is increasingly clear that one of these ways was romantic. And I did begin to think about what an incredibly wonderful husband you would make for some woman, and, surprise of surprises, it started to make me a little jealous. Actually, a lot of jealous, if I was to tell the truth.

I said to myself, "Why couldn't I have a man just like Jonathan? They must be out there somewhere, but I haven't seen many, or quite frankly, even one such man yet." This really meant, of course, that I was starting to compare all the real men I knew with you. You became the standard, although I was not aware of that at first.

Of course, I wasn't seeing anyone during that summer, but there were plenty of old reminders I could use. Guys whom I had previously discarded or who had thrown me aside. And I did compare them against you. None of them quite measured up.

So you see, my dear, I had begun a long journey. The journey that would someday take me to a point for which our friendship, our beautiful, beautiful friendship, had not prepared me. I guess that is why summer 1968 holds such fond memories for me. I had begun a long journey, a very long journey . . .

Midway through the summer, it was time once again for politics. The first national political convention had arrived. Sarah and Jonathan geared up for them in their usual manner. They fed off each other's intellect as they watched events unfold.

Disbelief and anger dominated their reaction to the Democratic Party's convention in Chicago. Events both inside the convention center and outside in the city's parks and streets were making them lose faith in America's new penchant for guaranteeing political liberties to everyone. The convention leadership seemed more intent on stifling all dissent—whether it related to convention business or the Vietnam War—than on trying to rally Democrats around the country to the party's candidate, Hubert Humphrey. Convention guards roughed up members of the press for little or no apparent reason. It was during the Chicago convention that Dan Rather, then a young reporter for CBS, uttered his famous line about reporting from "somewhere in captivity" as the guards ushered him off the convention floor.

Even delegates were denied an opportunity to voice objections to anything taking place on the podium. It didn't matter if they were complaining about a campaign issue or a particular candidate. Demonstrators outside the convention center and throughout city streets and parks became targets for overeager cops who thought they were on a divine mission to save America from its wayward youth. Chicago's Mayor Richard Daley became the symbol for abuse of power.

Jonathan and Sarah watched the convention at his condo. It allowed them freedom to relax and also to work on other responsibilities when convention activities slowed. And it afforded them the opportunity to cook together. Nothing fancy, of course. Each night Sarah arrived close to dinner-making time with a bottle of wine tucked under her arm. It was Jonathan's responsibility to determine the menu, purchase the food, and do the cooking. Their respective assignments represented a real role reversal from the normal male-female pattern of preparing a meal, and they joked about it almost every evening.

One of Jonathan's favorites was a meal called "slop." The name usually turned people off, but when he could convince them to be a little adventurous and try it, they typically asked for seconds. It was a simple recipe, really—ground beef, beans, an onion, ketchup, and some seasoning, with cheese melted on top after the other ingredients had cooked for awhile. After the mix finished cooking, it was poured over Fritos corn chips on a huge plate. Beer completed the meal. Sarah, who loved it, nonetheless insisted that the bottle of wine she bought for the occasion replace the Budweiser.

Because they were in the privacy of Jonathan's condo, they could vent their feelings much more freely in reaction to what was happening on the television screen. And vent they did, with conviction and without restraint. It was not a good week for those who believed in individual rights and due process before the law.

The Democratic convention finally ended, and they returned to their pre-convention routines. The Republican convention, which did not hold as much interest for them anyway because Richard Nixon was already a lock for the nomination, took place later that summer. But by then, Jonathan and Sarah could have cared less. She was off to her home in Pennsylvania, and Jonathan had already traveled to Colorado.

It had been a good summer for both of them, and for their friendship. Under less stressful circumstances than what had confronted them during the first half of 1968, both their fondness and respect for each other flourished. Jonathan returned to his parents' home with a feeling of really being connected with Sarah. He believed, with substantial justification, their relationship had blossomed under clouds of tragedy. Now it was growing under rays of sunlight. He felt good. Really good.

His week in Colorado passed quickly. While he wanted to retreat to the mountains for the duration of the visit, Jonathan knew he had to spend most of the time with his parents. They made a point of eating all three meals together every day, either at home or out somewhere. He played golf with his father virtually every afternoon.

It was during the course of one of their rounds that General Hawthorne raised the question that had obviously been on his mind since Jonathan's last visit. "Who was the woman who kept calling the last time you were home? Are you dating her?"

The query caught him completely off guard. Neither of his parents had said anything at the time about Sarah's calls. Now his father was raising the issue. Jonathan wondered why.

"She's a good friend, a really good friend, Dad," he said. "Why do you ask?"

"Well, the woman called several times, and your conversations were, shall we say, long. More importantly, although I didn't hear a word you said, I could tell how you were saying it. Your voice was different, nothing like I had ever heard from you before. I can't describe it exactly, but I could tell she was really special. How I don't know."

"She is special, Dad. Very special," Jonathan said. No one yet knew about Sarah. He'd had no reason to share the most important relationship in his life with friends or his parents. Now, though, the time seemed right to tell his dad. "Her name is Sarah Matthews," Jonathan continued. "She's a student. Just finished her junior year at Duke. I met her last fall when she was enrolled in one of my classes."

For an hour Jonathan told his dad about Sarah. Everything. He left nothing out. Well, almost nothing. His discussion of salacious fantasies was not complete but he told his father enough to give him a solid picture of his feelings. He ended the story by saying she had really touched his soul. He couldn't explain it. All he knew was that she was the first one to have done so. Yet he was ambivalent about it and did not know how to proceed further because of their respective positions. "It's really difficult, Dad. I value her friendship so much that I don't want anything to happen to it. And I worry I might be taking advantage of her because of my position."

"It's a tough call, son," his dad replied. "I can't tell you what to do. But it seems to me that each of you has settled into a rather comfortable and fulfilling relationship. If it's meant to go further than that, it will. But give it time. You both have lots of time. Don't jeopardize what you have, because, as near as I can tell, you already have a very special relationship. Few can say that about another human being. And I will tell you this. It's obvious from your reaction that she has made her way deep into your heart."

"That she has, Dad," Jonathan agreed.

"Well, good luck with Sarah, son. May the relationship go wherever you both want it to. I hope you are lucky in love as I was with your mother," his dad said.

Jonathan felt good that he had shared the story. It pleased him that his dad had been so interested and so perceptive. They had not talked often enough over the years about such personal feelings. Perhaps now with Ben gone, his father had come to realize how important it was to open up to his son, and to invite him to do likewise. There was no telling when the opportunity might be lost forever. His father did not share Jonathan's story, though, with his mother. General Hawthorne told him that when he was ready, he should be the one to tell her.

The episode with his father made him yearn for Sarah. It had only been a few days, but he already missed her. As he looked toward the Rockies each day, he thought about all the wonderful things they could be doing up in the mountains. He would have the same thoughts about the beach the following week as he lay on the sands of Avon on Hatteras Island near the southern end of the Outer Banks.

Before he knew it, Jonathan was lying on the beach. It had only been twenty-four hours since he left Colorado, but the time seemed much longer. Avon could not be more different than the Rockies. The Outer Banks was a long, thin strip of land that jetted just off the coastline of North Carolina. If one loved sun and sand, no place in the United States could match the beauty of the Banks.

Jonathan had rented a house about fifty yards from the beach. As with most of the newer places on the Outer Banks, it was situated one story off the ground because of periodic flooding. And it had a deck on top. Here one could sit facing the usual ocean breeze and watch the waves hit the shore. The rhythm of the waves was seductive, and one could watch their dance for hours.

Jonathan alternated between observing this ancient ritual and reading. Novel in hand was his preferred way of relaxing while at the beach. His material tended to be fiction. Contemporary and World War II spy stories were his favorites. One book a day was his norm. That summer, unlike the past two, he had another diversion to occupy his mind. Thinking of the woman he loved also formed part of his daily routine.

How much better it would be if Sarah was there. Their days would be filled with many wonderful things to do. Playing in the surf was much more fun with a woman at your side. Reading the same novel and then comparing notes. Running along the beach. Soaking up the sun's rays. Relaxing, simply relaxing, during the day and long into the night. Sarah's presence would light up the Outer Banks. And it would warm his heart as well. But perhaps it was better that she was not with him. They had spent so much time together that he had begun to lapse into periods where he thought of her as his lover. Not that he acted on the thought. But it was a dangerous one, nonetheless.

Before he knew it, Jonathan was well into the second week of his time at Avon. It had been a good ten days. The weather was perfect, with a continuous ocean breeze that made the days temperate and the nights cool. The unwinding that had begun in midsummer and continued in Colorado once again delivered its therapeutic effect in Avon. Jonathan's mind cleared itself of burdens occupying it since his brother's death. The initial grieving process was long over, and he was moving forward. His brother's memory was still with him, but thinking about Ben was just as likely to evoke a smile now as it was a tear.

It was Wednesday afternoon, and Jonathan was doing what he had done every day since his arrival. His beach chair was situated so that the sun's rays hit his body with maximum impact. The ocean breeze kept him comfortable as it competed with the heat for his body's attention. The breeze was winning that day. He felt good. Life was good. His novel lay at his side. His eyes had tired of reading and were, instead, closed and directly facing the sun.

"Surprise! I hope this is okay. I hope I'm not intruding and you're not mad at me for doing this," he heard. Jonathan almost fell out of his chair. Turning quickly, he looked in the direction of the voice. He couldn't believe what he saw. There was Sarah, directly in front of him.

Her next words were lost on him as he surveyed the beautiful twenty-one-year-old form in front of him, her bathing suit accentuating every sensuous curve of her frame. This first vision of her body now exposed by a bathing suit that was probably designed to arouse deep passion in men remained imprinted on his brain for as long as he lived.

"I tired of Lancaster and decided to surprise you," Sarah explained. "But as I drove down Route 12 from Nags Head, I became increasingly scared. I didn't know if you would be alone, although you had told me earlier that you intended to be. I kept thinking perhaps you had found a gorgeous blonde in a skimpy bikini and were lost in her arms. So I looked for your car. It took a while, but I finally found it. I breathed a sigh of relief when it was the only one in the driveway. That was a good sign, I told myself. But I still wasn't sure you would be alone. So I sneaked onto the beach to see if I could find you. When I saw no one beside you, I decided not to turn around and make the long trip back home. So here I am. Surprise! You are alone, aren't you? There aren't any blondes hiding somewhere?" At that, a huge smile crossed her face.

"Guess what? No gorgeous blondes, or brunettes for that matter either," Jonathan responded, laughing all the while. "It's really good to see you. But you should have given me some warning. I just lost five years off my life being surprised like that. Have you come for awhile? Are you going to stay? Or is this just a quick pass through? I hope this was to be your final destination."

"Well, I didn't know when I drove up. But you could easily twist my arm. If it's okay, I'd like to stay for your last few days. But if you have anything planned, just say so. No problem," Sarah said.

"Okay? Of course, it's okay. It's more than okay. It's terrific," Jonathan said. His heart pounded excitedly. What a surprise! His mind raced with ideas. He hoped she would stay for the rest of his vacation. *It would be wonderful,* he thought.

And it was. Their three and a half days together were filled with much excitement and adventure as they took advantage of all the Outer Banks had to offer. The first day began with a climb of the giant dunes at Kill Devil Hills. A cruise on Pamlico Sound on a rented sailboat followed. There they relaxed with a picnic lunch, complete with bottle of wine. They consumed a second bottle as dusk fell on the sound. The evening outdoor drama, *The Lost Colony,* chronicling the story of the initial settlers in the region, concluded the day's activities.

They spent the next day just relaxing on the beach at Avon, soaking up the sun. The morning began with an early stroll along the edge of the water just after dawn. It was a time for contemplation and conversation, and think and talk they did. About most anything. Anything, that is, except what was foremost in Jonathan's heart once again. Still taboo was any talk about their relationship evolving into something other than what it had been.

A hearty breakfast followed the stroll on the beach. Then off they went, from their cottage across the high dunes protecting the village of Avon from the ravages of the sea to Jonathan's favorite spot on the beach. There they spread out their beach towels and other paraphernalia, including a couple of novels, and positioned their chairs to maximize the effect of the sun's rays on their bodies.

Before beginning to read, however, they carried out a beach ritual that brought such a sense of sexual excitement to Jonathan. The previous day in the sailboat they had performed the same rite at Sarah's request. Since then, he had looked forward to a repeat with the anticipation of a lion about to enter the arena against the Christians in early Rome. *Suntan lotion. Thank God for sun and suntan lotion,* Jonathan thought. He was taken aback the previous morning when Sarah turned to him and asked for help.

"Jonathan, would you please put some lotion on my back?" she had asked. "I don't want to get burned. And could you rub it in? If you miss a spot, I'll be sore tonight."

Jonathan overachieved. No inch on her back went untouched. And rub it in? He rubbed and rubbed until his movements took on the character of a massage rather than simply the application of lotion. Interestingly, Sarah did not once suggest it was enough. Instead, she appeared quite content to allow him to complete the task at his own pace.

As Jonathan moved his hands first vigorously and then slowly over the curvature of Sarah's back, his mind began to fantasize about the two of them locked in passionate embrace. Visions of their lying in bed together danced through his head. Foreplay had just begun. His hands moved first along the contours of her back. Then lower and lower, until he was caressing her buttocks. Slowly and rhythmically they moved up and down, then in a circular fashion until settling in the indentation in the middle. His one hand then turned sideways as he softly caressed its sides. Lower and lower his hand dropped, still keeping the rhythm that had characterized his movements for some time. Finally he was close to her warmth. He was in no hurry, content to watch as her breath grew heavier and heavier.

Finally it was time. Gently turning Sarah over, Jonathan started once again to caress her body with the softness of a tissue on a baby's bottom. He could sense her moaning as his fingers moved closer and closer to the spot that, when touched directly, would make her begin to lose all control. His touch finally threw her helplessly into the most wonderful set of contortions imaginable as her total body responded as it was meant to respond to this most mysterious of rhythmic touches. But patience has its rewards, he thought in his dream, and he was content for the longest time to move close, then away, then to brush slightly up against the spot, then to circle it, penetrating with his finger ever so slightly and for just a fleeting moment. All the time he focused on bringing her to a level of sexual desire in which her wetness would immediately engulf him as he entered her.

As his fantasy was about to move him deep inside her, Sarah's voice jogged him back to reality. Her words were foggy and meant nothing to him. All he knew was his dream had ended. It was back to reality. And reality was three days on the beach with his best friend, nothing more.

Since Sarah's arrival, Jonathan had dropped his reading pace from one novel per day to a few chapters. But it did not matter how much he read. The important thing was that Sarah was beside him. They had one more night together before beginning the journey back to Durham—back to the real reality and Sarah's final year at Duke.

They decided to celebrate their last evening on the Outer Banks with a meal at the beach house. So they headed for Oregon Inlet, about a half hour north, to wait for the fishing fleets to return after a day at sea. There they could get all the fish they wanted at little or no cost. The fishermen on the incoming boats didn't care. They were only interested in catching fish, not eating or selling them. They just gave them away. Dolphin—not the type one finds entertaining at Sea World, but the kind akin to mahi mahi—was a usual catch. It made for excellent cooking on the grill, with just a touch of butter and spices to give it the right flavor. If cooked properly, it simply melted in one's mouth. They had made the right decision. Plenty of dolphin awaited them at the end of the fishing day.

Back they went to Avon, load in hand. Dinner proved splendid. The wine provided just the right effect on their senses. Dusk settled over the screen porch as Jonathan and Sarah finished their meal.

"Let's take one final night walk on the beach," Sarah suggested with a look of contentment on her face.

Jonathan agreed, so they headed for the beach. The wine warmed them as they climbed the dunes, then the fifty paces to the water's edge. Turning north, they began to explore the shoreline. They reflected on the events of the previous twelve months. The most difficult year of their lives, yet a year filled with so many good things. If only they could have eliminated the bad and kept the good. But life didn't work that way. Sarah and Jonathan had come to understand that all too clearly. They also pondered the unusual circumstances of their relationship. This discussion was soon accompanied by Sarah's taking Jonathan's arm and, clasping it around hers, walking as one along the shore.

The beach was deserted. He longed to pick her up in his arms and gently place her on a blanket on the dunes, then slowly undress her as she lay back, content to allow him to have his way with her. For an hour they walked northward toward the village of Salvo, barely a dot on the map. Then they turned around, retracing their steps back toward the spot where they had crossed the dunes. A silence came over them both and lasted the better part of fifteen minutes. As he caught glimpse after glimpse of Sarah out the corner of his eye, he continually noticed a smile on her face. It was always present. He knew then their relationship was right.

About forty-five minutes later, they were close to the place where they would leave the beach and head toward the house. It was now dark, but the full moon on the water provided a clear picture of the beauty of the scene in front of them.

"I think we'd better be getting back," Jonathan suggested.

"I guess so," came Sarah's soft reply.

As if on cue, both Jonathan and Sarah turned toward each other. It was as if each didn't want that moment to end. Jonathan slowly and gently placed the tips of his fingers of both hands on her cheeks. Deliberately directing her face upward toward him with the gentle touch of his fingers, he reached down and kissed her with all the tenderness his body could summon. His lips stayed on hers for only a few seconds—long enough to inhale her scent, but short enough to avoid increased passion that would emerge at any moment. Their lips did not part. It was a gentle kiss. A soft kiss. A kiss borne out of the sensitivity for the moment. A kiss full of many feelings and many signals. A kiss to which Sarah responded somewhat eagerly but also with restraint.

But it was also an ambiguous kiss. Certainly ambiguous to Sarah, but also to Jonathan as well. Subconsciously he meant it to be. It would allow him to retreat if need be. If she called him to task, he was prepared to define it as a kiss of friendship. It was certainly a kiss of need, of continual need for her for the remainder of his life. And it was also a kiss of thank-you. *Thank-you for friendship. Thank-you for being you, dear Sarah. Thank-you for caring. Thank-you for being there when I needed you most,* Jonathan thought.

As their lips slowly moved apart from each other, Jonathan stared at Sarah. She returned the stare. He thought the phrase "and time stood still" had never been more true. A slight smile overtook both of them as they continued to look at each other, apparently searching for a cue as to what to do next. Jonathan was the one to take the next step. It was pivotal in defining their relationship, at least as they would consciously interpret it, for a long time to come.

In the years ahead he often wondered what would have happened had he chosen an alternative path at that juncture. But it would always be too late for "Monday morning quarterbacking," for second-guessing himself. Much later, when the situation repeated itself, Jonathan would have the opportunity to, once again, follow a different path—one that could bring him total and unconditional happiness.

"Thank you, Sarah, for your wonderful and precious friendship," he whispered so softly that his words hardly disturbed the gentle breeze flowing about them. He had made his decision. He was going to do nothing to jeopardize their friendship. He wanted to take her in his arms, lay her gently in the sand, slowly undress her, and make love to her over and over again. But the fear, as irrational as it might be, that he would lose her friendship was too powerful to withstand.

"You have no idea how much it has meant to me this year," he continued. "I don't know what I would have done without you. I pledge this evening to be your friend for life, if you want me, with all that means. Just say the word. Just confirm what I believe to be the case. That's all," he said in a somewhat pleading voice.

Sarah continued to stare at Jonathan, giving little clue about how she was internalizing his remarks. She did not respond at first. But soon a combination of sigh and smile graced her face.

"I like you, dear friend for life. Thank you for returning my friendship tenfold," she answered in a voice with a softness that matched his own.

Jonathan was too swept away by the emotion of the moment to discern whether Sarah was being facetious. He later learned that she was not. But he also found out something else. Her kiss awakened in him far deeper feelings than he had experienced to date. His heart pounded as it had never pounded. His soul had not only been touched. A truck full of emotions had invaded it. He doubted the smile now appearing across his face would ever go away.

And Sarah?

. . . Jonathan, do you remember our last evening at Avon before the beginning of my senior year? I remember it all too well. It was the night of our first real kiss. And yet it was a simple kiss, a kiss hard to characterize. Or at least its implications were difficult to figure out. But it was a wonderful kiss. I wanted to respond much more, shall we say, vigorously, but in many ways I was relieved I didn't have to. Its tenderness overwhelmed me. Guys my age did not understand the concept of a tender kiss. But you did, many times over.

That first kiss set in motion one of the most amazing things that has happened to me. I have continuously dreamt about our kissing since then. Simply kissing. And yet it hasn't been so simple. In my fantasies, have we ever kissed and continue to kiss still, and in so many delightful ways!

My love, you taught me so much in my dreams about the art of kissing. How I have loved allowing you to take the lead as we spent an inordinate amount of time kissing, touching one another about the face with soft, gentle caresses, and with tongue and fingers alike. I have loved how you have alternated among your different ways of kissing me. Each has reached my heart and my soul in a slightly different way. Collectively, they have warmed me in a way only you have been able to. When I awoke, I felt no different than if we had actually been locked in each other's arms, totally spent from the most incredible love-making. Perfect dreams are like that.

But back to the beach on Avon. As you pulled me toward you that first time, I wondered what was happening. I had no idea what I wished to happen. It was so beautiful. If at that moment you had asked me to come with you to a spot on the dunes where we could lie unobtrusively, I probably would have. Would I have made love to you? Good question. I have no idea whether I would have done so or whether I would have run away as fast as I could. I suspect, though, we would have found ourselves in each other's arms.

I will tell you what your kiss did to me, or perhaps, for me, however-er. I never forgot it. I'm not now talking about the dreaming part. I'm talking reality here. When I chose to over the years, I read much into it. When it suited me otherwise, I saw less in it. But it never left my mind. I repeat, it never left my mind. In reality, it later—after the breakup with Gordon—became part of my fantasizing about a life I didn't have. That is, a life with you. It would be safe then to fantasize about you, because the ground rules were clear. And they had been reinforced by how you reacted to our first kiss. But I wondered if they would ever change. . . .

Jonathan took Sarah's hand and started over the dunes toward the beach house. The defining moment had passed. Henceforth, both would continue to be clear about their relationship. But they would also indulge in alternative thoughts, he more so than she.

They awoke early the next day. After breakfast, they began the trip back to Durham. Jonathan thought that perhaps it was good they were in separate cars. He needed the time to think, to reflect about all that had happened. They decided to take the southern route home. This meant they would first travel to Ocracoke Island via a ninety-minute ferry ride. This quaint little fishing village lay south of Avon. It could only be reached by ferry from either direction, so it had resisted any kind of commercial and tourist development. Instead, it had maintained the same character it had fifty years earlier, when fishermen plied their trade from the island's harbor.

Sarah and Jonathan spent the better part of a day on Ocracoke, first exploring the town proper, located at the harbor, then driving to the far corner of the island to enjoy the privacy of a deserted beach. They went back to the harbor for an early dinner at a quintessential fishing village restaurant, The Channel Fish. The shrimp, fried in a light beer batter, had never tasted better. After dinner, they boarded a second ferry for the journey across to the mainland. They arrived back in Durham around midnight.

It was one day short of a year since Jonathan had first cast eyes on Sarah. He would not have traded that experience for anything. A new academic year was about to begin. And so was Sarah's final year at Duke. He awaited the new year with the anticipation of one who was uncertain of what was about to happen but who believed that whatever took place would warm his soul.

Part Two

~ 15 ~

Returning to Campus for Another Year

September 1968. Jonathan's third year at Duke. It didn't seem possible that two years had already passed since he first set foot on campus. He had always heard that the older one becomes, the more quickly time flies. It was probably true. But there was another reason as well. The excitement of his new friendship with Sarah had contributed to the haste of the previous twelve months. It caused him to rise each morning with newfound enthusiasm. Not that he had been bored with life before. But affairs of the heart, even if they only exist in one's mind, awaken increased levels of anticipation and excitement that fuel the body like a shot of adrenaline. The condition is likely short-lived, but in the interim, the smitten ones appear to possess boundless energy, and life seems to accelerate at an ever-increasing pace.

Jonathan's newfound stamina had to compete, though, with rival forces tearing at his body. The past spring's tragic events had overwhelmed him, each new incident coming on top of the previous one and each taking its toll on his ability to respond. He had discovered that coping with personal crises taxed his mental and physical resources, leaving him emotionally drained and physically exhausted. It was as if he was swimming upstream against an ever-increasing current.

Jonathan also noticed that summer that once the crises passed, a return to normal was not long in coming. A few weeks after Kennedy's death, his zest for living returned. Physical exercise helped. Memories would always remain with him, but the good ones rapidly pushed the bad ones aside. Life went on, and life was good. He didn't know where it would take him, but he was ready. By the end of summer, his old self was back.

Jonathan was in no hurry for the new academic year to move forward so quickly. Quite the contrary. If he had his way, the calendar would meander in slow motion, held in check by some powerful force with the capacity to retard time. Sarah was entering her senior year. She had but nine months remaining on campus, maybe fewer. Their precious moments together were soon going to be limited.

She had applied to spend second semester in Washington, D.C., as part of Duke University's political internship program. That spring experience had been especially popular with political science majors since its inception fifteen years earlier. Students lived on Georgetown University's campus and attended classes each weekday morning. Afternoons during the first three weeks found them somewhere throughout the three branches of the federal government—executive, legislative, or judicial—observing the political process in action. Following that brief orientation period, they spent afternoons working as unpaid volunteers in some governmental agency or for a member of Congress.

Sarah would likely be accepted into the internship program. Her grade-point average was outstanding, her work experience in Senator Erwin's Raleigh office had gone well, and she had superior letters of recommendation from a number of faculty members. She had asked Jonathan to write one just as the summer term drew to a close. His letter praised Sarah's talents and accomplishments. He had mixed emotions as he composed it. His heart wanted her to stay in Durham, but his head pushed her toward Washington.

The experience would be good for her career. They had discussed it at length during one of their last get-togethers before leaving for their end-of-summer vacations. Washington was where she wanted to be. Where she could eventually make a difference. The events of the previous year, rather than turning her away from politics, had awakened a renewed passion inside of her, a desire to make the country and world a better place. Sarah believed that meant working within the system at the highest levels.

Not everyone in the late 1960s felt that way, though. Many students protested against big government and the capitalist corporate structure. Some had opted to drop out of life's mainstream altogether. A few had even decided to change the system by whatever means available, no matter how destructive or violent. No matter who was hurt or killed.

Not Sarah, though. She might not begin her career in a governmental agency. It was more likely she would become a lobbyist, trying to affect change by influencing the power brokers. But she would end up working in government before long. After all, she believed strongly in America's system of governance.

Jonathan was happy and excited for her, while his heart suggested he would have trouble coping when the fateful departure day arrived. So he put visions of her inevitable farewell out of his mind. He didn't want to think the glass half empty. Rather, he would ponder only good thoughts, those that focused on their friendship, and on any other wonderful path their relationship might take them during the next four months. He was determined to make their remaining time together as perfect as possible. At a minimum, he wished their friendship to be far deeper in December than it had been in August. The best scenario— well, he didn't dare dream that wonderful fantasy.

And Sarah.

. . . I returned my senior year a far different person than I was the previous September. A young woman who, while still timid, had experienced far too many sad moments in such a short period of time not to have been profoundly affected, had replaced the somewhat shy girl not far removed from high school. The death of a friend's brother—the first death of a contemporary, you should know—hurt me the most. It gave me a solid sense of mortality, I would say. My biggest regret so far in my life, my love, is that I never knew Ben except through the vivid pictures you've painted over the years. I've cried often, though not in front of you, for this loss.

Being dropped by some guy—not a new experience for me—wasn't much fun either, I should say. Although I shall always cherish our long walk throughout the golf course when I appeared at your office the night Michael gave me the bad news.

The deaths of two public figures who had stirred my political soul, coming right on the heels of Ben's death, added to my misery. Particularly

Bobby Kennedy's murder. It was so soon after I had seen him. After I had worked my heart out for him. His death really affected me. Even after I appeared to be over it, the tragedy still had a major hold on me. I guess because it came just a few short years after his brother's death. I was only a high schooler when JFK was assassinated, so I really didn't understand the full implication of the country's loss of his vision and vigor forever. But by the time his brother was killed, I could better measure the nation's loss. And let me tell you, I knew it was great. I wasn't certain the country could recover. The Chicago convention didn't help any either. Quite the contrary. It only reinforced the idea we were destroying ourselves from within.

But the most profound episode of my junior year was not one of the many tragedies that came my way. Instead, it was the most beautiful experience of my entire life. Meeting you. Getting to know you. Each of us coming to need the other and having that need met so completely. The evolution of our friendship was the most important and wonderful thing to have happened to me up until then. Nothing had ever come close to it. It gave me more confidence in social situations, much like I had in academic matters.

So, on balance, I came to cherish my junior year at Duke. For the bottom line, my dear Jonathan, was that it brought me you. It led to a friendship that, even if nothing else had ever happened in our relationship, would have been more than I could ever have hoped for. I looked forward to my senior year with much anticipation. I knew I could count on you for strength and comfort should I need either. And I started to think about my future.

The internship in Washington was part of that process. I returned to campus re-energized about politics and about helping solve the problems confronting our nation. The political tragedies of the previous year only reinforced my resolve. So I wanted to jump-start my life's work. Second semester in Washington would do just that.

But I was ambivalent about leaving campus a semester early. I knew I would never return to live there again. It's not that I didn't want to graduate and get on with my life. As I filled out the application for the internship, it occurred to me that, if successful, I would be cutting short the happiest period of my life—being a Dukie on the best campus in the country. So the decision to apply for the internship was far more difficult than I let on to anyone.

I hoped you would be supportive. I can't begin to tell you how important it was to me to have your approval. I don't know what I would have done had you thought it a bad idea. But you didn't, even though it would cut short by four months the time we spent living in the same town with each other. . . .

First semester 1968 was certainly different from the same time the previous year. Jonathan was well on his way toward tenure. He anticipated no huge roadblocks in front of him. He knew it would not happen for at least two more years, but he was confident that his early success as a research scholar would continue. His ability to apply modern data analysis techniques to large bodies of information was quickly paying dividends. The leading political science journal, *The American Political Science Review,* accepted another of his articles for publication, which would bring him many accolades over the next few years. The summer work on his book had been productive as well. He felt it would be in press before the end of the new school year. If so, he would be a lock for tenure and promotion to the next rank, associate professor.

Universities had a clear caste system. If a young faculty member arrived on campus without the doctor of philosophy degree—Ph.D. was its more common name—in hand, he or she received the title of instructor. The next rank, assistant professor, was reserved for new faculty members who had already received their doctorates before assuming their faculty positions.

In 1968, only about half the new faculty members arrived on American campuses with Ph.D.s in hand. There was a good reason for this. The baby boomers of the late 1940s and early 1950s began to appear *en masse* on campuses across the country. Universities were expanding rapidly, and graduate programs were hard-pressed to keep up with the increased demand for new faculty. As a consequence, many graduate students were tempted to enter the job market as soon as they passed their qualifying exams, the next-to-last hurdle to the Ph.D. degree. Their only remaining obstacle was the dissertation, the name given to the several-hundred-page report of the student's major research project. A dissertation usually took at least a year to finish but could be written, however, away from one's graduate school campus.

With the lure of a paycheck awaiting them as soon as they had begun work on their dissertations, many did not wait until they had met this final Ph.D. requirement to assume teaching positions. A large number would later find out they had made a huge mistake, particularly if they had accepted a position at a major research university. They had to play catch-up with their research agenda, which usually meant they had not published enough by the time the final decision on lifetime job security rolled around. Even prestigious universities like Duke hired young faculty without their degrees in hand.

An assistant professor had to labor for five to seven years before a university would consider promotion to the next rank, associate professor. During that time, the assistant professor had to excel, university rules typically suggested, in three distinct areas—teaching, research, and public service. All major universities were alike in this respect.

Small colleges and universities that did not aspire to major research institution status tended to emphasize only teaching and public service. The latter meant young assistant professors were good citizens on campus, for example, by serving on extra committees or advising campus student organizations. They were also expected to contribute to the intellectual life of the community, whatever that meant.

In order to be successful, political scientists needed to turn up from time to time on television offering their expert opinions whenever some particularly newsworthy event happened. They were also expected to write letters or "op-ed" pieces for local or national newspapers. Speaking about current affairs before service organizations such as the Rotary Club was also a plus. Running for public office was considered a bonus, as long as it didn't interfere with their faculty duties.

It had also become increasingly important that faculty at smaller and less-prestigious institutions spend some time on research. But given the huge demands that heavy teaching loads and public service obligations brought on, it was unlikely they could ever establish top-notch reputations.

Expectations were far different, however, at research universities from those at both small colleges and second-tier universities.

Administrations still paid lip service to teaching and public service. But the third criterion was the key. Publish or perish. It was an unambiguous choice. And better to publish in prestigious, "peer-reviewed" outlets. Such assessment involved critiques from the most outstanding scholars around the country. These research stars judged whether the proposed article was worthy of publication in a top journal—one on which leaders in the field had placed their *Good Housekeeping* Seal of Approval.

At Duke, the expectation was that by tenure-decision time, an assistant professor had to have at least one book published by a respected publication house, usually a university press. Two books were preferable but not necessary, particularly if one had several articles in good journals as well.

Students at research universities often complained, as did their parents—and, in the case of public institutions, state legislators—that faculty members ignored their teaching and public service responsibilities in the quest for publications. In many cases, the criticism was justified. Their faculty, at least the smart ones among them, had figured out that review committees, by and large, paid only lip service to teaching and public service as criteria for tenure and promotion. So they learned to play the game. Spend most of one's time on research and do what was only absolutely necessary in the other two categories.

Of course, research university presidents, when called upon to respond publicly to such charges, denied them completely. But anyone who talked to committee members privy to tenure-decision deliberations heard a different story, if the latter had the courage to admit it. In the same breath, university administrators defended the need for ongoing faculty research as an essential step in maintaining the lifeblood of the university, including its teaching function. Those from land-grant institutions such as Ohio State would also point to their responsibility to address state problems through research.

Although it was a private institution, Duke University had bought into the publish-or-perish syndrome. Its scholars had made contribution after contribution to the advancement of knowledge. Nobel Prize winners had resided on campus. National policymakers turned to its faculty for advice. Alumni were happy. Contributions poured into the fundraising office. Eager applicants for admission to the university abounded.

Interestingly enough, most students would say their professors were also excellent teachers. But Duke was unusual in that respect. Its administrators were aware of its reputation for good teaching and took pride in it. Jonathan was the quintessential young Duke faculty member. He excelled in all three areas—research, teaching, and public service—expected of professors.

Once a faculty member rose to the rank of associate professor, obligations in these three areas did not end. This rank was only partway to the top rung of the ladder. Faculty would toil for another five to seven years as associate professors. Then, and only if the candidate was recognized as a leader in his or her research specialty, promotion to the rank of full professor—professor was its more common name—occurred. The candidate had then arrived at the top of the faculty hierarchy.

There was a more prestigious title that only a very small handful of faculty acquired during their careers. It was a "named professorship" or "named chair." If a benefactor donated a large sum of money to the university and designated it to be used to enhance a faculty member's salary and/or for other perks such as a personal research laboratory, the professor carried the name of the benefactor.

In Jonathan's department, one of his colleagues was the Ernest Downing Professor of Political Science. Matthew Downing, class of 1965, who had inherited the family business, had contributed a million dollars to Duke in honor of his father, Ernest Downing. The elder Downing was a Duke graduate, class of 1942, who met his untimely death in an auto accident in 1960. Universities like Duke spent much effort trying to convince wealthy alumni and other supporters to follow the example of the Matthew Downings of the world and endow a faculty chair in the name of a family member.

Jonathan was comfortable with the mores of university advancement. He knew if he chose to stay at Duke, he would become an associate professor by the end of the 1960s and would achieve full professor status by about the middle of the next decade. Perhaps he might even close out the 1970s as a chaired professor. That would place him at the pinnacle of the Duke faculty ladder.

Of course, it was also likely that numerous job offers would come his way from other campuses across the country. Universities were known to raid other institutions for their bright and successful young faculty with promises of early promotion and huge raises. It was a rare faculty member who could resist such temptations. Musical chairs played out across every university campus in the late 1960s as good, young professors jumped at opportunities for early advancement and financial rewards.

Jonathan thought himself somehow different, immune to such temptations. He was content at Duke. Of course, his happiness in the past twelve months had increased by leaps and bounds because of Sarah. It would change when she left Durham for Washington, either at the end of first semester or after graduation in the spring. Her departure was inevitable. Only the timing was uncertain.

He was also content with Duke's faculty salaries. His needs were minimal, and he was certainly not materialistic. His only indulgence was international travel. It certainly wasn't his car. He drove a 1961 two-door Corvair Monza, bright red with white interior. The engine was in the back and the trunk up front. It had seen over 100,000 miles, but it still ran well. Ralph Nader had targeted the Corvair as a dangerous lemon because of the car's penchant for mechanical malfunctioning leading to all sorts of accidents. Nader's book, *Unsafe at Any Speed*, became a bestseller and forced General Motors to introduce new safety features. Jonathan's experience with his Monza was far different, however. He loved the car and couldn't imagine himself in another.

But travel was a different story. His strategy was to acquire outside grants to help pay the cost of his foreign adventures. He would fine-tune his entrepreneurial skill of finding someone else to pay for his travel over the next decade.

So Jonathan thought that in all likelihood he would spend his entire career at Duke. This assumption brought a smile to his face. After all, he would always be near the spot where Sarah has first mesmerized him. Every day, he would pass the places where the two of them had walked and talked, where their friendship had blossomed and grown. He hoped that when she left the campus for good—hopefully later rather than sooner—he would have added to his wonderful memories of their time together.

Jonathan's teaching schedule was similar to that of the previous year. He was responsible for an undergraduate class—the same one where he had met Sarah—and a graduate seminar. For the rest of his teaching days, he would look fondly at that first course and the students who would occupy the thirty places each time.

He and Sarah had arranged to have dinner the first day of class so they could exchange notes. She was trying to complete her formal course requirements that autumn in anticipation of her acceptance into the internship program. She was carrying a heavy load, four courses, to accomplish that task. Her horror about the amount of work before her was evident at dinner.

"Well, Jonathan, I must say today wasn't much fun," she said. "I have about five books per course to read, huge term papers in all four of my courses, and several smaller reports to give in class. I guess I can forget about sleep and fun until December. I may have to call on you to have my meals delivered to the library."

Jonathan laughed at her last comment. After a second, Sarah joined him, but hers had an edge about it that revealed a sense of hopelessness at her predicament.

"Ah, Sarah, it probably won't be as bad as you think," Jonathan reassured her. "Professors like to impress—actually the correct phrase is 'scare the hell out of'—their students on the first day. You're going to have to budget your time really well, though. Start your research early for your papers. Don't wait until the last moment. That's usually where students get into trouble. They wait until it's too late. Then they throw themselves at the mercy of the professor when they find they don't have time to finish them."

"Oh, Jonathan. I'm not a novice. I know the pitfalls of procrastination. I've already been to the library stacks today looking for topic ideas," Sarah replied. "It's tough, though, because we're just beginning to talk about the course material. In most cases, I have no idea what the classes are about. So I can hardly be expected to select a research topic so soon."

"Actually, that's a good point," Jonathan agreed. "The other piece of advice I can give is to use your time on weekends wisely. Blow off

Friday nights. But put some time in at the library on Saturdays. You'll be surprised at how much you can get done. Sundays too."

"Whoa, Jonathan! When am I supposed to play?" Sarah wanted to know. "I'm twenty-one now. I have to visit the bars from time to time. I have my reputation to protect. I may even get asked out on a date once in a while. Duke guys do that on occasion, you know. Tell me, did you ever work in the library on Friday nights or Saturdays when you were an undergraduate? Be honest now."

"I plead the Fifth Amendment . . . No, I confess. Of course not. I didn't have that kind of discipline. I was just your regular average Joe student who blew off most of the weekend until Sunday night," Jonathan admitted.

Jonathan didn't like Sarah's remark about dating, although he knew it was inevitable. He dreaded the moment when he would run into her on a date. It hadn't happened yet. He figured it was because she had done little socializing since her breakup with Michael. Too many other things had gone on in her life over the past year. But now it was different. He assumed it was only a matter of time before he saw her with some guy. That would really hurt.

"You'll have plenty of time for fun," Jonathan said. "But I guess you're right, about Saturday anyhow. It's kind of silly to think about working on Saturdays. But you would be surprised at how much you could accomplish. That's an assumption. Remember, I never did that myself.

"I'll tell you what I think will work, if you're interested. Let's hit the library together on Sunday during the day. At least, let's go there together, then off on our separate ways. This is a pivotal year for me, too. If I use my time right, I can really get on top of my research. I could finish enough to leave no doubt about my getting tenure. That would also allow me to plan the next phase of my research agenda.

"You see, once I have the luxury of tenure, I can create a more elaborate research design—one that requires several years to complete. Now I'm just concerned with how long it takes to get something published. I haven't had the freedom to take risks. After I get tenure, I can do that. Take risks, I mean. But planning my next research endeavor will take a lot of time. So I have two tasks this year: finish some more research pieces and get them published, and plan my next several years of work.

"I could use some extra time. You could use some extra time. Separately, we probably won't have the discipline to find it, at least after the first couple of weeks. But if we work together, we are more likely to stay on track and follow a schedule we set up. What do you say, Sarah? Let's try it. We could head to the library for about five or six hours on Sunday afternoons. Then we could go to my place and cook a nice dinner. That would start off our week just fine, wouldn't it?"

Sarah paused for a minute, then responded, "That's intriguing, Jonathan. It might just work. But you don't have to follow that kind of schedule. I do. You would be making a big sacrifice for me. Do you really want to do it? What about pro football games on TV on Sunday afternoons?"

A seriousness immediately came over Jonathan's face. He measured the words he was about to speak. "First, it would be a big help to me. I would benefit from it, not just you. But second, we're friends. Friends help one another. I want you to get as much as possible out of your last semester at Duke—if it is, indeed, your last semester here. I want to be able to help you."

"Okay. It's a deal, Jonathan," Sarah agreed. "Let me see. I'll blow off Friday night and Saturday completely. I'll probably get drunk one night and stoned the next. Might as well have all the experiences of college, don't you think? Actually, both are around everywhere in the dorms and student apartments. Does it surprise you I might have tried grass?"

"No, not really," Jonathan said. "Doesn't everyone try it sometime or another?"

"I think so, at least everyone I know. Why don't I meet you in front of the library around one on Sunday. Then we can plan how much time we want to spend studying and what time we're going to eat," Sarah suggested.

"Sounds good," Jonathan agreed. "After we finish at the library, we can drive over to Piggly Wiggly—you know, the big grocery store out on Route 501 toward Chapel Hill—and pick up some stuff for dinner. Then we'll head over to my place and cook a really nice meal to start off the week with. Okay?"

"Sounds great to me," Sarah replied.

"We'll call it the Matthews-Hawthorne Sunday night seminar,"

Jonathan suggested. He was careful to put her name before his on the seminar title. The early days of the women's movement had sensitized him to the correctness of such a step. "If any of your friends ask what you're doing that Sunday night, tell them you have a seminar. You don't have to reveal what kind of seminar, or the fact that it includes dinner."

"And wine?" Sarah ventured.

"What an awful seminar it would be if there was no wine," Jonathan said. He thought his remark funny, and Sarah's slight grin suggested the same.

"They'll be curious, of course, but I'll just keep my friends in the dark a little, at least for a couple of weeks," Sarah said. "It will be fun. It's a deal then?"

"It's a deal. We'll start this weekend," Jonathan answered.

Sunday at one o'clock found their new schedule underway. They agreed to meet back out in front of the building at six. Five hours later, both emerged from the library stacks hungry and ready for food. Off they headed to Piggly Wiggly. Ribeye steak was the first Sunday's choice, along with baked potatoes, asparagus, and salad. To be served, of course, with a bottle of French red wine, cabernet sauvignon, purchased earlier because of a state law that prohibited the sale of alcohol on Sundays. Back to Jonathan's condo they went, where he lit the grill, put some music—a new Simon and Garfunkel album—on the stereo and prepared the potatoes.

They ate on the outdoor deck. North Carolina evenings in early September were perfect. Moderate temperatures, little humidity, no wind, and lots of light blue sky left. Dinner was a time for all sorts of conversation. Sarah talked about her term papers while Jonathan described his research. But they also spent time talking about the future—mostly about Sarah's future. Jonathan loved to listen to her describe how she wanted to make a difference in the world somehow, making it safer and more humane. Many students talked that way, that is, about wanting to bring about world peace or solve the mysteries of cancer someday, but somehow he knew in her case it was going to happen. The world would be a better place because of her work some day.

"I'm really interested in international affairs," Sarah explained. "But I'm not that excited about trade and other kinds of business stuff. My work in Senator Erwin's office convinced me of that. I think I want to help poor countries, maybe join the Peace Corps."

Sarah is just the type of person for that organization, Jonathan thought. "Do you know where the idea of the Peace Corps originated? I'll give you a hint. It was with a future president." He determined to put her to the test.

"I think with John Kennedy, during the 1960 presidential campaign," Sarah answered.

"That's right, but do you know where he first announced it?" Jonathan asked.

"Is this a trick question?" Sarah wanted to know.

"No, not really," Jonathan replied. "But I'll give you a clue. It was on a university campus."

"Well, I really don't know. And nothing I've read about Duke suggests JFK announced it here. I give up," Sarah said.

"It was on the steps of the student union at the University of Michigan. I don't remember the date. But I do know it was an idea that caught on quickly, particularly with students. So I think joining the Peace Corps would be a good idea," Jonathan said.

"Well, it's one of many ideas I have," Sarah continued. "People in Senator Erwin's office said they would help me find a job in Washington next year. And I'll probably have lots of contacts if I do the internship next semester."

"Oh, you won't have any trouble finding something in Washington," Jonathan assured her. "It probably won't pay much, but it will get your foot inside the door. Then the city will soon be all yours, Sarah Joan Matthews." Jonathan's comment amused him. The two spent the rest of the evening talking about topics both frivolous and serious. He found the conversation comfortable.

"I hope today worked out okay. The key, though, is to keep it up. That's where I can be a help. My job's to keep you on track, to not allow you to waver. In a couple of weeks the temptations will be greater, and you simply cannot succumb to them. I won't let you," Jonathan told Sarah.

At that remark, Sarah first feigned a frown, then laughed and said, "I'm sure you won't. It's tough having a professor for a friend. I won't be able to get away with anything." Sarah was teasing him, and he knew it. She then changed directions. "How'd your work go today, Jonathan? Did you get as much accomplished as I did?"

"I think so," he replied. "I'll have a better sense in a couple of weeks. So I need your help too—that is, in keeping me on track. Can I count on you?"

"Of course, particularly since I have to be at the library," Sarah said. "I can guarantee you I'll hound you into joining me. No fear of that not happening. Misery loves company."

"So it's misery, Sarah, is it?" Jonathan asked playfully.

"No, not really. I'm just kidding. Actually, it's kind of therapeutic. It signifies a new beginning, I mean. So many things went bad last year that I would just as soon forget it. But now it's a new year with a whole new set of classes and a brand new schedule. It all helps put the bad things about last year further and further behind me. Does that make sense to you?" Sarah asked.

"It certainly does," Jonathan answered. "I know exactly how you feel."

Years later in her letter to Jonathan, Sarah wrote about the one beautiful rose in the previous year's bed of thorns.

> . . . As those terrible events of my junior year got pushed behind me, the one super good thing that happened to me then took on an even greater importance as I began my senior year. I mean you, our friendship. As comforting as it was to have you there when my crises hit, it was really nice just to get to know you in situations outside those tragedies. Summer was special. After we dealt with Bobby Kennedy's death, we settled into what I would call a normal routine. I liked it. I grew up a lot my junior year, so I guess our friendship was the first one I had cultivated since I had passed into a "more mature" stage of my life.
>
> I remember one rather silly conversation we had that summer about how I orchestrated Michael's dropping me. You said it forced you to stop thinking about your own coping and to start helping me through mine. When I told you I would thank Michael the next time I saw him, you responded that you would do it too. You had it all figured out. You would walk right up to him and in your most pleasant voice, say, "Thanks, jerk, for dropping Sarah Matthews last year. You turned her into such a

basket case that I was forced to stop feeling sorry for myself so I could direct all my attention toward her." I laughed so hard. It was that kind of give-and-take that made me so comfortable with you. More so than I realized at the time.

How our friendship evolved was a totally new experience for me. My world until then had centered around people my own age. Adults were just people of another generation who shared nothing in common with me. They were really authority figures for the most part. So I never had what you would call a friendship with an adult before you. My friends had been all peers, both guys and girls. I had had lots of guy friends, but they were my own age. And to be truthful about it, most of them were probably more immature than I was. They couldn't help it. Girls mature faster than boys.

I don't know if I was so ready for an adult friendship that I would have gravitated toward anyone who showed a similar interest in me. Or whether it was, as you would say, fate that brought us together, creating situations in which we each needed someone to lean on. It didn't matter. What was important was that we both seemed drawn to each other like two magnets.

What I'm trying to say is that from the first day that autumn when I entered your class and watched as you began to teach us, I felt some kind of closeness. It was silly, I know, but it seemed, once I heard you speak, that I had met you someplace before. I couldn't place it, however, and I know now our paths hadn't crossed earlier. That's why I think fate did play such a strong role in all of this. I was destined to find you as a friend, just as it was preordained that you would find me. There's no other explanation. . . .

Jonathan took Sarah to her dorm at ten. As he drove back to his condo after dropping her off, he found himself in a rather reflective mood. He and Sarah were in somewhat of the same boat. After all, there weren't many people his age in similar positions at Duke. There were very few women faculty, and virtually all of them were either already married or much older than he was. The same situation existed with the men on campus. There was a handful of young male faculty. But they spent most of their waking hours trying to get promoted and receive tenure. They didn't have time for much socializing that could eventually lead to friendship.

Add Jonathan's usual reluctance to make friends to the mix, and one could see why he felt such intensity about his friendship with Sarah. It was not an everyday occurrence with him. He couldn't explain why he had allowed her to get as close to him as she had. It hadn't been just being at the right place at the right time, with Ben's death and everything. It had to be something else.

Obviously, the fact that she stirred him in a deeply physical way had initially led to his wanting to know her better. Not that he would have acted on it, but Jonathan certainly was willing at least to fantasize about a physical relationship. Ben's death changed all of that. While he still harbored delicious thoughts of a romantic interlude—or two, or three, or a hundred such encounters—with Sarah, his desire for her had mushroomed into a need for her friendship.

The first weekend of their rigorous study schedule was a success, so Jonathan and Sarah agreed the routine should continue. The autumn semester moved forward, with Jonathan and Sarah leading separate lives six days a week, although they managed a couple of late night phone calls between Monday and Saturday. But Sundays at one o'clock found them at the library ready for another day of study and dinner. Both activities paid off. Their friendship moved into new terrain, with each learning more about what the other thought about, dreamt about, and worried about. Finding out new things about the other only a close confidant would notice. For Jonathan, each new revelation about Sarah intensified his fondness for her. He wanted more, but he gladly took what she offered.

● ● ●

Sarah received the wonderful news in a letter a few weeks before the middle of the term. She had been accepted into the internship program second semester. She called Jonathan immediately with news of her good fortune. Cheers emanated from both sides of the phone as she read the letter to him.

They agreed to celebrate that Sunday night at La Chandelle rather than cook at his condo. The restaurant had taken up a special place in their hearts, so it seemed the perfect choice. It was during dinner that the reality of her pending move sunk in.

"I'm really excited about next semester, Jonathan. But I'm scared too," she said.

"What are you afraid of?" Jonathan asked. "Remember how nervous you were last winter about going over to Raleigh and working in Senator Erwin's office? Yet in just a few weeks, you were on top of that job. Next semester won't be any different."

"But it will be," Sarah insisted. "I'll be plucking up my Duke roots, not entirely, but for all practical purposes. I'll be living in a new city, meeting new people, doing different things. I won't even be considered a real Dukie anymore." With that last remark, Sarah feigned a sob. That elicited a fake sigh from Jonathan as well.

"But really, Jonathan," she continued, "it is a huge passage in my life. I didn't realize it until I received the acceptance letter and started to think about it a little more—a lot more, actually. My whole life uprooted. Maybe I shouldn't go to Washington."

Sarah's insecurities were now taking hold of her. Jonathan was not about to let that happen. "Now, now, Sarah. Life is all about passages," he reassured her. "No matter how wonderful and how fulfilling one stage is, we mustn't pause too long there, or else it will lose its allure. Better to jump too quickly into a new phase of our lives rather than to move too slowly. That's where the excitement and the challenges are. Think about it, Sarah. Think about what you want to do with your life. Next semester is a giant step in that direction. You'll arrive in Washington with the entire city at your feet, ready for you to conquer. And conquer it you will!"

"You make it sound so certain. How can you be sure?" Sarah wanted to know.

"Because I know you, Sarah Joan Matthews. I've watched you from afar, and I've watched you up close for more than a year now. You have what it takes, in spades, to succeed in that town. You'll do it. You'll knock their socks off. I know it. I just know it," Jonathan said.

"I don't know what it is, Jonathan, but you always make me feel so good about myself," Sarah commented. "I always have a lot more self-confidence after I've been with you. I guess I should thank you."

"Of course you should thank me," Jonathan said and laughed. "But I'm not just doing it to boost your ego. I believe in you. You don't think I would have allowed myself to become friends with a dodo-head, a loser, do you?"

"I don't know about that. But I do know I feel like I can conquer the world after listening to you. I just hope I can conquer Washington," Sarah answered.

Jonathan wanted Sarah to subdue the nation's capital, but he longed to be part of her triumph. He knew, though, that his role would be a minor one. For he now realized she was walking out of his life, perhaps not psychologically but certainly physically. They would not be living in the same place. Probably never again. They would never be in such close contact as they had been, almost continually, since Ben's death. Others would enter Sarah's life. One would sweep her off her feet. This new guy would replace him as the most important man in her life. He would have an intimate physical relationship with Sarah, something that Jonathan could only dream about.

The thought deeply saddened him. But the mind has a way of finding a method to ease such blows. And so it did in this case. Jonathan reflected on what he would really lose if Sarah found a lover, or even a husband, in Washington. What did they have? Really have? A friendship, that's all. They weren't lovers. If he had had that opportunity, he had blown it that last night on the beaches of the Outer Banks two months earlier. But what a friendship they had! No one was going to tamper with that. Not a lover. Not a husband. No one.

He rationalized that he had never really had the opportunity to make love to her. Besides, he told himself, friendship—particularly the intense friendship he and Sarah enjoyed—is more special than romantic love. It's more enduring and more rare. They were not going to lose it. Ever. Another person entering her life would not diminish their friendship.

Then Jonathan's rationalizations reached new heights. Maybe the acquisition of a lover would find new tasks for their friendship. After all, romantic liaisons were always characterized by peaks and valleys. Sarah would need him during the valleys. The more valleys, the greater the need. He smiled to himself as he envisaged a much larger role for himself in Sarah's new life. He hoped he wasn't kidding himself.

The evening at La Chandelle came to a close.

❧ ❧ ❧

The semester moved onward at what seemed like an ever-increasing pace. And then it finally happened. The moment he had dreaded. It was a Friday night. Jonathan had decided to take in a movie—a big hit, *The Graduate*, with Dustin Hoffman. It was playing in Chapel Hill, ten miles to the south, in a theater on Franklin Street, its main thoroughfare. He opted for the early show, as it would be less crowded. As he was leaving the theater, there they were, Sarah and some guy. They didn't see him at first. They were laughing and obviously having a good time. He looked like your typical undergraduate. *Obviously too young for Sarah,* Jonathan joked to himself. He wanted to hide, but there was no place to go.

"Hi, Sarah," he said. The words flowed somewhat haltingly from his mouth. He didn't know what else to say. He had caught her off-guard. She hadn't seen him. Jonathan could see her face quickly turning red.

"Oh, hi . . . Professor Hawthorne," she replied. Sarah seemed to pause before saying his name. He guessed it was because she was now used to calling him Jonathan. She hesitated again, searching for something to say, and then continued, "How was the movie? Did you like it?"

She was searching for small talk, he guessed, as she struggled to gain her composure. "Oh, it was great," Jonathan answered. "You'll like it. It has an interesting May-December twist to it."

Jonathan wasn't going to pass up an opportunity to introduce the idea of a relationship between two people who were far apart in years. He ignored the fact, though, that *The Graduate* had it backwards. Anne Bancroft was older than Hoffman.

"Good. Well, we must hurry or we'll be late. See you, Dr. Hawthorne," she said. With that remark, off they went. Sarah had not introduced her date. It had been a quick exchange. It was just as well. He didn't want to know anything about the guy. Sleep came slowly that evening.

Sarah mentioned the incident only briefly when she saw Jonathan the next time. She apologized for not introducing him, but he said he understood. He did understand, he told himself, all too well. Sarah was dating again after a break following Michael's departure. He assumed she would get lots of offers. She was incredibly attractive and the kind of woman men like. It had happened to him, and it would happen to others.

❧ ❧ ❧

The semester continued. Thanksgiving vacation. They celebrated much like they had the year before, but with one difference. Ben was in his thoughts as much as Sarah the day after the holiday as Jonathan made his way, just as he had done a year earlier, to the foothills outside Aspen. He pondered the experiences he had shared there with Ben. While he knew they would never be repeated, he now wanted to enjoy that exquisite place with Sarah at his side.

❧ ❧ ❧

Before Jonathan realized it, only one week of classes remained, and final exams were just around the corner. Their Sunday venture into the world of study had continued. Their solid work ethic found its rewards. Jonathan finished two articles and touched off the final draft of his book. He was also well on his way to laying out his research agenda for the next five years. He was proud of himself. And he was proud of Sarah. She had worked hard. The only task remaining for her was to take all of her research findings and tie them together into her four term papers. Thus, her phone call.

"Jonathan, I have a big favor to ask. If it won't work, just tell me. I have to finish my writing and type my four papers by Monday," she explained. It was then Wednesday morning. "Could I hang out at your place, use a table, and borrow your typewriter until I finish? That way I can avoid all the interruptions in the dorm. I'll bring over enough food and drink to take care of myself. I'll stay out of your way."

Jonathan laughed at her last comment and replied, "Sure, no problem. When do you want to start?"

"Last week. Just kidding. Actually, that's when I should have started. As soon as possible, okay?" Sarah asked.

"Cartainly. When can I expect you, so I can clean up the place?" Jonathan asked.

"Don't do that. Can I come in about an hour?" she wanted to know.

Sarah spent almost five days at Jonathan's condo, working every minute. It was the classic last-week crunch time. By Friday night she was not even going back to her place but instead was using the second bedroom to catch a few hours of sleep. He took care of her meals that weekend. He loved doing it. It allowed him to fantasize that she really belonged there.

She completed her four term papers on time, the last one at six on Sunday evening, and earned an A on each of them. Jonathan suggested they celebrate the last Sunday night of the semester not with a cooked meal but, surprise of surprises, with one last dinner at La Chandelle.

Of all the perfect evenings there, none surpassed Sarah's final one as a Dukie. Jonathan had bought a rather expensive bottle of wine for the occasion. Both noted its smoothness as they drank a toast in celebration of their friendship. Jonathan offered it. "To our friendship, our wonderful, wonderful friendship! May it continue to warm our souls, no matter where the next months and years take us. May it be the link to each other as we each search, in our own ways, for happiness. And may it be the catalyst that propels us to reach for the sky as we ponder what future paths to take. I love our friendship."

"Oh, Jonathan, that was wonderful," Sarah said. "You special, special man. You touch my heart. Thank you, thank you, thank you, dear friend."

The evening was a perfect ending to Sarah's last semester on campus. It would be over all too soon.

~ 16 ~

Off to Washington for Sarah

January 1969. Second semester was about to begin. Jonathan's Christmas was the first since his brother's death and it was not an easy one. Although Ben had not been physically with them the previous holiday season, at least he was alive in the jungles of Vietnam as the Hawthorne clan gathered around the Christmas tree to open their gifts. Included among the wrappings then had been three presents from Ben, one for each of the family. Jonathan received a waist-length blue jacket made in Hong Kong. Ben had visited that Oriental jewel when he took his leave from the fighting in Vietnam, his "R and R"—rest and relaxation. Jonathan hoped his brother had enjoyed himself there—the last chance he would have had for some fun before he died. Visions of Ben tasting the fruits of some Asian beauty in the most spectacular of Far East cities brought a smile to Jonathan's face.

Christmas had brought back some of the pain of that fateful day the past spring. But Jonathan and his family had worked through it somehow. Family members played that much harder in the mountains the week after Christmas. He assumed they had wanted to fall into a deep sleep each night, rather than to toss and turn while thinking of Ben.

Jonathan was sad for another reason. Sarah took all of her belongings with her when she left campus following her last exam. He had helped her pack. Once again she had a late final, so all of her friends were gone before she left. He was thankful for that because he wanted her all to himself during her last hours on campus. He had made a small batch of eggnog for her to sip as he loaded her car for the next morning's journey. He joined her in some eggnog as he helped her with box after box.

The only really bright moments over the holidays were his phone conversations with Sarah. He regaled her with tales of the Rockies while she shared stories of her time with family and friends in and about Lancaster. She was really excited because they had had a white Christmas for the first time in memory, with two inches of snow having fallen on Christmas Eve.

As Jonathan's plane circled the Raleigh airport on its final approach following the holidays, a sudden loneliness came over him. He caught himself looking to the far corners of the horizon as if searching for something or someone. Of course, he knew the object of his exploration. But Sarah was nowhere to be found. He understood that. His mind was simply playing games. As Jonathan disembarked from the plane and made his way across the tarmac and into the airport lounge, she was some two hundred thirty miles away settling into her dormitory at Georgetown.

Spring semester began inauspiciously enough. He had the same teaching schedule as he had the previous year. His department chair tried to make his professional life as easy as possible so he could maximize his research productivity to increase his chances for promotion. Jonathan was grateful to Larry, although he knew he was already on top of his research. He felt he was now a lock for tenure and promotion.

He wished his colleague would make his personal life as satisfying as his professional one. Fat chance. His best friend and the woman whose presence stirred him like no other ever had was not around. Gone. Living four hours away. He already missed Sarah. He thought back to the same time a few months earlier during autumn semester, the end of the first week. He had already seen her several times by then. Now all he had was an image of her laughing that silly laugh and smiling that seductive smile.

Her phone call that evening was just the tonic he needed. They talked for more than an hour. Sarah was several days into her internship. Mostly she had just gone through orientation, but nothing of substance yet. Jonathan noticed at once that the excitement of the moment and a self-confidence he had only seen in his classroom first semester the previous year had replaced her nervousness and insecurity of a few weeks earlier. It pleased him. She had made the right choice by taking the internship. He hoped she would not be disappointed.

"Oh, Jonathan. I'm so excited. I don't know where to begin," Sarah said.

She didn't and jumped from topic to topic as she tried to capture the kaleidoscope of images running through her brain. She hadn't been to Washington since her high school senior class trip. Everything seemed so different. Jonathan laughed at her runaway enthusiasm. After twenty minutes, Sarah appeared to slow down. Only then could he get a word in.

"Of course everything looks different, Sarah," Jonathan said. "You now have a far greater understanding of how our government works. The buildings should mean a lot more now. And besides, the city is now your home. Maybe temporarily, but probably not. I have a feeling you will be there a long time. You will come to know every inch of the place before too long. From now on, you will look at the monuments, the buildings, the streets, and all that green space differently. Just don't become jaded about the place. That would be really sad."

"Don't worry about that, Jonathan. Washington will always be exciting," Sarah assured him. "I could never become jaded about this place. It is too beautiful, too exciting, and too important for that to happen. Last night I took a walk down Pennsylvania Avenue from the capitol building to the White House. Just by myself. It brought back one of my fondest memories, President Kennedy's inauguration. More than twenty inches of snow the day before. The poem by Robert Frost, who struggled to read it in the glaring sun. JFK's inspiring speech. Remember those famous words: 'Ask not what your country can do for you; ask what you can do for your country.' The parade down Pennsylvania Avenue later that afternoon. The inaugural balls the same evening. I was glued to the television. My parents allowed me to stay home from school so I could watch it all. I loved it so much. It will be awhile before I visit President Kennedy's grave, though. I'm just not ready for it yet."

"I can understand how you feel," Jonathan said. "It still brings tears to my eyes when I visit Arlington National Cemetery. Such a waste. You know, I sometimes stop and think that if Kennedy had not been shot,

Ben might still be alive. I can't believe JFK would have escalated the war the way Johnson has. Maybe I'm wrong, but I don't think so."

"You may be right," Sarah said. "I remember reading somewhere in one of my courses at Duke—I forget which one—that Kennedy's advisors are now saying the President was trying to find a way to get us out of the war, not plunge us deeper into it. I don't know if it's true or not. But I believe them."

"I do too," Jonathan concurred. "That's another reason why the loss of Ben is so hard to take. A stupid assassination started a chain of events that led to my brother's death. Why didn't Kennedy put the bubble on top of his car? It's because he was a politician, that's why. Politicians take risks in crowds. How stupid!"

Sarah suddenly remembered that JFK had chosen to have the protective, bullet-proof bubble removed from the car so the people of Dallas could see him.

"How are your new roommates?" Jonathan asked. He wanted to steer the conversation in another direction.

"Fine," Sarah answered. "There are two of them, Melissa Richards from Brown and Jill Brooks from Penn. We seem to have a lot in common, so I think it'll work out okay. They both want to get jobs in Washington after they graduate. Wait until you see them. They're really attractive." Duke shared its internship program with three other universities. Princeton was the fourth institution.

"So that's makes three beautiful women in a dorm suite. Those poor guys in the internship program won't have a chance keeping their minds on their work," Jonathan joked.

"Jill and Melissa are much prettier than I'll ever be," Sarah said.

"I thought we already covered this ground before. Where's that self-assurance of yours?" Jonathan asked her.

"The same place it always is, Jonathan. Far, far away," she answered. They both laughed at this exchange about the relative beauty of the three woman in Suite 615.

"So when are you coming to Washington?" she wondered. Sarah was now changing the subject. The question caught Jonathan completely off-guard.

"I hadn't thought about it. Is that an invitation?" he asked.

"Come on. You knew I would invite you up. You're my best friend. You knew I would want to show off Washington and what I was doing here," Sarah said.

"Okay, maybe I did. I at least certainly hoped you would. Let me look at my schedule for the next month. I'm sure I can break away on a Friday and stay until Sunday afternoon, if that's not too long. I'll be putty in your hands. You can show off everything to me," Jonathan said.

The thought of spending a couple of days in Washington with Sarah excited him. Visions of the two of them spending time at one place after another danced in his mind and brought a smile to his face. The conversation had been a good one.

"Well, Sarah, I'll call you as soon as I know my schedule," he concluded. "You take care of yourself. And soak up everything you can."

"I will. I'll be like a sponge," Sarah promised. "Good night, Jonathan. Talk to you soon."

"Good night," Jonathan said.

The following day Jonathan checked his calendar. He was tied up with events on campus the next weekend, but he was free the following Saturday and Sunday. Off to Washington he would go then.

The next two weeks seemed to drag on very slowly as Jonathan thought about the two of them sightseeing together in the nation's capital. He couldn't wait for the time to pass. As he stood at the lectern a few days later waiting for his undergraduate class to begin, his face broke into a wide grin as he thought back to the same time just a little over a year earlier. The students watching him now would have no idea what was making him smile.

He remembered how excited he used to get at the thought that he would have an hour and a half in which to stare at Sarah as he lectured, and how impatient he grew until the moment arrived. The idea always amused him. How disciplined he must be and what skill he must have, he would mockingly say to himself, to be able to impart great words of wisdom to those impressionable intellects in front of him while slowly undressing Sarah in his mind.

In his fantasies, he removed each piece of clothing so delicately and with such tenderness, while all the time kissing and caressing her. He was in no hurry. He had the entire class period to bring her to climax. It would take him at least thirty minutes into his lecture before her body lay before him, totally exposed, each curve eliciting an excitement that yearned to be satisfied. The next hour saw him exploring every inch of her nakedness, exciting her with each stroke of his hands and kiss from his lips. Only the harsh sound from the end-of-class bell would break his trance.

He knew none of Sarah's classmates had had a clue about what raced through his mind. Neither did the current group of students in front of him. He laughed at that notion. Someday he hoped to tell Sarah about this daily classroom fantasy ritual.

Now, as Jonathan stood at the lectern, he longed for the day when he would see her again. He found it curious how his emotions traveled back and forth across the imaginary line between friendship and passion. He reflected on how certain situations pushed the friendship button, while other moments aroused his sexual appetite for her. As he thought about it some more, he came to the realization that there seemed to be a strong correlation between their needing one another because of some crisis in their lives and the predominance of friendship feelings. When things were back to normal, Jonathan's physical yearning for Sarah intensified.

That was the pattern of the previous year. His desire to make love to her probably began the first moment he saw her. It grew until it was almost out of control, consuming his thoughts day and night. Then Ben's death intervened. Suddenly, his needs for Sarah were of a different kind. A series of crises and tragedies continued to intrude for several months. It was during that period that their friendship grew significantly. It was a time when they came to realize they had something very special. They had nurtured this bond, making it so strongly intertwined that he eventually realized no future friend would ever be as close to him as Sarah had become. Some day he wanted to discover that no lover would arouse stronger feelings and emotions as his experiencing her would bring.

No crisis now confronted either of them. Things had been "normal" since about midsummer. Not surprisingly, therefore, Jonathan's passionate longing for Sarah occupied an increasingly larger part of his consciousness. There's an old saying that absence makes the heart grow fonder. Maybe so, maybe not. But Jonathan did know that only being able to visualize Sarah in his mind contributed to his sexual fantasies.

There was another factor to consider. Sarah was four months from graduating. Four months until she would no longer be a student and he her professor. Just as importantly, her being in Washington seemed to accentuate the beginning of her transition from Duke student to Duke alumna. He knew, though, the wrong spin put on their being together in Washington would cause quite a scandal back on campus. Jokingly, he could see the headlines in the student newspaper now. "Political science professor caught in bed with senior!"

The story would reveal how a sex-crazed, sleazy, lecher of a professor who preyed on young students seduced a young, poor, naive, impressionable, and beautiful senior. None of his protests would convince anyone of how really sacred their love-making had been. He would have called it "making beautiful love between two enthusiastic consenting adults who wanted more than anything else to express their intense longing for each other."

The newspaper would have reported the incident much differently, calling it a "dirty professor forcing himself on an unsuspecting senior in some vulgar manner, after, of course, getting her stoned and drunk." He was lucky, he thought to himself, that they had avoided scandal while Sarah was living on campus the past year and a half.

Now what would his current students think as he walked into class the day after the newspaper article appeared? All of them would probably have copies of the paper in their hands. The bolder ones would read it conspicuously to see what kind of response it would evoke from their professor. The boldest of the bold would ask him to autograph the paper, right next to his picture covering three column inches. The shy students would simply stare at Jonathan and wait for him to say something.

He had always thought the biggest potential embarrassment wasn't a professor caught in an affair with a student. Rather, it was to discover midway through a lecture that his fly was unzipped, knowing there was absolutely nothing he could do about it. One of the little-known secrets passed on from one generation of male faculty to the next—in the same manner that secret handshakes are passed along from fraternity brother to fraternity brother—was the technique for checking one's zipper during lecture without being observed. While the technique was well-established, no one had yet discovered a method for closing an open fly while lecturing without the students' knowledge. Future generations of male professors would hail the inventor who unlocked that secret as a hero.

The image of Jonathan's name in headlines reporting the "mother of all indiscretions" might be just as embarrassing as discovering one's fly down in the middle of lecture. He laughed an uneasy laugh, though, as he thought of an alternative student newspaper headline: "Professor caught with fly unzipped during lecture. Students rejoice!"

On second thought, however, maybe being caught in an uncompromising position with a student was actually worse than having an open fly in front of the class. One incident was a result of carelessness or a bad zipper. The other incident grew out of a conscious stupidity— using as one's brain something much lower on the male anatomy. One was the result of being an absent-minded professor. The other was a consequence of an overactive sex drive and an underactive moral code.

His humorous focus on this absurd scenario continued. He pondered how he might deal with the issue in class. Simply ignore it. Probably not. Too many copies of the student newspaper were in evidence. Deny it. Impossible. Too much evidence. He would, instead, tell his students the whole enchanting—at least to him—story about Sarah. How she mesmerized him that first day. How he fantasized about her. Yet how he had been more pure than the driven snow until after she left Duke, at least until after she left the campus proper.

He hoped his confession would evoke sighs of sympathy from the class. He was uncertain about the probable response, however. The women would likely think it a wonderful story, particularly the part about his being more pure than the driven snow. They might even be brought to tears if Jonathan was dramatic enough in his storytelling. The men would not be able to relate to it at all, having not one romantic bone in their bodies.

The ringing of the bell signaled it was time to begin the day's lecture. Jonathan put the silly thoughts about campus retribution behind him and began to speak. As he gazed around the room, he saw no one who had the potential to move his soul like Sarah had done a year earlier.

❦ ❦ ❦

The two weeks finally came and went, and Jonathan made his way north to Washington. His mind and heart were filled with anticipation as its city limits edged closer and closer. He wondered what the next two days held for him. Although sensual images of Sarah increasingly bombarded him, he knew any expectations along sexual lines were unrealistic. Rather, their visit together would be as two dear friends spending time together after one of them had recently arrived in a new city.

Jonathan made his way past Interstate 495—better known as the Beltway—the huge circle of traffic lanes surrounding the city. It had given rise to a popular phrase political commentators used to describe the attitudes of Washington insiders, particularly those who had spent their professional lives working in government or quasi-government agencies located inside the Beltway. This experience often led to their developing a "Beltway mentality." Whenever the media believed government leaders did not have their pulses on the country's mood, they made disparaging remarks about the need for politicians and bureaucrats to travel "outside the Beltway" to find out what America really thought.

Soon Jonathan found himself on the George Washington Memorial Parkway, the most beautiful road in the Washington area. The twenty-plus mile long Parkway followed a route from Mount Vernon to the Great Falls of the Potomac along the river's edge, but rose high above it once it had passed the Key Bridge. Soon Jonathan saw the sign for the bridge looming in the distance. That was his exit, which took him across the Potomac into the District and deposited him on the edge of Georgetown University.

They had agreed to meet not far from campus at the corner of M Street and Wisconsin Avenue, the center of the Georgetown section of Washington. That was the current "in" spot for the younger set of Washingtonians, where the action was. The Kennedys, who lived there prior to JFK's presidential victory, had made it famous a decade earlier. Housing prices had shot through the roof in the past few years. Trendy shops vied for commercial space. Restaurants sprung up faster than spring grass following an April shower. Visitors and locals alike crammed its streets at the end of the workday and long into the night, taking advantage of both shopping and entertainment opportunities.

One of Jonathan's favorite restaurants was right at the intersection of M and Wisconsin. Nathan's had had a huge following for about a decade. Its bar was a preferred watering hole for government workers at the end of a long day. But it was its traditional Italian cuisine that caught the fancy of the town's diners. Nathan's pasta and bread were unsurpassed in the city. And the city's best wine connoisseurs savored the wines on its list. Jonathan had eaten there often during his frequent trips to Washington. On one occasion, the waiter had jokingly told him he had set a new indoor record for the amount of bread consumed during one sitting. He had no doubt it was true.

Jonathan had suggested Sarah meet him at seven o'clock. They had reservations for dinner thirty minutes later. Since he had no classes on Friday, getting to Washington by that time posed no problem. He parked about two blocks away in a rather overpriced lot and headed on foot to the rendezvous point. He could feel his excitement grow as the time for their meeting approached.

About a hundred feet from the intersection, he saw her. Sarah was standing about midpoint between the building and the curb. Although it was still winter, the temperature was surprisingly mild—about fifty degrees. She was wearing a light tan raincoat, the kind that both male and female Washingtonians favored. He slowed at first so he could observe her persona before she became aware of his presence. Oh, how he had missed her! Seeing her then just accentuated the point. After a few moments, he couldn't contain himself, so he picked up his stride and moved quickly into her field of vision.

"Well hi, Washington woman," he said in his best semi-pompous tone. "It's great to see you."

"Hello, professor man," Sarah shot back, laughing. "It is really good to see you too, Jonathan."

With that exchange, they kissed a soft kiss and embraced the warm embrace of friendship. Their hug lasted a full twenty seconds. It felt so good holding her, he thought, even if it was the touch of friends, not lovers. As he let go, Jonathan stepped back and, examining her from head to toe with an expression that revealed exactly what he was doing, spoke. "Well, being close to the country's power structure hasn't changed you yet, Sarah, at least outwardly. What about inside that pretty head of yours?"

"I haven't noticed any difference yet," she said. "I'm just the same old me, a college senior studying in the big city."

"It's too soon for any noticeable changes. But they will start soon enough," Jonathan assured her. "A more urbane, sophisticated lens through which to see the rest of the world will replace those Duke habits and outlooks on life."

"Probably so," Sarah agreed, "but I'm in no hurry for that to happen. I like being awe-struck by all my surroundings. It's so incredible. I can't take it all in."

"How about taking in dinner then? I could use a drink or two, and some food too. We need a toast to celebrate your first three weeks in Washington," Jonathan said.

"I'm ready," Sarah answered. "I can't wait to tell you everything that's happened. So much is going on in this big city."

"Well, let's go then. Maybe our table will be ready. If not, we can probably squeeze in at the bar somewhere," Jonathan said.

Their table was waiting for them. Washingtonians eat late on Friday nights, so the dining room was only about half full. The chianti went down smoothly. They had decided to get a bottle of wine right away rather than some other drink. Jonathan thought they might even have a second bottle if dinner stretched out long enough. Good chianti was worth two bottles.

"A toast then," Jonathan said in a jovial but dramatic voice. "To our nation's capital, whose beauty and wisdom have just been enhanced by the arrival of Sarah Joan Matthews. We salute you, fair city!"

Sarah blushed, as she always did when Jonathan talked about her that way.

His voice then turned serious. "And to you, Sarah Joan Matthews. May your internship be the first step in a long, happy, and successful voyage in this enchanting city. May you find a career that excites you, challenges you, moves you, and, finally, rewards you. May your current dreams about what the future holds for you fall far short of what reality eventually brings you."

With that, he raised his glass, the signal for Sarah to do likewise.

They both sipped a little wine, each looking into the other's eyes. Again, it was not the look of lovers, but of friends.

It was Sarah's turn. "And to our friendship. How much it sustained me in the last year. May it continue to grow, and may it be strong enough for us to help one another as we each draw from it in the years ahead."

"To our wonderful friendship," came Jonathan's soft response.

Not spoken in the toast was Jonathan's desire that Sarah find someone in Washington with whom to share all those dreams. If truth be told, he did not want her to find someone in the nation's capital, or anywhere else for that matter, who would move her to such feelings.

"I've missed you, Jonathan," Sarah replied. "There have been so many times in the short period I've been here that I just wanted to be able to ring you and share something."

"What stopped you? They have this new invention now. It's called long-distance telephone service. Perhaps you haven't heard of it yet," Jonathan joked.

"I know. I know. I could call you," Sarah said. "But somehow that seems so much more difficult now that we aren't in the same city. I will say I have come to value our friendship even more now that we aren't in the same place. It's kind of like a security blanket or a savings account I know I can tap if I run into a problem. That makes me feel more at ease, more secure."

"Good. I want you to feel that way," Jonathan said.

"Well, I do," Sarah assured him. "The other thing that has happened is that, when I just now saw you for the first time in weeks, we picked up right where we left off the last time we were together. It's as if we have never been apart. I like that."

"Me too," Jonathan agreed. "That shows how strong our friendship is. Time and distance are not going to chip away at it. Quite the contrary. It now has a momentum of its own. It's just going to grow and grow. Nothing will stop it, I'm afraid. So I guess you're stuck with me as a friend."

"I guess so. I could think of worse things to befall a helpless person," she said and laughed.

"So tell me all about what's happening," Jonathan said.

With that cue, Sarah proceeded to share details of her first several weeks in Washington with Jonathan. Her initial schedule was diverse enough to enable her to sample much of what official Washington had to offer. She had been to the capitol building and the several office buildings for members of Congress, the White House and the Executive Office Building across the street, the Supreme Court, the National Archives, many of the buildings housing the various Cabinet departments, and assorted popular monuments.

Interspersed with her sightseeing tours were daily seminars detailing the inner workings of the city. She was in the final stages of the orientation phase of the internship. The following week would find her beginning work in the afternoons somewhere within the government. The particular assignment had not been determined yet. There was much to absorb and Sarah was a huge sponge. Her excitement shone through loudly and clearly as she described her initial experiences. Jonathan enjoyed listening to her. Although he thought of her primarily as friend and lover, he had never ceased to view her as his student and himself as her mentor. Throughout all of their sadness and all of their crises the previous year, he had always managed to play the role of teacher when it was appropriate. He assumed that position now as he listened to adventurous tales flowing from her tongue.

Dinner was wonderful. Sarah didn't stop talking about her experiences until the entrées arrived. At that point, she turned the conversation toward Jonathan, starting with the same question she had asked early in the previous spring semester. "So tell me, Jonathan. Are there any pretty girls in your classes this semester? Any who have turned your head?"

"About forty of them. No, just kidding," Jonathan said. "Remember, I don't notice that stuff. I told you that once before. I'm all business when I walk into the classroom." He laughed to himself at the memory of how he had juggled delicious images of Sarah with profound thoughts of world politics as he stood in front of the lectern a year earlier. "I suppose there are several whom one might call attractive. But they look so young for a man of my age," he mockingly said.

"You're only twenty-eight now," Sarah reminded him. "Still young enough to think about such things."

"Yeah, but too old to do anything about it. I guess I'm doomed to bachelorhood," he said.

"Come now. You're much too handsome not to sweep some girl off her feet. I know every friend of mine who had you for a class developed a serious case of the infatuations. You had to have known that," Sarah said.

"I didn't know anything of the kind. I didn't even have one clue," Jonathan answered.

"I simply don't believe you, Dr. Jonathan Hawthorne. If you had enough smarts to get a Ph.D., you must have enough brains to figure out every female student in your course usually falls for you. They're just waiting for you to sweep them off their feet."

Jonathan took the boldest step yet in their relationship, at least since he had kissed her on the beach at Avon the previous summer. "But you didn't—fall in love with me, I mean—when you were in my class. So how can you say that every female did?"

Sarah was now laughing. But she was also blushing. A bright crimson color overtook her face. "Our situation was different. We were friends before I had a chance to fall in love with you."

"What's the matter? Can't friends fall in love?" Jonathan was treading on new and dangerous ground. He knew that. That's why he was acting as if it was a silly discussion without any serious merit to it. But he also was challenging Sarah. He wanted her to address the question of falling in love with him, even if he had raised the subject in a most circuitous fashion. He at least wanted her to ponder the possibility. He wasn't prepared for a full-blown discussion of the topic, however. He laughed to himself as he thought he hadn't yet consumed enough wine for that conversation.

"Of course friends can fall in love. But when that happens, it does so after the friendship has been established. Not simultaneously," Sarah said.

Jonathan suddenly felt very uncomfortable. That always happened when he didn't quite know where the discussion might lead. This was one of those occasions. It was time to change its direction. "Tell me, Sarah. You were really kidding me when you said many Duke women thought me interesting, weren't you?" he asked.

"I didn't use the phrase, 'thought you interesting,'" Sarah corrected him. "I said they had developed a serious case of the infatuations. They had fallen for you. That's a heck of a lot different than they simply found you interesting. I find Johnny Carson interesting, but I haven't fallen for him. Of course I was serious. The women line up the night before registration to make certain they get into your class. Those who are shut out can be found weeping uncontrollably or throwing themselves in front of speeding trucks."

Sarah was starting to have some fun with Jonathan. Her last comment made his face flush, which, in turn, brought that sweet little smile to the corners of her mouth. How he loved that smile.

"The wine has obviously gotten to you," Jonathan joked. "Now I won't be able to go into class without blushing. I'll probably have to keep my sport coat buttoned because of all the illicit thoughts I might have." Jonathan was now having some fun with her. They both broke out in loud laughter. Any serious discussion of the topic had just ended. "Oh, it's so good to see you. I'm glad things are going well here."

"Thanks, but you haven't really told me any news about Duke," Sarah said. "I miss it so much."

"Duke is fine. I'm fine. Everyone's fine. Actually, everything is going rather well. Nothing of any consequence has happened on campus, except for the public seduction of a male English professor by a crazed female student and the beheading of the captain of the cheerleading squad by the captain of the basketball team." Jonathan paused for a moment as a sly grin came over his face.

"Just kidding" he continued. "Everything is running smoothly. Our one month of winter is about to end. The Duke Gardens will be aglow in color before we know it."

"And the Duke coeds will soon be out in full force, sunbathing nearby in their skimpy outfits," Sarah reminded him.

"Oh, I forgot about that. Wait a minute. I never saw you sunbathing on campus in a skimpy outfit. Or any other outfit for that matter," he observed.

"There's a time and place for everything. I sunbathe at the beach. I study on campus. Simple as that. One shouldn't really mix them," Sarah theorized.

"Why not? Did you follow this rule religiously?" Jonathan asked.

"Of course I did," Sarah responded in mock indignation. "Actually, no. Not all the time. But I really did try to. I must admit it was tough sometimes those first few really warm days of spring when everyone was outside, either throwing Frisbees around or lying fully exposed to the sun in some kind of ancient pagan ritual of sun worship. But I was well-disciplined, at least most of the time. Besides, it took me a lot longer than most students to get my work done, so I didn't have as much time to sunbathe as the other females on campus did."

"I'm still debating on whether or not it would be okay for a professor to sunbathe—on campus, I mean," Jonathan said. "By the Duke Gardens or the lake on the golf course."

Jonathan's revelation that he might consider sunbathing on campus clearly amused Sarah. "I can just see the campus headlines now," she said. "'Professor in skimpy bathing suit attacked by a dozen demented female students gone berserk. Professor saved by fast action of the campus police, who threw a huge fish net over the students and an equally large blanket over the professor while ushering him out of the sun.' What a scandal that would be!"

Jonathan joined the spirit of the conversation. He remembered his earlier thoughts about the headlines detailing his being caught in bed with Sarah on this trip, or having his fly unzipped during his next lecture. "You're quite funny, Sarah. But I'm really serious. Do you think I could sunbathe on campus if I was discrete about it?"

"Sure, 'discrete about it.' Are you kidding? The campus horns would sound in unison the moment you emerged from your office or car wearing your bathing suit. The campus chimes would reverberate as they never had before. A horsewoman would blare the alarm, riding faster than Paul Revere sounding his call of the British coming. 'One if by land' would signal you're off to the Duke Gardens. 'Two if by sea' would mean you're heading for the lake. The dorms would immediately empty in hot pursuit as the rider made her way across campus. Sympathetic faculty might even cancel classes. Reporters would appear shortly thereafter, fighting with one another to scoop the story. The nightly TV news would make it their lead report."

"My, you have a wildly vivid imagination," Jonathan said. "I knew you were smart, but three weeks in this town have caused you great difficulty with reality. It's a Washington disease, by the way. But it usually takes longer to materialize. Most of the politicians have it. It's called 'reality impairment.' The cure? There is no cure. The treatment? Simple. Get out of town for two weeks. It works every time. The symptoms reappear soon after returning to Washington, however. Unfortunately, the government has not yet seen fit to allocate research dollars to find a cure, probably because no politician's loved one has died from the disease yet. Perhaps medical science will deliver a major breakthrough someday. Doubtful though. It's so sad." Jonathan clearly also had a flare for the absurd. Both of them broke out giggling.

"Oh, Jonathan, I haven't laughed so hard in I don't know when," Sarah said.

"Me either," Jonathan agreed. "This has been good, really good. Actually, I was semi-serious. Do you think I could join the coeds by the Duke Gardens when the warm weather hits? Since I'm on top of my research, I'll have the time."

"Why don't you just stick to the golf course?" Sarah advised "Then you might get good enough to play with me this summer."

"Good enough. I'll bet I'm good enough now," he asserted.

"Perhaps, and perhaps not," Sarah teased. "We shall see soon enough. Is it a deal? We'll play golf this summer if I make it back to Duke for a visit?"

"It's a deal," Jonathan said. He didn't know when he had enjoyed himself so much. It had been a long, long time. He was seeing a side of Sarah he really hadn't noticed before. Too much sadness had intruded on their relationship during the previous year. Now things were different. They were normal. He liked normal. Normal meant a rather humorous Sarah. He found himself being seduced deeper and deeper into that wonderful state of total infatuation with the woman in front of him.

And Sarah?

. . . *What a marvelous evening we spent together soon after I had gone off to my Washington internship my senior year. Remember, you came up for the weekend a few weeks after I had arrived? We met in Georgetown and had dinner at Nathan's. I never laughed so hard in my entire life. I knew you to be funny, but after that evening I was convinced there was not a funnier man alive than Jonathan B. Hawthorne.*

Of course, I now know it was another big step toward my seeing you in a completely different light. Unfortunately, my conscious self missed that step completely, at least then. But no matter. Let me go on. I have come to understand how important humor is in sustaining a relationship. If both individuals are laughing at something else, they don't have time or the inclination to fight with one another, become bored with one another, or even laugh at one another. I now know that, my sweet Jonathan. But I didn't know it then, sad to say.

It was also the first time the subject of student and professor falling in love came up. I guess I was responsible for the topic, because I asked you if you had any pretty students in class. I liked asking you questions like that. It forced you, us, to talk about male-female relationships, even if obtusely. It also made your face turn red.

I remember conjuring up a rather silly scenario of campus females going wild at the thought of you sunbathing somewhere nearby. Your face turned crimson. I liked seeing you blush then, and I like seeing it now. Of course, now I like it to happen when we're in bed together and I ask you if you'd like me to engage in some rather scandalous and delicious behavior that sends you climbing the wall while squealing in absolute and uncontrollable delight. Interestingly, your blushing never seems to lead you to say no to my suggestion. I think you know exactly what I'm talking about, my love.

Your visit was also important for another reason. It showed me exactly what kind of friendship we had and how deep it was. When I first saw you walking briskly toward me as I stood on the most famous corner in Georgetown, it seemed no different than when we met each Sunday a few months earlier during that Herculean research schedule we followed. We picked up right where we had left off a few weeks before.

Prior to that time, I had told you I had come never to doubt the permanence of our friendship. But you know little old insecure me. I can find the smallest of clouds in a totally blue sky. I worried as I lay in bed over the Christmas holidays right before starting the internship whether you really were going to be my friend for life. I know, you had told me that you would always be my friend. But I couldn't help it, I guess. The moment I saw you and held you, I knew better. By the time I had laughed with you the entire evening, I had forgotten my earlier fears.

The rest of the weekend was wonderful too, particularly our walk in the winter solitude of Bethany Beach. But I shall never forget our first dinner at Nathan's.

The meal was soon coming to a close. The second bottle of wine had been an easy decision, although nearly half of it remained. No matter. Jonathan hid it under the table away from the waiter's watchful eye. The empty bottle would soon grace Sarah's dormitory room for the remainder of the semester. She later packed it away among her most treasured possessions.

Still later, Jonathan hoped it would once again become a bottle of wine, if only for an evening. He fantasized that Sarah poured the contents of a rather expensive bottle into it on the night they made love for the first time as husband and wife. They began to drink the wine before Jonathan reached for her that evening. They sipped its final drops as they basked in the warm afterglow of love totally fulfilled.

Jonathan imagined he would discover her switch of wine bottles that future fateful night and would identify its origin without any prodding from Sarah. She would be pleased, he hoped. How she loved his sentimental nature, she would tell him. The empty bottle would occupy a special place on the fireplace mantel of their new home, its secret closely guarded by both of them. How he wanted those things to happen.

Jonathan walked Sarah back to her Georgetown dormitory, a journey of about twenty minutes. The fresh air felt good. As they reached the entrance, they hugged their usual hug and kissed their usual kiss—with one exception. It seemed to him that each time they parted, the hug and kiss became a little longer than the previous time. Maybe he was imagining things, but he thought not. Perhaps he would put a stopwatch to it, he mused, if only he could find some subtle way to do so. He grinned as he thought about the possibilities. He wasn't quite certain how he could hide a stopwatch or even use one if both hands were engaged, however. And the idea of counting "one-thousand-one, one-thousand-two, one-thousand-three" when they were kissing seemed to have a rather impersonal ring to it.

They agreed to meet early the next morning—very early, Sarah kidded him when he showed up at eight o'clock. He simply wanted to maximize their time together, he had responded when she raised a question about the hour. She suggested that since both of them now knew Washington, they drive around for about an hour until they were hungry, then head east toward Annapolis, thirty minutes away, for breakfast. If they were in the mood, they might then cross the Chesapeake Bay Bridge—Bay Bridge the locals simply called it—about ten miles east of Annapolis, perhaps even going as far as the Delaware beaches hugging the Atlantic Ocean, at least another hour and a half eastward. He couldn't wait for the next day to dawn.

Jonathan was glad he had walked Sarah back to her dorm rather than driven her. He needed the extra time in the winter air returning to where he had parked his car. As he slowly made his way back to the center of Georgetown, he reflected on the entire evening. Helped by an overabundance of wine, Jonathan smiled the entire trip. It had been a fantastic evening. They were so comfortable with one another. Until that moment, of course, when Sarah started to explain that she hadn't had time to fall in love with him because she had been too busy becoming his best friend. She had joshed him with tales of coeds wanting to throw themselves at his feet. But he knew she was kidding— about the hordes of Duke women and about her own situation. At least he thought so. Being only human, he told himself, it would be fun, at least for a little while, to have lots of women desire him. Too much of a good thing, though, would eventually wear out its welcome. Unless, of course, that good thing was Sarah.

Jonathan stayed at a small, intimate hotel up Connecticut Avenue just beyond the Washington Hilton, the rather curved edifice about a half-mile north of Dupont Circle. He had discovered the Normandy Inn a few years earlier. In a couple of years, the Democratic Party presidential candidate George McGovern would use its entire sixth floor of ten rooms during his unsuccessful bid to unseat President Nixon in 1972. An Irish chain owned it, and the hostess had come from Paris a few years earlier.

Madame Jeannette Ballard was a lovely lady of about sixty years old who tended to "mother" her regular guests. Although Jonathan did not get to Washington as often as he had in the past, she would still remember him, he was quite certain. They had befriended each other a few years earlier when he made periodic trips from Penn State. She even offered her personal driver from time to time to take him toward the center of town as far as Dupont Circle, if the chauffeur was free.

Madame Ballard would not be there when he checked in that night, however. She only worked during the day. But he knew she would have looked after him, so his room would be one of the better ones. He was not disappointed when the night clerk, a sweet old man by the name of Albert who had held his job for more than twenty years, gave him his room key. Sleep came quickly that night.

Early Saturday morning was the perfect time for sightseeing, particularly since most government workers were still in bed in the suburbs. Sarah's and Jonathan's travel took them quickly around the more famous tourist spots. It would be enough. All he needed was a brisk patriotic fix, and one hour would be quite sufficient.

Soon they were off to Annapolis. They ate breakfast at The Crab Pot, a lovely, intimate place overlooking the dock, with the Naval Academy just across the waterway. The selection was unplanned. Sarah worried as they took their seats, she later told Jonathan, that the restaurant's location—within sight of a major service academy—would put him into a grieving mood about Ben because of his West Point background. The connection didn't seem to affect him, though, for which she was grateful.

They spent the better part of the morning walking around Maryland's capital city. Time had done the old place justice. The red brick buildings and the narrow streets combined to give it a charm unmatched by any other capital in the country. Throw in the countless water inlets and the nearby bay itself, and one might be moved to say there was no city more beautiful than Annapolis. It was a temptation both Sarah and Jonathan might easily have succumbed to as they absorbed the sights, smells, and sounds of the city. Around midday, they decided to move on to the treasures of what was popularly known as the Eastern Shore.

The Shore encompassed the parts of Maryland and Virginia between the east coastline of the Chesapeake Bay and the Atlantic Ocean some sixty or so miles due east. Some even included the southern part of Delaware. All of this land was called the Eastern Shore, although technically, professional geographers would have defined the eastern shore of the Chesapeake Bay as only the sliver of land immediately adjacent to the bay's eastern edge. For more than a century, its inhabitants had ignored this formal definition and were proud to be called residents of the Eastern Shore. The Chesapeake Bay Bridge connected this landmass to the rest of Maryland. Built only a decade earlier, the Bay Bridge had opened up the Eastern Shore as well as the entire Delmarva Peninsula—the territory comprising the remaining parts of Delaware as well as the eastern sections of both Maryland and Virginia—to Washingtonians.

The bridge stretched for almost five miles across the bay. It reached its huge height, necessary for the passage of ships, somewhere near the middle of the span. Over the years, the U.S. Coast Guard had come to expect that from time to time a driver would panic at some point while crossing the bridge, come to a complete stop, and cover both eyes in a self-induced catatonic state. Authorities would then have to dispatch a professional driver to take over the wheel and transport the person safely to the other side.

Jonathan had been across the bridge many times. He always watched the reaction of first-timers, though, because he knew fear was likely to be a part of the set of experiences they encountered during their initial trip. But Sarah did not disappoint him. The height didn't bother her as she perused the beauty of the Chesapeake Bay. Soon after they completed the crossing, he pulled off to the right.

"Sarah, there is a crusty old restaurant over there that's terrific. See it? Seafood and more seafood. And your first taste of Eastern Shore crab. What about it? Did you work up an appetite walking around Annapolis?" Jonathan asked.

"I sure did. I'm game. Let's do it," Sarah said.

Fisherman's Inn was as advertised. Still unspoiled despite the encroaching civilization from across the Bay Bridge since the span's opening, the restaurant catered to local fisherman and a handful of tourists who had probably discovered it on a whim. Jonathan had stumbled onto it about five years earlier on his way to Ocean City, Maryland, a beach resort some eighty miles away just south of the Delaware border. He never passed the spot without stopping for a bite to eat. The crab soup was a specialty the regulars rarely ignored. Jonathan and Sarah ordered it as well and decided to share a seafood platter between them. He had suggested that they sample the restaurant's seafood wares for future reference. An hour later they left the Fisherman's Inn, their stomachs happy and content like clams at high tide.

They decided to push forward until they reached the ocean about ninety minutes away. The next stop, though, occurred at midpoint in their journey. Intrigued by a sign at the entrance to the first town that appeared about five minutes after they had crossed the Maryland border into Delaware, they couldn't resist pausing awhile for a cup of coffee. A sign reading "Bridgeville: if you lived here you would be home now" had announced the quaint little place to weary travelers for decades. If its intent was to entice passers-through to stop, it certainly worked that time. Jonathan would not be sorry for their decision.

Swain's, the only restaurant for miles, was along the main street in the center of town. An old-fashioned place, it served traditional meals to locals and visitors alike. There were no fake mashed potatoes at Swain's. Only the real thing! As Jonathan and Sarah sat down at a window table, it suddenly occurred to him that he had read something a while back about Bridgeville's successful coping with the State of Delaware's implementation of the Supreme Court's school desegregation decision in *Brown v. Board of Education* more than a decade earlier. The issue piqued his interest, so he put the question about the town's acceptance of the Court's decision to their waitress.

Karen, as her nametag so identified her, was well-suited for the role. Then a senior at Bridgeville High School, she had entered first grade in 1956 in a school that was off-limits to blacks, despite the Supreme Court ruling two years earlier. She had watched in sixth grade as the first black student appeared. There was only one in the entire district that first year, as the county black secondary school and the local black elementary school still serviced the bulk of the area's school-age blacks. More trickled in over the next few years. And, as Karen arrived for her sophomore year, she discovered that the state had finally closed the black schools and totally integrated her school system, as well as all the others throughout the state. Enrollment suddenly doubled, split evenly between the two races. Although it was slow in coming, Delaware finally found itself in compliance with *Brown v. Board of Education*.

"So, Karen. I understand your school is totally integrated now. How's it working?" Jonathan asked her.

"Fine. Things are going so well that I honestly don't know what the big deal was all about earlier, to tell you the truth," Karen explained. "You know, all that fuss about trying to keep black and white students apart. Except for the fact that I have an extraordinary memory, I probably would think that we had always been integrated. We even elected a black girl to be class secretary this year. And the rest of the town is dealing well with the implications of the recent Voting Rights and Civil Rights Acts too. Look around town for yourself, if you have time, before you head out for the beach. You'll see what I'm talking about."

Jonathan was impressed. "So, I bet you learned about these pieces of legislation in high school."

"You bet. We have this great teacher in our problems of democracy class this year. Just finished his master's degree in political science and wants to return to graduate school full-time to get a Ph.D. Taught us all about the civil rights movement, from *Plessy v. Ferguson* in 1896—you know, the Supreme Court decision that allowed separate facilities as long as they were equal—to the efforts of Martin Luther King, Jr. He's great. Our teacher, I mean. The entire class now has a social conscience because of him. By the way, why are you interested? Are you a teacher? You must be. I can tell," she said with a slight smile.

Jonathan laughed. "Sort of. I'm a professor at Duke University," he told her. "I teach political science, although my specialty is international politics. But I'm interested in the civil rights movement too."

"And I'm one of his students," Sarah devilishly chimed in.

The waitress was surprised by her revelation but hid her astonishment well. Sarah was amused by the entire exchange, deciding to move slightly closer to Jonathan, thus implying a somewhat more naughty relationship than the usual one between professor and student.

"Well, Karen, I hope that teacher of yours does pursue a Ph.D. We need good college teachers as well," Jonathan said.

"I plan on getting a Ph.D. too, Mr. . . . I'm sorry, what's your name?" Karen asked.

"Hawthorne. Jonathan Hawthorne," he said. "That's great. You ought to look at Duke. We have a great political science department."

"Well, I'm more interested in English, particularly creative writing, actually," Karen explained. "Civil rights is really kind of a hobby with me, particularly since my POD class. But I'll tell you what, Professor Hawthorne. If I end up at Duke, I'll enroll in one of your government courses, even if I'm in the English department and your course is in international politics. Maybe you'll mention civil rights once in a while, okay?"

Jonathan was clearly enjoying the exchange. "Sure, on one condition. You come up after class the first day and remind me you were our waitress in Bridgeville, Delaware, spring of 1969. Is it a deal?"

"A deal. I may just surprise you," Karen replied.

And so Karen did, a decade later, keeping her promise as she pursued her dream of graduate study in English at Duke. Jonathan remembered her as she made her way to the podium after the first class but before she had a chance to reveal her identity and remind him of their earlier encounter.

After they finished their coffee, Jonathan and Sarah pushed on to Bethany Beach on the east coast of the Delaware shore. He selected it because it was rather small and isolated. Its sandy beaches were the finest on the entire Delmarva Peninsula. Sarah applauded his choice. Twenty years later, high-rise condos and traffic jams littered Bethany, as the local population called the place. But in 1969, one could barely see signs of the pending bulldozer invasion.

With the winter temperature hovering around fifty degrees, Sarah and Jonathan set out on a walk not unlike the one they took on their last night on the Outer Banks some five months earlier. Only this time they walked in broad daylight. Two hours later, they had traveled almost to Fenwick Island, just north of the Maryland border and about four miles to the south of Bethany. The beach was deserted except for a few hardy birds who had all the small sea creatures to themselves.

Winter was not very harsh on the Delaware coast, except for an occasional storm. There had been a major northeaster, as they're called, in March of 1962. That violent storm came out of New England without warning and pounded the Delaware coastline until damage ran into the millions of dollars. But repairs had been complete for several years now, and the great storm of 1962 was fast becoming a distant memory. Looking out at the calm surf on this journey, Jonathan found it hard to visualize that fateful day some seven years earlier when residents feared for their lives.

Their talk moved among several subjects, from the humorous to the serious, from about nothing in general to where their professional lives might take them. They said little if anything about what their personal futures might hold. Both were in what might be called a transition phase. Sarah, knowing nothing of Jonathan's affections for her, was not contemplating any serious relationship, or frivolous one for that matter, with anyone in the coming months. Jonathan was lost in his usual place, somewhere between the reality of his code of ethics regarding student-faculty relationships and his deep desire for Sarah. He hoped that, when she graduated in three months, this self-imposed albatross would finally fall from around his neck.

How Jonathan loved walking on the beach with Sarah. He wanted some day to make love to her while lying on the sand under the moonlight. Some warmer night. They retraced their route back to Bethany Beach, moving at a somewhat faster pace than they had kept. Hunger pains began to appear as they approached the exit point from the beach. They had walked many, many miles that day.

"Shall we have dinner before we start back?" I know this great place about ten miles north of here in Lewes. You should see Lewes anyhow before we leave. It's an old town with lots of history," Jonathan suggested.

"If I hang around you much longer, I'll have to double my exercise routine," Sarah said jokingly. "Just kidding. Sure. I'm ready to eat again. I haven't had my fill of seafood yet."

Off to Lewes they went, passing the most popular Delaware beach, Rehoboth Beach, just to its south. Jonathan gave Sarah a history lesson about the area as they made their way past several historic sites. Now it was time to eat.

"Angler's is absolutely the best restaurant around here," he told Sarah. "I've probably eaten there ten times. A must dish is their crab imperial, their signature entrée. It's like a crab cake, though more spicy. I've never ordered anything else."

The crab imperial was as good as advertised. Sarah and Jonathan washed it down with a few bottles of beer as they watched the solitude both inside and outside the restaurant. Late January wasn't quite high season, Jonathan joked to Sarah. Hell, it didn't even qualify as low season. It was no season, so to speak.

"I like it deserted. It's perfect, Jonathan. I'm glad we stopped here," Sarah said.

"Me too," Jonathan agreed. "But we'd better be going so we can get back in time to enjoy a drink somewhere."

"You're really socializing me into the world of alcohol, Professor Hawthorne. What would the campus fathers say?" The beer had put Sarah in a good mood.

"They would approve of all the individual attention I'm giving you, Miss Matthews. I'm not certain about the alcohol, though. And the Duke catalog doesn't say anything about field trips, but here we are. See what you get for all those tuition dollars?" Jonathan joked.

"Thank you for the personalized program of study, Dr. Hawthorne. I think I'll nominate you for Duke professor of the year," Sarah said.

"The problem is that you would have to state your reasons. I'd like to see the faces of the judges when they read your letter of nomination," Jonathan teased her.

Both of them enjoyed each other's company. As they walked to the car, the sun was setting in the west. Its reflection on the water brought a smile to both of their faces. A little over two hours later, they were back in Georgetown searching for a cozy bar. They found one, O'Shannon's, an Irish pub just off Wisconsin Avenue. A few drinks later, Jonathan was saying good-bye to Sarah at her dorm entrance. In less than a day, he would return to Duke.

Sunday brought only brunch at Second Watch, a trendy restaurant in the area. At two o'clock he bid his farewell. "It's been a good weekend, Sarah. Thanks for inviting me up."

"My pleasure, as they say," Sarah said. "Thanks for showing me a good time. I liked getting away from the world of my internship to more familiar grounds. You're those familiar grounds. It was a great two and a half days. Think about coming back sometime later this spring. It'll be warmer then, although it still won't be skimpy bathing suit weather yet," Sarah said. She smiled, joined by Jonathan as he made his way to the car.

He headed south through the beautiful countryside of rural

Virginia and on to North Carolina. Back to tobacco country, where the warmth of early spring beckoned him. But his heart was already warm, made so by his time with Sarah. Memories of their time together would sustain him for a few weeks. And he would return in a few months to once again enjoy whatever came his way in their relationship. But his heart felt a twinge of loneliness as well. Already he missed her.

~ 17 ~

Devastating Revelation

Second semester rolled on toward spring. Jonathan's classes, not much of a challenge this time around, were going smoothly. He now required much less preparation time, which allowed him to focus on his new research agenda. He was content to do so. The need for a social life in Durham wasn't pressing. Perhaps if Sarah had never entered his life, he would have a heavier social life—hell, he told himself, he might have a social life, period. Even though theirs was only a friendship, it had intruded on Jonathan's desire to become involved with another woman. His fantasies of her added to his lack of interest in pursuing an active social life as well. The result was predictable. Jonathan's love life was nonexistent, zero, and going nowhere.

It was just as well, he thought. Now was not the time for serious involvement. Although if Sarah was to beckon, he would jump at the opportunity. But his lack of attachment to anyone allowed him to maximize his work time. He also planned to visit his parents during spring break in early March. The trip was important. It had been almost a year since Ben's death. While his parents were coping about as well as could be expected, the loss of their youngest son was still difficult for them. Jonathan knew they really looked forward to his visits. While he might have preferred a warm water port, he felt his parents would be terribly disappointed if he did not return home for the week.

Colorado in mid-March was a special time. The sun moved higher and higher in the sky, expanding the path of its warmth to those who ventured outside. In the higher elevations of the Rockies, one could receive the same therapeutic feeling, as well as a similar major league sunburn, as he or she could get on an August day at the beach. The vacation resorts called it spring skiing. Skiers removed layers of ski clothes and applied suntan lotion in anticipation of the warm rays of the sun that replaced the cold chill of a gray January day before they set off for the slopes. Nothing was better than a windless, sunny March day at ten thousand feet in twenty inches of new snow, all powder.

Colorado Springs, at the foot of the Rockies, also enjoyed the encroaching warmth at that time of year. Golfers quickly refurbished their games, which were rusty from the winter hiatus. Hikers were eager to return to their favorite mountain trails nearby. Restaurants readied their outdoor patios in anticipation of diners enjoying a meal under the sunlight or moonlight.

Jonathan carefully balanced his time between his parents and the mountains. He went skiing west of Denver on two different occasions but returned home each day in time for dinner. On a particularly sunny day with the temperature pushing seventy degrees, he and his father toured the Eisenhower Golf Course on the grounds of the Air Force Academy. The three of them ate dinner one night in the dining room of the Antler's Hotel, a downtown landmark.

His parents were happy to see him. They asked lots of questions about his year. His mom, who did not yet know of his infatuation with Sarah, quizzed him about his social life. Whether or not Jonathan had a special girlfriend yet was the direction her convoluted questioning seemed to be going.

It was at that moment that he brought up his visit to Washington to see Sarah. "I haven't really had any dates this year, Mom. But guess what. I did visit a woman in Washington one weekend."

His mother's ears perked up and her eyes widened as she waited for Jonathan's explanation. He had the feeling his dad knew precisely who the woman was. "Well, Mom, you remember my student friend I talked to on occasion when I was home before. She is spending this semester in D.C. as part of a Duke political internship program. She invited me up for a weekend, so I went. What a great time!"

Jonathan phrased his announcement in such a way so as to conjure up all kinds of wild thoughts in his mother's mind. His strategy was successful. "You spent a weekend with a student, of the opposite sex, out of town?" she asked. His mother's voice clearly revealed much surprise and a lot of indignation. "I don't believe it. You could get in trouble, Jonathan. What if you lost your job because someone found out?"

"Mom, Mom, Mom. It's not what you think," Jonathan explained. "Not exactly, anyhow." He then proceeded to tell his mother much of the story of his trip, starting with the fact that he had stayed at a hotel far-removed from her dorm. He didn't relate to her quite as much as he had revealed to his father earlier, however. He didn't think she was ready for all the details, most especially his vivid fantasies of Sarah. His mother's reaction convinced him he was right. She would never be ready for even an outline of his fantasies, let alone the details.

"You see, Mom," he continued, "Sarah has become an important person in my life. I turned to her when Ben died, and she was there for me. No one else at Duke could have comforted me the way she did during that awful period. Then I later helped her when her boyfriend dropped her without any warning. Consoling her was actually good for me, because it took my mind off Ben and turned it on to someone else's problems. And besides, she is only seven years younger than I am. She's twenty-one, an adult, and about to graduate from Duke. And, I must emphasize again, we are only friends."

"What if she suggested your relationship move into, shall we say, friendlier directions? What would you do then?" his mother wanted to know. She was taking the initiative now, clearly on the attack in her quest to direct Jonathan's life toward marriage and, of course, children.

"First of all, Mom, nothing will happen as long as she is still a student. Once she graduates . . . good question. I could fall madly in love with her very quickly, I think, without much effort. But right now it's our friendship that's so important to me. And besides, I don't want to do anything to jeopardize it. I'm not certain what I would do if she hinted at anything else." With a sly grin, Jonathan continued, "But I sure would like the opportunity to find out."

His mother seemed satisfied. His father, meanwhile, knew exactly what was going through Jonathan's mind. His wry look suggested amusement at the exchange between mother and son.

Both parents nodded toward one another later that evening when Sarah called. Jonathan just smiled and took the call in the adjoining room. An hour later he emerged, and without additional comment went to bed. The next day he would return for the final weeks of the semester. More importantly, he would soon make his way once again to Washington. He and Sarah had confirmed the arrangements during their phone conversation.

One thing did trouble Jonathan, though, as he lay in bed that last evening in Colorado. Sarah had indicated she had some news for him. But she didn't want to reveal it until she saw him face to face. He wondered what it was.

The trip back to Durham was long but uneventful. Longer still were the next six days as he waited for Saturday. He would then be on his way toward Washington. Unlike his previous trip when he arrived in D.C. on Friday, he had a command performance on campus that evening. It was awards night, when the administration recognized students who had made special achievements. Faculty were expected, actually required, to attend both the ceremony and the reception that followed. Political science faculty mingled with award winners who were department majors. It was a rather important evening.

In other years, Jonathan would engage in deep conversation with students he knew. Not this year, however. His departure for Washington was but twelve hours away. As always when he was about to see Sarah, his level of excitement climbed as he thought about what awaited him. This time, though, it was mixed with some apprehension because of her teaser about some important news. He went through the motions that evening, counting the hours before he would see her again.

Sleep did not come easy that night. In fact, if truth be told, it hardly came at all. He tossed and turned most of the evening as a montage of images floated continuously across his mind. Some good, some bad. The clock seemed to move so slowly, as if each glance from Jonathan impeded its journey toward daybreak. But at last seven o'clock arrived, and Jonathan was up and showering, getting ready for the long drive north.

By noon he had crossed the Key Bridge and was heading for Sarah's dorm. She was intrigued about his description of a great Cuban restaurant just off Connecticut Avenue up Columbia Road, so they had agreed to try it for lunch. Jonathan, who had eaten no breakfast, could smell the black beans and rice as they made their way across town toward The Omega.

They settled at a table in the back of the restaurant. Sarah seemed pleased with his choice. Both of them were starved, so they shared a shrimp appetizer complete with savory island spices, followed by a Caribbean-style chicken dish with a side order of black beans and rice.

Sarah had much to tell Jonathan, so lunch would extend into mid-afternoon. While he was most interested in "her news" for him, she obviously was in no hurry with any bulletin important enough to be labeled as special. Like it or not—and he clearly did not—he would have to wait until she was good and ready to announce the big news.

Her initial conversation focused on her current internship responsibilities. When Jonathan was in Washington earlier, Sarah was just about to conclude the orientation phase of the program and embark on some actual work somewhere in the government. She had decided to join a Department of the Interior task force dealing with Great Lakes pollution, especially in Lake Erie. It was part of the department's responsibility to address environmental issues within the sovereign waters of the United States. Lake Erie was a good place to start, as many industries in and around Cleveland were discharging thousands of gallons of polluted matter daily into the lake via the Cuyahoga and other rivers that emptied into it.

Lake Erie's fish had recently lost their battle with industry for use of the lake. Their deaths signaled the need for intervention by the federal government. The Department of the Interior had assumed responsibility as the government's point agency in spearheading the effort. So Sarah was able to get in on the ground floor of this new endeavor. At that time, the department focused its attention on documenting the extent of the problem and figuring out how to clean up the lake. Solutions would follow these steps. It was challenging but exciting work and crossed several academic disciplines, from the physical sciences to public policy. She was in her element. Her initial experiences had reinforced her desire to pursue a career in Washington.

"I just love it, Jonathan. It is so exciting! There is so much to study.

We have about ten different groups examining various parts of the problem. Hopefully, we'll have a position paper to issue before I leave in May. If not, maybe I'll have to stay on as an unpaid volunteer," Sarah said.

"Or they may find a paying position for you," Jonathan added. "This could be a great break. The one you need to get your foot in the Washington door."

"Do you think so? Really think so?" Sarah asked.

"I do," Jonathan replied. "How do you think most of the people in this town started? Either they knew someone before they arrived, or else they fell into something. Just like might happen to you. I think you should pursue a regular job with the department as soon as possible. That way you might just stay on without interruption."

"Except for going through graduation exercises. I can't miss that, Jonathan. It's too important to me," Sarah said.

"Of course not," he replied. "It is always a beautiful and moving ceremony. The quad is just the perfect place for it. If the weather is nice, and I hear it usually is, it makes for a memorable experience."

"Do you realize how soon graduation will be here? I can't believe it. In six weeks. Six more weeks and I'll be a university graduate, out in the real world," Sarah said.

"The real world, Sarah? Even if you stay in this town?" Jonathan asked.

"Of course! Don't be too harsh on this place. It gets more interesting every day. I can't wait until I have a really important position. Then maybe I can make a difference," Sarah answered.

"You can make a difference now with the work you're doing on Lake Erie pollution," Jonathan said. "You don't have to wait until you have your diploma. Let's see. You graduate in six weeks. That means in seven weeks you'll get your first solicitation letter from Duke asking you for money. The requests won't end until you die, and maybe not even then."

"What do you mean?" Sarah asked.

"Private universities depend on financial gifts in order to survive. Alumni are their favorite targets. The assumption is that your success in life is due to your Duke education and your Duke degree. Therefore,

you are expected to give some of the financial rewards back in grati-
tude for what your university experience allowed you to accomplish in
life. The more successful you are financially, the greater the expectation
of the institution."

"I hope Duke will have great expectations of me." Sarah laughed at
her remark.

"But I thought you wanted to help the country, Sarah, not make
money?" Jonathan was challenging her a little.

"Who said anything about their being mutually exclusive? In the
best of worlds, one ought to be able to accomplish both goals simultaneously. Don't you agree?" she asked.

"Yes, but it's difficult," Jonathan replied. "One usually has to make
a choice about which way to go. Good deeds or a fat wallet. Rarely can
you have both."

"I know, but I can dream, can't I?" Sarah asked.

"Of course," he replied.

Jonathan could see Sarah now. Struggling to decide between serving her country or serving her pocketbook. If she had to choose, he
knew which way she would go. She had good values, the right values.
She would opt for helping make this world a better place.

"How is everything else going, Sarah?" he asked.

"Just fine," Sarah answered. "My parents were down last weekend.
We really didn't have a spring break as such because of the internship,
so their visit kinda served as one. It was good to show off the city, my
dorm, and where I work. They were très impressed, I'd say."

"Good. I know how my parents were always interested in what I
was doing. I remember they came to Penn State one football Saturday.
October weekends in State College are incredibly beautiful, with the
leaves a collage of bright colors and crisp smells in the air. I miss Penn
State a lot, but especially in the fall.

"The Army football team was in town that weekend. So I showed
them around every part of Happy Valley, as the locals call it. Ben was
there as well, but he was with the cadet corps, so we didn't see much of
him. We were able to eat dinner together, though, before he and the rest
of the corps had to board buses for the trip back to West Point. It was
a really wonderful weekend. I showed my parents my little office, my

small apartment, and the classroom where I taught. I think they were pleased with what direction my professional life was taking. Of course, Mom always had the same question for me. Was I seeing anyone? Did I have a steady girlfriend?"

Sarah laughed at Jonathan's remark and asked, "And what did you answer, Dr. Jonathan Hawthorne?"

"The truth. That I was dating someone once and a while, but there was nothing to it. In fact, I didn't even introduce her to my parents that weekend. That's how important she was in my life," he said.

"Well, Jonathan. That's what I wanted to talk to you about," Sarah said. "That's my news. I've met a guy, and we've been dating the last several weeks, pretty regularly recently. I couldn't wait for you to know, but I wanted to tell you face to face, not over the phone. I wanted to see your reaction myself."

But Sarah was not going to get the opportunity to know Jonathan's real reaction, not now, and probably never. At that moment he had two simple choices. He could fall on his knees, confess that he had loved her since the day she first walked into his classroom and ask for her love in return. Or he could choose option two. Act like a close friend who was excited at the good fortune of one whose friendship he valued deeply.

The first option, of course, was never a serious alternative. Years later he wished he had been brazen enough to try it. But Jonathan was too conventional. Besides, the thought of disclosing his love for Sarah scared the hell out of him. Perhaps if she had already graduated. Maybe if they had then found themselves in a romantic situation not unlike that at Avon that warm August evening a year earlier. Possibly if she had not just revealed to him that she had just started to see someone. Certainly if he had had more courage. "That's just terrific. That's exciting news. Really exciting news."

He was lying. The words did not come easy. It took every ounce of deception to convey a sense of happiness at her good fortune. In truth, Sarah's words cut through Jonathan like no others, with the exception of the phone call telling him about his brother's death. He had long dreaded hearing those words from her. But he knew, as well, that she would likely utter them some day. At least he knew that intellectually. But psychologically was another matter entirely. He had never really prepared himself for that moment, nor could he ever have. It was simply too devastating. Now was the time for quick composure. He hoped he could pull it off. "Who is he? Where did you meet him?" he asked.

"He works at the Department of Interior as a staff member, on the same stuff I'm involved in. He graduated from Brown two years ago and came here soon after that. Been here ever since. Name's Gordon Conway. He's from Albany," Sarah said.

"So you've been dating him for several weeks now. Is it getting serious?" Jonathan didn't want to ask the question, fearful of the answer. But he had no choice. It was the next logical step. He simply couldn't avoid it.

"Good question," Sarah said. "I think he's really neat. Reminds me of you, actually. Remember, I told you that you would make a great husband for some woman. I guess I've been looking for someone like you, without even knowing I've been searching. I need to know him a lot better, though, before I can tell you exactly how I really feel about him. But the first signs are good."

Jonathan wanted to shout, "Why haven't you gone after me since you've wanted someone just like me?" She could have had the real thing, not some pale imitation. But he knew that to be an irrational response. "That's great," he said instead. "Now you have another reason for finding a job in Washington after the internship is over. That way you'll be able to see whether it's going to go anywhere."

Jonathan could not believe what he was saying. Here was Sarah telling him she may have just found the man of her dreams, and Jonathan wasn't protesting. Wasn't making a play for her. Wasn't revealing how he really felt about her. Why couldn't she have waited until after she graduated? Then maybe he would have bared his soul before she had a chance to find another. Or at least he could have competed for her affection. He rationalized that such behavior would have been difficult, however. One just doesn't subtly switch gears. It would have had to have been an earthshaking announcement. Something like that very moment, though, if he was honest with himself. He pretended to carry on a conversation with Sarah.

Sarah, I know we've been close friends for more than a year now. But there's something I must tell you. I've fallen in love with you, deeply in love. It just happened somehow. I don't know why. It just did. I couldn't help it. I now believe it started not long after I met you, but I was unaware of it at first. Then I began to deny it when the thought of falling in love with you penetrated my brain. But I can't hide it any longer. I'm sorry. Now I don't want you to get mad at me or run away from our friendship. I hope we can remain friends, and I'll deal with my feelings somehow. Of course, in the unlikely event you have similar thoughts about me, then let's talk about it or even do something about it. But I know the idea that you might harbor romantic feelings about me is really silly. So just forget I brought the subject up, okay?

Jonathan knew he couldn't reveal such thoughts to Sarah. Certainly not now. If this fling with Gordon didn't go anywhere, perhaps. But she was only in the early stages of a newfound relationship. He had to wait until he saw where it was going. If it went nowhere, then he might be able to summon enough courage to reveal his love for her. If, on the other hand, her relationship became serious, then he knew he would remain silent, never to disclose how he felt. Why couldn't she have waited until he was free to make a move for her heart? He wanted to shout it from the rooftops so he could free himself, somehow, of the burden of loving her without any chance of her returning it in kind. But he knew that was impossible. "So when do I get to meet the lucky guy? This trip?" he asked.

"I'm afraid not. He's out of town. Back home visiting his folks," Sarah explained. "Besides, it's much too early. Let's see where it goes. The relationship, I mean. If it does get serious, then of course you'll meet him. I need your *Good Housekeeping* Seal of Approval. If you don't approve, then I'll just throw him away." Sarah's seemed to make her last remark in jest, given away by the laughter rolling off her tongue.

"So I might get to pass judgment on him, then, before it's allowed to get too serious?" Jonathan asked.

"Well, maybe after it has just gotten a little serious. That way you'll know enough about him to give me your honest assessment," Sarah replied.

"You would value my judgment that much?" Jonathan wanted to know.

"Sure. I don't know what I would do, though, if you had severe reservations about Gordon or about my relationship with him," she said.

"Well, I'm certain that, if it comes to pass, I'll think him terrific for you. So don't worry," Jonathan answered.

He was convinced he was pulling off his charade. He hadn't revealed his true feelings. Sarah didn't suspect a thing. She didn't know that he loved her deeply. And she might never know. That thought brought a sense of profound sadness to his heart, but he would deal with it. He would get on with his life as well, if Sarah's initial reaction to this new guy continued to grow in the direction of some permanent arrangement. This changing circumstance would not affect his friendship with her. He had no doubt of that. They would always have a special bond no matter who or what intruded into their lives. They had pledged their commitment to each other. He was secure in the knowledge that no one would interfere with their own relationship.

The tears flowed later that evening. Long after they had visited the Washington Zoo. Long after they had walked among the inspiring monuments near the Potomac River. Long after they had enjoyed a quiet dinner at La Residence, an elegant French restaurant not far from Embassy Row, home in Washington to emissaries from many foreign governments. Long after he had taken Sarah back to her dorm and bidden her good night. As he lay in bed at the Normandy Inn, he reflected on the opportunity now apparently lost to him. His fantasies that evening were less of passionate love-making and more of the quiet solitude of lovers snuggling together. The two of them walking on some far-off deserted beach on a moonlit evening. Hand in hand. Savoring all life had to offer. Oblivious to anything but each other. Hearts beating as one as they reflected on their good fortune to have found each other. Then, Jonathan taking her and gently laying her on a secluded part of the beach. Undressing her in a lingering fashion with a tenderness that came from the soul. Slowly exciting her ever so delicately with soft strokes of his hand until she was ready for him. Entering her only after prolonged foreplay and all the while gazing into her eyes, watching as the sweet smile of fulfillment appeared over her entire face. Moving further inside her and then out again with much deliberation, observing her as an uncontrollable sense of sexual desire soon overcame her. A desire mixed with satisfaction brought on by his having filled her body with his own as their love for each other filled their hearts. A sigh of love gently fulfilled, rather than the scream of wild orgasms. Finally, falling asleep with the ocean breeze blowing faintly against both of their bodies.

That was the fantasy that captured Jonathan's mind as he pondered the future. Sleep was a long time in coming that night. The next day he would awaken as usual, but to a different world than the one he had known—a world without Sarah. He was determined to find happiness someday, though. His search would prove difficult, but the treasure at the end of his journey would make the wait worth it.

The next day came much too soon. Jonathan needed more time to rest his body and clear his mind. He and Sarah had agreed, though, to check the Tidal Basin for the first signs of cherry blossoms, a gift from the Japanese government years earlier. They rendezvoused at nine for the short drive to the grove of trees. But it was too early in the season. It would be another couple of weeks before their beauty would awaken and delight thousands of visitors to the nation's capital.

Disappointed, they headed for Alexandria, a Virginia suburb just south of the district, for breakfast. The old part of the city was in the process of restoration. Many restaurants and shops had recently sprung up in the area adjacent to the Potomac River. Weekends always found an invasion of both locals and tourists searching for the perfect brunch.

Jonathan and Sarah joined them that Sunday. The River's Edge proved to be just such a spot. He was amazed at how southern parts of Washington could be. When he left North Carolina, he thought he was leaving grits country. Not so. It was a featured item on the menu, along with biscuits and other Southern favorites.

Neither of them made any mention of Sarah's new love interest that morning. Instead, the conversation focused initially on her work with the task force but soon moved on to life at Duke. Jonathan could tell she missed the campus. She bombarded him with question after question about the comings and goings of the Duke community. Feeling her days there had been cut too short, she was eager for any news he might bring. He knew time would eventually have a way of dulling her appetite for information, particularly after everyone she knew had also left campus. But not now. Sarah wanted to hear everything about James B. Duke's legacy.

Jonathan was happy to oblige her. He had run into a couple of her friends a few times. And he was a regular at most important campus events. The social highlight of the semester had been a Simon and Garfunkel concert at Cameron Indoor Stadium. Their rendition of the title song to *The Graduate* was the hit of the evening. Cameron rocked that evening as the duo played song after song from their albums, both new and old. "You would have really liked it. Even we old folks enjoyed it."

"Oh, Jonathan. There you go again. Talking about how old you are," Sarah complained.

"I'm sorry. You're right, as always. I'm not very old. Not one student who has accidentally bumped into me on the quad has said, 'Excuse me, sir.' That's my unobtrusive measure of 'old.' When a Dukie first calls me 'sir,' then I'll consider myself old. Not before that, however."

"That's the old spirit! Excuse me. That's the spirit! Don't you ever let anyone convince you you're old," Sarah insisted.

"I won't. In fact, tomorrow I'm going to go into my class, peruse the entire female population, and see if any of them pique my interest," he said.

"Oh, you silly man! Do you really mean that?" Sarah asked.

"Really? Yes, I mean it. Of course, I won't do anything about it. Now is the time I start looking for a woman, though, don't you think? I mean, it's been awhile since I've had a real date. Not that I have missed it, you understand. What with working to crank out the publications, then Ben's death."

"Then my problems entered the picture. I'm afraid I've kept you from an active social life the past year," Sarah said apologetically. "I'm sorry, Jonathan. But now that I'm out of your hair, you can move full steam ahead."

Sarah's comments made them both smile, although his reason was different from hers. Out of his hair! Jonathan would welcome Sarah in his hair. And any other part of him she chose to invade. But he had to stop thinking of her that way. Their friendship was beautiful. It would be enough. It would have to be enough. And while he would not devote every waking moment to securing female companionship, he would not go out of his way to avoid it either.

"I don't know whether I'll move full steam ahead, as you say, but I guess it's time to see what's out there. I don't want to spend all my life going to bed alone every night, or during the day once in a while, for that matter," he said.

"Well, she will be a lucky girl, I'll tell you that. Do I get to approve her also, seeing we're best friends and all that?" Sarah asked.

"Of course you do. I value your opinion as much as you do mine," Jonathan replied.

"Good. It's a deal then. We each get to offer our take on the other's partner, or should I say pending partner, in case the person flunks the 'best friend's evaluation' test," Sarah said.

"It looks like I'll have to pass judgment a lot sooner than you," Jonathan commented.

"Maybe not. You never know. You could return to Durham and meet someone tomorrow who will sweep you off your feet, while Gordon and I may end up going nowhere," Sarah retorted.

"If I had to wager, Miss Matthews, I'd bet on my having to evaluate your pending mate first," Jonathan ventured.

"We shall see, won't we?" she teased him.

"Maybe so. We'll just have to wait for what the future brings," he said.

Sunday brunch was coming to a close. Jonathan knew he had to get back to Durham soon. Besides, he wanted the solitude of the long ride home in order to sort things out. Although, if truth be told, there wasn't much sorting to do. Sarah was either in for a long-term relationship, or else it would end in a few months. In either case, there was nothing Jonathan could do in the meantime.

They took a leisurely drive throughout the Virginia side of the district, stopping from time to time to look at some early spring flowers waking from their winter doldrums. Jonathan thought how perceptive those early leaders who had selected this parcel of land for the nation's capital were. Washington was far better than New York, the initial choice. There wasn't a finer setting within the thirteen original colonies than where they now stood.

Two hours later, they were back at Sarah's dorm. It had been a quick twenty-fours hours. But it was a twenty-four hours that would change his life for a long time to come.

"Are you going to take part in graduation?" Sarah asked.

"Oh, yes. All faculty march in front of the graduating class. It's quite impressive. It's very hard to be excused from the event, particularly if you are a junior faculty member," Jonathan said.

"Good. I want you to meet my parents. We're coming in two days early so I can have my last fling in Durham and show my parents around some more. It's been more than two years since they've been to campus. A lot has happened there since then. I'd like you to have dinner with us the night before graduation. Can you do it? I hope so. Please tell me you're free," Sarah pleaded.

"I think so. My social calendar appears to be empty that night," he said.

"But you haven't even looked at your schedule book. How do you know you're free?" she wanted to know.

"I know my social schedule. Believe me, it's empty that evening," Jonathan said.

Laughter flowed from both of them. It was clear to Jonathan, and probably also to Sarah, that he needed a social life more than ever. His mother would certainly concur.

"It's a date then, Jonathan. What do you think about one last meal at La Chandelle? Or do we want to keep it just our little place? Where we might meet every five years for a quiet dinner? Just the two of us—no spouses, no kids. Anyone else in our lives would be banned from the restaurant that evening."

"Sounds like a good idea—both dinner at La Chandelle with your parents and every five years for just the two of us, as long as we have incredibly reasonable spouses. We'll call it our pent-annual dinner," Jonathan said.

"I think that'll be a litmus test when we're deciding whether we want to spend our entire lives with them. If they balk at such an arrangement every five years, then we'll know they aren't the ones for us," Sarah reasoned. "On the other hand, if they accept that we are close friends and a private dinner every five years is important to us, then it will be an indication we selected our mates wisely."

"We're in business then. Call me when you and your parents know your plans. I'll keep everything open until I hear from you," Jonathan promised.

"Thanks again for everything," Sarah said. "I do enjoy seeing you. Not only do you boost my ego, you also make me laugh. You make me think about important things as well. Things I ought to think about. And I can unwind with you. I need that from time to time. Good-bye, Jonathan."

"See you soon, Sarah. Take care of yourself. And if you need me for anything—anything at all—just call. You know how to reach me," he insisted.

"I will. Bye," she said.

Jonathan gave her an extra big hug, then turned and walked toward his car. After reaching it, he looked back. Sarah hadn't moved from her spot. She threw him a huge kiss and then waved almost frantically.

He wanted to turn around, run back, grab her, and plant the most enthusiastic kiss he could muster on her lips. But of course he didn't. Instead, he waved back, paused for an extra second or two, then turned and climbed into his car. He honked softly as he pulled out into the line of traffic. Sarah was still there, standing on the spot where he had kissed her good-bye.

As Jonathan discovered years later when he read her letter, Sarah was already in the midst of contemplating the weekend's events as he drove off that day.

. . . As your car pulled away at the end of your second visit to Washington, a number of emotions tugged at my heart. The internship was going well. It had convinced me that Washington was where I wanted-ed to be. I was also excited about the new guy who had just entered my life. And I really had the sense it was a serious relationship that just might lead somewhere. I couldn't wait to tell you all about it.

Your reaction was one of shared excitement and happiness, at least it appeared to be on the surface. The more I thought about it, though, particularly as I lay awake in bed that night after telling you, the more I had a sense you were holding something back. Something you didn't want me to find out. At first, I wondered if you had already heard of Gordon and knew some dark secret of his that you didn't want me to uncover, that would hurt me. I dismissed the notion, though, after a few moments. But I still couldn't quite put my finger on it. So I tried to rethink the entire conversation that day when I first told you. You said all the right things. But somehow your heart just didn't seem in it. I couldn't figure out why. And then the next day you talked about the need to restart a social life after a few years' hiatus. You seemed to stress how important it was. Then you kidded about surveying the group of females in your class the next day to see if any of them interested you. At least I think you were joking.

It made me a little jealous, I can now tell you that. I probably wouldn't have thought twice about your falling in love with an older woman or at least one who wasn't my peer. I defined an older woman, by the way, as someone nearer your age. Not that I thought of you as old, just older. Sorry about that. But the thought that some Dukie might sweep you off your feet, that she would get to know you even better than I did, aroused a little jealousy in me, I confess. Actually, it was more than a little jealousy. It was a huge amount.

I tried to figure out why that was so. And I came to the conclusion I had rather enjoyed our special relationship during that last year and a half. For the rest of my life, I selfishly wanted to be the most special of all those at Duke with whom you had already come into contact or would ever get to know over the years. I know that sounds rather silly. But you were so special to me. I didn't have the good sense or the experience to understand just what kind of specialness it was—that it might be coming close to being in love with you, and quite frankly, maybe even spilling over into love. But I did feel like I had a proprietary relationship, and I would resent anyone whose actions diminished that bond.

When you left that Sunday, I had a feeling that another was about to share the special place I occupied in your heart. That was sad enough. But I didn't want her to be a Dukie. . . .

Jonathan's drive back to Durham was different than the trip he had taken a few short months earlier. The last time, his sense of loneliness grew from the knowledge he would not see Sarah for a month or so.

This time it was an awareness that she was probably walking out of his life for good. They would remain friends. But never again would they have the physical closeness they had experienced for more than a year. Never again were they likely to live in the same town. Never again would they be psychologically attached to no one but each other.

He was wrong about this, of course. At least about some of it. But it was some time before he found himself in a position to address the possibility of something more with Sarah.

~ 18 ~

Graduation and Good-Bye

Early May. Graduation arrived almost before Jonathan had a chance to catch his breath. It was scheduled for the first Sunday of the month. The Matthews family was arriving Friday evening. La Chandelle was on for Saturday night. Sarah told Jonathan she planned to announce in the middle of dinner that they had eaten there about a half a dozen times. She wanted to see her father's reaction. The idea scared the hell out of Jonathan, but Sarah just laughed when he tried to explain why that probably wasn't such a good idea.

"You're just afraid my father will think you took advantage of his little girl, aren't you?" she teased.

"Precisely. What's he supposed to think? La Chandelle isn't exactly your campus-style eatery. It has atmosphere. Lots of atmosphere. Romantic atmosphere. It's a restaurant for lovers, not professors and their students," Jonathan reminded her.

"Then how did we end up there, Jonathan?" she asked.

"You found it. Remember? When you picked me up at the airport after Ben's funeral, we went there. So, were you trying to seduce me, young lady?" Jonathan asked.

"Of course, but you were more pure than the driven snow, as you like to say. You rebuffed my every advance. I was so devastated," Sarah replied.

"What advance?" Jonathan wanted to know. "I don't remember any advances."

"They were so subtle you obviously missed them completely," Sarah explained. She could not contain her amusement at the discussion.

"Well, my loss then," he replied. Jonathan said it in such a way so that Sarah could not really tell whether he was serious or joking. If she thought him serious, she did not admit it. A pity. He wanted to plant a seed in her brain. One small enough so he could disavow any romantic intentions if she called him on it, but large enough so she could easily interpret his real purpose if she so chose. He didn't have the courage to confess his true feelings toward her. But he was at least brave enough to hint ever so subtly at them.

"So, how should we get together for dinner?" Sarah asked. "My parents are staying at the Carolina Inn in Chapel Hill. Everything in Durham was booked. I'm with friends in the dorm."

"Well, the Carolina Inn's on the way to La Chandelle. Why don't I pick you up at the dorm, then we could drive over to get your parents?" Jonathan suggested. "It will be a tight fit in the Monza, but we can do it. Alternatively, they could follow us in their car, after we greet them at the Inn and you make the introductions."

"Let's let them drive too," Sarah said. "That way they can speculate as they follow behind us on what kinds of sinister designs you've had on their little girl and how successful you've been. I'll even tease them by moving close to you when you're driving, snuggling up a little. Then they really will think the worst—or the best."

"Thanks a lot, Sarah. You have a devilish streak in you that I'm just discovering. Is this something new, or have I just been blind?" Jonathan asked.

"I think I've always been that way, although the events of last year kinda stifled my impish side a bit. You left yourself wide open for my assaults, and I couldn't resist them. Come on. You know I'm just kidding. My parents will love you. I've told them all about you," Sarah said.

"Just what exactly have you told them?" Jonathan wanted to know.

"Everything. How we met. How I thought you one terrific professor. How you called on me when Ben died, and how I leaned on you when I had my troubles. How you encouraged me to take the internship. That you visited me twice this semester in Washington. They even know I surprised you at the beach last summer. See. I've told them everything. So I left nothing out, nor did I embellish anything for that matter."

"How did they react? Did they think I had some ulterior motive for my interest in you?" Jonathan asked.

"No. Of course not. At least I don't think so. Remember, Mom's a college professor. She understands these things," Sarah explained. "Millersville is a really strict, old-fashioned place, however. They would not tolerate such behavior between faculty and student. I remember Mom told me once about a new young male professor—single, from Pitt. He was in the history department, although he was really a political scientist. They don't have a political science department.

"Well, he arrived on campus in autumn 1960 just as the Kennedy-Nixon campaign was heating up. He befriended the president of student government, a senior, who had just developed a belated interest in political science after spending most of his undergraduate career as a math major. This new professor became the student's mentor, in effect, tutoring him in political science every evening. Since he wasn't married, he had no obligations at night. They usually ended up at the Hotel—that's spelled H-o-t-e-l but pronounced 'Hótel'—the only tavern in town, for a sandwich and a beer or two, where they would continue their discussion of political science.

"They even watched the first Kennedy-Nixon debate on barstools at the Hotel bar. You know, the one where Nixon looked like he needed a shave and Kennedy appeared with a Florida tan. The student body president learned a great deal that year and is now finishing his Ph.D. in international politics and Russian studies at Indiana University, almost the same fields as yours. Mom told me he's at the top of his class and will probably get a teaching position himself at some first-rate university when he finishes. And all of it is due to the special interest this fresh young professor showed him.

"But some stodgy old faculty members raised their eyebrows at the new instructor who took such an interest in that first student, and in several others the following year. Somehow, inviting students to his apartment or joining them at the only bar in town was considered inappropriate behavior for a young faculty member. The whispers circulated, more loudly by the week, until finally the dean was forced, reluctantly, to speak to the young professor.

254 • *Memories of Ivy*

"The dean's chastisement crushed him. He had been brought up in the Socratic system of dons so prevalent in the English higher education system, where student and professor engage in a one-to-one, give-and-take, individualized program of study. The young prof was really playing Socrates. He lasted only three years there, then left for a job at another university. Future generations of Millersville students lost out as a consequence.

"So you see, Jonathan, that Mom is predisposed to think your behavior rather exemplary. And she's awfully curious to meet a young male professor from a major university. Wants to compare notes, I think. Dad's the one you have to watch out for, though. . . . No. Just kidding."

Jonathan picked Sarah up right on schedule. Then they drove off to Chapel Hill. Her parents were waiting outside as they approached the Carolina Inn. He could have picked them out of a police lineup. There was enough of each of them in Sarah to make identifying her parents an easy task. She introduced her mom and dad. He immediately saw why Sarah was such a special person. Her mother, an attractive woman of about fifty with prematurely gray hair, had the same persona as her daughter did. In an instant, Jonathan knew exactly what Sarah would look like and how she would act thirty years from then.

Her father was also about fifty, of medium stature with a full head of graying hair. He appeared to be the quintessential corporate executive who carried himself in a regal manner, yet he displayed a warmth that put everyone at ease. Jonathan liked them at once. Of course, he thought he wasn't being entirely objective, as he relished everything about Sarah. Why wouldn't her parents appeal to him?

The evening's events bore out his initial assessment. Her parents were wonderful conversationalists and very funny as well. They had a knack for saying the right quip or asking the appropriate question. They were interested in his work as a professor and in his personal life as well, although they pried more discretely into non-academic matters. They also probed, delicately to be sure, into his and Sarah's relationship. She had told the truth. They knew much about the past year and a half. Jonathan sensed they were pleased that Sarah had found a close friend who could also play the role of mentor as she sought to figure out what she wanted to do with her professional life.

Her father asked the first question about her future. It was not an idle query. "So tell me, Jonathan, what do you think of Sarah's decision to stay in Washington and work for the government on the pollution problems of the Great Lakes?"

"The important thing, as I told Sarah, Mr. Matthews," Jonathan began, "is that she wants to work in some aspect of public policy. She has sufficient classroom training and practical experience both in Raleigh a year ago and now in Washington to make a success of herself. The key is getting her foot in the door, in Washington if possible. Sarah has done just that. Now she has to produce, and she will. Believe me, she will. She was one of the top political science majors at Duke. And I am being objective. My colleagues think so too."

"So you really think she's ready? What about graduate school? Shouldn't she get her master's degree before starting to work? Won't the lack of an advanced degree come back to haunt her?" her father wanted to know.

Sarah suddenly interjected herself into the conversation. "Wait a minute, you two. What about me? It's my life you're talking about. How about including me once and a while in your discussion?"

"Sorry, Sarah," Jonathan said. "You and I have already had this talk. But you're right. We shouldn't be so rude and ignore you. Will you forgive us?"

"Of course I do," Sarah replied. "Please continue and I'll just absorb your pearls of wisdom."

"You're right, Mr. Matthews," Jonathan said. "Sarah needs to think about an advanced degree. But the beauty of working in Washington is that there are plenty of opportunities at night for her to work on a master's degree in public policy. At least four universities in the area offer them. Their programs are full of people just like Sarah who work during the day and go to school at night."

"That's right, Dad," Sarah chimed in. "Lots of people in the Department of the Interior do that. My boss was going to class two nights a week. It wreaked havoc on his personal life, but he was committed to getting his master's degree."

"There's no doubt, Mr. Matthews," Jonathan explained, "that it's certainly easier to go to graduate school full-time. But in D.C. the norm is to do just the opposite."

"I believe you, Jonathan," he replied. "I just want to make certain Sarah doesn't run into a roadblock someday. Look at us, her parents. We have three advanced degrees between us. Of course, only one is mine. Her mother is twice as smart. She has two."

That remark brought laughs from all of them.

"And you got that by going part-time at night, Dad. I remember when I was a little girl that you were always studying late at night. You would put me to bed, then tell me you could only read me one story because you had to go study. I couldn't understand why a grown-up was going to school. We used to make little jokes about it," Sarah said.

"I never joked about it," Sarah's mother jumped in. "It doubled the amount of work I had at night."

"You were just being punished, my dear, for being so smart and so efficient in going straight through school until you had your doctorate," Sarah's dad retorted.

The tone of her father's voice suggested that Mr. Matthews was really proud of his wife's accomplishments and her career. It made it easy for him to want the same thing for Sarah.

There was one particularly good aspect of the evening. He sensed her parents had little clue about their daughter's changing personal circumstances. Gordon's name did not enter the conversation one time the entire evening. Sarah was a private person, not one to announce every facet of her existence to the whole world, or even to her parents. Nevertheless, her failure to mention Gordon did not sadden Jonathan. Quite the contrary.

The rest of the evening went much like the conversation about Sarah's future—serious talk mixed with a little banter. While Jonathan would have preferred to be at La Chandelle alone with Sarah, he enjoyed her parents' company. Seeing them also helped him acquire a more complete picture of her. But then the thought occurred to him. Wasn't he supposed to be putting thoughts of love for Sarah behind him? Weren't moments like this really counterproductive? Didn't he have to get on with his life? He knew the answer to all those questions.

But he couldn't quite bring himself to exhibit such discipline during Sarah's last weekend on the Duke campus. Too much had happened the past eighteen months for that. He might as well indulge himself for a few more days, he rationalized. On Monday, when Sarah was gone, he would resolve to move forward with his social life, unencumbered by unrealistic expectations about her. Sarah would remain his dear, dear friend. But he could no longer allow himself the luxury of fantasizing about her. It would lead nowhere but to self-destruction.

Two hours later they were in his car heading back toward Chapel Hill. That was always a special moment for Jonathan—Sarah sitting next to him in the front seat as he made his way to one destination or another. That night, though, there was sadness in the air.

Neither of them said anything for at least five minutes, until Sarah broke the ice. But her voice talked not about their parting, at least not yet. She was curious about his reaction to her parents. "What did you think of my mom and dad? I hope you liked them."

"It's more important they like me," Jonathan said. "After all, I'm your friend. They would want you in good company."

"I already know they like you a lot. Mom told me so when we went to the restroom," Sarah assured him.

"How did she know what your father thought? Did your parents use hand signals?" Jonathan wondered.

"No, silly," Sarah retorted. "She knows him like a book. She could tell. So could I. Believe me, if Dad didn't like you, it would have been quite obvious. He has never shown any hesitation in the past in letting my male friends know when he was less than enthusiastic about them. I watched it happen a couple of times. More than a couple of times, actually."

"Well, I like them a lot. We just seemed to connect, if you know what I mean. I usually form opinions quite early about someone, and I have always been on target. So I'm quite confident they're terrific. But then, I knew they would be. Look at you," Jonathan said.

It had been a long time since Sarah had blushed in front of him. But blush she then did. Crimson red, as always. The darkness in the car could not hide it. "You always have a way of making me feel good and of boosting my ego. Remember when I told you I was basically a rather shy person? I still am. But you've done your best to change that. I guess when I need a booster shot in the future, I'll have to call you."

It was time for some serious talk about the future—not their work futures, but their personal lives. Sarah was first to speak. "It doesn't seem possible that my four years at Duke end tomorrow. I can still remember when my parents brought me down here for the first time. It seems like only yesterday. But when I think about what I was like then, it really seems like an eternity. I was just a kid. . . . I know, I'm still a kid," she said.

"I didn't say that," Jonathan retorted.

"I may only be twenty-one, but I really have grown up a lot," Sarah said.

"You won't get any argument from me. Whom are you trying to convince?" Jonathan asked.

"Oh, I don't know. I'm just rambling, I guess. But if tonight isn't the time for reflection, when is? Will you indulge me? And will you give me your handkerchief if I start to cry?" Sarah asked.

"Of course I will. As I always say, 'what are friends for?'" Jonathan replied.

"I'm really glad I came to Duke," Sarah began. "The first year was all a blur. Just getting acclimated to college. Before I knew it, the year was over. I didn't feel like I had accomplished very much. But when I returned my sophomore year, I sensed that I was a slightly different person. I knew the ropes. I was beginning to think about a major. I had friends whom I had missed during the summer. When I went home at the end of that year, I said to myself, *You're halfway there. It's going fast. It's going great.*

"But it was nothing compared to the last two years. Such a difference! My experience in Raleigh took me to the next level of intellectual maturity. And I think social maturity as well. Then there was meeting you and experiencing all that our relationship brought, both in and out of the classroom. That was the icing on the cake. No, it was the cake itself and the icing. I learned so much from you. In so many areas. And the top layer of icing was our friendship. Of all that Duke has given me, nothing compares to the gift of your friendship. I really mean that, Jonathan.

"It provided me the confidence to go to Washington this past semester. It gave me the courage to face all sorts of new challenges. It gave me a security blanket. And it brought me laughter, so much laughter, at least this past year. It has also given me the assurance that, if I ever need someone, no matter what the circumstances, you will be there for me. That feels really good, you know."

"I hope so," Jonathan said. "I feel the same way. Our relationship was totally unexpected. But I welcomed it. And I look forward to what your changing situation will mean for our friendship. But I'm going to miss you, Sarah Joan Matthews. It won't be the same around here. In fact, it hasn't been the same since you went off to Washington. So, in many ways I know what it's going to be like. It won't be as much fun. And now that you're going for good, I might even get into trouble."

"I seem to remember, Dr. Jonathan Hawthorne, that we shared a bottle of wine by the first green of the Duke golf course one night," Sarah recalled. "That would have meant trouble if we had been caught."

"Not a chance. Remember, if anyone had approached us, we were going to run further and further deep into the Duke woods. We were safe the entire time," Jonathan assured her.

"I know. Just kidding," Sarah said.

The Carolina Inn loomed in the distance. Sarah said she simply wanted to say good night to her folks, then they would go back to Durham. Her parents made a point of saying how much they enjoyed meeting him and what a good time they had had. Jonathan guessed they had spent the entire drive back from La Chandelle comparing notes about the evening. He knew he had passed their test. They wanted to know if they would see him tomorrow. Sarah jumped in with a reminder that all political science majors would be attending a reception sponsored by the department following graduation.

"You are going to be there, aren't you, Jonathan?" Sarah's dad asked.

"Of course," Jonathan answered.

"Then we'll see you at the reception," Sarah's mom suggested. "That's great. See you tomorrow. And Sarah, we'll meet you outside the dorm at eight for breakfast, okay?"

"That's fine, Mom. I love you both," Sarah said.

"We love you too," her mom replied. "Good night, sweetheart."

Jonathan and Sarah watched as her parents entered the Inn. Then they turned and walked the short distance to where he had parked. She took his arm as she often had done a year earlier in times of crisis. It was a welcome touch, and Jonathan moved to put his arm around her ever so softly. Since he had two more days before he was going to ban

forbidden ideas from his mind, he felt he could engage in some fantasizing as they walked. His thoughts during the one-minute hike to the
car taxed even the wildest part of his imagination.

As they headed back to Durham, it was Sarah who spoke first. "Let's
have one last drink together. It may be awhile before we have the
opportunity again."

Jonathan had a third bottle of wine left in the car. The four of them
had consumed the first two at dinner. The Duke Gardens, bursting all
over with spring flowers, offered a seductive and secluded spot. Sarah
and Jonathan were seduced. A full moon provided just enough light to
accentuate the beauty of the flora. The aroma from the wine, coupled
with the fragrance from the nearby flowers, completed the perfect
scene.

They spent a good part of the next hour in silence. If one was
watching the two of them from a distance, he or she might think them
lovers who had stolen a private moment together, away from the
crowds. Not that they were locked in a passionate embrace. Rather, a
simple contentment seemed to fill the air around them. They each
appeared to offer a series of toasts. They drank from each other's glasses. Sarah sat with her head on Jonathan's shoulder as the late evening's
chill reminded them spring had arrived only a month earlier. He was in
no hurry to see the evening come to a close. And it appeared that she
wasn't either. So time moved slowly as each pondered the significance
of their last evening together and the unknown future in front of them.
Finally, it was time to call it a night. Only their spoken good-byes
remained.

"Well, Sarah, it's time we go," Jonathan said. "Think about me once
and awhile. Allow a few seconds a day for an old friend. For I shall be
doing the same."

"Oh, Jonathan. I shall always treasure our moments together," Sarah
assured him. "And I look forward to all those times during the next fifty
years when our paths will cross, not by chance but by design, so we may
savor our friendship over and over again."

They walked to the dorm where she was staying, arm in arm, in
silence. Nothing else needed to be said. Everything was understood.
Clearly understood by both of them. As they reached the door, each

turned to the other and embraced that wonderful embrace of deep friendship. Each then looked toward the other and moved forward for their final pre-graduation kiss on the Duke campus. As always, it was the sweet kiss of friendship. Its memory would never leave Jonathan. Each pointedly stared at the other as they parted.

Jonathan's mind worked overtime during the drive back to his condo. He wanted to store every memory from the evening's events so he could play them back whenever the desire or need to arose. He always cherished his time with Sarah. None of those earlier times with one another had been any better than her last evening at Duke.

Surprisingly, sleep came easy that evening for Jonathan. Later he understood why. Certainty had replaced uncertainty. Not the certainty he wanted, but an unambiguous certainty nonetheless. He could get on with his life. He would begin to do so Monday morning.

And Sarah?

. . . My dear Jonathan, nothing surpassed the emotion of our last evening together the night before I graduated. I was in a sentimental mood anyhow because I was leaving a place I had come to love very much. I know. I hadn't been there for several months, but I was still a Dukie. Now I was about to lose that status. Having you meet my parents and the four of us having dinner at La Chandelle was important and special.

Our hour at the Duke Gardens brought home how much you meant to me and how much I was going to miss you. It wasn't the wine talking. Not at all. It just suddenly dawned on me what an incredible passage I was about to go through. And my best friend was not going to be physically there when it happened. I knew I could call on you at a moment's notice for help. But you were going to be more than ten minutes away. Much more. A feeling of loneliness suddenly came over me. That's why I probably held onto you a little more tightly and a little longer that evening. I was entering the unknown, both professionally and personally, and I wanted you nearby. That's why I was so sad, I guess.

But you were terrific that night, as always. I went to bed with a smile on my face. It was a nervous smile, but a smile nonetheless. I knew, once again, you would have a spot in my heart forever and would always be part of my life some way. How I didn't know. That was part of the unknown that scared me so much. But I left Duke the next day with such fond memories of my four years there. And you, my dear Jonathan, were at the top of the list. . . .

The sun broke brightly the next morning. Graduation was never better. For Jonathan, the day was mostly a blur. He marched in the procession and mingled with the political science majors after the ceremony was over. He spent a substantial portion of time in the company of Sarah and her parents.

He and Sarah had said their real good-byes the night before. As she and her parents bid him so long and left the reception, Jonathan rapidly sank into a deep depression. His tears flowed freely as the Matthews' car sped away in the distance.

~ 19 ~

Life Moves Forward

Summer 1969 was uneventful for Jonathan. The campus was virtually deserted. Most of his colleagues were off somewhere doing research or simply vacationing. A few were holed up in the library. Jonathan had no teaching responsibilities for four months. He spent most of his time during the first part of the summer at the computer center analyzing large bodies of information about international conflict. The age of the personal computer had not yet arrived. Its invention would make life much easier for research scholars. But in 1969, the best technology could offer was a huge mainframe computer, usually placed in some obscure part of the campus away from sunlight and anything else that signified quality of life. Its speed paled in comparison to machines people used at the end of the millennium.

Sarah was off in Washington at her new job as a staffer on the task force for Great Lakes pollution. Jonathan had no idea how her personal life was going, although, if he was a betting man, he would place his money on her relationship with Gordon continuing and even flourishing. He talked to her about every other week, mostly about her new job. He never asked questions about her social life, nor did she volunteer any information. He had resigned himself to the inevitability of her falling in love with another, if she had not already done so, and marrying. So the less he knew, the better.

He could have adopted a different strategy. Sarah was no longer his student, or, for that matter, a Duke undergraduate. He was now free from any moral prohibitions on his behavior toward her. If only she hadn't confided to him that she was seeing someone. Then he could plot how he might initiate a more intimate relationship.

But Jonathan was now bound by another part of his moral code, or at least his operational pattern of behavior. He would never ask a woman for a date or make any other kind of similar move if she was already involved with someone else. It was a complete hands-off policy. Only after the relationship had run its course would he then take steps to indicate an interest.

Thus, he waited for a clear signal from Sarah that her relationship with Gordon was over. After all, she had confided in him when her previous affair had ended. In fact, she was a basket case who needed his comforting that evening. So there was no need for him to inquire. He would find out soon enough if they had split.

Jonathan also began to take steps to improve—start actually—his social life. He joined a health club, where he worked out three days a week. They were a new phenomenon, replacing the antiquated YMCAs of a by-gone era. This new version was coed, with lots of amenities. He also joined the University of North Carolina Golf Club. He chose it over the Duke University course because he assumed he would meet more people, particularly women, in Chapel Hill than in Durham. His instincts were good ones, although he would not take advantage of them.

Jonathan's progress toward tenure was such that he now had some time to play. And play he intended to do. If a new circle of friends entered his life, so be it. If an especially attractive woman emerged as a consequence, that was also fine. If not, his mind and body would still benefit from all the physical activity. He loved the outdoors, whether in the cool, dry summer months of Colorado or the hot, humid ones of North Carolina. It made no difference. He would spend three weeks in the mountains in late July and another three weeks at the beach in August. He was aware that six weeks of formal vacation time was probably obscenely excessive, but he didn't care. He was so confident about his research that he could afford the time.

He spent June and part of July in Durham. Jonathan was on campus about forty hours a week. It was not a nine-to-five, Monday-through-Friday schedule, though. Instead, it varied so he could play golf two weekday afternoons as well as exercise three days a week. He usually worked out in the evenings, but sometimes he headed for the health club in the middle of the afternoon to avoid the post-workday crowds. He often put in twelve-hour days at the computer center and office. Once and a while, he even spent Saturdays working. In that way, he could accommodate his desire to enjoy life a little more.

Jonathan loved the flexible nature of a professor's schedule. His hours were not set in stone during the regular academic year either, although he was expected to be on campus every day. And his summers were completely free to do with as he pleased, as long as he was productive. The university didn't care if he ever came to the office when the students were gone from campus as long as the publications kept coming. If he was especially proficient, he could even have substantial leisure time throughout his career. If, on the other hand, he was compulsive about work, he could ignore his personal life in favor of a workaholic's existence.

Some of Jonathan's colleagues were like that. They lived, breathed, and slept political science. In fact, there were more who, he believed, overachieved rather than underachieved in the amount of time they spent working. One facet of university life that greatly amazed him was the failure of many of his colleagues to have much genuine contact with what he would call the real world. They lived solely in the world of the academy—a rather artificial world, in his judgment.

Jonathan took his job seriously. All aspects of it. But he looked at it as just that. A job. It was a means to an end. Not an end in itself. He wanted a life outside the university and was determined to achieve it. He had really committed himself to that during the weeks of soul searching following Sarah's revelation about Gordon.

Strangely enough, he soon discovered his research productivity was increasing, despite the cutback in his number of work hours. He attributed it to a renewed vigor achieved through his workouts and outdoor pleasure activities. His mind had become less cluttered, and he had an additional supply of energy. His research ideas were coming much more easily, and his writing—both its clarity and its speed—improved greatly.

So did his golf game. He was now back to the regular skill level, an eight handicap, of his graduate school days, when he used to hit the links on Penn State's scenic blue course about ten times a month. He was now part of a regular foursome that met a couple of times a week. Two were faculty members in other departments at the University of North Carolina—history and chemistry—and the third was an UNC alumnus who had stayed in Chapel Hill and owned several successful businesses.

Golf gave him such pleasure that he vowed never to stray from the game during the rest of his life. It had not yet brought him any introductions to beautiful women, though. But he was working on it. A few regulars on the course caught his eye. And they appeared to be single—at least cursory looks at the second fingers of their left hands suggested so.

Soon it was the end of the second week in July. Time to head home to Colorado. None of his research notes accompanied him on the plane. He vowed not to look at them again until early September when he returned from the beach. He wanted six weeks of pure, or even impure, relaxation and fun. As the plane headed west toward the Rockies, Jonathan reflected on the past six months. The biggest change, of course, was with Sarah. She had gone through two transitions—from student on campus to intern in Washington to Duke graduate now making her way in the world of politics in the nation's capital. Her last phone conversation revealed much optimism about her future there.

She did not, however, divulge any clues about her personal life. There were hints, however, both spoken and unspoken. Mostly the latter. In fact, Jonathan had engaged in some detective work during the phone call. Remembering Sarah had surprised him at the beach the previous August, he made certain she knew his schedule for the rest of the summer. He made a point of saying he had rented the same house at Avon as he had the previous year, but for the last three weeks of August instead of the final two. He suggested that if she was free, she was welcome during any part of his time there. No problem. She didn't have to give any advance notice. Just show up.

Jonathan had hoped Sarah would be delighted and respond positively to his invitation. She didn't bite even the slightest, however. Instead, he sensed a firm hesitation. She replied that her schedule—she did not indicate whether it was her personal or work one—precluded her getting out of town any time that summer. This, Jonathan thought, despite the well-known view that Washington essentially closed down in August. Not like Paris did, but it was not far behind. He thus took her lack of interest as a sign that her relationship with Gordon was flourishing. Either they had plans for later that summer, or else she was afraid he would be offended if she visited an adult male, even just a good friend, alone for several days. So he didn't pursue the subject any further.

No matter. He had anticipated her continual involvement with Gordon, so the disappointment, while strong, was not unexpected. He had conjured up all sorts of vacation plans for the new couple. Much as he had done earlier for Sarah and himself. Now, though, another had replaced him. It was much less fun, he mused, to think about her in some exotic port of call with someone else. He had better get used to it. That's what the future held. All his earlier dreaming was just that, dreaming. Nothing more. It would never be anything else but wild fantasies.

Colorado was wonderful, as always. The dry air was a welcome relief from the humidity of North Carolina's Piedmont region. Especially the mountains. Jonathan split his time between his parents' home in Colorado Springs and the family house in the Rockies. His parents joined him for a week in the mountains. He thought it good for them to spend time in the higher elevations of the Rockies among the lush green of the meadows and the pure white of the nearby snow-capped peaks. The atmosphere was therapeutic for two souls who needed some therapy. His parents went for daily strolls along the footpaths that unknown hikers had carved decades earlier. Jonathan joined them each morning for their hour-long walk.

It was always a pleasant time. He was never one who disliked being around his parents. Even as a teenager, he didn't rebel against family vacations like most kids that age did. And he always looked forward to his visits home from college. He and his dad were really pals. Jonathan had respected him for as long as he could remember, and the admiration grew as he did, until he came to realize that his dad was the most positive influence in his life.

He and his mother had a special closeness as well. As with all boys and their mothers, over the years their relationship had changed. He had gone from the protected to the protector, even with his father still around. His mother did not mind this transition, although from time to time she reminded him that she was still his mother. When she had something to say—something really important to tell him—she still expected him to give her the proper respect and attention.

So his second week in Colorado at the family retreat northwest of Denver went well. Jonathan had decided he would spend the last week of his Colorado vacation driving around the mountains and towns of the central Rockies. Aspen, of course, was high on his list. He liked to use the mountain resort as a base. His favorite hotel of all time, The Prospector's Inn, looked out over Wagner Park, home to local rugby players for most of the summer. Years later the owners tore down the snug little Western-style hotel and replaced it with sterile condos. But in 1969 the Inn still reminded one of old Aspen, a town full of individuals who loved it for its beauty and outdoor allure. Just beyond the park were the ski slopes. In the summer, they offered a challenging climb to all those who were brave enough—or stupid enough—to try it.

His favorite Aspen restaurant was Little Annie's, also much preferred by the local crowd. An unpretentious and informal place, it catered to those who had come to Aspen to live and work, not simply to visit and be seen. From time to time, tourists stumbled onto the place, discovered its hidden secrets, and then returned every vacation. In 1969, Aspenites would not have been caught dead in a Hard Rock Cafe. Of course, one would open in the early 1990s and immediately attract the new in-crowd of beautiful and wealthy people who had taken over the city. But 1969 was different, very different.

Jonathan's favorite dish at Little Annie's was its chicken-fried steak with an overabundance of french fries. The steak was pan-fried in a light coating of some flour-based set of ingredients, then smothered with gravy as it was served. As importantly, he loved making conversation with the restaurant's regulars. They were a varied lot, having come from virtually every state in the union and from every blue-collar occupation, drawn to Aspen by its breathless outdoor surroundings and steady work.

John Denver would soon be seen often on the town's streets looking for furnishings for his new home. His song "Rocky Mountain High" captured the essence of Aspen. A later song, "Aspen Colorado on a Saturday Night," added to the town's aura. Jonathan was once warmed at the sight of a family—father and mother with their eight-year-old blonde daughter Marie—playfully dancing down the snow-covered streets of Aspen on a bitterly cold January Saturday evening singing "Aspen Colorado on a Saturday Night" at the top of their lungs.

It was at Little Annie's on his second night in town that Jonathan met someone—a woman. A high school art teacher from New Hampshire who had just decided after five years in the classroom that teaching art to mostly unappreciative kids was probably not quite as stimulating and rewarding as she had once thought. So she had headed for Aspen the day school ended in June, lured there by an article she had read six months earlier about the opportunities for adventurous people who loved the excitement and the beauty of the western mountains. *So,* she had thought, *why not? Give it a chance.* There was nothing to lose. She was a free spirit. Better to feed it than to stifle it. Her letter of resignation to her school board lay by her bed. In another week she would decide whether or not to send it.

She was sitting alone at the next table when Jonathan was seated. She cast a quick glance at him as he reached for the menu, smiled, and returned to her meal, which had arrived only moments before. Jonathan ordered his usual chicken-fried steak and sat back with a beer in his hand, waiting for the food to arrive but in no particular hurry. The woman continued to eat until most of her plate was empty. He observed that the restaurant was full, and a line had just formed by the entrance. An idea suddenly entered his mind. If she ordered coffee and/or dessert, he would ask her to join him in order to free up a table.

The thought scared him. It was most uncharacteristic of him to be so bold. The primary reason, of course, was his heightened fear of rejection. That worry had resulted in many lost opportunities over the years, he was certain, but he couldn't help it. Why then the sudden boldness? He knew the reason why. He had made the decision at Sarah's graduation. He would pursue a social life, perhaps not with a vengeance, but at least with some serious diligence.

After the server had taken her coffee order and left, Jonathan bit the bullet. "Excuse me. There seems to be a lot of people waiting for a table. If you want, you can join me to drink your coffee. That would free up a table. . . . Besides, I just thought that up as a new line to meet beautiful women. I would be disappointed if I thought it didn't work."

The woman across from him immediately echoed his laughter and then replied, "Actually, that's a new one. I like it. Subtle, allowing for a hasty retreat if brutally rejected. Of course, it would have been better if you had dropped the last part about its being a pick-up line. That dramatically lessened its effect." She grabbed her coffee cup and slid into the seat across from Jonathan.

"I'm Jonathan Hawthorne," he introduced himself.

"Michelle Morgan," she said. "Nice to meet you. Tell me. Is that really the first time you used that line?"

"The truth? Yes. Just thought of it the moment I saw the crowd by the door," Jonathan replied.

"Pretty good. Do you live here?" Michelle asked.

"No. Just visiting for a couple of days," Jonathan answered. "How about you?"

"That's a good question. I don't know yet whether I live here or not," she said. The quizzical look on Jonathan's face prompted Michelle to relate the story of how she happened to find herself in Aspen that late July day.

"Wow! You've been rather impetuous, don't you think?" he said.

"Impetuous? You must be a teacher," Michelle commented.

"I'll answer that in a minute, but I'm more intrigued with your story. It's probably much more interesting than mine," Jonathan said.

"I don't know about that," Michelle replied. "But I figure you only go around once in life, as the saying goes. I was falling into a rut. Afraid I would spend the rest of my life in a small New Hampshire town teaching art to a bunch of disinterested high school ingrates, and then wake up some morning and regret it. I hedged a bit though. I didn't up and resign immediately. I decided to come out here to see if the grass was greener on the other side. Actually, to see if there was any grass at all. Hell, any grass would probably do it for me. It doesn't have to be greener."

Jonathan smiled at the way she put it. There seemed to be a lot of spunk sitting across the table from him. He'd better watch it. "Well, did you find any grass, and is it greener?" he asked.

...

"Oh, there is plenty of grass all right. And it doesn't get any greener," Michelle replied.

"Then you've made up your mind. You're quitting teaching and starting over out here?" Jonathan asked.

"I think so, if I don't get cold feet. I've given myself another week before I make the final decision," she explained.

"I think that's terrific. I wish I had enough guts to do something like that. I like my job though," Jonathan said.

"What do you do? Was I right? Are you a teacher? A high school English teacher?" Michelle asked.

"You're close. I'm a teacher, at Duke University. Political science. Just finished my third year," Jonathan explained. He always called himself a teacher rather than professor in front of pre-collegiate teachers. He didn't want to appear pompous. His tactic usually worked.

"That's terrific. So you're free in the summertime then?" Michelle asked.

"Not exactly. We're supposed to do research," Jonathan replied. "But I had done enough by the middle of July, so I said, 'The hell with anymore time in the computer center,' and here I am. My parents live in Colorado Springs, and we have a place up in the mountains outside Denver. I just finished spending two weeks with them, and now I'm off on my own for a week. See, my story isn't nearly as exciting as yours is."

Jonathan thought her interesting. Michelle was attractive as well—blonde hair, blue eyes, and about five and a half feet tall with a figure he found inviting. They carried on a lively conversation during the remainder of Jonathan's dinner, which took about half an hour. As he paid the bill, he turned to Michelle and took the next step. "I had planned to go over to The Red Onion after eating. They have a good western country-type band playing tonight. Want to join me?"

"Love to," Michelle said.

Funny how all the moves come back so easily, Jonathan thought. *Like riding a bicycle, people say. Once you learn it, you never forget.*

The Roaring Fork Boys were as advertised, a western version of country music. Loud, funny, and good enough after one had consumed a few beers. It was hard to ruin live music in a bar—not impossible, but hard. Jonathan and Michelle listened and laughed while each downed about three more apiece. Coors, of course—the beer of choice for those who fancied themselves Rocky Mountain types.

"I've never gone drinking with a college professor before," Michelle said. "It's kinda fun."

Jonathan's comeback was in keeping with the emerging mood of the evening. "I've never had a Coors with a high school art teacher before, and I agree. It is fun."

After an hour and a half, during one of the band's breaks, Jonathan suggested they leave. So off they went, ambling along the streets of Aspen. Window shopping was a popular sport in the old mining town, even at night. The temperature was still about seventy degrees, although it was almost ten o'clock. With the low humidity, one needed a sweater to keep the mountain coolness off the shoulders. They studied each window while leisurely strolling up the first street. After about ten minutes, Jonathan took her hand, which slipped nicely into his.

"I've never held hands with a high school art teacher either," he said and laughed.

"You know what I'm going to say next, don't you, Jonathan? . . . I've never held hands with a college professor before either," Michelle replied, as a huge grin appeared on her face.

They were both in fine spirits. The alcohol had done its job. Any social inhibitions they might have harbored were quickly disappearing. Another ten minutes, and he had his arm around her shoulder. Michelle nuzzled up to him, making walking a little easier. Jonathan found the experience really satisfying. It had been so long since he held a woman that way. Sure, he and Sarah had also walked hand in hand. But it was different. It was clearly understood that theirs was the embrace of friendship. No matter what he had thought or hoped for. It was only friendship. This was different. There was sexual tension in the air. He could feel it. And he knew she sensed it too.

After another twenty minutes, they had covered most of the stores in downtown Aspen and had started walking toward the edge of town, away from any passersby. Michelle then turned to Jonathan and, with a smile on her face, issued an invitation. "Would you like to see my apartment? We could have a cup of coffee or a nightcap if you'd like. I should tell you I've never invited a college professor to my Aspen apartment before—or a high school teacher, school board member, lawyer, or anyone else, for that matter."

Jonathan laughed, or rather giggled, then said, "And . . . you probably know what's coming now."

But before he could finish, she interrupted. "You've never been to the apartment of a high school art teacher before, in Aspen or anywhere else."

They bent over exhausted from the laughter. Then, straightening up, they turned toward one another and paused. Both seemed serious all of a sudden.

Jonathan took both her hands in his and pressed her close to him. "At the risk of making you laugh again, I have something else to say. I've never kissed a high school art teacher."

But she didn't laugh. Quite the contrary. She reached up toward Jonathan, and their lips touched, gently at first, then passionately. Soon their lips parted and their tongues searched wildly for each other. Her taste quickly covered his mouth as she licked the outside of his lips. She was already breathing heavily as she continued to kiss his face. At the same time she pressed her body against his, wrapping her right leg around the back of his left one. His hands probed her back, rubbing it gently while at the same time holding her firmly against him. He was hard, harder than he could remember being. It served as a magnet for her, as she started to move her lower torso in a circular fashion, using his groin as the center point of the circle.

Their embrace lasted a full five minutes. Jonathan was fully aroused and now breathing out of control. So were the images floating through his brain. He wanted her—really wanted her. Her lips tasted so good that he wished to savor the rest of her. It had been so long since he had made love to a woman. She had aroused him so much that he was afraid he would climax before he had a chance to enter her. He knew she was also sexually excited. He imagined how wet she must be. Slowly he pushed her to arm's length, looked her in the eye, and, in a soft voice, asked to make love to her.

"It's been a long time since I slept with a woman, a very long time. I had almost forgotten how good a woman tasted until we just now kissed. I know we just met a few hours ago. But I want to make love to you tonight. I'd like to take you back to your place and explore every inch of your body. So please say yes," Jonathan pleaded.

Michelle gazed at him but said nothing at first. Then a smile slowly covered her face. "It's not far from here. Only three blocks. But I have a better idea. Let's go to your hotel. I want to watch the sun come up tomorrow over Wagner Park."

A huge smile appeared on Jonathan's face as he led her in the opposite direction toward The Prospector's Inn. They quickly climbed the steps to the second floor. Once they were inside, Jonathan didn't turn on the light. He preferred the darkness. They both walked tentatively toward the bed. Only the sounds of their breathing broke the quiet. The outline of her body against the moonlight made her even more desirable. He couldn't wait to reach for her.

Two hours later, Michelle started to giggle, which brought a puzzled look to Jonathan. "What's so funny?" he asked with a sly grin on his face.

"I just thought. I've never made love with a college professor before. Or had that many orgasms with a college professor, or anyone else for that matter."

They both laughed.

"You really do know what I'm going to say next, don't you?" Jonathan said.

"Yeah, I think I do," Michelle replied.

In unison, they shouted the next refrain, "I've never made love with a high school art teacher before."

"Want to do it again?" Michelle asked.

And so they did, until they both fell back on the bed exhausted. Sleep overtook them both, the soft Rocky Mountain breeze from the open window seducing them. Michelle never saw the sunrise.

~ 20 ~

Life Without Sarah

Jonathan had planned twenty-four more hours in Aspen before moving on. He spent all of it with Michelle. They awoke at ten o'clock, made love for another two hours, then took a shower, dressed, and headed for some place to eat. They spent the day hiking in the mountains and skinny-dipping in a cold mountain lake, the evening at a restaurant and bar, and the night together in bed once again. By the next morning, Jonathan figured he had had five orgasms total. Enough, he mused, to satisfy his lust for awhile. It was clearly the deprivation of the previous couple of years that had caused him to keep going for most of the night.

He could not estimate how many times Michelle had come, but it was far more than he had. While there weren't many reasons why he had ever wished to change genders, the ability to have multiple orgasms at a moment's notice was clearly at the top of any list he might create. He remembered his first experience with a woman who had the capacity to achieve a series of orgasms much like Michelle did. She confided to Jonathan that she thought it was a blessing, although she wasn't certain. He was, however.

The two of them did manage to see the sunrise the second morning. It had been a wonderful thirty-six hours. His body had welcomed it. His mind had also. Michelle appeared to enjoy it as well. He thought her exciting—witty, very attractive, and with a sexual appetite like no other he had ever experienced. She was clearly a free spirit. They had had a good time, but it was nothing more than that. In the midst of their love-making the second day, Michelle decided to resign her teaching job and stay in Aspen. She invited Jonathan to visit her when he returned to Colorado at Thanksgiving. He promised to repay the favor at the beach sometime in the future. Not during the next three weeks, however. It was too soon. Besides, he still subconsciously harbored the hope Sarah might change her mind and show up at Avon.

He didn't know how he would react when he saw his best friend the next time, given his enthusiastic romping in bed with Michelle over the past couple of days.

One part of him defended his behavior. *Look, you two aren't an item. Sarah has a boyfriend. Even if she didn't, there is no romantic commitment between the two of you anyhow. Nothing at all. So what's the problem?*

Another voice countered, *You're hopelessly in love with Sarah. Every thought, word, and action of the past two years took place in the context of her. Granted there was nothing formal between you. But she had "stretched the envelope" just enough to suggest she thought you a real catch for some woman. Why couldn't it be her?*

Jonathan wasn't certain which voice he would hear when he next saw her. But he couldn't worry about it. He had to get back to Colorado Springs for his trip home to Durham, and then on to the beach. It couldn't come soon enough. He told his parents just enough about Michelle to start them wondering. Nothing more.

❦ ❦ ❦

It was on to Avon, which was lovely as always. It was his third summer there. Nothing had changed. He hoped nothing ever would. He liked it there. The Outer Banks served as a refuge from the daily travails of both his job and his personal life. The trip also acted as an opportunity to rejuvenate his entire body, which Michelle had run into the ground just a few days earlier.

Sarah did not surprise him as she had the previous year. He had expected that, but no amount of preparation could shield him from disappointment. As he walked on the beach the last evening before returning for the first day of class, he thought back to the same place and night, one year earlier. Once again, he wondered whether or not the opportunity on the beach to take their relationship to the next level had really existed.

His rational self had always answered no to the question. But his heart wasn't certain. When it dominated, he was haunted with second thoughts about how he might have responded after their kiss. He knew it was silly of him to think anything, particularly anything permanent, could have emerged from any move he might have made that fateful August evening. He thanked the rational side of his brain for conveying a sense of reality about its potential. One tear after another, however, appeared, rolling down his cheeks as he walked alone among the sand crabs of Avon.

❧ ❧ ❧

Jonathan returned to Duke the next morning. The first day of class reminded him he was one year closer to tenure. A new group of coeds filled with the normal anticipation associated with a new semester would be making their way to his classroom. His reputation as a good teacher had grown considerably since the day Sarah first walked into his classroom two years earlier. He didn't have to worry that his classes would be half empty.

Jonathan intended to call Sarah that evening. He hadn't talked to her since his family retreat to the Rockies almost four weeks earlier, pre-Michelle. It was the longest amount of time without any contact between them since their friendship had blossomed. He gazed around the classroom for any especially attractive women, knowing that would be one of Sarah's first questions. He was right. She posed it early in their conversation.

"Where have you been? Well, I know where you've been. But I was worried because I hadn't heard from you. Are you all right?" she asked when they finally talked.

"Of course I'm okay. I know it's been a few weeks," Jonathan answered.

"A few weeks? It's been closer to four. I thought when I hadn't heard from you, you had been seduced by the Rockies or the beach, or perhaps by some beautiful blonde," Sarah said.

Jonathan laughed an uneasy laugh. He ignored her reference to a blonde. "Well, I took a vacation from all my responsibilities to my job, friends, and family. I became a hermit, I guess. First in the mountains and then at the beach. Sorry. I guess I didn't think you would worry about me very much, with your new job and other intrusions in your life."

Sarah let the last part of his remark pass without comment but said, "Things are well here. The job's going great. And I'm settling into my new apartment. Took a six-month lease."

Jonathan didn't ask her why only a six-month lease. Before he pondered the possible implications of the short length of time, Sarah turned to the expected topic. "Today was the first day of class, wasn't it? I cried this morning when I thought about it. I miss Duke already. Remember two years ago when I walked into your class?"

"I sure do," Jonathan said.

"Me too. It changed my life," Sarah acknowledged.

Jonathan wanted to shout that it had changed his life as well, but he decided to keep quiet.

"So tell me. Are there any cute coeds in your class? Did you check them out today?" Sarah asked.

"You bet I did," Jonathan said. "In fact, there are a couple with some potential. It might even be a decent crop."

"Some potential! Is that all? No drop-dead beauties? What's a stud professor like you to do?" Sarah asked.

Jonathan ignored the reference to his studness, although he now had a higher opinion of it than he had had a few weeks earlier, thanks to Michelle. "None of the new students are as pretty as you are, fortunately. That might create some real problems for me."

"What do you mean, fortunately? Are you sorry, Professor Jonathan Hawthorne, I ever took your course?" Sarah asked.

"You know the answer to that," Jonathan said.

"I do, don't I?" Sarah remarked, somewhat slyly. There was a mischievous tone to her voice. They talked about half an hour—about nothing out of the ordinary at first. Sarah indicated she was still seeing Gordon, but she didn't elaborate. Jonathan chose not to pursue it.

And then, surprise of surprises, he told her about Michelle. Not entirely everything about their time together, but enough to paint a picture. A very small picture. "Well, I did actually meet a blonde. In Aspen. At Little Annie's, one of my favorite restaurants. She's an art teacher at some high school in New Hampshire but was in Aspen trying to decide if she wanted to chuck the whole thing and move to the Rockies.

"Did you take her out?" Sarah queried.

"We went to a bar with live music the night we met, then we went hiking the next day. Went to dinner the second night too," Jonathan replied.

"I see. Well?" Sarah wanted to know more.

"Well, what?" Jonathan said.

"How'd it go? Was she fun? Was she gorgeous? Did you kiss her? Did you go to bed with her?" Sarah asked.

"You don't think I'd choose a dog, do you? I may not have dated much recently, but I haven't lost my pickup skills—at least not yet," Jonathan remarked.

"No, of course not. But what kind of pretty?" Sarah pressed.

"What do you mean, 'What kind of pretty?'" Jonathan asked.

"You know. How tall was she? Was she well-built? Long hair or short? And so on. And so on," Sarah continued.

"I don't remember asking you those kinds of questions about Gordon. How come you're asking them to me?" Jonathan retorted.

"Women are different," Sarah explained. "We're curious. We want to know such things. Did she flirt with you? Come on to you? Were you poor and defenseless?"

"No to all three questions," Jonathan answered. He could have said that she didn't have to come on to him. That he had initiated most of the advances. Although he wasn't quite sure of that now. No matter. He had told her enough about Michelle. No need to go into all the details. Or any details for that matter.

It was good to hear Sarah's voice again. But he had better watch himself, he thought. He was in the process of psychological disengagement from her. No need to take two steps backward. They ended the conversation without any talk of visiting each other.

❧ ❧ ❧

The semester continued. It was a normal one. His two classes were full of bright and eager students. His research was back on track after the six-week layoff. His golf game did not suffer—he managed at least two rounds a week. And his body was becoming finely tuned once again as a consequence of a regular workout schedule. Ready to do battle. Ready to make love all night. Not much of the latter was happening, however. In fact, no love-making was occurring. The female prospects at the Carolina golf course still looked promising, but no occasion had arisen yet that would allow him to strike up a conversation with any of the members he'd singled out earlier for attention.

Sarah called a couple of weeks later. She said she was coming down for a football game and was bringing Gordon, and she wanted the three of them to have dinner after the game. Jonathan agreed. Dinner would not be at La Chandelle, however. He would eat peanut butter and jelly sandwiches while nude on the campus quad before he would include Gordon at a La Chandelle dinner. He thought Sarah would understand. After all, they had an agreement that every five years they would return there for dinner, just the two of them. He was beginning to realize any future meals together might just be confined to their pent-annual rendezvous at La Chandelle.

As it happened, Michelle called the same night, about an hour after he had talked to Sarah. He was glad she did, especially after Sarah had mentioned Gordon coming with her to Durham. "Hi. This is Michelle, from Aspen. Remember me?" she said.

Jonathan pretended to pause before answering. "I've never made love to a high school art teacher before. . . . Yeah, I remember you."

"I've never had twenty orgasms with a college professor before," she shot back.

Jonathan laughed. She was quick with the quip too. "How are you, Michelle? Are you still glad you made the decision to stay? Or are you homesick now?"

"Not yet. I love it," she said. For the next ten minutes, she confided how life was going for her in Aspen. She had a new job as an artist for a local magazine and had already submitted her name for a teaching position, although she wasn't sure she wanted to go back into the classroom. Her purpose in calling, she said, was to invite him to Aspen over Thanksgiving. They had talked about it when they parted, but she wanted to do so formally so he knew she was serious.

With the thought of Gordon and Sarah on his mind, he responded, "I'd like that. How about Friday? I can be up around noon. I can probably stay until early Sunday."

"Good. Do you care if I have a turkey the day you arrive?" Michelle asked. "I'd like to celebrate the holiday in the traditional way with someone, even if it's a day late."

"Sounds good to me," Jonathan said.

Visions of Michelle completely nude while locked in his arms took over his thoughts. It brought a smile to his face and a hardness to his groin. While he would have preferred making love with Sarah, the time with Michelle had felt really good. Hearing her voice, not to mention her reference to the twenty orgasms, made him want to be with her again. He decided he was happy and excited he was heading for Aspen.

➤ ➤ ➤

Sarah's visit to Duke took place three weeks later, homecoming weekend. It was everything Jonathan thought it was going to be, unfortunately. She and Gordon showed up at his office late Friday afternoon. They stayed about thirty minutes and agreed to meet Saturday at the post-game receptions in the dorms along the quad. "An okay guy" was Jonathan's first reaction to Gordon. He knew, though, that he could never be objective about anyone who was, in essence, going to prevent him from being with the woman he loved.

The campus was in a festive mood following a 45–24 victory over the University of Virginia Cavaliers. The beer and the bantering flowed freely at the post-game parties. Jonathan caught up with Sarah and Gordon about an hour into the frivolities. Thirty minutes later they were at The Carolina Cookery enjoying a pre-meal drink from the two bottles of wine Jonathan had brought with him. Barbecue, southern style, and steak were the specialties. It didn't matter. Jonathan was less than thrilled about the whole weekend anyhow. Sarah had no idea, however, about his true feelings. He pulled the evening off well, he thought. Everybody imagined everyone else had had a wonderful time. Nobody asked any questions. Jonathan didn't want to know anything about the two of them, from the weekend sleeping arrangements to a possible life-long relationship. He would find out soon enough, he figured.

He was right. The call from Sarah came two days later, on Monday. "Well, what did you think?"

"Think? About what?" Jonathan asked.

"You know, Gordon," Sarah said.

"Oh. Don't you remember? Guys don't get into that nearly as much as women do," Jonathan replied.

"I know, but you had to have a reaction," Sarah insisted.

"I like him. He seemed like a good guy. About his hair though. Do you think that's his right style?" This last question, said in a mocking voice, was Jonathan's attempt to keep the discussion humorous. He was successful for awhile.

"Oh, come on, Jonathan. Be serious. You're making fun of my questions about that blonde in Aspen," Sarah said.

"I am, aren't I?" he replied.

"Yes you are. And I'm trying to be serious," Sarah said.

Jonathan paused, then asked, "Why?"

"Well, because. Just because. No. There's a reason. I think Gordon is about to ask me to marry him," she replied.

Her words shot though him like a bullet. "Why do you think so?" Jonathan wanted to know.

"I just have this feeling, from things he's been saying lately," Sarah answered.

"Well. How do you feel about that? Do you love him?" he asked.

"I don't know how I feel about it. Yeah. I love him. At least I think I do. But I'm worried I might be rushing it," Sarah said.

"Only you can decide that, Sarah. Remember, he's been out of college and on his own for a couple of years. He's probably been lonely for awhile. You're a welcome addition to his life. Why wouldn't he want to get married?" Jonathan observed.

"I see what you mean," Sarah said. "He's further along than I am in deciding how he wants to spend the rest of his life."

"Exactly. First of all, although you didn't ask, I put my *Good Housekeeping* Seal of Approval on Gordon, okay? Second, remember that it's a big decision. I've never confronted it, although that girl at

Penn State probably figured we were a lot closer to marriage than I did. So I really haven't thought through the big picture, if you know what I mean. Just don't get pushed into anything you aren't sure about," Jonathan advised. "I don't want to see my best friend get hurt."

Jonathan wanted to introduce their own relationship into the discussion. He wished to do more than that—much, much more. His time with Michelle had made him realize that he really needed a woman. While she had provided the physical intimacy missing from his life, she had not furnished the psychological closeness he now knew he desperately also wanted and needed. Only Sarah could fill both requirements. He could tell her to wait, that he loved her and wanted her to give him a chance to show why they could be the happiest couple in the world. But, of course, he said none of that. Instead, they talked for awhile about Gordon and about her job. As he put down the phone at the end of the conversation, he suspected what the future held. He didn't like what he saw.

◄ ◄ ◄

He was not surprised at Sarah's phone call the weekend before Thanksgiving. Gordon had popped the question. She told him she would give him an answer before Christmas. Jonathan tried to put her out of his mind during the next few days. He was not successful until Tuesday when the plane carrying him home for the holidays came into view of the Rocky Mountains. His parents would be waiting for him at the airport. He also thought rather lustful thoughts of Michelle as the aircraft circled for its landing at Denver's Stapleton Airport. He couldn't wait until they were again caressing each other's bodies. He knew it was pure lust. Or rather impure lust. But he didn't care. They both enjoyed it. No one was getting hurt. A huge smile of anticipation crossed his face as the plane's wheels touched down on the runway.

The three days home were pleasant. Wednesday was reserved for the immediate Hawthorne family, while Thanksgiving Day found the extended clan around the dinner table enjoying the traditional feast once more. It had been two Thanksgivings since Ben had been alive on this holiday. Last November had not been a good period for them, but time had a way of healing. The relatives were far more festive this year.

They also kidded him about his pending weekend sojourn to Aspen. His mother's joy that Jonathan would finally be with an eligible woman balanced out her sadness at his not being there the entire Thanksgiving vacation. She had relayed the good news to the entire Hawthorne clan immediately following the pre-meal grace. In fact, she gave a hint of it during grace when she thanked God for both the "turkey and Jonathan's weekend companion."

He decided to fly to Aspen rather than to chance a drive in the weather. Given the early season snow, it was unclear how much longer Independence Pass would remain open. If it closed while he was in Aspen, he would have to take the long way back around the mountains—an eight-hour drive under normal conditions. Jonathan didn't want to risk it.

Michelle was waiting for him when the small jet touched down at eleven in the morning. Dinner would be at five. As they drove toward her apartment, she painted a vivid picture of what the afternoon appetizer was going to be. Jonathan experienced a first that Friday. Making passionate love with the smell of turkey permeating the air was certainly different, but it served to accentuate the development of an appetite—for food, that is. He devoured the turkey and everything else on the dinner table later that day. His appetite for sex was already in the midst of being fulfilled, over and over again, that afternoon.

Years later, modern science would uncover the secret of the aroma of pumpkin as an aphrodisiac. Had Jonathan known that, he might have attributed his physical staying power to the pumpkin pie cooking in the oven. Instead, he assumed his constant hardness was the result of Michelle's wide-ranging skills. No matter. The huge smile on his face, and on hers, would have been no different.

Sleep came easy for both of them prior to dinner. It seemed strange he was sleeping before a big holiday meal rather than afterward, but it was the first time in his life that particular appetizer had been served. He knew sleep would come just as easily after dinner, or more specifically after the post-dessert "dessert."

Jonathan and Michelle alternated the rest of the weekend between the external sights and sounds of Aspen and the sights and sounds of her bedroom. They took trips around town actually only as much-needed respites from their constant love-making. It was certainly different, he thought, from two Thanksgivings earlier when he spent the Friday after the big day hiking alone in the nearby foothills while contemplating his infatuation with that new student of his, Sarah Joan Matthews. This time Sarah and the foothills were far from his consciousness.

It was a fun weekend as well—fun beyond the sex. Jonathan liked Michelle. He enjoyed her company. The sex was a bonus, a huge one to be sure. She was great in bed. But she had more to offer. He left Sunday at noon with a promise to see her soon, perhaps over the Christmas holidays if she was going to be in Aspen. If so, given the length of that holiday season, he thought they might even get some skiing in—during their breaks from love-making, at least.

As Jonathan walked into his class Monday morning, he reflected on where he had been and what he had been doing just a short twenty-four hours earlier. One might have described the smile on his face as slightly naughty. He wondered if any students had picked up on it.

The semester could not end quickly enough for Jonathan. He anticipated an early return visit to Aspen. And he waited for a call from Sarah telling him of her decision. The latter came, but not by phone. It was in a letter. One might call it a sweet note from one good friend to another. Sarah had made her decision. The wedding was scheduled for June. The third Saturday, but only if Jonathan was free, she told him. Otherwise, she would have to change the date. He doubted if that was true, but it didn't matter. He was available that weekend. He would deliver a command performance. He had no choice but to be there and suffer through the entire schedule of events. Then he would get drunk, by himself, and engage in the most prolonged episode of self-pity an adult male had ever undertaken. He wondered, though, why she had written him instead of phoning. That question haunted him for years afterward.

A call came from Michelle the same day. She would be in Aspen for the duration of the holidays. Work prevented her from traveling outside Colorado. Her parents were visiting the week before Christmas, but were leaving on the 26th. She hoped he could come out for several days between Christmas and New Year's. He saw no reason why he couldn't. So they made arrangements.

Christmas in Colorado was as good as it had ever been, certainly

better than the year before. The Hawthorne family enjoyed a wonderful Christmas, made special by a five-inch snowfall on Christmas Eve.
Jonathan joined his extended family at the mountain retreat the day
after Christmas. He planned to stay only a short while before heading
for Aspen. The snows had been plentiful all along the front range of the
Rockies, which was unusual for that time of year. It made his short time
at their mountain home more exhilarating as the cross-country trails
were open.

A few days there were enough. He bade farewell to the family,
noticing as he pulled away that a huge smile adorned his mother's face.
He obviously had her blessing. He doubted, though, that she had any
inkling of what had transpired during his last Aspen trip or what was
certain to happen this time. After all, parents don't do such naughty
things or even think such dirty thoughts. Aren't all children immacu-
lately conceived? The drive from the Hawthorne mountain home was
about four hours. He anticipated he would arrive around noon.
Jonathan wondered if Michelle had another afternoon delight waiting
for him.

She did. Big time. Michelle obviously loved sex, and she certainly
loved it with Jonathan. He had been away from her just long enough
to develop his own strong sexual appetite. He wondered whether or
not, if he saw her more often, his level of desire—or hers, for that matter—would remain the same. Quite frankly, he didn't want to find out.
The spacing between visits was just about right. He was not interested
in a commitment. But he certainly enjoyed his visits to Aspen. He justified them to himself on the grounds that he was making up for lost
time.

Make up for it he did that visit. It was a repeat of Thanksgiving.
Some minimal sightseeing. A lot of Michelle's bedroom. The one difference was that they did manage to get some skiing in—three afternoons' worth actually. It felt good to hit the slopes, particularly to clear
his mind of the sexual fantasies continuously playing out in her apartment. It also felt satisfying to be with a woman doing anything, not just
making love. Jonathan left four days later feeling really okay about life,
with one exception. But with the scent of Michelle's body all over him

as he began the journey back to Colorado Springs, there wasn't much room for thoughts of Sarah. Or so he assumed.

The drive afforded him time for thinking about the big picture and life in general. His professional life was in fine shape. Outward appearances would suggest his personal life was also. Any of his colleagues in his department, he suspected, would gladly have swapped their schedules between Christmas and New Year's with his agenda. But outward appearances can be deceiving. He ached, and ached deeply. He had lost any opportunity he'd had to make Sarah his wife. Likely gone forever. He knew, though, he would get over it. Time heals. He had discovered the wisdom of that old saying in the past year as he coped successfully with Ben's death. He would do the same with Sarah's departure.

PART THREE

~ 21 ~

Twenty Years Apart

Twenty years now
Where'd they go?
Twenty years
I don't know
I sit and I wonder sometimes
Where they've gone
Like A Rock
—Bob Seger

If Jonathan hadn't had any feelings of love and desire for Sarah, he would have thought her wedding perfect. But time and distance were still not long enough. So he bit his lip, hitched up his pants, and toughed it out. No one knew the difference. Sarah certainly didn't. She looked radiant in her traditional wedding dress. Jonathan tried not to look at her often. It hurt less that way.

Sarah had suggested he bring Michelle with him, but he demurred. It didn't seem right somehow to mix his two lives together. He wanted them separate, compartmentalized. It didn't matter anymore, though. One of his lives, the world of Sarah, was gone. Accepting it would require lots of time alone for reflection and self-pity. There had been several moments during the weekend when he wished he had brought Michelle. She could have made him forget Sarah, at least for awhile. Time he spent in bed with her seemed to take his mind off anyone and anything else.

But there was another reason why he didn't ask Michelle to join him. She might have sensed his long-term infatuation with Sarah. He didn't want that to happen. Not so much because it might affect what she thought of him. Rather, he wanted the story to be his alone, his secret. It was okay that his dad, and even his mom, knew about Sarah. But he didn't want to share it with anyone else, and certainly not with a woman with whom he had been sleeping.

Sarah's parents were extra-friendly during the whole weekend. They had sensed a year earlier at her graduation, Jonathan later found out, that a special bond existed between their daughter and him. Her dad had felt that Jonathan harbored feelings somewhat stronger than friendship for Sarah. Her mother had detected something else—Sarah was captivated by Jonathan. He didn't know at the time that they were disappointed Gordon, rather than he, was standing next to her at the altar. They certainly didn't convey that message at her wedding. But they did make him feel special. He appreciated their kindness.

Jonathan did allow himself one step backward. The day after the wedding, he traveled throughout the Lancaster area, searching for landmarks of Sarah's youth. The high school, the Colt Inn, her home. He wanted to take back to Durham some additional memories of the woman whom he loved so much but who had just walked out of his life.

Jonathan's drive back to North Carolina was a pivotal point in his life. He decided he needed to search for happiness. He wasn't owed it. It wouldn't just come to him. He had to find it. Sarah's marriage had motivated him to look at the big picture. And that picture no longer included her, at least as his lover or wife. If he wanted a woman to be part of that life, it was going to be another. Michelle quite likely would not be a permanent part of his life either. He enjoyed her company. She made him laugh. They were great in bed. They were good friends, but not in the same way he and Sarah were. His conversations with Michelle never quite approached the depth or intensity as those with his best friend had. He had been seeing her for a year and had come to realize she would never replace Sarah as the focal point of his life. Their relationship, while comfortable, was not going anywhere, nor was it going to.

Michelle joined him at Avon two months later, and he visited her twice more when he was in Colorado. These visits reinforced his view of their relationship as one of sexual intensity but casual emotion, rather than one in the early stages of a lifelong commitment. So when she gave him an ultimatum nine months later, Jonathan didn't hesitate. He liked Michelle, even loved her in a small way. But he didn't want to spend his life with her. It was an easy decision. Sarah, rightly or wrongly, was the litmus test. She would always be the litmus test. His feelings for a woman had to equal or surpass those he had harbored and still did for Sarah. His feelings for Michelle came up short. While he was content to continue the relationship as it was, he was not prepared to go further. So he walked away. Michelle cried when he told her. So did Jonathan.

❧ ❧ ❧

There were two others over the years, Paula and Deborah, but he found them wanting also. Or, more accurately, his feelings for each were wanting. He reluctantly came to the conclusion that whoever said there was one, and only one, perfect match out there somewhere for each of us was right on target. He had found his perfect match, his soul mate, but she was married to another.

Jonathan resigned himself to a life alone. He plunged into his work. He had been right about his career. Tenure and promotion to associate professor came a few years later. He earned the rank of professor in 1975. By 1980 he was the Carter Hamilton Professor of Political Science. Carter Hamilton was the son of an alumnus, David Hamilton, class of 1947. Hamilton had been killed in Vietnam in 1968, and his dad had endowed a chair in his memory. Jonathan cried during the investiture ceremonies as he thought about Ben's death the same year in the same awful place.

The years passed. He moved into a new house overlooking a lake in Chapel Hill. A bachelor's house, he told everyone. His colleagues, or more precisely the spouses of his male colleagues, fixed him up from time to time with the current most eligible woman in the Durham-Chapel Hill area. But nothing ever came of those encounters, except for several brief interludes of sexual satisfaction, for him as well as his partner.

There were even some whispers he might be gay. A few women immediately came forward to report Jonathan Hawthorne was nothing if not the most enthusiastic heterosexual they had ever met or gone to bed with. The rumor died quickly, replaced by one that came much closer to the truth. He had been unlucky at love, some said. The love of his life had married another, had perhaps died of some mysterious disease, or maybe even had joined the convent. Such a pity, the faculty wives would say. Here was a handsome gentleman, now in his late forties, who oozed both sexuality and sensitivity—two of the most sought-after male characteristics by American women.

Jonathan ignored the whispers, no matter the origin or the substance of them. Everyone sought perfect happiness, but few ever achieved it. He had made a satisfying life for himself. His career was the envy of his peers. His health was good. He had a rich circle of friends as well as a handful of regular lovers. His parents were alive and well. His mother had even come to understand there would be only one woman in his life, Sarah. She had stopped bugging him years earlier about her desire for grandchildren. His dad admired him, recognizing how powerful his love for Sarah must have been to drive his resignation with being alone.

◆ ◆ ◆

And Sarah? Her story can best be told in her own words. Jonathan came to understand her tale when he read her letter.

> . . . *Life is a series of missed opportunities, wrong paths, and mistaken turns. Why did I marry Gordon? Good question. To be honest with you, I can't explain it. Perhaps it was the culmination of a long list of rapid changes occurring in my life at the time. Or conceivably the glamour of Washington and the picture Gordon painted of it. Or a very insecure girl's ultimate search for a security blanket. In the final analysis, though, I would have to admit that it was probably because he was the first to ask me.*
>
> *The initial five years were okay. Good even. But as my self-confidence grew and I matured, I came to realize something was missing. Something very big. It was, in truth, the essence of totally unconditional love. You had defined it for me during one of my early visits to your office that first year.*

Do you remember? I hope so. When it finally hit me that I had merely satisfied—remember when you explained that word to me?—I sank to the depths of depression. Not severe depression, mind you, but a healthy—what a choice of words—dose of depression nonetheless.

I fell into a pattern of simply going through the motions of love. I was good at it, primarily because Gordon didn't care. He was not around very much. He was too wrapped up in himself and his work. So I stopped being around. I sought refuge in my own work. I wanted children, but not with Gordon. Only with my soul mate. But I was probably suppressing who that might be. Until I allowed the light bulb to turn on years later.

Do you know what I cherished most during my nineteen years of marriage? Maybe I should feel guilty for saying this. Darn it, I don't feel guilty at all. It was three special nights out of nineteen years. Our pilgrimage every five years to La Chandelle. That should have told me something, but it didn't. At least at first. I had explained to Gordon when he married me that I came with some baggage. One of the bags was you and our friendship.

Gordon wasn't very pleased about that, but it didn't matter. My La Chandelle trips were the only times Gordon ever showed the slightest bit of jealousy. Of course, I never gave him any reason to be jealous. But it made him mad that I would not allow him near La Chandelle, even in the "off years." He once tried to stop me from our pent-annual dinner. Remember when that was supposed to be the litmus test for approval by each of us of the other's initial choice of a mate? I would not agree to it.

The pact to meet every five years proved to be the one constant in my life. It always gave me an extra boost of self-assurance. It was only twenty-four hours or so each time, but I cherished it. As the date approached, I grew really excited. I guess because it brought back such good memories.

I know, it wasn't the only time we saw each other over the years. Your visits to Washington from time to time were always a treat for me. And I savored our periodic talks on the phone. I calculated that we probably talked about four or five times a year long-distance. They always left me with a good feeling. The thing that struck me more than anything else was our ability to resume a conversation as if we had talked only yesterday. It was uncanny. Also uncanny was your ability to predict what I was going to say next. You knew me better than anyone, certainly better than Gordon did.

And I came to understand that I knew you too, so well. Except for one thing. I couldn't figure out why you never married. I heard what you were saying, that you hadn't found your soul mate. But I guessed that after awhile, you might have "satisficed." You didn't, though. Today I am so thankful for your perseverance.

Finally, I came to the realization I did not love Gordon and probably never really loved him. I felt so sad and very, very guilty. Did I have the courage to do something about it? At first, no. But I sensed Gordon felt the same way. When we finally got around to talking about our marriage, I found out I was right. There was nothing to save. Inertia and indifference captured his feelings.

The divorce was amicable, at least at first, and very quick. We argued over some possessions and fought a little over blame. The emptiness I felt when Gordon was gone had nothing to do with him and everything to do with me. I hesitated to tell you at first. I didn't want you to think me a failure. Your approval had always been important to me. But you knew me too well. Your initial question when we talked for the first time suggested you sensed something major had happened and you were almost certain what it was.

You were wonderful in the way you helped me through the emptiness. You didn't have to fly up to see me, but you did, the very first Friday. We talked nonstop for eight hours before exhaustion took over. The next day you took my mind off my troubles, or at least changed the setting so I could talk more clearly about them. Do you remember? We went over to Annapolis and the Eastern Shore, retracing the steps of our journey during my internship almost twenty years earlier. Fisherman's Inn and Angler's were still there, which brought a smile to my face. The stroll on the beach had the usual effect on me. The combination of the salt air, the sound of the waves, and the panoramic beauty in front of me cleared my senses and allowed me to think straight.

I wasn't consciously thinking of you yet as my soul mate. That wouldn't become a possibility until later, sometime between the time your father died and our fourth pent-annual trip to La Chandelle. I was just trying to get my life in order and move forward. I realized then that my

marriage had stunted some very important areas of growth that I want-
ed to experience. And I knew, because you had given me that self-confi-
dence, that I would find it.

You were such an angel! I think of how intensely you loved me, how
long you had loved me, and how much you had desired me—yet you
kept your actions that weekend focused entirely on helping me through
my psychological and physical transition. I was just awe-struck at how
powerful our friendship had become.

When you left to go back to Chapel Hill, I think I began to see you
in a different light, or perhaps, an additional light. I even entertained the
notion that you might have been my soul mate all along. But it scared
me, so I laughed at the thought and quickly dismissed it. Today I simply
smile at the idea. . . .

After comforting Sarah, Jonathan returned to North Carolina with
mixed emotions. Although he had rationalized away his failure to marry
her two decades earlier and had come to accept his life as one of much
satisfaction, Sarah's revelation of her divorce rekindled in him feelings
that had long lay dormant. He struggled with the security of his present existence with all of its certainties versus the possibility, however
remote, that he might have a life with her after all.

He had always told himself that all he wanted was for Sarah to be
happy. Had that meant spending her life with Gordon or someone else,
that's what he would have wanted. He understood that perfect love is
unselfish love. He would have been happy in the knowledge that Sarah
was happy—an affirmation of his unselfish love.

But she had not found happiness with Gordon. She was still searching for it. Not very hard yet. But she would. Jonathan knew he and
Sarah were soul mates. He was convinced of that. At that moment, he
decided to risk the security of the present for a chance at total happiness in the future.

When he walked into his office Monday morning, his secretary—
it was one of the perks of his chaired professorship—sensed a difference
in him. He was not the same Dr. Hawthorne. Something extraordinary
had occurred. Propriety prevented Mrs. Walker from asking what on
earth had happened over the weekend. The transformation in Jonathan

that day was just the first of many wonderful changes that would soon overtake his life.

Word spread quickly among the "Dr. Hawthorne's look-afters," that unofficial group of women who had been looking after him for years trying desperately to find him a mate, that something wonderful had happened. Dr. Hawthorne was a different man. No one dared inquire about the reason, at least not at first. A week later, a colleague's spouse finally cornered him at a reception and asked, "My, you look pleased about something, Jonathan. Anything you wish to share with us?"

But he just smiled and said nothing. After a few weeks, the campus chattering slowed, until it finally came to a stop a month later.

Jonathan talked with Sarah every week. They were conversations between friends, one helping the other. He had performed that role more than twenty years earlier, she reminded him. They talked about the walk in the rain one night long ago, his arm around her. She confided to him what a source of strength he had been then. He smiled as the memory of that evening grew more vivid.

He still had his grandiose plan. Actually, it wasn't a plan yet—only a conviction that they would finally be together. But before he could design the grand strategy, something intervened—a tragedy. Jonathan's father suffered a massive stoke. The call from home told of the suddenness with which General Hawthorne had been struck. Could Jonathan come home quickly? His father may not make it. He took a plane the next morning and arrived in Colorado Springs in the early afternoon.

As he waited for his luggage, he thought how eerie the trip had been. *Deja vu.* Twenty-two years earlier, he had made the same journey. Although he had come to grips with Ben's death years before, thoughts of his brother stayed with him every single day. Now his father. The difference was that his father had led a full life. His time was soon, if not imminent. But the hurt in his stomach was no less than it had been when Ben died. He loved his father. Their relationship had been a good one.

It was *deja vu* with Sarah as well. Just like before, his first call to a friend after he received the news was to Sarah. She was home that evening, just as she had been twenty-two years earlier. She consoled him once again.

"Oh, Jonathan, I'm so sorry. What can I do?" she asked.

"As you have always done. Be there with me in your thoughts. That will give me the strength I need," Jonathan replied.

"But I want to be there in person for you, to help you. May I come? You need someone there with you. Let me be that one," Sarah offered.

"You've always been that one, haven't you, Sarah?" Jonathan reminded her. "Okay. I'd like you there with me. But I should warn you. Everything is up in the air. The early reports aren't good. Dad may or may not make it. It's too soon to know one way or the other. He could completely recover. He could die today or tomorrow. Or he could linger for a long, long time."

"I have some vacation time due me. I'll be there as soon as possible. Is that okay?" Sarah asked.

"Thanks, friend. I really am glad that you are coming. I do need you. Bye," Jonathan said.

"Bye, Jonathan. Take care of yourself," she said.

Jonathan arrived at the hospital and went straight to the intensive care unit. His mother, relatives, and friends were there pacing as he walked in. Within seconds, he was hugging his mother as tears flowed down their cheeks. She immediately took him in to see his father. The General was unconscious, hooked to a number of machines that helped his breathing and monitored his every bodily function. Sadness overtook Jonathan as he viewed his father. Although he had held out hope during the trip home for his dad's recovery, he saw immediately that there was no chance his father would make it. It was simply a matter of time.

Sarah made it there later that day and was with him continuously during the three-day vigil that followed. They were returning from a thirty-minute walk break the afternoon of the third day when his uncle met him at the hospital entrance with the news. His dad had died peacefully five minutes earlier. The tears flowed freely as Sarah and Jonathan embraced.

"How I loved that man! He was such a wonderful father." Jonathan had difficulty getting the words out.

"Oh, I'm so sorry, Jonathan. You gave him the greatest gift you could. You were a perfect son," Sarah reassured him.

"Thanks for being here with me. It means so much. I really need you," he told her.

They turned and scurried to where his mother was. She reached for him instinctively as he ran into the room. Sarah would later tell him how touched she was at what transpired between mother and son at that moment.

The viewing took place two nights later, and the funeral the following day. Sarah remained the entire time, leaving the day after the burial. It was a sad scene at the airport when Jonathan saw her off. He stayed a week more to help his mother take care of some necessary affairs before returning to Chapel Hill.

His dad's death had had a profound effect on Sarah.

> . . . *Your father's death was so sad. I didn't know why, but I had a real need to be with you. I don't know what I would have done had you said no to my coming. I felt so sorry for you, and helpless too. I had seen you grieve for your brother. Now I was watching you mourn your father.*
>
> *I couldn't understand at first why I also viewed it as my loss. But I did. Later I would figure it out. I didn't want to leave you the day after the funeral. But I had to. When I said good-bye and boarded the plane, I felt lonelier than I had been for a long time. I thought about that the whole way home. . . .*

The late autumn turned to winter, then to spring. His dad's death was still on his mind, but the grieving process was moving forward, helped by Sarah's frequent calls. Her last phone call reminded Jonathan their pent-annual event was near. They decided to extend the visit a few days longer than usual. They made plans to meet at the Raleigh airport when her flight arrived the afternoon of June 2. Sarah had reserved a room at the new hotel built on the Duke golf course.

PART FOUR

~ 22 ~

Soul Mates

Sarah's plane was on time as it approached the Raleigh-Durham airport. June was the beginning of the hot summer season in the Piedmont region, but the view from the sky still revealed a lush greenness. There was a haunting beauty to the tall, thin pines with their blanket of pine needles resting at their feet, serving as an outline to the airport's boundaries. She could always tell when the plane was near the Research Triangle, as the area around the airport was called. The trees appeared more stately, more inviting. And the clay soil took on a somewhat darker shade of red than found elsewhere.

Sarah seemed excited as she scurried through the jetway and into Jonathan's waiting arms. It was 1990, twenty-three years since they had first met. As much as she mesmerized him as she walked through the doorway and into his classroom for the first time, he thought her even more beautiful now.

The drive to the Washington Duke Inn, the massive new hotel complex near the eighteenth green of the Duke golf course, took thirty minutes. Sarah was continuing her pre-divorce practice of staying at a hotel rather than at Jonathan's house during their pent-annual visits. He was going to suggest his place this time, the first visit since her split from Gordon, but he decided against it. It was better that she initiate such a move.

Sarah had not seen the new hotel, which had opened only a few months earlier. Its magnificence overwhelmed her. Jonathan waited in the lobby while she put her luggage in her room. They planned to sightsee around campus for awhile before returning—she to her hotel room and he to his home—to change clothes. Although the spring flowers were long gone, the campus was never more beautiful. They walked up and down the quad, laughing at all the funny memories they had shared there. Across to the Duke Gardens they went, where they jointly replayed the story of Sarah's last night on campus. It was then that Jonathan confessed to her that he had saved the wine bottle from that evening. It rested on his bookshelf in his den. Sarah smiled at his revelation. Across the golf course they ambled, pausing at the first green in homage to their mischievous evening there, the night of Bobby Kennedy's California primary victory.

It was good to be with Sarah again, he thought. It was their first time together since his dad's death. As she had always been able to do, she made him laugh. She also made him lust. The prohibitions he had held tightly in place for twenty years were quickly crumbling. He no longer felt constrained about fantasizing again about her. Quite the contrary. He had dreamed often about her in the months since her divorce. He had allowed the dreams to explore freely anywhere they wanted to go.

Sarah and Jonathan went back to the Washington Duke Inn for a drink in the bar overlooking the course. Liquor laws had changed in the late 1970s. It was now possible to buy alcohol by the drink in most parts of North Carolina. Sarah had a vodka and tonic to celebrate late spring. Jonathan ordered the same, but without the lime.

"Well, this will be our fourth pent-annual visit to La Chandelle," Jonathan mused. "Do you remember when we took your parents there the night before graduation? That was really a wonderful evening."

"I remember how nervous you were about how my parents would react to 'the professor,' as they then called you," Sarah said.

"Of course I was nervous. You had told them all about us," Jonathan remarked. "I was afraid they might think I had some less-than-honorable motives for befriending you."

"Well, didn't you?" Sarah asked.

"Of course," Jonathan replied, laughing. "But that's beside the point. I was helping their daughter."

"They knew that. They loved you for it. They still love you for it. For what you did then and what you do now," she told him.

Forty-five minutes later, they parted to get ready for dinner. Jonathan was back at the hotel at seven. He stopped in his tracks when Sarah emerged from the elevator. Her red sundress, buttoned in the front, flowed freely as she walked toward him. As often as he had seen her dress up, he couldn't remember when she had looked more radiant. His red tie with blue dots matched her outfit.

La Chandelle never changed. That was one of the two reasons why Jonathan liked it so much. The other was because of all the memories of the time he had spent there with the woman he loved. It had been twenty-two years since they first ate there. Sarah appeared ravishing that first evening, and she looked captivating now. The years had been good to her. Very good. The mature grace and loveliness of early middle age had replaced the youthful beauty of her early twenties. Sarah was now forty-three. She would still be lovely when she was seventy-three, he was convinced.

Jonathan had aged well too. His weight had not changed much, thanks to his vigorous workout schedule. His hair had a touch of gray in it, and it was beginning to recede somewhat. But he carried himself elegantly, Sarah told him, particularly for a man who had just left his forties. She laughed at her little joke, but he pretended to be offended by it.

Dinner was splendid. Never had La Chandelle touched his soul like it did that evening—the setting, the music, the food, the wine, and the company. How he enjoyed Sarah so! She mesmerized him that evening as she always did. But this time it was different. He could feel it. He also sensed a change in Sarah. It was a distinct change, but it was subtle at the same time. Only his many years with her allowed him to see something different about her behavior.

He couldn't quite put his finger on it, though. She was just a little more open, a little more "touchy-feely," and a little more intimate in conversation. It wasn't just the wine, although the alcohol did contribute some. Rather, Jonathan sensed a freer Sarah, or a more flirtatious Sarah perhaps. It was hard to say. They had been such good friends for so long that they had enjoyed a freer type of give-and-take than most new friends or acquaintances have. The longer the evening wore on, the more extended the eye contact between them grew. It was as if each was afraid that glancing away would cause the other to vanish.

It was a leisurely dinner. But all good things must come to an end or continue elsewhere, Sarah said, so Jonathan paid the bill and they left. Arm in arm, they made their way to the car. Neither appeared eager to pick up the pace. It was a moonlit night, with relatively low humidity for an early June North Carolina evening. Jonathan hugged her shoulders as she prepared to enter the car. The drive to the hotel was unusually quiet. Midway back, the song "Lady in Red" began to play on the radio. Both smiled at the coincidence of Sarah's dress and the song. "Lady in Red" came to symbolize his lifelong fascination with her.

Jonathan parked in a regular parking space rather than in a short-term spot closer to the hotel entrance. If Sarah picked up on the significance of the move, she gave no indication. If truth be told, Jonathan had selected the place subconsciously. As they entered the lobby, he paused, turned toward her, and asked, "Would you like a nightcap?"

"Just one, out on the patio, maybe," Sarah suggested.

A glass of sherry warmed each of them as they sat under the stars. They snuggled a little against the soft breeze blowing toward them from across the eighteenth fairway. Soon their glasses were empty. Each rose without a word and started toward the patio door that would take them back into the hotel. Turning instinctively toward each other after a few steps, they slowly pressed forward until they were locked in an embrace. They had often held each other. But this time it seemed different to Jonathan. Sarah was pressing herself against him more intimately than she ever had before.

Both stepped back a pace, stared at each other, and then came forward once more. This time their lips met each other in a soft, gentle, but prolonged kiss. Jonathan placed his hand on the back of her head and turned it slightly so that her cheek pressed against his lips. After another soft kiss, his lips moved to her hair where he patiently inhaled its scent, pressing his lips tightly against its blackness. They were still locked in each other's arms. He could feel their hearts beating against each other.

Sarah backed a short distance away, smiled, and simply said in a soft voice as she held out her hand, "Come."

Jonathan reached for her hand, and, without a word, they entered the lobby, headed for the elevator, and took it to the fifth floor. Room 525 faced the eighteenth green. The huge window allowed the moon's dim light into the room. They entered it and walked slowly toward the window, peering outside for a few minutes, his arm across her shoulders, until they could make out the shape of the golf course below.

Sarah slowly turned toward Jonathan, and in a soft and tender voice uttered those words he had waited to hear for twenty-three years. "I think I've finally found my soul mate. I love you, Jonathan. Come undress me, my love. And look me in the eyes as you do. I want to watch you."

"You have found your soul mate, my precious Sarah. I've loved you from the very first moment I saw you," Jonathan confessed. A tear flowed down his cheek.

Sarah noticed it, and with her hand she gently brushed it away. "You dear, dear, wonderful man. Come make love to me."

And so he did. The red dress was first. Five buttons down the front. Jonathan unbuttoned each one of them deliberately while his eyes never left Sarah's. His hand, shaking, briefly touched her skin as the dress parted further with each move. As the last button came undone, the front of the dress separated completely. Jonathan slowly pushed the one side back over her right shoulder, then repeated it on the other side. The dress dropped to the floor. His heart pounded. The moonlight framed the outline of her nearly nude body. Sarah looked so beautiful!

While still maintaining eye contact, his hands began to touch, ever so gently, the part of her arms, shoulders, and lower chest that the dress had covered. Very rhythmically and tenderly, his hands moved over her warm body with a touch as soft as he could summon. Sarah signaled her pleasure with a muted sigh. Jonathan's smile revealed his feelings. He couldn't believe it was finally happening.

Next, he moved to the upper part of her breasts not covered by her bra. Gently, he moved his fingers over the soft skin, again barely touching it. His index fingers followed the outline of her bra but never transgressed on its space. That would come later. Ever so gently, his fingers moved over and over the same part. She smiled as their eyes continued to watch each other. Despite the fire in his groin, he wanted so much to be patient. He wished to bring her alive slowly but completely. He desired to give, not take from her. He wanted to see the smile of utter satisfaction and exhaustion on her face when they fell back, finished.

Sarah's bra fastened in the front. Despite a clumsiness arising from his shaking hand, Jonathan unfastened it and slowly pulled each side away from her body, letting it join her dress at her feet. His eyes left hers to absorb the beauty of her swelling breasts, unleashed from the constraints of her clothing. But only for a moment. He had been right about her breasts years earlier. They were beautiful. He told her so in a hushed voice, bringing a smile to her face. For the rest of her life, she never tired of his constant reminders of how ravishing they were.

Sarah's smile was his reward. So were her hands. She placed them under her breasts and began to massage them rhythmically as if to music from somewhere off in the distance. Slowly Jonathan began to caress them, observing at once their roundness and firmness as they pushed outward and upward from her chest. But he didn't feel the nipples— not yet. He wanted his first encounter with the most exquisite nipples he had ever seen to last as long as possible. So he caressed only the outer edges of her breasts at first. His touch alternated from fleeting softness to moderate pressure. Her groans suggested he had found the right mix. Soon he began to close his fingertips over the middle of each nipple. He continued to caress them, again not moving his eyes from hers.

"I love your nipples. I have thought about how beautiful they must be since that day I first saw you. My fantasies came up short though. They feel so good!" he said.

Sarah smiled at Jonathan's comment, then placed her hands over his as he continued to caress her breasts. "Do what you want with them. They're yours!"

As she uttered those words, Sarah moved her hands from her side to his chest. She began to rub it gently, slowly unbuttoning the top three buttons of his blue shirt. She slipped her hand inside and caressed his chest, all the while staring at him intensely. Her touch on his body caused his heart to beat even faster.

Jonathan's hand moved to his mouth, where he moistened his fingers. Returning them to Sarah's breast, he focused on her right nipple, caressing it, moving his fingers at first back and forth, then in a circle around its outside as the nipple became harder and bigger. Her sighs increased as he expanded the motion, wetting his fingertips from time to time so as to sustain the warmth of his touch. Soon a second set of moistened fingers was caressing her other nipple, inducing the same hardened pointedness.

Jonathan's eyes now left Sarah's as he brought his lips to her breasts. At first the kisses were gentle with lips not yet parted. But soon they separated, and his tongue moved forward to kiss each nipple, now more pointed than ever. The warmness of his tongue made her squirm as he continued kissing and sucking each nipple.

Sarah responded by lowering her hands until they moved over the warmer part of his body. They strolled across the entire front of him.

Jonathan could tell she sensed how hard he was. It was time to move toward warmer pleasures. He reached down and removed her black shoes, then her hose. He laid her gently on her side on the bed. Sarah's only remaining piece of clothing was her panties, barely covering a small part of her. Jonathan quickly removed his clothes and lay down next to her.

His hands then moved deliberately over the back and sides of her panties. He loved the feel of his hands there. The simplest caress awakened in the depths of his body even stronger desires for Sarah. He tried to keep his touch as light as possible, gently moving his hand first in a vertical fashion over the middle of her bottom, then outward to the sides.

Placing Sarah on her back, he began to caress the front of her, again taking care to move only partway to her warmth at first. His hand alternated from the burning flesh on the inside of her thighs to her stomach. It felt so good to feel the warmth of the woman whom he had desired for so long. He was content to take his time. His hard penis might have disagreed, but it was not going to dictate the pace of the evening—at least not yet.

Jonathan's hand began its slow journey toward Sarah's warmth. Delicately, very delicately, he flirted with its edges, his fingers exerting a minimum of pressure, each time for only a brief moment. Each caress propelled him a little closer to her wetness. He moved his fingers around the edges of her panties and onto her bare skin. Sarah gasped as he inched forward into wetter and wetter territory.

Jonathan slid her panties down over her ankles and onto the floor.

Separating her legs further, he bent down close to her warmth and, using his fingers, gently pushed the folds of skin apart. He brought his tongue down on her, inching ever so slowly toward the spot that would, he knew, unleash such wonderful pleasures. He was not wrong. His tongue began slowly to taste her wetness, then darted wildly from side to side, searching for the magic place. An uncontrollable shaking throughout her entire body—beginning slowly but then escalating quickly as sexual desire took over every sensory nerve—soon gave it away. He had found Sarah's spot. Her wetness permeated every fiber of the skin on his face, leaving a taste that would still be there twenty-four hours later. Its familiar scent, left untouched by the next morning's shower, would remind him of the happiest night of his life.

As Jonathan brought Sarah to climax, he could wait no longer. He entered her with a hardness he had never known before. At first his thrusts were powerful and fast, until she came once again. But he didn't want to come yet. He simply wished to make Sarah totally happy and completely satisfied. That would give him more pleasure far longer and far greater than his climax would. So he paused for awhile.

This gave Sarah the opportunity to take the initiative. She did so excitedly, reaching for his penis, still hard as ever. Slowly she began to caress it, taking care to touch all of him. Jonathan could not move. She touched him in such a way so as to prolong its hardness. She smiled and told him she didn't want him to come yet. As his breathing began to rage out of control, she backed off. As he quieted down, she increased her stroking.

Sarah then moved her body so that her face was close to his stomach. Ever so delicately she began to kiss his midsection, moving her lips in a circle that grew larger with each revolution. Finally her tongue found his penis, and she began to kiss its sides in a somewhat tantalizing manner. She moved in a deliberate motion over the entire surface, careful not to excite him too much for fear he would come. She wanted his first time with her to be deep inside her. Sarah's lips then moved toward its top and began a slow back-and-forth motion, characterized by a gentleness that only served to excite Jonathan even more. After a few moments, she directed his penis inside of her. A huge smile appeared on her face as she felt Jonathan filling her.

"I want to see your eyes when you come inside of me for the first time, my darling," she said softly.

They began a slow movement of their bodies, increasing the speed until both were on the edge of coming. Faster and faster they moved until there was no longer any doubt it was time. Jonathan exploded inside of Sarah as she thrashed about widely, herself now in the midst of a deep orgasm. Shouts of "I love you!, I love you! I love you!" echoed across the room.

Of all the fantasies of making love to Sarah that had flowed throughout Jonathan's brain over the years, none had come close to capturing their first real life experience. Making love with one's best friend, one's soul mate—well, there was nothing better or more satisfying. His smile was never larger. It would never be the same again.

Their entire bodies went limp, hers resting on his, the sweat falling from both of them as if they were in a steam bath. It seemed like forever before their breathing returned to normal. They were content at that moment to lie there motionless, basking in the afterglow of their first love-making. After what seemed like an hour, Sarah began to kiss Jonathan's face. She moved to his ears, then to his neck. He was content to allow her to explore his upper body. He had dreamed so long of this moment. Sarah's kissing continued. Again she aroused him, so he once more went deep inside of her, penetrating as far as possible. Soon they both came, simultaneously as before.

There would be no more love-making for awhile. They lay there in each other's arms, not saying a word. There was no need to. Everything was understood. Clearly understood. Soon Jonathan was caressing her body once again. He quickly found her spot, the thin piece of skin that stood out from the rest of her. Slowly he moved his finger back and forth over it with just a slight amount of pressure. Within fifteen seconds she started to stir. Within thirty she was moving quickly. Within forty-five, she was out of control. At one minute she was climaxing, with only a pillow pressed against her mouth keeping her from waking the entire cadre of guests at The Washington Duke Inn. They both fell back, exhausted, in each other's arms.

Sleep overtook both of them for about half an hour. Sarah awoke first. When Jonathan opened his eyes, she was staring at him with that smile that had captivated him the first day he saw her decades earlier. Jonathan began to speak, but before the first word flowed from his mouth, Sarah put her fingers against his lips and softly whispered, "Hold me. Just hold me for awhile. This feels so good. So perfect. I love the warmth of your body."

And so Jonathan took her in his arms, their legs wrapped around each other, and held her. He was content to do so. Twenty-three years of desire had been unleashed that evening. He was in heaven. His hands would not stop. He began to caress her once more, slowly. Her sigh revealed her pleasure at his touch. For fifteen minutes they lay there, locked together, while they engaged in light touching.

Finally, Sarah spoke. "Well, well, well. What have we just done, my dearest Jonathan?" She was still smiling and appeared very content.

"I will tell you what I've just done," Jonathan replied. "I have just made love to the woman who first mesmerized me a long time ago, and has captivated me ever since. I have just lived every fantasy that had entered my mind since the day I met you. Actually, no. It was more wonderful than any fantasy I ever had. I have just experienced what I thought would never be mine to experience. I thank you, my sweet Sarah. And I will tell you. I love you. Three short simple words, but they convey everything I feel. Absolutely everything. I love you. I love you. I love you."

"You adorable, wonderful man," Sarah said. "I should be the one to thank you—for waiting all these years. Why didn't you tell me a long, long time ago how you felt?"

"You know the answer to that. But now's not the time to talk about what might have been. Let's just experience what is," Jonathan replied.

"You're so right. I've had such a warm feeling for you for a long time, an incredibly long time. I don't know when it passed over into love, but it did, probably years ago before I married Gordon. But I had an unmistakable sense of it when I was at your parents' home when your dad died. I wanted to take you into my arms that day and say, 'Make love to me tonight. Let me help you take your mind off your dad.' But that would have been silly.

"When I returned home, I wondered if I just felt sorry for you. Or if I had really gone through one of life's big passages. I couldn't be certain, at least at first, but soon I was convinced. And when I walked through the jetway today and saw you, I knew immediately that my recent instincts had been correct. It had nothing to do with feeling sorry for you. I did love you, so much, and probably had for a long, long time. Far longer than I dare to admit to myself, even today. So come kiss me again, my favorite professor."

And Jonathan did, everywhere. Sarah returned the favor. They could not stop repeating how much they loved each other. It was as if, since they had waited so long to utter those words, they could not stop now that they each had the chance. And they didn't.

Deep sleep came easily to both of them as they lay locked in a tight embrace of their entire bodies. The morning sunrise was never more beautiful. But Jonathan and Sarah never saw it. The smiles on their faces as they both lay buried in sleep told the whole story.

Sarah reflected on that night not long thereafter when Jonathan asked her to marry him.

. . . What can I say about the night we first made love and told each other we had found our soul mates? I know you had waited for that evening far longer than I had. It was years measured against months. So your anticipation had to be incredible. How can I put it to capture what the evening was and what it meant to me? It was simply the most wonderful night of my life.

First, my taking the initiative. I guess I surprised you that night when I took your hand and told you with one word—"come"—that I wanted you. All of you. I had spent the time since my divorce really thinking through my entire life—where I had been, where I was, where I was going. And with whom I wanted to share the rest of my journey. I kept coming back to you, my dear.

When I was with you as you grieved for your father, I came to a startling discovery. I loved you! Really loved you! Had loved you! Probably for a long time! That realization brought the biggest and longest smile to my face. But it scared me as well. What if you didn't love me? I tried to retrace our entire existence together. Boy, did it take a long time! Six months. As I fitted one piece after another together, I came to the conclusion you probably loved me, or could be induced to do so. I smiled right then and there. I also concluded you had probably loved me for a very long time, although I didn't realize it was since that first year we met. It really blew me away when I found that out. So when you revealed your love for me as we turned to one another in Room 525 for the first time, I was not surprised. But greatly relieved? Oh, yes!

Let me also tell you about our love-making that first night. Was it good! Really, really good! Better than any I had ever experienced before. I've come to expect it routinely now, but the first time it was totally unexpected. I knew it would be wonderful because I had already discovered I loved you. Making love with one's best friend should be the ultimate. But every part of it exceeded any thought I might have had about how it might go. You were marvelous. What you did to my body! I felt the physical warmth for days, I believe. You aroused in me a previously unknown sexuality. I responded to your touch much, much more intensely than I had ever done before.

It just seemed so natural. I wanted to please you. I don't know if I surprised you that night, but I surprised myself. What I discovered later when our love-making became even more intimate was that these new things pleased me too, greatly. You now know how much I love to kiss every inch of your body, and how much I want your tongue to explore every inch of mine.

We had been best friends for so long and yet had not been to bed before. That made it so special. Our love-making was so different than anything I had experienced before. It was the intimacy that overwhelmed me that night and continues to astound me today. What makes it so intimate? That's an easy question. Giving—that's the first thing that comes to mind. Trust. Complete trust. Gentleness. Wanting to satisfy the other person, over and over again. Desire. Continual desire. Anything goes. And finally—it is really love-making, joint love-making, one soul mate to another. It is love being demonstrated unconditionally, without reservation, without fear, and with total commitment. That's what our love-making is. I love you, best friend. . . .

~ 23 ~

Dream Realized

Jonathan awoke slowly the next morning. He thought he had been dreaming. The images dancing across his brain were too good to be true. As his hand moved deliberately across the bed, it touched something. Someone. He knew then he had not been dreaming. He realized Sarah was lying next to him, sound asleep. The smile that had graced his face as he fell asleep in the wee hours of the night immediately returned.

He sat up partway in bed, careful not to wake her. He wanted to look at her, stare at her. Sarah was lying on her stomach. She was so captivating! The sheet did not cover all of her, so Jonathan began to explore every visible inch of her body. After about five minutes, he could contain himself no longer. Slowly he began to move his fingers gingerly over her exposed flesh, careful to touch her only so lightly. There was not an uncovered inch that did not feel Jonathan's gentle graze. As each moment went by, he could feel himself becoming aroused again. He was so much in love with her. To have his desires fulfilled after all those years was simply incredible. Too much to ask. But it was happening. Oh, was it happening!

His lips soon replaced his hands. Again he used them ever so gently. He began to kiss and lick every part of Sarah outside the sheet. He was so aroused that it was all he could do to continue his gentle touch. His tongue moved across her back, wetting each point of contact. Lower and lower his lips moved until he had crossed the small of her back. Still he did not stop. They searched for her bottom, gently kissing each cheek. Then Jonathan moved down the back of the one exposed leg. Her skin was so soft. He remembered her calf muscles from that first day in class so many years before. Now he was kissing and caressing them. They had lost none of their beauty or allure.

Although she was still asleep, Sarah began to moan and stir. Jonathan's touch was having an effect on her. A wonderful effect. Soon she was alert enough to know where she was. The same smile that had crossed Jonathan's face when he awoke now appeared on Sarah's. She was content to have him caress her body. He was eager to do so. Soon she could not lay idly by. Her hands began to move across Jonathan's body. They were a welcome touch.

"Good morning, my love," were the first words from her mouth.

"Good morning, sweetheart. In case you don't remember from last night, I love you," Jonathan said. Sarah smiled at his remark.

"I hope you haven't forgotten what I said, or did, to you last night, my love. I haven't. Every single word spoken then was true, and long overdue. So take them, my dear, and place them somewhere deep in your heart. I love you, my sweetheart," he continued.

With that, Sarah raised her parted lips toward Jonathan and kissed him, softly at first, then with a passion remarkable for the short time since she had been awake. He was ready to respond. Soon he was deep inside her making love once more. This time both were on the edge of climax for what seemed like the longest time. They both looked passionately at each other as Jonathan moved, just fast enough to keep both of them on the edge, but slow enough to avoid a climax. He was glad it was morning, as he could see her face clearly. It had the unmistakable look of someone deeply in love, who was at that very moment enjoying the pleasures of being made love to by her soul mate. He knew his smile conveyed the same message.

Her face was so beautiful. His eyes could not leave hers as he continued his deliberate movement in and out of her. Sarah moaned a happy sound while holding onto him tightly. Jonathan did not want it to end. He was determined to keep her pleasure at just the right level so she would not beg him to come. It was a fine line, he knew, but he didn't want to cross it, not yet. He wished to make up for all those lonely nights the previous twenty-three years when their only love-making had occurred deep inside his mind.

On and on it went, with Sarah increasingly wet from the flashes of heat permeating her body. And still Jonathan moved in a deliberate manner. She wasn't going to be able to control herself, she shouted, but Jonathan slowed the speed and the intervals of his thrusts. Once again Sarah was simply in a high state of arousal.

"You're incredible, sweetheart," she screamed as she gasped for air. "What you're doing to me. Don't stop. Don't ever stop."

But Jonathan and Sarah were only human. A minute later they both came at the same time, thrashing wildly about and shouting uncontrollably.

Back to sleep they went for about an hour, locked in each other's arms. Jonathan again was the one to awaken first. Once more he simply looked at Sarah until she stirred about ten minutes later. Sarah was smiling that wonderful smile again. They instinctively reached for each other and hugged the embrace of lovers.

"You're not leaving me today, are you, Jonathan?" Sarah asked.

"As long as you want me here, I'm here. How's that?" he said.

"That's what I wanted to hear. How about for forever? Is that asking too much, my dear?" Sarah said.

"You know the answer to that, my love," Jonathan replied.

With that, they both smiled and kissed each other. Sarah was the first to speak again. "How about a shower together? I want to wash every inch of your body."

"Only if I can reciprocate. We may not make it out of this room today at this rate," Jonathan joked.

"What's so bad about that?" Sarah wanted to know.

Jonathan only smiled. He had never taken a shower with a woman before. He found out quickly what he had missed. Sarah took the soap and started with his chest. But she didn't stay there long. Before he knew it, she was washing his groin, then his bottom. It was clear he would never be cleaner when she had finished. He soon detected how hard he could get in the shower. He also discovered how readily he could slip deep inside her. And how easily they could move, even with the water pouring over their bodies and the floor slippery from the fallen soap suds. He also found out how quickly he could come.

He discovered something else as well. Sarah loved to have him wash her body. Her entire body. It responded eagerly to his rubbing. Jonathan felt he was going through a whole bar of soap in his effort to satisfy her every desire. He was successful, more than once. They locked themselves around each other as the hot water pounded their bodies and their senses.

Soon they were back on the bed. It was unclear which one was preventing the other from dressing. They were laughing and giggling so much, interspersing it with kisses everywhere.

"Do you know what I want to do today, my love?" Sarah had apparently been thinking and planning.

Jonathan smiled. Whatever she wanted to do that day, no matter how outrageous, was okay with him. He was in heaven.

"I want to first check out of here," she continued. "Then I want to walk every inch of the campus. Arm in arm. I want to kiss you publicly, at every place we've ever been together. The quad, the Gardens, the golf course, the library, your office—all have special meaning for me, for us. If you're adventurous, I even want to make love in your old office. Can we get a key? Then I want to go back to your place and soak in the hot tub. I can't guarantee I'll keep my hands off you either. Then let's return tonight to La Chandelle, our special place. Finally, I want to come back to your place, make wild, wonderful, passionate love, then fall fast asleep in your arms. How does all of that sound?"

Jonathan thought it sounded perfect. So off they went. It was a day for new lovers. And the two of them were well-suited. Their three-hour stroll around campus was especially sentimental. While they were not obscene about it, they exhibited a continual public display of affection the entire time. They were usually hand in hand. He had an occasional arm around her shoulders. They stole a quick kiss every so often, and three passionate kisses when they thought themselves alone. It was "down time" on campus, so it was virtually deserted. It wouldn't have mattered. Jonathan would have stood with Sarah in the middle of the quad during the change of classes the first day of the autumn semester and kissed her passionately. Dr Hawthorne's "look-afters," who would have been forewarned, would be lined up along the sidewalk watching closely, happy that they could finally breathe a sigh of relief. Their work was over, their job complete.

As they walked along the golf course, Jonathan remembered that moment long ago when he and Sarah were arm in arm on the rainy night Michael had left her. They came to the precise spot, the seventh green, where he had been tempted to take her in his arms, tell her he loved her, and then kiss her with abandon.

Jonathan paused, then said, "Sarah, do you remember that night we walked in the rain here and I tried to comfort you? Well, when we passed this very spot, I was severely tempted to tell you to forget Michael, confess all, and ask for your love. And, of course, kiss you fervently." He paused for a second, then turned really serious. "I'm twenty some years late. If you'll forgive me, I'd like to do now what I so desperately wanted to do then."

It was a tender kiss, at first, then a passionate one. A prolonged kiss. A kiss that said everything. The extended embrace that followed was icing on the cake. Their hearts, so close, pounded against each other.

"You wonderful, sweet man. How could I have been so blind?" Sarah whispered. "Why did I not see what your heart and your eyes were telling me? Why didn't I have enough sense to realize it was you, deep down, I loved all along?"

"The mysteries of the heart are just that, sweetheart. Wonderful mysteries," Jonathan answered. "We can't explain them. You were young, very young. I was your professor, for goodness sake. I can't tell you how often I had wished I had been just another student."

"I'm glad you weren't. You had such an influence on me. Our resulting friendship has been my most prized possession . . . until now."

The rest of the stroll conjured up similar memories of lost opportunities. Jonathan confessed each one of them, begged her forgiveness each time, then proceeded to do what he had wanted to do two decades earlier.

Sarah loved every moment of it. She feigned surprise at parts of his confession with comments like, "Oh, Jonathan, I don't believe a word of it. You lusted after me where, when?" But he just laughed and told her, yes, it was true. Every word of it. As much as Sarah loved him when that day started, she loved him so much more at its end.

There was only one campus goal that they hadn't met that day, she reminded him. "My dear, we didn't make love in your old office this afternoon."

He smiled and told her they had to leave some things undone for the next trip. They soon left campus and headed for his house by the lake. The hot tub was as advertised. It was Jonathan's first experience in a hot tub with a woman. It would not be his last.

They saved the best for later. Enchanting La Chandelle. Wonderful La Chandelle. Romantic La Chandelle. They finally spent an evening there as lovers, not just as friends. Jonathan was on target the first time he saw the place. It was a restaurant for lovers. He calculated they had eaten there at least a dozen times. None approached that night's excitement of sitting across from the woman he loved, had taken to bed for the first time in his life in the past twenty-fours hours, had told of his undying devotion to her, and who had his loved returned in kind. Of all the nights Jonathan had spent there with Sarah, this was the one he didn't want to end.

Conversation that evening centered on their experiences the previous twenty-four hours, their love for one another, and the implications of it all. Jonathan kept thinking it was all too good to be true. He was hesitant to assume anything beyond the moment.

Sarah, on the other hand, was not her characteristically shy self. She obviously sensed Jonathan's timidity. And she was now secure in her knowledge of his enduring affection for her. So she took the initiative. "Wow! What do we make of all of this, my love?" She later told him she had wanted him to come forward, but thought that might be difficult.

"I don't know. I'm afraid to think of the future, I guess," Jonathan said.

"Why?" she asked. But Sarah knew the answer. All of this she revealed to him later. Jonathan had desired a life with her for so long that he didn't dare dream it just might happen. His fantasies over the years might have been fantasies, but they were familiar fantasies. Secure fantasies. He was never hurt in his fantasies. Sarah understood all too well what was going through his mind. She had loved him for only a short period of time. Or at least she had only recently come to realize she loved him. Instead of making her less certain of what she desired for the future, she was as convinced as she could be of what she wanted. It was Jonathan. A life with Jonathan. As his lover. His companion. His soul mate. His wife. She was as certain of that as of anything in her entire life.

"Listen, my dear Jonathan," she continued. "I will tell you what the future holds. What I want for us. We are soul mates. That is reality. Our love is reality. Twenty-some years of missed opportunities are a reality. I want the reality that should have been but wasn't. Simply put, my sweetheart, I want a life with you. I want to spend every last day I have on this earth loving you and showing my love for you. And having you love me. Anything short of that simply won't do. Do you understand me? Do you really understand what I'm saying?"

Tears flowed down Jonathan's cheeks as he explained, "I love you so much that I've been afraid these last twenty-four hours to contemplate the implications of all of this. I want the same things you do. Oh, how I want them!"

The drive back to his house found Sarah snuggled close to him. The music on the radio was for lovers. "Those Were the Days," a song from her time on campus, played.

Sarah looked at Jonathan in the middle of the song and compared the past, present, and future. "Those early days were wonderful, these days are better, but our best days are still ahead," she said. With that, she reached up and kissed his cheek, then fell back into the snug position she had been occupying.

Their love-making that evening was different, less intense but more intimate in a way. They were already becoming familiar with each other, with the other's body, and with yet another aspect of each other's hearts. They fell into a deep sleep, their arms wrapped around each other in a lock of profound contentment and security.

Sarah went back to Washington two days later. But she did not return to her old routine. She and Jonathan were now committed to each other. It was a lifelong pledge. She immediately began the process of disengagement from the city that had been her home since her senior year at Duke.

❧ ❧ ❧

Most of the remaining summer weekends found her in Chapel Hill. They spent one August week in the mountains of Colorado and another on the Outer Banks. It was twenty-two years late, but they made love under the moonlight on the beach at Avon. It was while they were lying on the blanket basking in the warm afterglow that always accompanied their love-making that Jonathan officially asked Sarah to marry him.

And it was at Avon the next day where she began to compose the wonderful letter detailing her journey from student to friend to soul mate. She finished it a few days later, while the sea gulls serenaded them as they lay contently on the beach.

◄ ◄ ◄

Autumn found Sarah in Chapel Hill as much as possible. Their feelings for each other continued to grow, and their commitment strengthened. Their love-making took on more intense pleasure and greater intimacy as they came to know each other's bodies the way they had always known each other's souls.

◄ ◄ ◄

Jonathan and Sarah were married in mid-December in Duke Chapel. The night before the wedding, his mother and her parents joined them at La Chandelle for a most special dinner. There they toasted his dad and brother. The next day, the wedding guests raved about the Christmas season eggnog served at the reception. To a woman, "Dr. Hawthorne's look-afters" drank to excess, now freed at last from the years-long responsibility of finding a spouse for him.

As he repeated his vows, Jonathan's six-month-long smile was exceeded only by his mother's. She now knew she would go to her grave a happy woman. Her son had married the woman who had captured his heart years earlier.

Jonathan's and Sarah's life together, really together, had finally begun.

~ 24 ~

Life Together

Jonathan and Sarah honeymooned across the ocean. Their initial stop was Paris, the city of lovers, for a few days. A small, left-bank hotel that used to function as the British Embassy served as their headquarters. They searched for a Parisian version of La Chandelle for their first official meal abroad as husband and wife. They found it at L'Ambroise in the 4th arrondissement. The restaurant passed the test. Its high, ornate ceilings and book-lined shelves on the walls gave the impression of dining in someone's home—someone important.

They walked the streets for hours in search of the Paris they both knew and loved, holding on to each other against the wind of the mildest winter weather on record. Notre Dame, the Louvre, the Arc de Triomphe, the Eiffel Tower, the la place de la Concorde, the old opera house, and, of course, Montmartre. Sacré-Cœur, the beautiful white-domed cathedral, sat at the center of this most romantic of Parisian neighborhoods.

Montmartre's narrow and winding streets, strange squares, and broad vistas of the rest of Paris were perfect for lovers. Jonathan and Sarah joined other romantics strolling leisurely among its quaint streets and buildings. As they climbed the steep steps that took them up the hill on a gloomy night to a favorite hideaway café, they remembered Brassaï's famous photograph *Les Escaliers de Montmartre*. Taken in 1936, it captured the essence of that famous district.

They were sorry to see their brief visit to Paris end. But both were eager to reach their final destination, Reutte, a small town nestled on the German-Austrian border in the Bavarian Alps. Sarah, who was not as keen on cold weather as Jonathan was, had to be persuaded the Alpine village would make a perfect spot for lovers. He convinced her with images of panoramic views of the Austrian Alps to the south, indoor and outdoor hot tubs, and room service. For seven days they rarely left their hotel suite. The view of the mountains from the bedroom so enchanted Sarah that she vowed to build a house some day with an equally awe-inspiring vista of mountains or the ocean.

They spent Christmas alone in nearby Innsbruck before returning directly to Colorado to be with Jonathan's mother. Sarah's parents met up with them a day later at the Denver airport. Then off they all headed for the Hawthorne Rocky Mountain retreat for five days of winter fun. It was there that Sarah ventured onto skis for the first time. This brought a huge smile to Jonathan's face as she tried to master the basic techniques of this outdoor sport. He thought her just as sexy in her ski clothes as she was in a bathing suit.

The Hawthorne and Matthews families would usher in the new year shouting at the top of their lungs along with the mountain animals, heard calling somewhere off in the distance. It was a time when the parents came to know one another better.

It was also a time when Jonathan and Sarah sat the three of them down and told them an abbreviated version of "that wonderful journey," as she liked to call their twenty-three-year odyssey. Tears flowed from both mothers when the newly married couple had concluded their story. And Sarah was convinced she saw a small tear in the corner of her dad's eye as well. When they had finished, the five of them toasted the new marriage—not with champagne, but with Christmas eggnog.

They returned to Chapel Hill three days after New Year's, aware that the Matthews and the Hawthorne families were now close friends. It pleased them both that their parents had clicked so well.

"But why wouldn't they?" Sarah asked in mock astonishment when Jonathan remarked at how well they had gotten along. "We immediately hit it off so well back when."

◆ ◆ ◆

Second semester was mostly a blur. Jonathan's memories of it centered around their adjustment to each other and his own acclimation to marriage. It was a piece of cake, he told himself over and over again. He awoke each morning wondering what fantastic circumstance would happen to him that day courtesy of Sarah. He retired to bed each night thanking her for how she had made his life more special.

Their love of golf took them to Augusta the second weekend of April for the Masters Tournament. Friends had given them tickets for the Saturday and Sunday rounds. All of their golfing friends were envious they had come upon the most prized ticket in all of sport, not just golf. The weather dawned beautifully the first morning as Jonathan and Sarah entered the grounds of Augusta National, as it was formally called. The azaleas were at their zenith, their redness and pinkness rendered even brighter by the spring Georgia sun.

They walked the entire course that first day, pausing from time to time at the most picturesque spots on the course. On the hill behind the sixth green was one favorite place. By the third green with a view of the fourth hole was another. Amen's Corner, the name given by Herbert Warren Wind, golf writer for *The New Yorker*, to three notorious holes at the far end of the course—eleven, twelve and thirteen—was yet a third desired area.

But their favorite spot was behind the sixteenth green, the par-three hole over water. Sunday would be their day at sixteen. They were at the gate bright and early when the course opened that morning. Rushing to the back of the sixteenth green, they placed two folding chairs purchased at the golf course gift shop at the most advantageous spot in the first row. The location was on a direct line with where the golfer would land his drive if he wanted it to funnel from high on the upper left part of the green down to the hole, positioned as always in its traditional lower back left Sunday placement. Sarah laughed when they had their chairs in place.

Written boldly on the backs of the chairs were the initials SJM-JBH, their identification code. Their plan was to wander around the course early until the first group of golfers made it to number sixteen. Then they would watch each group come through that hole for the remainder of the day before following the last twosome into the club-house.

"So that's why we brought four chairs today," Sarah said, laughing. "People actually put their chairs somewhere on the course, then leave for hours, and nobody touches them."

"That's right," Jonathan said. "It's one of the Masters' traditions that only those who attend the tournament in person know about. We put two down at the sixteenth green, then use the other two the rest of the morning until about one-thirty when the field finally reaches sixteen. We then hurry over to our seats. Works every time."

"Very clever, Professor Hawthorne," Sarah said.

They loved the Masters and vowed to return as often as they could.

◆　◆　◆

The semester soon ended. Sarah and Jonathan had decided to build a second home on the Outer Banks. Not south toward Avon, however, despite its wonderful memories. They selected a place in Duck, just north of Kitty Hawk and about fifty miles north of Avon, in large part because it had some elevation to it. Sarah had remembered her honeymoon retreat and wanted a place that hovered above its immediate surroundings. Development had begun a decade earlier in Duck, but its strict zoning laws had prohibited the helter-skelter pattern often found in resort areas. The area was clearly pleasant to the eye.

They wanted to move into their new winterized home by the end of summer. Jonathan had successfully applied for a sabbatical for the next academic year. They planned to spend the entire year on the Outer Banks. He had finished twenty months of research and needed another year to write a book detailing his findings. It was going to be a treatise on global public policy—how the international community had been working together to solve newly emerging world problems such as overpopulation, lack of food, and environmental pollution. He was pleased with his digging. If his writing went as well as his research had, he knew he would make an impact on the political science profession, and perhaps even on the government community.

Sabbaticals were a time for uninterrupted work. They were also a time for renewal—physically, emotionally, and intellectually. Jonathan promised to re-energize himself in all three areas. But he also looked at his sabbatical in another light. He and Sarah would be isolated from all their friends and he from all of his campus responsibilities, except for a few doctoral students who were in the final stages of their Ph.D. work. Jonathan would still see them every three months or so. What he really wanted most was the opportunity to share a leisurely year with Sarah. He wished to make up for twenty-three years of unfulfilled fantasies.

It was a good time for Sarah to be in Duck as well. She had recently accepted a consulting job with the government agency for which she had labored for over a decade. She could do the work at home, so why not Duck, she told Jonathan.

❧ ❧ ❧

Summer found them supervising the building of their new home, a traditional structure adapted to beach styles and codes. Its hillside location was perfect, allowing them an uninterrupted view of the ocean a hundred yards away. They managed two weeks in Colorado in early August, where they visited with Jonathan's mother and traveled throughout most of the major resort areas. They even joked about Michelle when they arrived in Aspen, although neither made an effort to see if she was still there. Then they were off to Lancaster, where Sarah showed Jonathan all the important places of her youth. It was then that he confessed that he had strolled the city the day after she had exchanged vows with Gordon.

❧ ❧ ❧

When they returned to North Carolina on Labor Day, their house was ready for occupancy. They had sublet their Chapel Hill home for the year, so they packed many of their belongings, bought some new furniture and other items for the beach, and headed for Duck a week later.

They celebrated the first night by christening the Duck beach the same way they had the Avon beach the previous August. They giggled about it as they toasted their new home while walking hand in hand along the beach with a bottle of wine afterward. They vowed to continue exploring each other's body while lying on the beach under a moonlit night as long as they lived.

September found them following their great love to Kiawah Island. The Ryder Cup, the bi-annual golf match between the United States and Europe, took place at the South Carolina resort after conducting its match two years earlier at The Belfrey in the English midlands near Manchester. Jonathan had befriended two British club pros—Ken, a Scot, and Bryan, an Irishman—at an earlier Ryder Cup in the States. The Brits had invited Jonathan and Sarah to the Ryder Cup matches two years later at the Walton Heath club near London.

Ken and Bryan were coming to Kiawah, so Jonathan invited them to visit Duck afterward. They, in turn, had two extra tickets for Kiawah, so off went Sarah and Jonathan to the South Carolina coast. For three nights they partied with a host of British PGA officials, all friends of Ken's and Bryan's. They discovered the Brits usually win any drinking contests with Americans. They also found out how friendly and giving the British can be once they take a liking to you. Their two friends from across the ocean enjoyed three days on the Outer Banks after the Ryder Cup matches, even taking it easy on Jonathan during their daily thirty-six holes of challenging golf on the links course in Kitty Hawk. Sarah and Jonathan promised to make an appearance at The Belfrey in 1993 for a return engagement with their British friends. There were no two better men than Ken and Bryan.

Autumn was special on the Outer Banks. The fishermen arrived then, although usually further south than Duck. Their numbers were much smaller than the summer bathers, so the beach was practically deserted. A day did not go by, no matter how bad the weather, that Sarah and Jonathan did not walk the beach for at least an hour, twice a day. They both thought October in Duck was simply the most perfect time and place in the world. His writing was going well. His loving was also. Both brought a smile to his face. The latter brought one to Sarah's face as well.

• • •

They invited their parents down for Thanksgiving. By then the town was a former shell of itself. No matter. Their home on a bluff overlooking the ocean was an ideal place for turkey and pumpkin pie. For four days the Hawthorne and Matthews families enjoyed the salt air and the magical waves beating against the shore. The turkey was gone by Thursday night, so they turned to seafood for the rest of their meals—either at nearby restaurants or at home. Their parents were introduced to some new delights from the ocean, accompanied by recipes from Outer Banks natives who had handed them down to one another from generation to generation. Their favorite was Hatteras style clam chowder. What distinguished it from its New England and Manhattan cousins was its clear broth. No chowder tasted better.

One day they drove to the south end of the Banks, where they boarded the ferry for the ride to Ocracoke. It hadn't changed in the twenty-three years since Jonathan and Sarah were last there. They stole an hour away from their parents so they might talk more intimately about their last visit to the isolated island the night Bobby Kennedy died.

They were sad to see their families leave, but happy to once again be alone. They were so into each other. There was no doubt that the words "soul mates" captured the essence of their relationship. It was uncanny the way they thought alike. The way each could anticipate the desires and needs of the other. Their constant togetherness did not tire them of each other. Quite the contrary. They thrived on it. They loved each other. They were in love. Really in love. Anyone who saw them together had no doubt about that.

Their parents remarked how happy and content they seemed to be. Sarah's parents, who had watched her go through the motions with Gordon, were so delighted for her. They saw love emanating from her eyes and from her heart. Jonathan's mother, who had despaired for years that he would never marry, was doubly pleased that not only had he found a wife, but that Sarah was the woman of his dreams. Their parents returned home secure in the knowledge that their children could not be happier, more in love, or more content.

❧ ❧ ❧

They traveled inland for their mid-December anniversary. Independently of each other, Jonathan and Sarah both had made reservations at

La Chandelle. They toasted their love and their good fortune in finding the greatest of gifts. They didn't return to Duck that evening, though. Rather, they were in Room 525 at the Washington Duke Inn, reliving that night eighteen months earlier when they moved from simply being in love to loving each other with every fiber of their bodies and souls. This sojourn was no less perfect, exciting, and fulfilling than that June evening a year and a half earlier.

❧ ❧ ❧

Christmas found Sarah and Jonathan in Colorado again, as they had been the year before, with both sets of parents. They knew their parents were aging and probably had few years left. They both wanted to make them a part of their lives as much as they could. There was plenty of happiness to spread around. Sarah and Jonathan understood that. So they were eager to share their profound joy whenever possible. Their parents always appreciated it. The three of them often talked about how lucky they were to have witnessed the extraordinary relationship in front of them.

❧ ❧ ❧

Spring on the Outer Banks was just as beautiful as the other three seasons, perhaps even more so. The flowers seemed to flourish as if they had found the secret of living side by side with the salt air. The reflection from the sea made the sun appear brighter. Jonathan and Sarah thrived during the dark winter months following Christmas, but they flourished even more in spring.

The Outer Banks came alive in the springtime. Tourists had not yet begun to appear, so the entire strip of land from Duck to Ocracoke belonged to the locals. By spring, Jonathan and Sarah were considered locals. And some good fortune would make them even more permanent fixtures on the Banks. Jonathan had won a prestigious fellowship that allowed him a second year of research and writing, uninterrupted by duties back on campus. After about two microseconds of discussion, they decided to spend another twelve months at what they had originally planned to be their summer home until retirement.

In fact, he had just figured it out. He was due for retirement in a year. While he did not have to take it, it was his for the asking. Sarah and Jonathan decided that if the next year proved as rewarding as the one that had just concluded, they were staying. Simple as that. They would not return to Chapel Hill and to the Duke campus. Their home at Duck soon began to take on a more permanent look.

◆ ◆ ◆

March came and went. So did April and May. The sun was higher in the sky, warming their bodies as they strolled along the beach each day. They were always hand in hand or arm in arm, and they never tired of touching each other.

The tenants who had rented their house were about to vacate. So Jonathan and Sarah headed west to Chapel Hill to assess the damage and make arrangements for their house to be cleaned. These obligations took a couple of days.

Jonathan then had some business on campus that required his rather undivided attention for a few days, so he urged Sarah not to stick around. "Sweetheart, why don't you go back to Duck? No need to stay around here twiddling your thumbs. You can fly back and be home in half an hour. I'll bring the car as soon as I finish, probably in two days. Three days max," he promised.

Sarah wasn't sure, but Jonathan prevailed. So the next day, he drove her to the Raleigh-Durham airport for the short commuter flight home.

"Do you realize, sweetheart, tonight will be the first night we have not slept together in the same bed since we've been married?" Sarah asked.

Jonathan seemed surprised. "By God, you're right. I hadn't thought about that. Maybe we ought not to break our streak."

"No, honey, you were right in the first place," Sarah replied. "As much as I love it here, I'll be bored to tears while you're working. At least at the beach I can carry on my normal routine."

So Jonathan walked Sarah to the door of the terminal and kissed her good-bye. He was not allowed beyond that point. "Good-bye, sweetheart. See you in a few days. I love you."

"See you soon. I love you too," Sarah replied. She started to walk away but turned back, laughing. "Come here, Professor Jonathan Hawthorne. I paid my tuition. I want a big kiss."

Jonathan grinned as he took her in his arms. How he loved her! Really loved her! Sarah then turned and headed outside toward the plane. She climbed the steps and then, just as she was about to board, turned back, smiled, and blew him a kiss while giving him a thumbs up. Jonathan just smiled and thought back to that day twenty-five years earlier when Sarah walked into his class for the first time. As beautiful as she was then, she was even more beautiful today. He returned the thumbs-up gesture. Sarah smiled, blew another kiss, then boarded the plane.

~ 25 ~

Time Too Short

After Sarah's plane took off, Jonathan went to his office, which was staffed by a couple of his advanced graduate students. He met with several of them who were working on their dissertations. He remembered back over twenty-five years earlier when he found himself in the same predicament. Consequently, he always took extra time to make certain each of them was on the right track. He wanted no unusual or unanticipated roadblocks placed in front of them. Over the years, his doctoral students had come to appreciate his attention.

Two hours later, he had finished with the last one. It was time to go over to the Chapel Hill house to make certain the cleaning crew had done its job. His car was parked behind Perkins Library in the usual place. He stopped on his way out and chatted with the department secretaries. To a person, they remarked that marriage apparently was good for him. Jonathan just laughed and went on his way.

Instinctively, he turned on the radio as he was leaving the parking lot. He was near the edge of the campus by the golf course when a news bulletin interrupted the music. A commuter plane from Raleigh-Durham to Manteo had crashed into the Albemarle Sound on its final approach to the airfield. There were no survivors.

Jonathan knew immediately that it was Sarah's plane. There could be no mistake. It was the only scheduled air service to the Outer Banks that afternoon. Frantic, he raced for a nearby phone on the golf course and called his travel agent. They confirmed the schedule and the number of the downed plane. There was no mistake. Jonathan was in a daze. His life, his entire life, had just come tumbling down on him.

"Sarah! Sarah! Sarah! Why did I urge you to fly home? Why didn't I tell you to stay? Why? Why? Why?" Jonathans screams could be heard a hundred yards away.

The tears rolled down his face. He could not stop them, nor did he want to. He began to wander aimlessly across the golf course, virtually deserted by an earlier rainstorm. After awhile, he found himself at the seventh green, where he simply sat down and stared straight ahead. The wonderful seventh green, the green that had twice played a role in his relationship with Sarah. Those memories didn't enter his mind now, though. His only thoughts were of Sarah in her final moments on this earth, her whole life probably passing before her as the plane came tumbling to earth. He prayed she had not been aware of the pending doom awaiting her. He hoped it had happened without warning, without her having to suffer. How he prayed for that. His beloved Sarah. His heart ached so much for her.

It was completely dark before Jonathan rose and walked back to his car. He was emotionally drained. But there were things to take care of. He knew that. The police were waiting in Chapel Hill when he arrived home. His office had told them he eventually would wind up there. They offered little information. The plane was to be raised from the shallow waters of the sound. They had confirmed the passenger list, and Sarah was on it. Jonathan already knew that. He had observed her board, watched her smile the smile of love and happiness, and had seen her wave good-bye and give their traditional thumbs-up signal. Thirty minutes later she was gone. The tears returned.

He dreaded the next two phone calls he had to make. He remembered what it was like to watch his parents grieve for the loss of a child. Now he was about to experience it once more. How he wished he didn't have to make the first call. Sarah's parents were devastated. Her dad, who had enjoyed a special bond with his only daughter, took it especially hard. Jonathan offered to fly to Lancaster, but they said no. They wanted to grieve alone for a day and then come to Chapel Hill immediately thereafter. They wondered if he knew anything yet. He understood exactly what they were talking about. He had heard little.

He had been told only that the plane would be raised the next day—at least the officer in charge seemed to think so. He didn't know when Sarah's body would be released to him. He hadn't thought about a funeral or burial yet. It was too soon.

"We love you, son," they both said into the speakerphone as they hung up.

It took Jonathan about ten minutes to compose himself for his second call. His poor mother. First a son, then a husband, now a daughter-in-law. She had been through so much heartache and sorrow over the years. He didn't know how she stood up through it all. She was especially relieved and happy when Jonathan married. He knew she had worried so over the years about his disinclination to take a wife. Now she would fret again about him. He could not let that happen. He had to be strong for her. And he had to be especially strong for Sarah's parents. They all needed him and would for a long time. He vowed to be there for all three of them, whatever they required.

But Jonathan realized he also had needs. He pondered whether he was strong enough to make it through another grieving process, by far the most difficult of them all. His beloved Sarah. He fought back tears and prayed for strength as he dialed his mother's number. He hoped she was home. He couldn't stand having to be the one to break the awful news about a loved one and wanted to get this ordeal over with as quickly as possible. He thought back to his friend, Denver Smith, who had had to perform that ritual numerous times. *Where did he get the strength?* he wondered.

"Oh, Jonathan! Jonathan! I'm so sorry. Poor Sarah! Poor you, my dear! What can I do?" his mother said upon hearing the news.

He told her there was nothing to do. He asked her if her health was good enough for the trip east. She said yes and that she would plan to come as soon as possible, hopefully the next day. Jonathan confessed he would like that since Sarah's parents would not arrive until the day after that. He needed his mother and was glad she would be with him. She told him she loved him and would see him as soon as possible.

Not long afterward, the phone began to ring off the hook. Colleagues and their spouses had heard the news. A couple of them stopped by the house to offer their condolences and to ask what, if anything, they could do. There was really nothing, he told them. But in his

heart he had one great need. It was for Sarah. It would never be fulfilled again.

After about two hours, Jonathan wanted no more intrusions, no
matter how good the intentions. So he left the house and headed for
the campus. It was now close to midnight, but he needed to walk. He
had to retrace his steps. His and Sarah's steps. He wanted to relive those
precious moments he shared there with the woman he loved so deeply.
He parked his car in the usual place and began his sentimental journey.
First the classroom where he initially laid eyes on her. The door was
open, so he walked in. He quickly found her seat, even after all those
years. He took his place at the front of the class and recreated in his
mind that instant when she walked through the door, later responded
to her name, and smiled that wonderful first smile. Image after image of
that fateful semester danced across his brain.

He visited the adjacent classroom where Sarah and her classmates
had enjoyed his eggnog after the final exam. Where she had stayed after
all the others had gone and volunteered to help him clean up. Where
he had bitten the bullet and asked her to go with him to get something
to eat. Where he had taken the first real step in his long journey to make
her his wife.

Jonathan then wandered over to his old office where Sarah first
appeared just before the initial exam. He remembered how she had
regaled and impressed him with her tales of Cairo, London, Edinburgh,
and Paris. And, of course, St. Andrews. They had planned to attend the
British Open in three summers when it returned to the Old Course.
He vowed to go alone in her memory. He would kiss the seventeenth
green, just as Sarah and her father had done some forty years earlier, in
her honor.

He was off to the old student union next. Jonathan and Sarah had
listened to the news about Martin Luther King, Jr.'s, assassination there.
The union was closed at that late hour, but simply seeing the building
satisfied his need for reflection. He moved on past Cameron Indoor
Stadium, past the football field and the other athletic fields, and on to
the golf course.

He walked every inch of it. The two of them had enjoyed many
rounds during the six months they lived there as husband and wife.

Sarah had been right. He had difficulty beating her. He remembered their drinking a bottle of wine by the first green. As he passed the seventh green, Jonathan paused. Unlike earlier that day, he thought about the significance of that spot, both twenty-four years before and just two years earlier. He lost his composure at that moment and the tears gushed from his eyes. It was a full half hour before he left the green.

Back toward the golf course entrance he wandered, near where the Washington Duke Inn stood. He walked to the patio behind it, where he and Sarah had kissed their first lovers' kiss and she had uttered that magic word, "Come." Jonathan smiled a sad smile as he remembered how nervous he had been that evening and how wonderful Sarah had been about it. His eyes moved toward the sky, searching for the window in Room 525. He soon found it. He had memorized its location soon after they first made love there, so that every time he approached the eighteenth green, he could look up and relive the most wonderful night of his life. Now, though, a sad smile graced his face as he thought about how they had finally made love there after all those years of desiring her.

Jonathan's last stop was the Duke Gardens. They had spent her last evening on campus before graduation drinking the evening's third bottle of wine among the flowers of spring. Sarah lamented that she was leaving the next day, never to live there again. But twenty-one years later she would return as his wife. As sad as the moment was, Jonathan would not have given up their short time together as husband and wife for anything.

After about half an hour, Jonathan headed for his car and the ride back to Chapel Hill. It was after three o'clock when his head hit the bed. The tears accompanied him as he struggled to fall asleep. Once it came, however, it was a deep sleep—the sleep of one whose emotions had been put to the severest of tests that day.

The phone awakened him around seven. His mother would be there shortly after two. He told her he would pick her up at the airport. The police called about nine with the news that the U.S. Coast Guard had recovered the plane. Sarah's body would probably be released later that day. Jonathan thanked them and replaced the receiver. How he dreaded having to identify her body. He spent the rest of the morning at the funeral home making the necessary arrangements. Assuming things went as planned, the viewing would be two nights later, a Thursday, and the funeral on Friday.

He contacted Sarah's parents with the information and to see how they were coping. Not well was the response, but they would be okay. He was not to worry about them. How was he doing they asked. About as expected, he told them. No need to bare his soul right then to Sarah's parents. They had enough to worry about.

His mother's plane arrived on schedule. The tears flowed freely when they saw each other. Jonathan remembered Sarah's remarks about mother and son the moment they embraced after his father's death. She was probably smiling right now at the repeat of the earlier scene.

He identified Sarah's body later that afternoon. His mom waited outside, not wanting to intrude at that very private moment.

She was a huge help over the next twenty-four hours, mostly in insulating him from well-meaning friends. He couldn't talk much with them. He wasn't ready and thought he might never be.

Sarah's parents arrived early the next day. They told Jonathan they wanted to be there, even though there wasn't much to do. He understood their desire—even need—to be present. He seemed so helpless. There was nothing he could do to ease the pain that permeated every part of his body. But he had to go on. They were counting on him. He would not let them down and would get through the next three days somehow.

The four of them joined forces to help one another cope with the tragedy. They all seemed to gain a measure of strength from one another. They needed it the next night when the viewing was held. Hundreds of mourners showed, which overwhelmed Jonathan. All of his colleagues who were in town, many faculty members from other departments, and others from the Duke family came to pay their respects.

The funeral took place the next day in Duke Chapel at eleven o'clock. *How ironic it is,* Jonathan thought, as he remembered back eighteen short months earlier when they had spoken their wedding vows at the same place. He had never been happier then. Now he had never been more sad. The Chapel was full, as hundreds came for the service. Many were simply former students of Jonathan's who had remained grateful to him over the years for how he had influenced them. He really appreciated those who had heard the news and traveled some distance to share in his sorrow.

Sarah was to be buried at Duck. She and Jonathan had picked a location earlier on their property not far from the house that had a perfect view of the ocean. They had often reaffirmed that that was where they wanted to spend eternity. He knew the exact spot and conveyed that information to the individuals who had responsibility for taking care of the grave.

Only the family was to make the five-hour trip to Sarah's final resting place. Jonathan wanted it that way. So a reception was held at the student union—the new one built since Sarah had graduated—to give the family an opportunity to thank those who had taken the time and made the effort to attend the funeral. It was two hours before Jonathan had a chance to greet the last guest.

At two in the afternoon, they left Durham and slowly began Sarah's final journey to the Outer Banks. Past Raleigh they went. Past Rocky Mount, past Williamston, past the town of Manns Harbor, and across Croatan Sound to Roanoke Island and its village of Manteo. *Almost home, Sarah,* Jonathan thought, as they crossed the final bridge to the Outer Banks. Turning left, they headed north past Nags Head, past Kill Devil Hills, past Kitty Hawk, then straight ahead a few miles to their home in Duck.

It was almost dusk when Sarah was finally laid to rest.

Epilogue

Jonathan smiled as he read the final words Sarah had written to him in response to his marriage proposal. He now knew for certain that every word he had been reading in her letter was real rather than a figment of his imagination. She had said yes to his proposal of marriage. He knew that, unfortunately, the events he had witnessed the past week were also real.

Sarah had been so confident about the future. Her final words in her precious letter to him had made that clear.

. . . I love you, dearest Jonathan. I pledge to spend every minute of the rest of my life making you happy.

Sarah had fulfilled her promise to him. Their time together was the happiest of his life.

With the sound of the waves pounding the shore in the background, Jonathan took the letter and slowly returned it to its envelope, careful not to allow any of the tears falling from his eyes to damage it. Then he placed it back in his pocket. He carried her letter with him for the remainder of his days.

He turned, as he found himself doing a hundred times a day, to the hillside behind him. It had been five days since he had buried Sarah. The grave was still covered with flowers that, until recently, were alive with the freshness of spring. Sarah would be pleased with her final resting place. As if it mattered. Well, it did matter.

Jonathan then took another letter from his pocket, opened it, and began to read it one last time. It was his final letter to Sarah. He had worked on it since the parents had left two days after the funeral. It had taken every minute of the past three days. He wanted to get it just right. He wished to leave her with a statement of his eternal love. He desperately wanted her to have something special of his. What greater gift than that which he had always given her without hesitation—his unconditional and unselfish love and devotion.

He had the empty wine bottle from the mantle—the one he saved from the Duke Gardens on the night before Sarah's graduation. He intended to place the letter inside the wine bottle, then bury it with her. She would be pleased with this gesture, he knew. His body ached so much. Oh how he missed her already!

My dearest Sarah. I've had many difficult tasks in my lifetime. But none compare to what I am doing just now—writing you a final affirmation of my love for you. You must bear with me. This isn't going to be easy. It hasn't been these last three days. I have searched and searched for just the right words, but they just wouldn't come. Perhaps if more time had elapsed between your accident and my writing this, I could handle this better. But it has been too soon, much too soon. My body still rebels against trying to do things that are impossible. It just won't let my mind work as well as I want it to.

Besides, as often as we told each other of our love—and it was every day, wasn't it?—much of our communication was by simple looks. Instinctively, we knew what the other was thinking. We communicated with our eyes and with our hearts. And the other instantly understood. I guess that's when I knew my feelings had passed from infatuation to love.

That means you now know, more than you ever did on earth, how much I loved you, worshiped you, adored you, and desired you. And how completely happy I was when you told me you loved me and wanted to spend the rest of your life with me. You can read my mind totally now. I hope you're smiling.

Then why am I writing this? I guess because it forces my brain to think directly and clearly about my feelings for you. That way you should be able to pick up my mental images more easily in heaven.

But there is another reason. A more important one. I have this need to do so. I must spell out my feelings. You were not only a special part of my life. You were my life. First as a figment of my fantasy world. Then as a dear, dear friend who helped me so much when my brother was killed. And who continued to be a source of strength until the day you died. Finally as my soul mate. How true it is that one has a soul mate somewhere out there. How you touched my soul, and I yours. You and I created something—us. A new being. It was wonderful, and it was perfect.

Before I began this letter, I once again read every word you had written me when I asked you to marry me. I came away thinking I was the luckiest guy in the world. The story of your long journey from my student to my friend to my lover to finally my wife brought tears to my eyes and joy to my heart.

Happiness is measured in quality terms, not in quantity moments. As an English poet once wrote: "For a day and a night Love sang to us, played with us, Folded us round from the dark and the light; And our hearts were fulfilled with the music he made with us."

We had only eighteen glorious months together, my love, as husband and wife. But what wonderful music! It was the most astonishing time of my entire life. Eighteen months during which we experienced the best there is between two people completely and unconditionally in love with each other. If there was another couple on the face of the earth who was happier than we were, then I'd like to meet them. I can't imagine a greater physical and psychological intimacy than we enjoyed. You responded to my every need—sexual, emotional, and intellectual. I was so utterly and totally fulfilled. God must have thought of us when he introduced the idea of partnership between a man and a woman. We were the perfect model.

I'm glad our parents came to understand the deep attachment and the great affection we had for each other. I know that gave them comfort—in your case their little girl had finally found happiness, and in my case her little boy had finally married his true love. I promise to look after your parents, to be a part of their lives until they're with you.

Thank you, my precious Sarah, for showing me a world only you could reveal. For making me the most fortunate man in the world because he was able to find total and unconditional love.

Someone once said the love we give away is the only love we keep.

I shall love you throughout eternity. And I shall carry your love with me forever.

    Good-bye, sweetheart. Until we're together someday in heaven. I love you.

Jonathan folded his letter neatly into the wine bottle and carefully placed it in the small hole he dug next to his beloved Sarah.

The sun was setting in the west. Jonathan turned, and, with a tear in his eye, blew a kiss its way. He knew Sarah would catch it somehow.